THE
BABY
MONITOR

BOOKS BY ROSIE WALKER

Secrets of a Serial Killer

The House Fire

THE
BABY
MONITOR

ROSIE WALKER

Bookouture

Published by Bookouture in 2024

An imprint of Storyfire Ltd.
Carmelite House
50 Victoria Embankment
London EC4Y 0DZ

www.bookouture.com

ISBN: 978-1-83790-946-9
eBook ISBN: 978-1-83790-945-2

To my mum, Hilary, with all my love.
Now that I have a daughter too, I understand even more what an
amazing mum you are.
I am lucky to have you.

My third comfort,
Starred most unluckily, is from my breast,
The innocent milk in its most innocent mouth,
Haled out to murder.

— HERMIONE TO LEONTES, *THE WINTER'S TALE* BY WILLIAM SHAKESPEARE, ACT III SCENE 2

'We're home!' Jeremy calls, pushing the front door open with his hip and manoeuvring the baby's car seat through the hallway.

I hobble up the footpath behind him, exhausted. The lights are on in our living room, the blinds half shuttered against the Edinburgh evening. From outside, our home looks cosy, a warm island flanked on both sides by the dark windows of our neighbours.

I fix a smile on my tired face as I step into the light of the hallway and check on the baby, who remains fast asleep in his seat despite Jeremy's shout. Newborns scare me. In those first weeks, they're so fragile it feels like every breath might be their last.

'Mummy and Daddy are back.' Jac's voice floats down the stairs. Liv's godmother. I steel myself for my oldest friend's bright energy and my daughter's excitement.

Jac appears at the top of the stairs. 'Liv's getting changed, bless her. She thinks the new baby will appreciate her *Frozen* dress.' She laughs, and then her gaze lands on the car seat and she rushes down the stairs. 'Oh my God, he's the most beautiful baby I've ever seen.' She leans over the seat, then straightens up and pulls me into her arms, gently but with force. 'I'm so proud of you, Miriam.'

Exhaustion washes over me and I struggle to stay upright in Jac's embrace. She smells clean, of laundry detergent and perfume. I feel a flash of envy for her child-free life where everything is in her control. In contrast, I smell of hospitals and fear and have very little say in the shape of my days for the foreseeable future.

Jeremy heads back out to the car, collar up against the autumn air. I packed so many bags: hospital stuff, post-labour stuff, baby stuff... going-home outfits in different sizes, nappies, wipes, blah blah. I'm the type of person who channels anxiety into over-preparation. In the end, everything was so quick there was no time for anything we'd planned. No birthing pool, no Jeremy wafting me gently with a hand-held fan. No time for snacks, massage, music. Just contractions, screaming, pushing, baby, and then trying to put me back together.

We spent so much time preparing for the hospital part and not enough for this bit: the strange, sleep-deprived twilight days after the birth. When you're home alone with no help and you have to somehow keep your helpless creature alive when every tiny thing could kill it.

'Thanks so much for looking after Liv for us,' Jeremy says to Jac as he re-enters the house, a bag in each hand. 'Meeting the baby might be strange for her, so having you here will have been a nice distraction.' He lugs the bags upstairs, calling for Liv.

'Speaking of which, time for me to get going, I reckon.' Jac grabs her jacket from the hook and pulls it on, then wraps a tartan scarf around her neck.

I nod, grateful for her perceptiveness. We've carefully planned Liv's introduction to her new brother, preparing her with books and chats about how exciting it will be to welcome a baby into the house.

Jac nods towards the sleeping infant. 'And I bet you want to get him settled too. You chose Samuel?' she asks.

I nod. 'Samuel.' His brand-new name seems unwieldy in my mouth. Panic hits me. There's so much to do. Unpacking, getting the baby settled. Finding clothes that fit his tiny body. Feeding him. Feeding ourselves. Introducing him to Liv. And I'm dying for a bath.

'He's adorable. Almost as cute as my god-daughter.' She points at a photograph on the wall: Jac and Liv at Liv's third birthday party a couple of years ago, both with matching tiger face paint. Liv has changed so much, my chubby-cheeked toddler turning into a young lady before my eyes.

The baby lifts his mitten-covered hand to rub at his face, his movements jerky and new.

'Samuel's awake. Ready to meet his big sister.' Jac's scarf muffles her voice as she looks down to zip her jacket. She pulls me into another hug. 'There's a basket of goodies in Liv's room. A bunch of your other parent friends chipped in too: Nicole, Zain and that lot.' She tries to suppress an eye roll at her mention of Nicole's name, but I spot it and look away. I'm too tired to try and make peace between them today. But a rush of love overwhelms me for them both.

As I close the door on the crisp September evening, Samuel's gurgles turn to wails.

'Where's my big girl?' I push open the nursery door with my hip. 'We've got someone to meet you.'

Liv sits cross-legged on her pink canopy bed, a Barbie in each hand. Jeremy is next to her, another doll on his lap.

'Don't want to meet anyone, Mummy,' she states, and bashes the Barbies' heads together. Despite the stubborn set of her jaw, she looks so picture-perfect with her blue tulle *Frozen* dress puffed up around her. I feel a pang of sadness as I wish I could give her more: more time, more affection, more months as my only child. I'm so afraid that I won't be enough for her, now I have two.

Don't force it, the advice says. *Give them space.* So I don't react to her comment, and although I'm aching to hug her, I ease myself into the rocking chair on shaky legs, unbutton my top and hold Samuel to my breast. I marvel at the inside of his mouth, wide open and all red gums as he screams. But as if by magic, he senses my nipple even with his eyes screwed shut, and nuzzles his face into my breast. His cries subside into adorable little sniffles. I allow myself a breath, and another. Until he arrived, I'd forgotten how breastfeeding feels. Relief and peace. The moment a plane's wheels hit the tarmac upon landing.

I look around the room: on the changing table next to me is the gift hamper full of nappies, wipes, dummies, muslin cloths... the small things that run out fast and are always useful. Over Samuel's head, I carefully pick up the card, written in Jac's swirly hand:

To Miriam, Jeremy and Baby,
Love,
Your friends xx

My eyes fill with tired tears of gratitude.

Jeremy watches me and Samuel for a moment with a blissful smile, then pulls Liv towards him with an arm around her shoulders.

I wipe at my eyes and clear my throat. 'Liv, I know it might not be easy to meet your new little brother. You're going to be a great big sister.'

She puffs up her chest and nods. 'I will, Mummy. I'll play with baby Samuel every day.'

'You two will have so much fun when he's a bit bigger. But

you'll always be my first baby, and Mummy's special girl. So we bought you a little present, from Mummy, Daddy and Samuel.'

She looks up from her dolls, brown eyes twinkling with reflections from the fairy lights.

Jeremy reaches into his pocket and holds out a gift-wrapped box. 'Want to open it?'

She shrugs, but he places the box in her lap and she abandons the Barbies and tears into the wrapping paper. She drops the paper to the floor, flapping her hand to get rid of the tape stuck to her thumb, then lifts the lid from the box and peers inside. 'There's two.' She thrusts the box forward to show me.

I reach in with my free hand. 'This one's for me.' I hold out the first bracelet: a delicate silver chain with a circular charm with a heart-shaped hole in the centre. 'And this one's for you.' The second charm is smaller and heart-shaped. I fit them together, Liv's inside mine. 'You see, Liv? You're always in my heart, every moment of every day.'

I feel a bit emotional, and swallow hard as I fasten my bracelet around my wrist. 'I'm going to wear mine every day, to show how important you are to me. Even when I'm busy or looking after Samuel, I'll wear this bracelet because I love you. OK?'

She nods. Her eyes linger on Samuel, watching him feed.

I hold out her bracelet. 'Would you like to wear yours?'

She picks up a Barbie and turns away. 'No thank you.'

I try not to react, not to let her know I'm hurt. I can't make her responsible for my feelings. A sudden wave of exhaustion renders my voice breathy and weak. 'That's OK. Maybe you can wear it another day.' I open her bedside drawer. 'It's in here when you're ready.'

'The present was from Samuel too,' Jeremy says. 'Ready to meet him?'

She gets off the bed and takes a step towards us, her eyes fixed on Samuel, the feathery layer of hair on his little head, his upturned nose pressed into my breast, and the starfish hands opening and closing while he suckles.

She watches closely. I hold out a finger and Samuel's fist wraps around it. 'Look, Liv. Do you want to let him hold your finger too?'

She shakes her head. Her lower lip sticks out and starts to quiver. I reach to her with my free hand, ready to comfort. But in seconds her expression shifts: her lip retracts and her mouth sets in a hard line of resignation.

I pause, giving her some space. This must be a lot to process.

'When are his real mummy and daddy coming to get him?' she asks, her voice uncertain.

Jeremy smiles, leaning forward. 'Me and Mummy are his real mummy and daddy, just like we are yours.'

Her lip wobbles once more, before she gets it under control again. 'Are you going to send me away now you have Samuel?'

I long to pull her close, cuddle her into my arms and kiss this better. But the baby huddles between us, little mouth attached to my nipple. 'Samuel lives with us now, just like you do. We will love you for ever and keep you here with us. We're one happy family: Mummy, Daddy, you and baby Samuel.'

She folds her arms, shaking her head slightly as if she can't believe what she's hearing. She stamps her foot on the rug. 'Take him back.'

I stifle a smile. She looks so serious. Poor little thing; this phase will pass, I'm sure. She seemed excited right up until this moment. Reality has hit: this isn't a ready-made playmate, it's a competitor for parental attention. I really, really understand how she must feel right now.

Samuel detaches from my nipple with a little pop. I look down to find him fast asleep, rosebud mouth upturned in a contented almost-smile. 'Liv, sit on the bed and you can hold him for a minute. Give him a "hello" cuddle from his big sister.' I fasten the strap of my nursing bra and pull my top down as Liv climbs back onto the bed next to Jeremy, taking her time.

I lay him on her knees and she holds him stiffly, unsure what to do with her hands. The corners of her mouth twitch as she looks down at him. I feel a stirring of hope. Here before me are the two most important things in my life. I created them, and they'll be on this earth long after I'm gone. They need to love each other and look after each other, because one day I won't be here to do that. I swallow hard.

Jeremy leans towards her and kisses her head. 'He looks so comfy. Look how peaceful he is, sleeping on his big sister.' After a moment, he stands, straightening the legs of his jeans as he steps towards the door. 'I'll go sort things out downstairs.'

As he leaves the room, Liv mumbles something I don't quite catch.

I lean forward. 'It's good you're whispering so you don't wake him. What did you say?'

She says it again, louder. 'I want to throw him.'

I take a breath. 'We don't throw babies. But I'm glad you can tell me how you feel. I'll take him now, and you can hold him again when you feel safe, OK?'

I reach out for him, but Liv makes a sudden movement, and her fingers wrap around his neck. Her knuckles bend, ready to tighten.

'What are you doing?' I scoop him into my arms. She doesn't have time to hurt him. To squeeze.

She wriggles her shoulders like a weight has been lifted from her. As if nothing happened.

'Liv, what was that?' I can't tell if I imagined it. Am I so tired I can't judge these things?

'Nothing, Mummy. Just giving the baby a cuddle.' She flops down on her bed, facing the wall. 'Go away, please. I want to be on my own.'

Samuel sleeps on, no idea of what just happened. Or did it?

Maybe I saw aggression where there was only clumsy affection. I take a tired breath. No matter which, it's my job to guide Liv through all her feelings about her new brother, I know that. But I don't have to start today.

Behind me, the baby monitor camera whirrs to life, and I turn to watch the little box slowly rotate, panning the room. Its black lens glints at us like the eye of a crow. It finds Liv and the movement stops. Is Jeremy watching us on a phone app?

I hold Samuel close and leave the room, pulling Liv's bedroom door closed behind me. Outside, I stop, taking deep breaths. It's not a big deal. She's five years old, and today was a difficult day. I press my forehead against the cold wood of her door and breathe some more. And that's when I hear it: a raspy, mechanical voice inside the room:

'She's lying. Mummy doesn't love you.'

2

I stumble downstairs. The mental exhaustion I felt in Liv's room has disappeared, replaced with fury. But my body keeps the score: my movements are sluggish and I'm one false move away from falling down the stairs with Samuel in my arms.

In the living room, Jeremy has opened a bottle of champagne and placed it in a silver cooler. The lamps are on, the curtains drawn against the dusky autumn evening. He has lit a fire in the grate, the flames beginning to catch at the smokeless logs, and is staring at his phone, a half-smile on his face.

'What are you doing?' I hiss through gritted teeth, trying not to upset Samuel in my arms. 'You think that's funny?'

His eyes widen in surprise. 'What?' He glances at the bottle. 'I know you're breastfeeding, but you can have—'

'This isn't about champagne.' I gesture at the phone in his hand.

He looks even more confused. 'I was reading this Reddit thread where—'

'You're watching me on the monitor. Talking to Liv through it. Saying things about me.'

He turns his phone around to show me a wall of text on his

screen. 'Mim, I'm not watching you. I have no idea what you're talking about. I'm just messing about on Reddit.'

'That's what you call messing about? Seriously, the camera was blinking at me and swivelling around on its little stand.'

He leans back on the sofa and tilts his head in concern.

I rub my eyes, eyeballs stinging. I'm so tired, but I can't leave this alone. It's too important. 'If you don't trust me to look after our kids, we have some serious problems.'

'I haven't even set up a monitor app yet.' He shakes his head, disbelieving. 'It's not about trust, Mim. Of course I trust you.' He sighs, rubbing his face. His voice is muffled through his fingers. 'What did you think you heard me say?'

'You told her "Mummy doesn't love you".'

He takes in a sharp breath. 'Oh my God, Miriam.' He moves his hands, places a palm on either side of his face. He's making a good show of not knowing what I'm talking about. 'Why the hell would I say that to her? It's insane.'

'Don't call me insane. That's what I heard.'

'I didn't mean...'

'Then say what you mean, please.'

He groans in frustration. 'I didn't call you insane. I wouldn't. But you're more vulnerable than most. You're *at risk*.'

I flinch at his use of my midwife's words. It's about last time. Everything's about last time. I have to be so careful what I say, what I do.

I'm too exhausted to argue any more. I sit in an armchair, Samuel still sleeping in my arms. I stare at him, admiring the curve of his cheek, the slope of his nose.

Jeremy stands and crosses the room, crouches next to my chair. He places a hand on my arm and I tense, but I don't pull away. 'Look, you've been through so much in the last forty-eight hours. Maybe your brain's playing tricks on you. Auditory hallucinations are common with sleep deprivation, right? It's so important you get enough rest.' He holds out a hand and helps me out of the armchair, pulls me into a hug with Samuel cocooned between us.

I rest my head on his shoulder and almost fall asleep right there, standing up in the middle of the living room. Enjoy this, I tell myself. We love each other. We have two healthy children. This is the dream: we wanted this so badly, and now it's here.

'I promise I haven't been watching you on the monitor, love. I think you're a great mum.'

My eyes flutter open, and over his shoulder I catch sight of his phone, face down on the sofa. I don't have the energy to be angry, I realise. I take a deep breath and exhale, letting go of my suspicions and choosing to believe him. It's easier. It's all I can do.

He clears his throat and steps back, startling me. 'I need to talk to you about one more thing before you have a bath and get tucked up in bed.' His tone is serious. Two red patches of skin emerge on his cheekbones. 'Something happened the other day at work.'

He busies himself pouring champagne into glasses, avoiding my gaze.

My stomach drops and I sit down. *Please don't have lost your job.* I don't know what we'd do with only my measly art therapist's maternity pay. We have no cheap childcare, and grandparents aren't an option: Jeremy's not close to his family, and my mother isn't a natural caregiver. Although I love my job, it's touch-and-go whether we can afford for me to go back. We need Jeremy's income.

'What's going on, Jeremy?' I try to keep the wariness from my voice. He can be impulsive, and sometimes doesn't think things through.

He hands me a half-glass of champagne and holds out his own to cheers. 'I've been offered a promotion.'

My heart soars and I take a massive breath, my relief masquerading as pleasure and pride, I hope. 'That's amazing!

Congratulations! What's the job? And what's the money?' If I wasn't holding Samuel, I'd jump up and throw my arms around him. 'We needed this. I'm so happy for you.'

He takes a big slug of champagne, and so do I. It's delicious: crisp and bursting with bubbles. It's been so long since I've had a glass, I almost forget how to drink it, swallowing hard and hurting my throat with the fizz.

He sits next to me and leans towards me to stroke a finger along Samuel's cheek. 'You remember Tabitha?' he asks in a quiet voice. 'You might have met at a work thing a few years ago. At the conference centre.'

I frown, trying to remember. 'I met a lot of people that night.'

'Red hair, lipstick to match.' He pauses, then waves a hand when he sees I've no recognition of her. 'Never mind. She wants me in her team. Says she likes how I fix problems. My "can-do attitude", she calls it.'

I smile in acknowledgement. Jeremy does not let a problem fester, that's for sure.

'I haven't accepted it yet.' The circular patches of red reappear high up on his cheekbones. 'I needed to talk to you first.'

He tells me the details: the salary increase, the posh new 'systems integration consultant' job title, the private health insurance, the share options.

I take another sip of champagne, savouring it, grateful for the opportunity to think. 'Of course you have to take it. The salary alone...'

'We can get that extension. Skylights in the kitchen.'

I smile. 'I have always wanted a skylight...'

His finger taps nervously against his champagne flute. I stare at the dark hair speckled across the back of his wrist. If this is such good news, why doesn't he seem happier?

'Are we celebrating, then?' I pull aside my top, attaching Samuel even though he's still half asleep. If I feed him while I drink this half-glass, it's possible I will have processed the alcohol before his next feed.

Jeremy drains his drink. 'But Mim, these next few months will be hard: a five-year-old and a new baby. The new job's a lot of travelling. Long hours. And after last time...'

There it is. *Last time.* Samuel's lips disengage from my nipple with a loud smack as the suction releases. I shift sides, try him with the other breast, but he's asleep again.

'What if I have to go away for work and you're not OK? And I'm not here for you, and Liv and Samuel?'

An icy dread creeps across my skin, prickling every pore. He doesn't trust me alone with the kids. I stand up, and he watches me lay Samuel in his bassinet, a slight frown on his brow.

'Look, if I have to go away, I need to know you're doing all right. That you haven't pulled your hair out and the house hasn't burned down. That you haven't run away and left the kids to live feral.' He laughs.

I don't move, my body frozen in place, my face a mask. *Too close.*

'And I know you can't check your phone all the time. You've got enough to worry about with these two.' He points at the bassinet and raises his eyes in the direction of Liv's bedroom above.

His unspoken words hover in the air: *It can't be like last time. You can't shut me out.*

I sit next to him again and reach for him, gazing at the white-gold wedding band he's worn every day since we married six years ago, so familiar it's almost part of his hand. My own hand looks minuscule in comparison. I smile. 'You're right. These first few months with a new baby are the hard bit. But it'll get better.'

I'll prove to him I'm coping this time. Especially if he's away a lot with work. We need a solid marriage if we're going to weather that. We need to trust each other.

'I love our life. Our family.' I feel a lump in my throat, and cough to loosen it. 'Baby hormones,' I try to joke, staring at the floor so tears don't spill.

'I love our family too.' He inhales, a sharp suck of air through his teeth. 'So maybe we make a deal?'

'Mm?' I keep my gaze fixed on the rug and his tartan slippers.

'I wasn't watching you tonight, but what you said made me think. Keep the baby monitor on in the kids' room. That way I can check on you all even when I'm on the other side of the world. I'll be able to see Liv at bedtime and Samuel at nappy changes.' He pivots so his knees touch my thighs, and holds out his little finger. 'And in return, I will always answer my phone and text you back. No matter what glamorous dinner I'm at. Or serious meeting, of course.'

I think about my side of the bargain: keep the baby monitor switched on at all times. Is that trusting me? Or just... surveillance?

His expression darkens at my silence and he drops his hand. 'I don't have to take the job. I can stay where I am, home every night at six and—'

'How can I agree to this?' Anger flashes inside me and my words come out louder than I intend. There's a grunt from the bassinet and I drop my voice. 'After what I heard on the monitor?'

He shakes his head, exasperated. 'I shouldn't even have brought up the new job tonight. It was too much to talk about today. I'm sorry, Mim.'

I pick Samuel up, ready to bring him upstairs for a final change and feed before I go to bed.

Jeremy kisses me on the cheek as I head out of the door. 'It's just an overtired brain making you a bit paranoid. You'll feel better in the morning.'

I freeze. *Paranoid.* How could he be so insensitive, after everything? I stare at him and he gazes back, eyes wide and guileless, totally unaware of how deep he cuts. But I'm too tired to address this. I force myself to unclench my jaw. Not tonight.

On the landing upstairs, I pause outside Liv's door, listening. Everything is quiet.

Then her door swings open.

She stands in the doorway, her pyjama top buttoned through the wrong buttons and her long hair falling over her face.

'Hey, Liv,' I say with a frown. She's usually such a heavy sleeper, especially for the first couple of hours after going to bed. Nothing can wake her. 'You OK?'

She doesn't move.

'What's up?' I shift Samuel to my chest and wrap my free arm around her shoulders.

She tenses and backs away from my touch. I frown. This isn't like her.

She whispers something.

'What did you say, baby?' I turn my ear towards her mouth to hear better.

'There's someone in my room.'

3

It's a relief when the sun finally rises the next day. During the night, the darkness of our bedroom felt like a prison. Through a gap in the curtains, I watch as Edinburgh's suburbs come to life and windows light up across the streets. The early risers, the shift workers, the insomniacs. And the breastfeeding mothers.

When Jeremy's alarm goes off, I'm propped up against pillows and fighting to keep my eyes open while Samuel feeds again. He has long since finished gulping the main part of his feed, the sucks turning to little flutters as he sleeps, his lips still wrapped around my nipple.

Jeremy swings his legs out of bed and opens his wardrobe door. 'So we have a deal? Baby monitor stays on, I accept the job?' He catches my eye in the mirror as he pulls out a couple of ties and holds them up. Trying to decide which one to wear to face his future boss and take the job offer.

Samuel's gums clamp down hard on my nipple and I inhale through my teeth. My eyes prickle with tears and I look down, stroking his head to soothe him.

Do I believe what he said last night? That he didn't speak to Liv over the monitor. Cautiously, yes, I think I do. But I do not agree it was an auditory hallucination, caused by an overtired brain.

So what does that mean? We've been hacked and a stranger is watching my babies?

And what about the person in Liv's room? I switched on the lights, checked the wardrobe. Nothing. Just a dream, perhaps.

He turns and kisses my hair. 'I'm so proud of you, Mim. You're coping brilliantly.'

I meet his eye. I need to know he means it. That he trusts me. 'I want you to take the job, Jeremy.'

He doesn't flinch. His eye contact doesn't waver. We link pinkies like schoolkids and my shoulders loosen in relief.

He pauses, gazing down at the baby in my arms. I can see Samuel's brain pulsating at his fontanelle, where the two plates of his skull have yet to fuse. His eyelashes rest on his cheeks, perfect little crescent moons that flutter while he suckles. His cheeks are round, with red blush and peachy smooth skin. He's perfect.

Jeremy straightens up and takes a breath. 'I don't want to go in today. I don't want to leave you so early. I'll be back as soon as I can, as soon as I've signed the paperwork.'

So I've only got a couple of hours to do what I need.

He shuts a drawer, and the dresser mirror tilts downwards. I look up, catching sight of my reflection. My pyjama top is unbuttoned, one breast hanging out and resting on the remnants of my bump, round and proud as if it still holds a baby. The other breast is mercifully covered by Samuel's head. I pull my top closed and smooth my hair. My cheeks burn, knowing this will be the image of me Jeremy carries with him while he's at work, surrounded by red-haired career women in pencil skirts and high heels. Who don't smell of sour milk and day-old sweat.

I smooth my hair again, hoping his last impression of me is a fairly attractive one, even though I feel like Medusa.

'You're gorgeous.' It's as if he can read my thoughts.

'Good luck today.' I run a finger under each eye, rubbing away the remains of what little sleep I had. 'Who are you meeting?'

'Tabitha, my new boss.' He runs his hands through his hair, leaving it sticking up. He looks so handsome in his suit. 'I'll talk to her about extra leave. She might let me take some time before starting the new contract, on top of the normal two weeks' paternity leave.'

I nod, not ready to get into it today. I know why he's saying this, and it's not because he wants more time with us. It's so he can keep tabs on me and make sure it's not a rerun of last time.

He leans over and kisses me on the cheek, his expression softening. 'I'm so sorry I have to go today. Look after yourself, OK? I'll call if I'm delayed. Ask for help if you need it: get Jac over or call your mum.'

I bite back a laugh at the idea of asking my mum for help. 'Mum's too busy living her second teenage phase.'

'Ah yes. The cruise.' He chuckles. I've been sharing the selfie-stick specials she's been sending for the past two weeks: Mum in a hot tub with five other pensioners, holding cocktails to the camera; riding a camel; hooked up to a parachute, about to be launched off the back of a speedboat. It's telling that her 'trip of a lifetime' coincided almost exactly with the birth of her second grandchild, who she therefore won't meet for at least a couple more weeks. 'She'll grow out of it,' I whisper, with a smirk at the phrase we use for Liv's more trying behaviours.

I place a palm on his face, smooth from his morning shave. 'We love you, Daddy.'

He takes sleeping Samuel from my arms and kisses his forehead before laying him carefully in his bedside cot. Then he stands back and surveys us both with a smile. 'Get some rest while he sleeps. I'll miss you all today.' His phone buzzes and he grabs it, turning the screen away from me and silencing its ring.

He's always got his phone in his hand. Has he always been this attached to it, or has something changed?

'That's Tabitha. See you soon. Kiss Liv for me.' He raises his phone to his ear and thunders down the stairs.

I leave the bedroom door ajar so I can hear if Samuel wakes up, and pull Jeremy's dressing gown around me as I cross the corridor. It smells of him: woodsmoke from the fireplace, the spice of his body wash, and a faint earthy undertone of his skin.

I stand in the corridor, listening to him moving around downstairs, chatting on the phone. 'No, I haven't heard from them yet... I'll check when I get to the office. I'm on my way now.' His voice fades as he closes the front door behind him.

It's time.

In the study, Jeremy's laptop sits open on the desk. I bypass his facial recognition and enter his PIN: Liv's birthday. The desktop wallpaper is one of my favourite pictures of the three of us: our cheeks squashed together in front of the penguins at the safari park, a fourth-birthday present for Liv from Jac, who took the photograph.

I open Instagram and click on one of the 'mumfluencers' I've followed for the last six months or so: Mummy_Talks_Straight. I try not to spend too much time on social media, and usually only follow people I know, but I made an exception for Jenna: her oldest son is about the same age as Liv, and she's got a new baby too, just a couple of months old. She felt like a kindred spirit, made even more relatable by her unashamed confessions: a self-described 'lazy mum', she encourages independent play in her son and prides herself on her ability to drink every cup of tea while it's still hot. #mumgoals, isn't that what they call it?

I click to open a new message and start to type:

Hey Jenna. Have you or any of your followers come across baby monitor hacking? I think my account might have been compromised but am doing a bit of research to make sure I'm not imagining it, ha ha! *cry-laughing emoji* You have so many followers, so I thought I'd check to see if you'd ever come across it. xx

I press send and sit back, arms folded across my still-rounded belly. The message delivers almost immediately, and the little green dot next to her profile picture flicks on. She's reading it.

I stand up and step back from the desk, considering whether to return to bed and try to get some more sleep, or go downstairs and make a coffee in the hope I can drink it before it goes cold. But before I get to the door, there's a beep from the computer.

I hadn't expected an immediate reply, but one line appears on the screen:

Hey friend!

Within moments, the three little dots appear to show she's typing again. I sit back down and lean forward, hand sticky on the mouse.

The laptop pings and a message pops up on screen:

No, sorry.

I type quickly:

Could you ask your followers? Like, run a poll?

She types again. I hold my breath as the three little dots dance.

Miriam, I promise you, these stories aren't real. The ones already out there have done so much damage; they're scaring parents enough that they're unplugging their baby monitors. It's never happened. All the stories are fabricated. X

My face flushes and I release the breath I was holding in one big gush of air. Why would someone make that up? I've heard about this, articles popping up in my newsfeed. I didn't imagine what I heard. But still, I feel foolish, as if I've somehow revealed myself to believe in a crazy theory like a faked moon landing or flat earth.

OK. Thanks anyway. xx

I close Instagram and open a new tab, where I log into the baby monitor website, which is called Guardian Angel: the portal where you can watch your monitor feed.

Liv's bed appears on the screen in black and white: she's lying on her side, arms outstretched in front of her, hair flowing behind her. Like a freeze-frame image of her leaping from a building. The image quality isn't great, but I can see her lips pursed in the serious expression she's always had while asleep, ever since she was a baby. It feels like someone is squeezing my heart: a love so big it hurts.

But I'm not here to watch my daughter sleep. I'm here to work out who else is watching her.

Down the side of the feed are some buttons: arrows to move the camera to pan around the room, and a little loudspeaker option that you can press to switch on the two-way intercom. The button someone presses to watch Liv. To tell her Mummy doesn't love her.

I open my account settings and look at the options. There are so many. *Account management. Account verification. Account linking. Authorised devices.*

To my sleep-deprived brain every option looks the same. I wish I could ask Jeremy to help. He's much more technologically minded. But I can't do that. He can't know the dark places my mind goes. I glance at the clock. It's nearly time to wake Liv and I've accomplished nothing but scrambling my brains.

I close the Guardian Angel tab.

I decide to start from the very basics and open a search engine in an incognito window.

Baby monitor hacking, I type.

Over four million results. They can't all be fake?

I feel sicker and sicker as I scroll through, opening pages here and there. I read stories of toddlers being woken over and over again during the night by disembodied voices, cameras panning around kids' rooms, women being watched while they breastfeed their babies, strange music playing into a nursery, someone watching nappy changes.

There are even recordings online: their grainy black-and-white images adorning the news articles from around the world, inviting you to watch someone else's life unravelling at the hands of... who? And why?

The Instagrammer was wrong. Baby monitors get hacked all the time. It does exist. And it's terrifying. I scroll until I can't scroll any more. I'm frozen at the desk, spit pooling in my mouth as I try not to vomit. Why would someone want to do this? That's what I can't fathom. What's in it for the voyeurs?

Some articles imply that it's trolls causing chaos for chaos's sake, lurking around sites like 4chan, upsetting people for the thrill of it. There's a weird superiority to it: showing people their passwords are weak, educating them with a demonstration of why they should *be better*. God, there are some dicks out there.

My thoughts shrink from the darker motives, but I can't look away from the screen. Paedophiles and traffickers, gathering footage to sell on the dark web. Collecting details of people's movements; of their children's ages, names, whereabouts. Befriending them. Infiltrating their lives. Watching them grow up.

I scroll and scroll.

Kidnap.

Abuse.

Murder.

I'm frozen at the computer, the hair on my arms standing on end.

I need to work out who's doing this to our baby monitor. I need to find out who it is and catch them, stop them doing it to anyone else.

This isn't only about protecting Liv and Samuel. It's bigger than that. If this person is part of a group of sickos all doing the same thing, I could get every one of them thrown in prison. I could protect hundreds of kids.

I've lost track of time, down this rabbit hole of horror. With a shake of my head, I bring myself back to the here and now. The sun has risen, casting an orange glow across the surface of Jeremy's desk.

It's time to wake Liv.

I close my tabs and shut down the laptop, and head to her room.

'Wakey, wakey, lovely girl!' I trill as I push open her bedroom door.

But her bed is empty.

Where is my daughter?

I rush downstairs, my hand slippery on the banister, nearly tripping in my rush to find her.

I try to calm myself. This reaction is out of proportion, I know it. Ordinarily I wouldn't panic; I'd assume she'd woken early and taken herself downstairs to sneak in some CBeebies before Jeremy and I arrived to nag about screen time. But after her strange reaction to Samuel, and everything I read this morning about the hackers, and the voice I heard in her bedroom last night... my mind can't keep a handle on things. Nothing seems safe or normal today.

The living room is empty, the television screen blank. The room smells musty, as though no one lives in this house, even though just hours ago Jeremy and I were curled up together on the sofa, sharing champagne. The bassinet stands empty in the corner.

Samuel.

My whole body judders in fear. I left him in our room, sleeping in the sidecar cot attached to our bed. Our door was ajar; I'd have heard if he woke. But would I have heard if Liv crept into our room?

I take the stairs two at a time, nearly tripping again.

At our bedroom door, I pause for a moment, listening. There's no sound. I can't gauge whether the silence is a good sign of a still-sleeping baby, or an ominous sign of horror. The door catches on the carpet, making a *shh* sound as I push it open.

There's blood on the carpet.

A trail of blood.

I inhale, almost choking on my panic.

The blood leads around the other side of the bed, where Samuel's cot sits. The bed quilt is rucked up in such a way that I can't see the baby inside the cot. It could be empty. He could be gone.

I hear a rustle from around the side of the bed, someone moving.

'Liv?' I whisper, my breath shaking.

I rush around the bed, and freeze.

'Liv, what have you done?'

Where is the blood coming from?

I stifle a scream, try to think. I scan the scene, starting with the things that fuel the biggest, scariest fears.

Samuel stirs awake in his crib. His sleeping bag and sheets are still crisp white. No blood. He stretches, his little hands opening and closing, limbs shivering as his underdeveloped brain fires impulses through his nerves. Samuel is OK.

Liv sits cross-legged on the floor, upright. Conscious. Not bleeding to death. She's alive.

Worst-case scenarios discounted, I drop to my knees among the mess, grab Liv's hands with my own. 'What's happened, Liv?'

She won't look at me.

She's holding something in her right hand. White fabric, covered in blood. 'Did you hurt yourself?' As I prise open her fist, I see my dressmaking scissors on the carpet next to her bare foot: the sharpest scissors in the house. Blood on the blades.

'Oh, Liv. What have you done?'

She tries to scramble away, but I hold her wrist tight. Underneath the balled-up fabric, there's a cut right across the palm of her hand. I try to keep my face neutral; I don't want to scare her. I replace the material in her hand and close her fingers around it, then kiss her fist.

She looks at me then, surprised at my tenderness. At my lack of anger. Her hair is mussed and matted at the back. For a moment she looks like a wild animal in a trap, eyes wide and watchful. *What has happened to my sweet little girl?*

'You did the right thing, finding something to stop the blood.' I smile at her, pleased that I've found something to praise. Then I look around, see the detritus scattered across the carpet around us and realise what she was cutting. 'Oh, Liv,' I whisper again, taking in the destruction.

She sees my face fall and pulls her hand from mine. She shuffles away, her back against the wardrobe door, arms wrapped around her knees.

I pick up the closest item. Samuel's hospital wristband, shredded. His time of birth, weight, length, all scratched off and illegible.

Next, his early scan pictures. Torn, scribbled on, cut to ribbons. The one where it looked like he was waving; the one where he was sucking his thumb. The one where we were certain we could see he was definitely a boy, but the ultrasound tech corrected us with a stern 'That's the umbilical cord.' The contents of Samuel's memory box, all destroyed. We've shown her this box so many times over the months to help her understand. She's even asked to get it down, to look through the mementoes.

I look at her, cowering in the corner. 'That's Samuel's vest, isn't it?' I nod to her hand, which is still clutching her knees.

She shakes her head, but her eyes say different. It's not just any vest. It's the first one he wore; the one we brought him home in from the hospital yesterday. The one I folded into a Ziploc bag and placed in his memory box for us to keep for ever. Covered in my daughter's blood.

'Are you going to hit me?'

I freeze, my hand outstretched towards the rest of the mess. 'What?'

'Are you going to hit me?' she says again, her tone cold and indifferent. She's not afraid. She's just asking, in the same way she'd ask, 'Do I have school today?'

I feel the sharp sting of anger and try to swallow it. I ask myself again, what has happened to my daughter? I've never hit her, and neither has Jeremy. We've always been so careful and measured about how we discipline her, how we address misbehaviours. From the moment she learned to exert her will, we researched toddler brain development, gentle parenting, how to guide her through her big feelings. We've never even done a time-out. Why would she ask if I'm going to physically punish her? Where is this coming from?

I look around at the destroyed memory box, at the ripped keepsakes, the destruction of irreplaceable memories. My heart aches for Samuel, for what Liv has taken from him. From me.

I want her away from me. I wish I could send her to her room. But I've got to approach this with love. My daughter needs more, not less. I swallow everything, the anger, fear and frustration, and open my arms to her.

'Come here, baby.'

She looks at me with her wild-animal eyes. She doesn't move.

With effort, I heave my tired body towards her, already feeling the exhaustion from my run up the stairs. I felt nothing in that moment, but now I ache to my very bones. She flinches away from me as I wrap my arm around her bony shoulders and pull her close. I lean my chin against her head and kiss her hair. 'Let's get your hand cleaned and bandaged, shall we?'

Samuel begins to cry, the animalistic wail of a hungry baby. I can't help it; I drop my arm from Liv's shoulders and turn towards the crib.

As soon as I move away from her, Liv stands. 'It was right,' she says in a whisper.

I look up from Samuel's searching little mouth, which I'm attempting to line up with my exposed nipple. I try to keep my tone kind, try to retain that feeling of tenderness I conjured while we huddled on the floor surrounded by mess. 'What was right, Livvy?'

She walks towards the door and pauses. Then she turns, casts a glare over her shoulder.

'The voice was right. You don't love me.'

I rush into the café at the soft play, Liv trying to wrestle her hand from mine. The screams and shouts of children echo and amplify off the walls and ceiling. Uncanny paintings of Disney characters peer down from the walls: to me, there's nothing cute about these distorted murals, with their gaudy paint soaked into the breeze block.

I feel like a packhorse, with Samuel strapped to my chest in the sling and the nappy bag banging into my legs with every step. My body feels like I've run a marathon. It's 10 a.m. and it should be bedtime already. But I need to talk to my friends.

Blowing a strand of hair from my face, I pause and glance around, finally spotting Nicole and Zain hunched over their coffees like every Tuesday, discarded shoes and socks littering the area alongside the table. They're deep in conversation, Nicole stopping talking only to shove cake into her mouth, Zain's forehead wrinkled into his constant funereal frown.

I can't help but grin at them as I cross to their table. 'I'm so glad to see you two,' I blurt, not even waiting for them to finish their conversation. In the last few days, I've forgotten how to talk to adults.

They stare at me in silence, mouths open, before replacing

their surprise with big smiles. 'Here she is!' They both stand to greet me, giving me careful hugs.

'Hello, stranger!' Nicole pats me on the shoulder. 'We weren't expecting to see you for at least a few weeks.' She looks concerned, and her eyes flick to Zain with a small frown. 'Shouldn't you be resting?'

I shrug. 'I'm tired, but I feel OK. And Liv needed to get out of the house or she'd be climbing the walls.'

Both give knowing nods, glancing up at the play structure to check on their own children: Lottie and Kai. They're the same age as Liv, and just as wild.

They coo over the baby for as long as they have to, but I can tell they're desperate to get back to adult chat: Zain and Nicole have retained their pre-parent identities, raising children as an addition to their lives instead of the centre of them. I'm grateful to be reminded that the world doesn't begin and end with the contents of your nappy bag or the number of baby classes you attend.

Liv tries to run off into the soft play to cause chaos with the other kids. 'Wait a minute,' I say, leaning down and putting a hand on her shoulder.

Zain and Nicole sit back down to their coffees while I help Liv remove her shoes. I stand up, expecting her to dart off to find her friends. 'You ready to go play, Livvy?'

'I'm a good girl?' she asks, her eyes on her bare toes against the grubby carpet.

'A very good girl.' I stroke her fine curls, so soft and light.

'Then you won't give me away?'

Nicole and Zain both glance up at this, then away, the unspoken understanding that these things fade faster when you pay them little attention.

My stomach clenches. 'What?' I crouch down once more. 'I would never give you away. What's this?'

'They said you won't want me any more now you have

Sam.' Liv's lip trembles and her plump cheeks flush. Nicole catches my eye again and I force a smile.

I pull Liv into a cuddle. 'Who said that? They're wrong. I love you, Liv.'

'Liv!' A shriek fills the air from high above us: Kai, Zain's son, in one of the upper levels of the soft play, his face pressed against the netting. 'COME PLAY!' he yells.

I want to ask more, but Liv wriggles away, her confusion forgotten.

I drop her shoes into the pile and sit at the table, taking a breath. 'Anyone want an extra kid or two?' I try to joke, but my voice trembles.

Nicole gives me a sharp look. 'Everything all right?' she asks. 'We were talking about the new reception teacher. Not very exciting.'

Work feels a world away from where I am now, deep in the moment-by-moment universe of keeping a newborn alive. But I would give so much to feel the hush that descends when I pick up a pencil and sketch an outline onto paper, or watch the face of one of my pupils as they create a piece of art that helps them see their world more clearly.

Zain grins and pushes his coffee over to me, the sleeve of the cup warmed by the latte inside. 'Have this. I haven't touched it yet. Hope you've got some gossip to cheer us up. War stories and terrible losses of dignity are most welcome.'

'Yeah, none of this "hashtag blessed" rubbish; save that for social media,' adds Nicole.

I nearly choke with laughter on the foam of my latte.

Nicole picks at her chipped nail varnish and throws me a look. 'As much as it's lovely to see you, why are you here, Mim? You should be in bed, breastfeeding, while your husband brings you toast and wrangles Liv. He's on paternity leave, right? Make the most of him while he's still around.'

My cheeks flush. 'I'm OK, honestly.'

She looks at me, sceptical. 'Where is he? Surely he wouldn't have let you come out so soon.'

I bristle. 'He isn't my boss, Nicole.'

'No, that's Jac,' she mutters, but then flashes me a smile to show she's joking. We used to be inseparable, the three of us. Learning dance routines together after school, talking endlessly about the boys we fancied... but somewhere along the way, Jac and Nicole's friendship diverged. Jac thinks Nicole's a weirdo. Nicole thinks Jac's controlling and bossy, interfering in my life. And Jac didn't go down the motherhood route when we did, which put more distance between them, too. Somehow I've managed to maintain close friendships with both of them, much to the other's annoyance.

I take a big gulp of coffee and remember why I'm here. 'Actually, I wanted to talk to you both. There's something going on and I need some help.'

There's a shriek from the play area, and all the parents in the café glance up, assessing whether it's their child and whether the sound is one of pain, danger or fun. There's no follow-up scream, so slowly the conversations start again.

'So what—' The tannoy beeps, and a crackling voice booms over the loudspeaker: 'Would the owner of a silver Audi estate, registration FY12 YHC, please come to the ticket desk urgently.'

My stomach flips. 'No.'

Nicole and Zain look at me, surprised. 'That your car?'

'Must have left the lights on or something.' I stand up, Samuel still strapped to my chest. I take a sip of my latte and place it back on the table. 'Will you keep an eye on my stuff, please? Oh, and—'

'And Liv, yes. Don't worry, babe,' Nicole says.

As I walk away, I see my friends lean in to talk across the table. I feel their eyes on me as I approach the desk. My ears heat up.

The girl behind the counter looks young enough to still be in school, her skin shiny and smooth. 'Can I help you?' she asks, her eyes barely leaving the computer screen. 'How many tickets?'

'Oh, no tickets, thank you. My car was just announced over the loudspeaker.'

She suppresses a smirk. 'I'll get my boss.'

I frown, glancing over my shoulder through the glass doors and into the car park, where a man is unloading trays of ready-made sandwiches from a van onto a trolley.

'Madam? You're the owner of the silver Audi?' The manager has slicked-back hair and is wearing a baby-blue polo shirt.

'Yes, what's the—'

'Your car has hit another vehicle. You must have left the handbrake off.'

I'm suddenly too hot, my hair sticking to my neck, moisture gathering on my forehead. I curse my body for refusing to fit any of my old clothes yet, forcing me to wear this awful thick polo neck. My cheeks must be bright red.

I swallow. I hate this. I hate driving, hate being an adult, hate owning things that cost lots of money. Hate being responsible for a vehicle so large that if it hits someone they could die. I'm not ready for this kind of life.

I want to turn around, to walk away and leave everything behind: the car, the kids, the credit card bill, the bank account teetering on overdraft every month, the marriage...

The manager clears his throat. 'Follow me, please.'

I trail behind him into the car park. The delivery van has now left, and I can see the damage my car has caused. How has this happened?

I parked on a slight incline, I see now as I survey the scene. As I pulled into the car park, Samuel started whining for milk at the same time as Liv realised where we were going, bouncing up and down with excitement in her car seat, throwing herself against the straps. I was faced with a conundrum: let Liv wait while I fed Samuel, or let Samuel wait until we got settled inside, risking a full-blown newborn meltdown.

It's possible I knocked the handbrake as I leaned over to pick Samuel up, or maybe I didn't put it on properly in the confusion. I have no idea: I'm so tired, I'm surprised I could even dress myself this morning. Samuel is three days old, and I have yet to eat a full meal, take a proper shower or drink a hot cup of coffee. I'm running on fumes and my brain is working at about fifteen per cent capacity. My body hurts, and this morning I tried to put the kettle instead of the milk into the fridge.

I wrap my arms around Samuel's tiny form, cuddled in the carrier against my chest. I shouldn't have come.

Who knows what happened? It doesn't matter. What matters is that the back of my car is caved in and the number plate is lying on the tarmac. And behind my car: a smashed-up Rolls-Royce, the little winged figurine bent and scuffed, the headlights cracked.

I groan. 'Why would someone park their Rolls here, of all places?'

The manager stands up straighter, offended. 'We share the car park with the business park,' he mumbles.

I shake my head, unable to process anything he's saying. My stomach heaves as I realise what this means: repair bills, increased insurance premiums... confessing to Jeremy.

The manager shifts, his shoes scraping on the tarmac. 'Well, I guess I'll leave you to exchange details.' He shuffles off.

For the first time, I notice the man standing six feet away, Bluetooth headset in his ear as he paces up and down. 'Of course I wasn't at fault. I wasn't even in the car.'

I wince at his tone. He must be speaking to his insurance company.

I swallow and take a step towards him. He freezes, noticing me, and then his face clouds as he realises I'm the owner of the car that smashed up his precious Rolls. I felt guilty until I heard him speak, saw the disdain on his face. Now I'm sad our Audi didn't do more damage.

He hangs up and folds his arms.

'I'm really sorry. I'll call my insurance. Let me give you my details.' I unlock the car and reach into the glove compartment for a pen and paper.

Once I've noted everything down, he takes the scrap of paper without a word.

'We'll sort everything out through our insurers, then?' I ask.

'I hope you realise how inconvenient this is.'

I frown. 'It was an accident. I'm sorry.'

'You already said that.'

I shrug, a wave of tiredness washing over me. I can't be bothered to argue and my boobs have started to ache. I need to straighten the car and get back inside to Liv. 'I've got to go, but look, can you text me your details? My mobile number's on that paper.'

He glares at me, gives a tiny nod.

I'm about to go back inside when the glass doors burst open.

'See? There she is, Mummy's right there.' Nicole rushes across the car park carrying a red-faced and howling Liv, her thumb in her mouth.

'Is everything OK?' I ask, scanning my daughter for injuries.

'She couldn't see you, thought you'd left.'

Liv reaches out for me, her incoherent sobs almost forming words: *Don't leave me just because you have Sam now.* My heart breaks for her, my poor, confused daughter. I pull her into my arms and bury my nose in her neck, mumbling words of comfort to reassure her. At first she snuggles in, but as soon as she realises Samuel is tucked into the sling on my chest, she pushes me away. 'No,' she snaps.

When I look up, the man has walked away; he's sitting behind the wheel of his dented car, glaring at me through the windshield, a cold look in his eye and the blue light blinking on his headset.

'Poor thing.' Nicole strokes Liv's hair. 'What made you think Mummy would leave you, Liv?' She turns to me. 'What happened out here?'

With my free hand I gesture at the mess I've made of the Rolls, and the wreck of my own car. My hands are shaking. My cheeks burn.

'What happened is I'm s-t-u-p-i-d,' I spell, and Nicole smirks. I make my tone sound jovial, but I want to say worse: *I shouldn't be allowed in a car when I'm this tired. I'm dangerous. Why did I go out?*

But I can't say that. Zain and Nicole and I share our TMI confessions and messy lives, but they still require a level of pretence from me. I don't have to be put together, but I can't be an emotional mess either.

'I'm sure I won't feel like this in a couple of weeks, but today...' I rub my face with both hands, then glance at Liv and lower my voice. 'Two kids feels like too many right now.' I force a laugh.

Nicole places a hand on my shoulder. 'This could happen to anyone,' she says, in a voice so soothing I could almost cry just like Liv did: huge, relieving sobs. For a moment I imagine sinking to the ground, pressing my face into the tarmac and letting go of everything I'm trying to keep inside.

The kids would be fine without me. They wouldn't even remember me. *I could just walk away.*

6

'You should get home,' Zain says, a comforting arm around me after I explain what happened outside.

'I'll head off in a few minutes. First I need to talk to you both.'

They exchange a glance, and I know they were talking about me while I was outside. I ignore it and carry on.

Liv's welded to my side, her head resting against my upper arm. 'Liv, will you go and find Lottie and Kai? They'd love to play with you.'

She hesitates for a moment, and then runs off.

I take a breath. 'Last night I heard a voice on the baby monitor. Talking to Liv.'

'Oh my God.' Nicole shudders. 'I've read articles about that kind of thing. So, so creepy. Stories of the camera panning across the room, the live-streaming lights coming on when no one else has access...' She drifts off with a grimace.

'These Wi-Fi monitors are a risk,' says Zain, who works in our school's IT department. His expertise is why I've dragged our new baby out of the house today when I should be resting, feeding and taking it easy. 'The non-Wi-Fi ones are a better choice. Even better if you can get one of those old-school audio-only ones.'

I shrug. 'Bit late now.'

'Did you disconnect it?' Zain asks.

I glance down, check Samuel in the sling. He's still fast asleep, his face pressed to my chest. 'Not yet. Jeremy wants to be...' I stop. There's no way I can explain the weird bargain we struck. So I tell the other truth, the plan that began to emerge this morning while I roamed around the internet uncovering the depth of depravity behind these hackers.

Zain and Nicole listen, their faces blank. When I finish, they exchange another look.

'So you want to keep letting this hacker talk to your daughter so you can trap him?'

My cheeks flush. I get out my phone, clicking on the Guardian Angel app. I slide the phone across the table to Zain. 'Can you tell me anything about who else logs in?'

'Mim, this is crazy. I know you think you're doing a good deed, unmasking some weirdo pervert or whatever. But from a tech side, it's not that simple. If your monitor is hooked up to your home Wi-Fi, they could be using your monitor as a way into other devices on your network.'

'It's more than that. They're messing with Liv's head. With *my* head.'

He rubs a hand over his stubble. 'It's more likely they're scammers looking for financial details.'

I push my phone at him. 'Please? Tell me what you can find.'

He holds my gaze for a moment before looking down at the phone. 'You need to change all your passwords. Set up two-factor authentication. Get password management software.'

I smile at him, pretending I understand what he's saying.

As he clicks around in the app, Nicole reaches across the table and lays a hand on my arm. 'We're here for you, you know.

You've got a newborn and a little girl barely out of the terrible toddler years. You're deep in the woods right now. One hundred days of darkness. Remember that.'

'One hundred days of darkness?' I repeat, puzzled.

'The first days after the birth of a new baby. The darkness starts to fade around a hundred days in.'

I swallow, fighting tears. I turn my face away, but it's too late.

Her hand gets heavier on my arm. 'It will get better.'

I shake my head. 'I know. It's not that. I...' I stop. All the things I can't say. That I don't remember the first one hundred days of Liv's life. Perhaps it was like this, only I wouldn't know, because I have no memories. It's still possible that this time I'll end up right where I was back then, in a darkness so deep I'm blind.

Zain clears his throat and slides my phone back to me. 'I'm sorry, Mim. I can't see anything unusual on the app. No recognised logins, no unusual activity. It's possible you'll see more on the desktop version; they sometimes have additional features you can't access on the app.'

I pocket my phone, nodding. 'Thanks. I'll have a look again on the laptop.'

I wave at Liv to come down. It's time to go home.

'You should contact their help desk. They might be able to detect IP addresses, that sort of thing. And help you increase your security.'

As Liv fastens the Velcro straps on her shoes, my thoughts drift to the smashed-up car, the increased premiums, the cost of nursery when I return to work, the credit card we struggle to pay every month. Jeremy's new job makes all the difference. We need him to take it. And for him to do that, I need a monitor he can check even when he's in another country, so he can see I'm taking care of our kids and myself.

It's just for today, I tell myself. I'm not willing to sacrifice my child's safety and wellbeing to save others. I will protect Liv with every fibre of my being, and that includes removing access to her on the baby monitor. I have until her bedtime to do my detective work, and then I'll change our password and lock out the hacker for ever.

'And unplug the monitor, Mim. Don't let the creeps in.'

My friends can't help me. I have to deal with this alone.

7

The front door whips open before my key touches the lock.

I smile, relieved. 'Thank you, I didn't have enough hands.'
I'm juggling Samuel in his car seat, the changing bag, and Liv,
who needs to be touching me at all times today, apparently.

'Where the *hell* have you been?' Jeremy hisses, taking the
car seat from my hands. He's pale and sweaty.

'Are you OK?' I ask. 'You look ill.'

'I was sick with worry, Miriam. We have a brand-new baby
and you're supposed to be resting, but you take our children and
disappear.' He turns and stalks into the house with Samuel,
leaving Liv and me on the doorstep.

Her eyes widen in surprise. 'Why's Daddy cross?'

'I'm not sure, baby. He's cross with me, though. Not you.
You've done nothing wrong.'

I settle her in front of the TV before bracing myself to enter
the kitchen, where Jeremy is banging around in anger.

'What's going on?' I climb onto a stool at the breakfast bar,
trying not to wince at the movement.

Samuel is still in his car seat on the floor, fast asleep. I'll
have to take him out soon; they say it's not safe to leave them in

those seats after the journey's over. Another little thing that might kill my baby.

Jeremy stops emptying the dishwasher. 'I went to work for a couple of hours, and when I got back, you were missing.'

'I went out. You could have called me.'

'You're three days post-partum, Miriam.' He turns and grabs a couple of highball glasses from the dishwasher, one in each hand.

'And I felt OK. I wanted some fresh air, and Liv needed to get out too. I wanted to see my friends.'

He pauses, one glass in the air halfway to the cupboard. His hand trembles. 'So you were with Jac? I knew it. She has no idea about the recovery time you need after having a baby. It's always Jac—'

'No, I wasn't with Jac, actually.' I feel a moment of triumph. He's always been a bit funny about Jac: saying I have one glass of wine too many when we go out, that she doesn't understand the responsibilities parents have to take on, that she's inconsiderate to drop in unannounced to people's houses when they have kids, that she goes through boyfriends too fast and picks unsuitable men because she subconsciously doesn't want to commit... His list of criticisms is long. But Liv adores her, and I like that she represents a version of me I don't get to see very often: the old me. The before-kids me.

'Look, I know I'm supposed to be resting. If you hadn't gone to the office, I could have done that.'

'This is how things go wrong, Miriam.'

'Liv needs entertainment. I can't drop everything for Samuel when we have Liv too. She's struggling; you know that.'

The tension in his face releases slightly.

'I took her to the soft play for an hour. It wasn't too strenuous. I got to have a coffee with Zain and Nicole, and Samuel slept in the sling. I could feed him when he was hungry, and they have a great changing facility. It's this big room with a couple of sofas—'

'I don't need to hear about the baby change at the soft play, Miriam.'

'Fine. But I was thinking about our family.'

'Not about me.' He's gripping Liv's plastic Minnie Mouse cup so hard it's warping.

'You went out. You went to work during your paternity leave, Jeremy.'

'To accept a job. I was thinking about our family too.'

I can't tell him about the car. Not now. I slide from the stool and bend over to unclip Samuel from his car seat. I manage to lift him into my arms without waking him, and sink into the battered leather armchair in the corner of the kitchen.

'Miriam, I'm very concerned about you. And now so's our midwife.'

'What?' My fingers freeze where they're fiddling to unfasten the cup of my maternity bra. 'What about our midwife?'

'When I got back from work, she was standing on the doorstep. Holding a weighing scale.'

No. *No no no.* 'The third-day visit.'

'Yes. She came to discharge you over to the health visitor and check that Samuel's gaining weight. And you weren't here.'

I grab my phone and flick to the calendar. There it is: *11 a.m. midwife.* 'How could I have forgotten?'

He folds his arms. 'I don't know, Miriam. Maybe because you've just had a baby and your brain isn't working? Maybe because you should be staying at home and resting, not driving all over the city meeting up with your friends for coffee. Jesus.'

I definitely can't tell him about the car. I get Samuel latched on and he suckles away, making little grunting noises. 'There's nothing wrong with my brain.'

'So far.'

'Leave it, Jeremy.'

He sighs and sits on a stool, his head in his hands. 'Look, I know you're feeling OK right now. I'm glad. That's good.' His voice is muffled through his fingers. 'But at this point last time you seemed fine too.'

My skin prickles and I stifle a shudder. My mouth is dry. 'Can I have some water, please?'

He brings me a glass and I down the whole thing, dripping a tiny droplet onto Samuel's forehead. He doesn't notice, keeps suckling as if nothing happened.

'Is she coming back?'

Jeremy looks at me from around the open fridge door. 'Huh?'

'The midwife.' I like our midwife, and this was her last visit. 'I was hoping I could thank her, maybe give her a box of chocolates or something.' Specifically, I'm grateful to her for being so discreet. She knows what happened with Liv, but made it clear we didn't have to talk about it. She kept an eye on me, but told me that every pregnancy is different, and just because something happens with one doesn't mean the same thing will happen with the next. I've clung to that hope, and a box of chocolates is the least I can do. Not missing our final appointment. God, she won't think it's happened again, will she?

Jeremy piles up his arms with items from the fridge: a tub of ghee, two peppers, garlic, and a box of chicken breasts. He dumps it all on the counter and grabs a chopping block. He must be making curry. 'Yes, Miriam, she's coming back. She has to. Today was important and you can't skip it.'

'That's not what happened.'

He shrugs, grabbing a knife from the block. 'They need to do Samuel's heel-prick thing and check your stitches. She's coming back tomorrow.'

I swallow. 'What time?'

'Why? Planning on going out again?'

I shake my head. I was planning to sneak the car to the garage tomorrow, get the boot fixed without Jeremy finding out. I guess that'll have to wait, and I'll have to hope he doesn't look at the Audi in the meantime. Luckily it's parked down the street because there weren't any spaces outside the house when I arrived home. Maybe he won't see it.

While Jeremy cooks dinner, Samuel and I join Liv in the living room, where she's watching CBeebies. She tells me about the silly games Bandit has been playing with Bingo and Bluey, and for a moment it's like before: Liv's content and I'm relaxed. Then I see a light blinking in the corner and everything rushes back. The baby monitor's parent unit, squatting in the shadows, goading me with its flashing lights. Is someone logged into our account now? Watching Liv's empty bedroom, waiting for her to return?

I lay Samuel in the bassinet and grab my laptop, angling the screen away from Liv. She doesn't notice, curled up on the couch with her thumb in her mouth. She hasn't sucked her thumb for years, but I guess regression is normal with a new baby.

I log into our monitor account and navigate to the help page. I click through the options until the chatbot connects me with a human being.

Debbie: How can I help you today? I'm Debbie.

Miriam: Increase monitor security.

Debbie: Thanks for your enquiry. Good news! Guardian Angel is at the cutting edge of digital security technology so your little one is safe. Only those authorised to access your monitor feed are able to do so. We've written a number of articles...

I skim the copied-and-pasted script, frustrated. As I'm reading, 'Debbie' sends over some links, one to a digital security checklist. I open it in a new tab and stay on the chat.

Miriam: Can you tell if someone accessed my baby monitor?

Debbie: If you're concerned about your monitor's security, we recommend changing your password to a new, secure and unique password made up of letters, numbers and symbols. We also highly recommend enabling two-factor authentication.

I roll my eyes. I just wanted someone to tell me if they could see whether someone else had logged into my account.

'Dinner's ready,' calls Jeremy from the kitchen.

I close out of the chat. 'Be right there.'

I switch off the TV despite Liv's protests. 'Go see if Daddy needs help setting the table, please.'

After she leaves the room, I spend one more minute on the laptop and change our password.

That's it. I've locked them out.

8

After that, I get my lovely daughter back. For the next few weeks, she's cuddly, happy and interested in Samuel. Sure, she's a bit resentful and struggles with a new baby in the house, but it's normal kid stuff: refusing to eat dinner, jumping all over the furniture, forgetting to be quiet when he's sleeping. We follow all the parenting advice: we talk to her on her level, try natural consequences, validating her feelings, time-ins, cuddles...

Then Jeremy's new job starts.

As he leaves for his first trip, he grabs his wheeled suitcase in one hand, his laptop bag in the other, and kisses each of us.

'Leave the monitor on, please.' It's the last thing he says to me.

As soon as the door closes behind his retreating back, Liv's behaviour escalates again. Her actions have a twinge of adult-hood that makes me believe the voice still talks to her, despite the new password.

There's hitting, kicking, spitting, and bed-wetting for the first time since she was toilet-trained. She runs away in the supermarket, throws tantrums on the way to school. Bleach appears in Samuel's bottle. Luckily I smell it before I pour any expressed breast milk inside.

Changing the password didn't work, and I realise I can't control my daughter but someone else can. They've got back in.

Two days into Jeremy's trip, the sound of smashing glass brings me running downstairs from the bathroom, Samuel dripping in my arms, shivering in his hooded towel.

Liv stands barefoot in the middle of the kitchen, surrounded by the sparkle of glass. My favourite Dartington crystal wine glasses. A wedding present from Jac's parents.

The cupboard door stands open, still swinging on its hinges. She must have climbed onto the counter to reach them. She looks up at me, eyes wide in mock innocence. Her big toe flexes, lifting from the tile and settling back down.

'Stand still, Liv,' I warn. 'I'll get you some shoes so you don't cut your feet.'

In less than a second, her expression switches to defiance and she looks away, setting her mouth in a firm line. She makes ready to move.

'No!' I step forward, but I can't do anything, standing there helpless with Samuel in my arms.

She walks backwards through the glass. The delicate crystal crunches under her bare feet.

Blood blooms across the tiles.

She doesn't cry. I wrap her feet in tea towels and carry her to the car, strapping her in and locking the doors before running back to the house to collect Samuel and the nappy bag. I drive us to the children's hospital on the opposite side of the city, and we sit in the waiting room, Liv on my knee.

'What happened here?' asks a passing nurse, directing the question to Liv.

'I didn't want to do it. Mummy told me to.'

The nurse's friendly, inquisitive look disappears. She

glances at me and looks away before I can shake my head in denial.

As soon as we return from Sick Kids, Liv with bandaged feet, I scrub the bloody footprints from the kitchen floor. I give up on my plan to entrap the hacker and abandon the stupid deal I made with Jeremy. There's too much at stake. He'll understand.

That's enough.

I unplug the baby monitor.

Three hours later, Jeremy notices. Both kids are upstairs – Samuel napping and Liv having some quiet time – and I've just sat down in front of the TV when my phone vibrates with an incoming call. My stomach flips like a kid who knows they've been naughty.

'Hey.'

'The monitor's off.'

I close my eyes and utter a silent scream of frustration.

'Miriam?'

I open my eyes again, focus on the muted TV. It's some cooking show: stressed-looking chefs in white coats bustling around a hot kitchen trying to cook without the proper ingredients.

'There was an accident.'

His voice turns urgent. 'With the monitor? Or something else? What happened?'

I tell him about the glass, about Liv's behaviour.

'Poor Liv. Poor you. What a day.' He pauses, and I know what's coming next. 'But why turn off the monitor?'

I sigh. He won't believe me. It'll make me sound crazy. I can't tell him. 'It's stopped working,' I lie. 'I'll order a new one.'

He sighs. 'I know that's not true.'

I let the silence continue.

'Look, I know Liv's not been easy lately. And you're still recovering from the birth. Why don't we get someone in to help?'

'A nanny? I thought you hated that idea.'

'A friend to come and stay, maybe?'

'They have lives, kids, jobs, things they can't drop.' Not to mention he's asking me to organise yet another thing. I know he's busy at work, but does he have to delegate at home, too? I have enough to do without my husband assigning me tasks.

'Jac, then? Or your mum.'

I let out a joyless laugh. 'I'll contact a child psychologist, Jeremy. Can we try one thing at a time?'

'I need to know you're all OK. Turn the monitor on, Miriam.'

'I told you, it stopped working.'

He pauses for a moment and I think he's going to let it go. Then, 'I saw you turn it off. I watched you walk into the room and unplug it before the feed went dead.'

I don't say anything.

He takes a shaky breath. 'I'm worried about you, Mim. When's the next health visitor appointment? I'd like you to talk to them about your mental health.'

'I'm fine. It's Liv we need to worry about. And this baby monitor. It's not safe to have it switched on.'

He groans. 'This again?'

I haven't mentioned it to him since the first night we came home from the hospital. I knew he wouldn't believe me. 'Jeremy, the voice on the monitor tells her I'm going to hit her. It tells her I don't love her and I'm going to give her away so that Samuel's our only child. It tells her to feed him bleach, to destroy his things.'

'Oh my God.' He sounds genuinely shocked.

My shoulders relax. He believes me.

I should have told him before. Perhaps all I needed to do

was include him. I wait, listening to the static on the line. He's going to know how to solve this. Even if we never plug the monitor back in, we still have a lot of work ahead of us to repair the damage done to our beautiful daughter. And we can do it together. With the right love and care, Liv can go back to being the happy kid she was before. The one who sings to herself when she thinks she's alone; the one who skips to the park because it's faster than walking.

'Oh my God,' he says again. This time he sounds afraid.

I stand up, pace from the fireplace to the bookshelf and back, gesturing with my free hand. 'We can fix this now. We'll get help for Liv and she'll—'

'Miriam, stop.' I can hear him typing something into his computer. 'I can't believe I didn't see this before. I was so afraid of it; I thought I was watching so closely. But in the drama of Liv's behaviour, I missed it.'

I stop pacing and slump to the sofa. 'Missed what?'

'It's not Liv who needs help. It's you.'

My breath catches in my throat.

'Plug the monitor back in, Miriam.' His tone is cold.

No matter what I say, he shuts me down in the same steely voice. There's no space for me, for my theories, for what I've heard, for what I've seen in Liv. All he says is 'Plug the monitor back in.'

'Where's the person I married? My teammate.' I hate how my voice sounds: whiny and forlorn. Pathetic and lost. 'I need your help.'

'Miriam, believe me, I'm going to help you. But the help you need and the help you *think* you need are different things.'

I rub my face so hard my skin feels hot. 'No, please. I—'

'I'm going to go, Miriam. I'm going to speak to my boss about coming home early, because you're not well. And I'm going to call someone to come over, to be with you until I can get there.'

My stomach twists and I bend double, still seated on the sofa. I close my eyes against tears of frustration. I have no idea who he'll tell or what he'll tell them. I'm so ashamed of how he'll make me sound, ashamed of who he believes I've become. 'I'm your wife, Jeremy. The woman you love. The mother of your children.' If I can remind him I'm still me, maybe he'll hear me.

I hear a sharp intake of breath at the other end of the line. 'Where are they, Miriam?' He sounds terrified.

'They're fine. I'm taking good care of them.' I hear it then: what Jeremy can hear, what he imagines when I speak to him. In his mind, I'm the crazed mother in the horror film, standing over the bloody remains of her murdered children, an axe in her hand, saying, 'I'm taking good care of them.'

I remember that 1960s study where mentally healthy people got sent to psychiatric hospitals across America. I think back to my therapy training. Rosenhan et al., I think it was. They wanted to know what it was like in the institutions and how easy it was to distinguish between sane and insane. It was simple enough to get in and get diagnosed, but then as soon as you were a patient, all evidence of sanity became observed as symptoms of the claimed mental illness that got you locked up in the first place. You were stuck.

I'm one of those patients: the more I claim I'm fine, the less fine I seem. I can't win. I stand up, switch off the muted TV. 'I'll go and get Liv. You can speak to her. She's playing in her room.'

'Thank you.' I hear the relief in his voice. Perhaps I've managed to erase that crazed image of me holding the axe. Temporarily.

Liv is singing to herself, sitting in the middle of the floor surrounded by clothes from her dressing-up box. They're mostly old outfits of mine and Halloween costumes. When she looks up, I see she's got into my make-up: her eyes are blackened with eyeshadow, her mouth smudged a bloody red.

'You look pretty,' I offer.

Her face darkens. I've said something wrong.

'Daddy's on the phone. Would you like to speak to him?'

She smiles and scrambles to her feet, reaching out to the phone. She clicks on the screen, switching on the camera. 'Hi, Daddy!' she trills in the friendly, happy voice she never uses for me any more.

'Hi, baby!'

She glares at me and points at the door. 'Mummy, get out.'

'How are you doing?' Jeremy is saying. 'Are your feet OK?'

Liv pushes me towards the door and tries to close it on me, nearly trapping my fingers. I push back. I need to stay.

And sure enough, there it is: 'Baby, can you do me a favour?'

'Yes, Daddy,' she says sweetly.

'I need you to plug in the baby monitor for me, OK?'

She's already heading towards it, one hand outstretched, the phone balanced in the other.

'No!' I shout, and run across the room, almost tripping on a high-heeled shoe.

Liv shrieks, a mixture of delight and fear. She's not used to me behaving like this: chasing and snatching. I grab the monitor and cables. 'Jeremy, I'm not doing it,' I call to the phone, still in Liv's hand. 'It's not safe.'

Liv rushes at me and tries to grab the monitor, her expression still switching between frivolous fun and seriousness. I hold it high in the air, out of her reach.

She jumps, arms swinging.

'I'm not giving it to you, Olivia.'

'But Daddy said—'

'Daddy's wrong. Jeremy, you can't use Liv like this.' I try to calm my voice, but I'm incensed.

'MIRIAM!' Jeremy shouts.

Liv stops jumping and looks at the phone screen, where Jeremy's face peers out at us ineffectually. He can't do anything.

'Plug in the monitor, Miriam. I need to see you're all OK.'

'Do what Daddy says, Mummy.'

I shake my head and walk towards the door. 'That voice that talks to you on the monitor, Liv. It's a bad person. It's not safe.'

Her face flushes red and her free hand makes a fist. She speaks in a low tone, with danger underneath. 'That's my friend. My friend loves me.'

I shake my head and take the phone from her hand. 'Did you hear that, Jeremy?'

But the screen is black.

Liv launches herself at me, trying to grab the monitor, my phone, anything. She's like a wild animal, scratching and biting. 'Give me the monitor. I want to talk to my friend,' she screams.

I hold her off, manage to toss the monitor into the corridor and shut the door. I pick Liv up and sit her on the bed, where she folds her arms across her heaving chest. Her hair is everywhere, the make-up smeared across her cheeks.

'We don't hit or kick. We don't snatch things from other people's hands.'

She glares at me through narrowed eyes. 'I don't love you. Daddy doesn't love you. I wish I had a different mummy.'

I stand up. I can't speak.

'I wish you'd given me away.'

9

It's just for a minute. I need some air. Some space.

As soon as I step out into the garden, I feel a release from the iron bands that were wrapped tight around my chest while I was inside. I breathe the damp autumn air into my lungs.

I close the door softly behind me and walk away from the house, following the flagstone path to the garden gate.

Samuel is napping, Liv is playing. The children are fine.

I am not.

I slide the deadbolt and the wooden gate swings open to reveal the old carriage lane behind our house. On the other side is the park, lined with ancient trees from the now-demolished estate that once owned this land. The grassland is threaded with paths, dotted with dog-waste bins and benches.

I cross the lane, the gravel sharp under my bare feet, and trudge to the nearest bench. It's so close to our house that I'm sure if Samuel cried I could hear him. I know I shouldn't be here, but I have no choice. A moment to catch my breath, and then I'll go back. They won't even know I'm gone. It's the same duration as a bathroom trip. That's all.

The wooden bench is damp under my thighs, and the feeling ignites a long-buried memory: sitting on another bench, shivering in the cold, broken and alone. But that time, Liv was with me in the pram, her newborn howls loud and insistent, animal-like cries that filled me with terror.

My memory of that time is patchy at best. Part of it is genuine amnesia: the doctors told me as I recovered that it was likely there would be things I wouldn't remember.

I remember her being born. I lay awake in my hospital cubicle after Jeremy left to go home for the night, and I stared at her through the plastic of her cot. Even though I hadn't slept for two days by that point, I couldn't close my eyes.

By the time we were discharged, my vision was blurred and a miasma trailed behind moving objects like a smudge.

'Why would they let me take her home?' I said to Jeremy in the hospital car park. 'We're nowhere near ready.'

He smiled indulgently, as if what I was saying was cute. 'I think everyone feels that way. It's overwhelming.'

I was too exhausted and spaced out to tell him I didn't think everyone felt this way, as if each of their senses had been hijacked by a new version of vision, hearing, taste. An impostor. How can you trust anything when you can't trust your own perception?

I heard Liv crying even when she was asleep. I smelled gas when there was no leak. I read an article about shaken babies and suddenly I imagined doing that every time I picked her up. *What if I did that?* I'd think. *Would I? Could I?*

I remember her ear-piercing shrieks as she cried through the night, every night. Reflux. Colic. The words meant nothing to Jeremy and me, clueless new parents. All we knew was that our baby was in pain and we couldn't fix it. And she wouldn't let me sleep.

When Jeremy was at work, I'd take long walks, pushing the pram while I tried to outrun my own brain. But no matter how far I walked, the thoughts came with me.

After those first few days, my memory is blank.

Jeremy has told me some of it since.

He told me they found me alone, walking along the side of the A720 bypass with no shoes. The soles of my feet were bleeding, gravel embedded in my skin. Someone called 999 when I nearly fell asleep and stumbled into the hard shoulder. When the police picked me up, I was talking incessantly, talking about shaking my baby, about her needing a new mother.

They told me I begged them not to take me home, not to make my baby live with a mother like me, one who would ruin her life.

I got what I asked for: they didn't take me home. They took me straight to the hospital, where they had to sedate me to get me to lie down and sleep. When I woke up two days later, I was in a psychiatric ward. And my new baby wasn't there.

But there was a small part from that time that Jeremy didn't tell me, that he couldn't tell me. Because I never told anyone. I had forgotten it until this moment, sitting here on this bench in the park behind our house.

It's the feeling of damp on my jeans, the echo of panic in my chest from my fight with Liv. It triggers something in my memory, and now I remember, for the first time in five years, and the recollection tears me in two. No matter how hard I try, I can't suck enough air into my lungs. I'm suffocating. I grip my knees with both hands, lean forward with my head between my legs. My breath comes in tight, high-pitched wheezes.

Because now I remember, and I can't take the shame.

That day, when Liv's cries got too much, I lifted her from her pram and held her against my chest. She was so small, curled up against me.

'I'm sorry,' I whispered into her little seashell ear. 'I love you more than you'll ever know.'

My whispers turned to sobs as I laid her back in the pram. 'But you're better off this way.'

10

The memory sears like a brand. *I love you more than you'll ever know.*

The mist turns to proper rain, snapping me into the present. I feel like I've washed up on the shore after a shipwreck: relief and exhaustion, combined with a feeling of being saved from a massive danger. I'm far away from that moment now. Years have gone by. And I didn't do it. It was a moment. A stupid moment.

No one ever knew.

But Liv's words today echo through me like a fist to the chest:

I don't love you.

Daddy doesn't love you.

I wish I had a different mummy.

I wish you'd given me away.

Is it possible she knows? On some level, even though she was a tiny baby, maybe she knows what I almost did. And now she wants to push me away like I did with her.

I stand up, no idea how much time has passed. I need to get back to the house, to my kids. I can't believe I left them alone.

I run from the bench, across the grass and the gravel lane,

ignoring the sharp stones under my bare feet. I slam the gate behind me, not bothering to close the bolt. I'll come back once I've checked on the kids.

I open the kitchen door and listen. The house is quiet. No one is crying, calling for me. It's all OK.

I'm shivering, rainwater dripping onto the kitchen tiles. I grab a tea towel from the drawer and ruffle it in my hair, but I don't stop: I've got to check on my children.

I run up the stairs and throw open our bedroom door. Samuel's bassinet is empty, his sleeping bag in a crumpled heap. I feel a twinge of fear, which I shove away. Perhaps he was crying. Liv must have picked him up to soothe him.

I whirl around and cross the corridor to Liv's room. It's empty too. And the monitor is back: plugged into the socket, its little red light blinking at me to show that someone is watching.

Someone knows I left them.

'No no no no no no.' I grab my phone from the floor, screen still blank from when Jeremy hung up. How long ago was that? I've lost track of time.

I try to unlock the screen, but my hands are shaking too much and I lock myself out. If I need to call the police, I have to be fast. Time is important in kidnappings, and I have no idea how long I've been gone. All I know is that someone knows I left them. And they came and snatched them away.

Whoever has been watching must live nearby. Close enough to get here fast as soon as my back was turned.

I need the landline. I need to call 999.

I run down the stairs as fast as I can, almost falling once more. My breath comes in ragged gasps.

I rush into the living room, and stop dead.

'Blinking hell, mate. What's happened to you?' It's Jac. She's sitting on the hearthrug, legs curled under her. Next to her, Liv is hunched happily over a jigsaw.

Liv doesn't look up, and I'm glad of it: I must look terrifying.

'Where's Samuel?' I ask, breathless.

Jac points to the bassinet with a puzzled half-smile on her face. 'Fast asleep once I gave him a bottle.' The half-smile disappears and she gets up from the rug, puts an arm around my shoulders and eases me onto the sofa. 'What's going on? You look like you've been... I dunno. Through some stuff.' She glances at Liv, who's humming to herself, not listening. It's as if our huge argument didn't happen. As if Liv never said those awful things to me.

'Why are you here, Jac?' I ask, knowing the answer but hoping it will be different.

'Jeremy called me.'

I knew it.

'He said you were struggling today.' She looks at my wet clothes, my dirty feet, my bedraggled hair dripping onto the sofa. 'Looks like he was right.'

If this was anyone else, staring at me in my worst moment, making a judgement, I'd bristle and shove them away. But this is Jac, my oldest friend. She's seen me through my worst moments with a shrug and a smile. And I've seen hers, too. I've been there for the death of her parents, her painful break-ups, the emotionally unavailable men, the times when she's been the 'other woman', and the times she snooped through their phones and found what she'd hoped wasn't there.

So when she says 'Looks like he was right', I half sob, half laugh.

I'm grateful that he called Jac, out of everyone he could have chosen. I know he's not a massive fan of hers, but I love that he respects our friendship nonetheless.

'Thank God he didn't call my mother.' I laugh again, but Jac doesn't.

She passes me a glass of water.

'He called my mother?'

She nods slowly. 'He called everyone. When Liv answered

your phone and said you'd gone, he tried everyone he could think of. Even the lovely Nicole,' she says with sarcasm.

She wraps a manicured hand around my wrist and guides the glass to my mouth. My hands are still shaking, and some water trickles down my chin.

The doorbell rings.

My eyes meet Jac's, and I know that panic is written all over my face.

She takes the glass from my hand. 'I'll get the door. You go upstairs, give yourself a moment. Brush your hair, get into some dry clothes.' She puts a comforting hand on my shoulder and squeezes. 'We'll get through this.'

I want to beg her not to go. I want to hide under the covers, like a child afraid of monsters.

I hang my head, a sudden rush of exhaustion crashing over my body. I don't even know who 'everyone' encompasses. I'm humiliated.

What did he tell them?

11

I'm halfway up the stairs when Jac pulls the door open. I glance over my shoulder to see a massive pink coat topped with a puff of candyfloss blonde hair.

'Jac, darling!' Jac is enveloped in a perfumed hug, her face thrust into the pink fluff of my mum's coat. 'It's wonderful to see you.'

I duck around the corner out of sight and pause for a moment, listening. They've always been close, ever since Jac used to practically live at our house when we were teenagers.

'Let's go get the kettle on. I can't wait to hear about your trip.'

I close my eyes in gratitude for Jac pretending everything is normal.

Without hesitation, Mum launches into tales of the cruise, which will go on for at least an hour if no one interrupts. 'My goodness, it was such bliss. And the aquarobics instructor. Adonis, that was his actual name. Jac, you would have died. Anyway, we docked at Southampton a couple of days ago and I knew Miriam was struggling. I couldn't go another day without meeting my new grandson. Where is he?'

Their voices fade as they head along the corridor, Mum chattering as she always does. I stand for a moment on the landing. I do feel a pang of regret that she is now holding my baby for the first time and I'm not there to see it happen.

I stare at myself in the bedroom mirror. My hair is wet and tangled. Mascara streaks my cheeks. I look monstrous.

From downstairs, I hear Liv shrieking, 'Grandma!' and begging for presents.

I hear the rush of the pipes as Jac fills the kettle from the tap.

As I remove yesterday's make-up and run a comb through my hair, I feel curiously removed, as if it's Jac's family downstairs, not mine, and I'm the guest in this house. I could walk out of the door and no one would mind.

Hair brushed and a dry outfit on, I head downstairs as the doorbell rings once more.

On the doorstep are Nicole and Zain, foreheads furrowed with concern.

'Hello.' I fix a smile on my face. 'I'm guessing Jeremy called you?'

I'm glad I'm the one who could open the door to them: it's an opportunity to show them I'm fine.

'He must have been worried, but everything's OK. Come through. The others are in the kitchen.'

'Jeremy said you were missing,' Zain whispers.

I give a puzzled shrug. 'I popped out of the house for a few minutes and he panicked. It's hard, working away as much as he does.'

Neither of them look convinced, but they brush past me, leaving their shoes by the door. In the kitchen, Mum has Samuel over one shoulder and Liv clinging to the other.

'Oh, that newborn smell. You can't beat it.' She shakes her head and whispers into Samuel's ear in a squeaky voice: 'No, you can't beat it, can you? Can you can you can you?'

I try not to roll my eyes. 'Mum, this is my friend Zain. He's the school IT guy.'

Mum greets Zain and turns to hug Nicole, immediately launching into invasive questions. 'I was so sorry to hear about your divorce. Your ex seemed so nice at Liv's last birthday. Just shows, you can never tell. And you wanted more kiddies, too, didn't you?'

Mum's never been known for her sensitivity or tact. I wince and turn to Zain before Mum can ask about custody issues, peri-menopause or anything even more nosy. 'And this is Jac, my oldest friend. She was at school with me and Nicole.'

'The famous Jac,' Zain says with a grin.

Jac laughs and shakes his hand. 'Nothing Nicole told you is true, I promise.'

As Nicole and Zain sit at the dining table and chat to Mum, Jac sidles over to me and leans against the kitchen counter, arms folded. 'Jeremy called your colleagues?'

I close my eyes and nod.

'Damn.'

'Yeah. That's one way to ruin my life.'

'Although I'm sure Nicole can do that by herself.'

I ignore her and turn my back to the room, reaching into a cupboard to get glasses for water. 'Nicole's my friend as well as a colleague. You know that. But still, he shouldn't have called...'

Once everyone has a drink and Liv's playing with her new doll from Barbados, Mum eats custard creams and tells us about the islands she visited, the bingo games she won, and the new friends she made on the cruise. They're all going to go again next year, apparently.

'And what are you doing nowadays?' I hear Nicole ask Jac on the other side of the room, her voice clipped. All very polite, as if this is a normal day and my life isn't falling apart in front of their eyes.

I sit in the old leather armchair and listen, cradling my

cup of tea, wondering what Jeremy said to them to make them feel they need to sit vigil with me here, watching me, waiting for me to do something insane so his suspicions can be vindicated.

Every few minutes one of them flicks a look over at me, checking up. My cheeks ache from smiling, pretending everything is fine. They're here for me, ostensibly to look after me and make sure I'm OK. So why don't I feel cared for? Why do I still feel so alone?

Even Liv seems to be making a special effort to seem like the perfect child: curled up in the middle of us all, putting on little voices for her new doll and bouncing it over to Jac. Next to her, Samuel coos from his bouncy chair, watching everyone happily.

I don't have to wait long before I hear the scrape of the front door on the hallway rug. Jeremy's home.

There's an immediate sense of relief in the air, as if the whole room has uttered a collective sigh. They must have been wondering the same thing I was: *Why are we here? How long do we have to stay?*

'Hey, everyone.' He rushes into the kitchen, laptop bag still over his shoulder, shoes leaving wet footprints on the tiles. He comes straight to me and pulls me into a hug. His wool coat still smells of travel. 'I managed to get a fast train. Thanks for coming over.'

'What's going on, Jeremy?' I draw away. I can't take this any more. I feel like a prisoner waiting for the guillotine to drop. 'You've brought everyone to the house and we've sat around for the last hour just waiting. Waiting for what?'

Zain shifts in his seat, and Nicole lifts her empty mug to her lips and pretends to drink.

Mum clears her throat.

Ah. They *do* know. I'm the only one in the dark.

Jeremy's cheeks dapple pink. 'Liv, can you pop upstairs and

find some pyjamas, please? I'll be up soon to help you brush your teeth. Maybe Grandma will read you a story.'

He indicates the chair next to him at the table, but I shake my head. I want to stay where I am, my cold tea still cradled in my hands. A small distance from the little conference of so-called concerned family and friends. Who have been conspiring against me.

When Liv has left the room, Jeremy lays his laptop bag on the table, pulls out a sheaf of papers and hands them to me. It's a brochure. Each page has the same letterhead: *Hermitage Well-being Centre, Edinburgh.*

'What's this?' I flick through.

Jeremy won't meet my eyes.

Jac half smiles at me in apology.

'A mental hospital?'

'No, no. God, no. Not at all,' blusters Jeremy.

'A retreat, darling,' says Mum. 'A quick break to recentre yourself. Yoga and mindfulness every morning. I did it on my cruise and it was marvellous.'

'Just a break, Smidge,' says Jac, reaching out and laying a hand on my arm. Her use of my childhood nickname warms me, but her fingers are cold. 'Some time to recuperate.'

I look at them all, gathered around my kitchen table like a war council. Conspiring against me. Sending me away.

I swallow the bile rising in my throat. 'What about Liv and Sam? I can't leave them. I'm still breastfeeding, for God's sake.' My voice cracks and I start to cry, tears of anger and panic. I can't leave my babies. They can't make me leave my babies.

Nicole looks over, a kind smile on her face. 'You said it yourself the other day: the transition from one child to two, it's tough. It's a much-needed rest, Mim.'

My hands shake as I place my mug on the worktop next to me. I scoop Samuel from his bouncy chair and cradle him in my arms, his face tucked into the space between my neck and shoulder. I turn away from the room, rock back and forth and sing to him under my breath, the song I've been singing to him every night since he came home from the hospital: 'You Are My Sunshine'.

I can feel their discomfort, their eyes on my back. I don't care. They're not my family, not my friends. I needed their help long before this and they weren't there for me. All of them telling me it's in my head, not one of them trying to see what I see. And now they're separating me from my babies.

Jeremy stands, puts his hand on my shoulder. I bristle, try to shake him off.

He holds firm. 'It's two weeks, Mim. That's all I've booked. If it goes well, you'll be home before you know it.'

If it goes well. I wonder what conditions I have to meet for that to happen.

'And I've taken a couple of weeks off work, so I'll be with the kids. We'll come for visits. And we'll call whenever we can.' He kisses my cheek. 'This is about you feeling good. About you coming home rejuvenated and ready to be Miriam again.'

'I *am* Miriam. There's nothing wrong with me.'

He turns me around, looks me in the eye. There's no love on his face, only determination. 'You left our children alone, Miriam. That can never happen again.'

My cheeks flush. I still have no idea how long I was gone. It felt like a minute or two. But Jeremy had time to call everyone, to reschedule his train, to get to the station. What happened? For the first time, I can't argue. He's right: it can never happen again. Whatever went wrong in my head in that moment was the same thing that went wrong all those years ago on the bench with newborn Liv. Something so painful and terrible I blocked it out until today.

Something broke in my brain. But both this time and that awful day when Liv was a baby, I managed to stop it and come back. Surely that counts for something?

I hang my head, wipe a tear from my cheek. 'Our children need to be safe, and you deserve to know they're safe with me.'

He exhales long and hard, his breath ruffling my hair. 'Thank you.'

'I'll go to the hospital—'

'Retreat.'

'Retreat, then. And I'll work hard to prove I'm OK. And I'll come home and we can go back to normal.' I reach out and grab his hand. 'I just want the four of us together and safe. That's all I need.'

Samuel starts to fuss, his limbs twitching and kicking against me. My mum stands and takes him from my arms. 'I'll go and check his nappy,' she whispers.

My neck feels cold without his breath against my skin.

I fold my arms. 'So it's two weeks. And what happens at the end of this two weeks? How do they measure whether I've improved?' I think again of the Rosenhan subjects trapped in the psychiatric hospital, their claims of sanity marked as indicators of the opposite. 'What happens if they decide I'm still crazy?'

'Not crazy, Mim,' Jac says.

'Just tired,' adds Nicole. 'We've all been there. After Lottie was born, I hallucinated ants crawling over her face. I ripped the sheet off her cot thinking it was a nest.' She shivers and rubs her arms, and a sad smile crosses her face. 'Still, it's such a joy for Liv to have a little brother, and both of them surrounded by so much love. You'll be home to your babies in no time. This retreat isn't a punishment. It's a gift.'

Jeremy looks at her gratefully, and for the first time I realise what he's gone through today: thinking I'd abandoned our children, worrying about me and them, the hoops he had to jump through to get out of work and catch an earlier train. Booking the retreat on the phone in the taxi from the station. How it must have felt on that train, powerless to make sure everything was all right at home.

'I'm so sorry, Jeremy.' And I don't mean I'm sorry about what happened today. I'm sorry for so many things. Sorry I can't cope with a new baby, like every other mother somehow can. Sorry he can't trust me to look after the children. Sorry he has to leave his brand-new job for two weeks so I can lounge around doing yoga and meditating. 'I'm sorry.'

He nods, and I think I see the twinkle of an unshed tear in his eye. 'If you still need help at the end of the two weeks, I'll stop work. Be at home for a while.'

My stomach contracts. 'But what about money? We need your job.'

He shrugs. 'It's more important that you and the kids are safe. If I need to find a job with no travel, or one where I work from home, that's what I'll do.'

'We'll help with all of it,' says Jac. The others nod, grateful for a role in the conversation and a way to help. 'We've all got contacts; we can put a word in for Jeremy if we need to.'

I shake my head. 'That won't be necessary. He's just got this job and it's what he wanted. We're not planning for him to give it up and stay at home. He'd hate it. He'd hate *me*.' I ignore his protests and carry on. 'I'll do whatever I need to do. I'll go there, I'll rest, I'll take whatever meds they need me to take. Just... no quitting the job. And at the end of this, I'll come home and be their mummy.' I start to cry in earnest then, my shoulders shaking with stifled sobs.

Mum returns, Samuel in one arm and Liv following her, holding her other hand. My babies. I wipe my face, hoping Liv hasn't noticed.

I hold out my arms and she runs to me and throws herself at me in a huge hug, her legs wrapped around me.

'Love you, Mummy,' she says, like she used to before all of this. As if no damage has been done. I feel the warmth of her cheek against mine, smell the buttery scent of her skin. More tears flow down my cheeks, but Liv can't see so I let them.

I can never, ever lose this. And as much as I will love Samuel with all my heart, Liv will always be my first baby, the one who made me a mother.

I open my eyes. The atmosphere has relaxed. The others chat like it's a dinner party, and my mum does the side-to-side dance to lull Samuel to sleep. Over Liv's shoulder, my eyes fall on the retreat brochure: the stack of printed A4 paper stapled in one corner with creases from days in a laptop bag. And the tell-tale stripe along one side, like our old, rickety printer leaves behind. Exactly like that, in fact.

I freeze, my arms still wrapped around Liv's narrow waist.

He printed that at home, before he left for his work trip.

I look up at Jeremy, who's laughing at one of Jac's jokes, his smile wide and genuine. He seems happy, I think. Relieved.

This isn't a hastily put-together scheme organised in the back of the taxi this afternoon. This has been days, maybe weeks in the works.

It's not anything to do with what happened today.

How long has he been planning to send me away? And how long have my friends known?

12

There are cameras everywhere. I can see them from the car window as we pull through the stone archway into the courtyard. They're dotted around the building at regular intervals, all pointing in different directions. They've tried to be discreet, but I can see them, their little red lights blinking at me: small lenses in black casings the size of an apple.

Jeremy pulls into a parking space labelled *Visitor* and switches off the engine. We both sit in silence looking up at the building, the car ticking as it cools.

There are no people around, and no movement in the windows that look into the courtyard from all four sides. It's eerily quiet, but I itch with the feeling of being watched.

I sink down in my seat, my knees touching the glove compartment.

The main entrance sits across from the archway we drove through, a big glass door to pretend it's not an institution keeping people inside.

'Ready?' Jeremy turns to me.

I shake my head. 'Not really.'

He sighs. 'This is supposed to be something nice, Miriam.

It's a treat, a break. Other new mums in your position would kill for a couple of weeks on a retreat. Some time to yourself without the kids. Try to enjoy it, OK?'

He keeps saying these things as if he's booked me into a five-star hotel in the Virgin Islands. But it feels like marketing spin. In reality, this is baby steps away from getting me sectioned, only there's a yoga teacher and the food's probably better than what you get from the NHS. We're lucky, apparently, that the private healthcare from his posh new job kicked in so quickly, which is why I'm not stuck at the bottom of a months-long NHS waiting list or talking to a student doctor in a broom cupboard once a week.

He gives up waiting for me and gets out of the car, standing with his hands on his hips and gazing up at the building. 'Looks nice.'

I open my door and climb out, trying to make myself as small as possible. I feel eyes on me from every angle: the cameras, the windows, the big glass door. I want to scratch off my skin.

Jeremy grabs my suitcase from the boot and wheels it towards the entrance, where a man in a smart grey suit appears, watching us with a fixed smile on his designer-stubbled face. As Jeremy approaches, the man steps forward, right hand outstretched.

'You must be Jeremy,' he says as they shake hands. 'I'm Dr Niall Stokes, clinical director and consultant psychiatrist here at the Hermitage Wellbeing Centre.' He straightens up and clasps his hands behind his back, his suit jacket flexing open to reveal a crisp white linen shirt. He looks expensive, like this whole place.

'And this is Miriam?' He raises his voice so he's half talking to Jeremy and half addressing me, still standing by the car pretending to get something out of the passenger seat.

I straighten up and smile at him. 'Hi.' I'm glad I'm still ten feet away and don't have to shake his hand. I bet he smells expensive, too.

He gestures at the suitcase next to Jeremy and the handbag slung over my shoulder. 'You can leave all your bags here; someone will get them shortly. Shall we go inside?' Without waiting, he spins on his heel and returns to the glass door, where he punches in a code so it silently slides open.

We follow him into a high-ceilinged entrance hall, where the carpet is so thick it feels rude to wear shoes. There's a slick reception desk, with *Hermitage* written on the side in backlit lettering.

The receptionist greets us as we pass by, flashing perfect white teeth.

We walk along a wide corridor lined with doors, the walls painted a light grey that perfectly matches Dr Stokes's suit.

His office is just as opulent, with large sash windows overlooking smooth grassy lawns that roll down to a pond with benches at regular intervals around the shore.

'Nice view, eh?' He catches me looking.

It's a big office lined with bookshelves, a massive Swiss cheese plant in one corner. He indicates that we should take a seat on the oxblood chesterfield sofa, then sits behind his desk, steepling his hands under his chin.

'So, welcome, Miriam.' He slides his keyboard out of the way to clear a space on his desk. 'We're so pleased you could be here. As you know, Jeremy, there's usually quite a waiting list for spaces here at the Hermitage, but luckily we had a last-minute cancellation so were able to fit Miriam in at short notice. Miriam, I've spoken with Jeremy, so I know a little about your story. But could you tell me in your own words why you're here today and why you feel the Hermitage is a good step for you at this time?'

I suppress a shudder. There's something uncomfortable

about a stranger using my name so many times. Like he's claiming ownership over me. I clear my throat. 'Erm. I just had our second baby. With our first I had quite severe...' I pause. I hate saying it.

'Postnatal psychosis,' Jeremy finishes for me. 'Miriam had postnatal psychosis after she had Liv five years ago. And she spent some time in the mother and baby unit.'

I close my eyes.

'I see. We have your records from the initial psychiatric unit intake and then your stay in the MBU, so we'll get up to speed before your first consultations. Miriam, could you tell me what's brought you to us this time?'

I open my eyes. 'Jeremy thinks I'm heading that way again.'

Jeremy picks up a jug of water and pours himself a glass, takes a drink. 'I think, with the right care at this early stage, we might be able to help Miriam this time. Before she gets too bad.'

Dr Stokes stares at me, not breaking eye contact even when Jeremy speaks. I feel like a butterfly pinned to a board. 'And Miriam? What do you think?'

The room feels like it's buzzing with electricity. In the six weeks since Samuel's birth, no one has asked me what *I* think.

I scan the walls, the bookshelves, the cornicing on the ceiling. I can't see any cameras in here. And surely, if my brain was inventing this, I'd see a camera in every room. But I spot ten, fifteen, even twenty places where Dr Stokes could conceal a lens, and there isn't one.

'I don't agree with Jeremy.'

'You think you're fine?'

I place my hands on my knees, my palms cupping the kneecaps. I will myself to sit still, to seem calm as I speak. 'No, I don't think I'm fine. I'm exhausted and mentally strained, like every woman who has recently given birth and also has a young child who needs attention.'

Dr Stokes nods his encouragement.

'I think my brain is scrambled. But scrambled in a totally normal way that doesn't need...' I wave a hand to indicate the whole place, 'incarceration.'

Dr Stokes looks from me to Jeremy and back again.

'Mim, you're not being *incarcerated.*' Jeremy takes my hand. I resist the urge to pull away. 'We've talked about this. This is voluntary. It's not a psychiatric unit. It's a private retreat.'

'So I can leave whenever I want, then? I can wander down to the local shops for a packet of crisps? I can stay for one night and decide I want to head home the next day?'

Dr Stokes clears his throat. 'We do encourage our guests to stay for the duration of their programme, to get the maximum benefit from our treatments.'

'And what if you don't think I'm better at the end of the two weeks?'

He places a hand on the desk in front of him, his fingertips resting on the antique leather surface. 'I'm sure once you know more, you'll be reassured that you'll get what you need here, and there's no need to worry about it not working.' He stands up and plucks at the legs of his suit to straighten the creases. 'Follow me, and I'll give you a little tour while I tell you about your programme.'

I count five cameras as Jeremy and I follow Dr Stokes into the corridor and back past the reception. As we walk, he gives us a short history of the Hermitage Centre: its origins as a posh boarding school and then its conversion into a private asylum in the late-Victorian era, inspired by the Quaker-run York Asylum and its humane approaches to mental health treatment.

We pause on the terrace at the front of the building and look out over the sweeping lawns down to the pond. 'And we're surrounded by tranquil grounds where our guests can reflect on their treatments.'

The deserted grounds look more like those of a stately home than a hospital. I scan the horizon, but there's no fence, nothing to keep us inside. There's no need for one: we're ten miles from the nearest village, and there's no public transport.

'What's a typical day for your patients...' Jeremy stops himself. 'Guests?'

I try not to roll my eyes. I spot two cameras trained on the terrace.

'Miriam will work closely with our nursing team. They administer the practical one-to-one support to ensure guests' care plans are delivered. They specialise in topics like sleep hygiene, nutrition and holistic therapies.' Dr Stokes turns to us both, brings his fingertips together to create a triangle. 'Our nurses are truly special people, and their main job is to relieve the pressure on our guests so they can focus on recovery and relaxation. Try to see your time here as a gift, Miriam.'

Jeremy wraps an arm around my shoulders and pulls me close.

'So Miriam will join in with the group during the day, eat meals with everyone in the dining room, get involved in activities, and then have regular therapy sessions either with me or one of my colleagues, depending on who she's been assigned to.'

Jeremy gives me an encouraging smile. I don't smile back.

'Our therapy team are amazing. We've got an occupational therapist, sensory specialist, psychologists and psychiatrists. I'm sure you'll have seen in the brochure that we offer person-centred counselling, relaxation, yoga, t'ai chi, creative therapies... all with a very low guest-to-staff ratio. There's someone here for you at every moment of the day.'

A cold wind whips around the side of the building and I shiver. Something about this place gives me the creeps. I've stepped into the *Stepford Wives'* version of a mental hospital.

'That's a chilly breeze. Let's get you inside.' Dr Stokes

opens the doors back into the building and guides us to reception. He glances at his wrist, but his sleeve doesn't move back far enough to reveal a watch. 'It's about lunchtime, so a good opportunity for Miriam to say her goodbyes, sign a couple of intake forms and then join the rest of the group.'

Jeremy hugs me long and hard, promising to call every night so I can speak to him and Liv. When the big glass door closes behind him, I realise that he saw only the parts of the centre curated for visitors: reception, the grounds and Dr Stokes's office.

We weren't shown any of the 'guest' facilities – the bedrooms, the dining area – nor did we see a single patient.

As soon as Jeremy leaves, Dr Stokes changes. The solicitous professionalism disappears, replaced with polite disinterest.

He strides over to reception. 'Tamara, can you please call Sonya for me? Tell her there's a new guest.' He glances over his shoulder at me, then leans across the desk, his words inaudible from where I stand by the entrance, hovering there as if Jeremy might return at any moment and change his mind about leaving me here.

Within moments, a tall woman in heels and a smart suit appears from a corridor I haven't been along yet, a big smile on her face and a clipboard in her hand. 'Miriam?' She shakes my hand as if I'm a business partner rather than a new patient. 'I'm Sonya, the ward manager. I'm the head of the nursing staff, so you'll see me in the ward and getting involved with the guests too.' She has a slight accent I can't place.

Her handshake is firm, her skin dry and soft. For the first time since arriving here, I feel like it might be OK.

She leads me away from Dr Stokes and down the corridor, through several doors that need a security code and a swipe card to access. 'You get your own en suite bedroom, so you'll have a private and peaceful space where you can relax. This isn't a holiday; you'll find it to be a rather intense, confronting experience but one that leaves you feeling better at the end. Like your brain's going through a car wash.' Her deep laugh shakes her shoulders.

We enter a lift, which she operates by scanning her fingerprint before pressing the button for the second floor. 'The best advice I can give you is to get it all out: don't keep any secrets. You can't hide anything here, so don't even try.'

I shiver and rub my arms against the sudden chill that creeps through my bones. My eyes dart around the lift, looking for cameras. 'Is there CCTV everywhere?'

She nods. 'Pretty much. All for guest safety, of course. Lots of great tech here. We used to have retina scanners before we realised they damage your eyes.' She gives me a thumbs-up. 'Fingerprints and access codes are much better.'

The lift pings and the doors slide open to reveal an open area with huge windows, natural light flooding the space. Large house plants sit in each corner, and two pillowy sofas face each other in the centre. 'This is the living room, for evening entertainment and downtime between therapy sessions. There's a TV, books, a stereo with headphones if you want to listen to music. We encourage our guests to socialise if they want to, but there's no pressure if you want to sit alone with your thoughts or curl up with a book.'

The ache in my chest relaxes slightly. I haven't read a book since before Liv was born. At the thought of Liv and Samuel, my throat aches. 'What about calling home?'

She smiles. 'We have a multimedia room, where you can video-call your family. It's open for three hours a day, from four until seven.' She guides me to a door that she opens with her swipe card and a code again. It's a little booth with a computer and a headset. She doesn't turn on the light, so the only illumi-

nation comes from the daylight behind us and a red LED light
in the far corner. More CCTV.

We back out of the multimedia room. 'Where are the other
patients?' I ask.

'The other guests,' she corrects me, and glances at her
watch. 'They've just gone into lunch. You should have time to
join them and grab some food too. Let's pop our heads into your
room, and then we'll go up to the dining hall.'

She leads me down another corridor. The carpet here feels
less opulent, more functional. We pass door after door, each
with a swipe slot and keypad and a frosted glass window.

'You'll get a keycard to your room,' Sonya says. 'Only you
and the nursing staff can access your space. Your belongings are
secure. We ask our guests not to go into each other's rooms; you
should meet in the public areas if you want to spend time
together.' She pauses at a door and swipes her card. 'Keeps
things simple that way.'

She opens the door for me and lets me walk in first. The
room smells of clean laundry and looks like a hotel room: crisp
white sheets on the bed, a desk, and a small flatscreen TV on
the wall. There's a door in the corner that must be the en suite.
'It looks lovely,' I say truthfully.

She pulls the chair from the desk and sits down, indicating
for me to sit on the bed. It's soft under my thighs, and I'm
already looking forward to climbing into it later, for a night of
sleep without any interruptions. The first in weeks.

My stomach contracts. Just thinking of Samuel makes my
milk come in, and I can feel the nursing pads in my bra soaking
up the fluid.

As if she can read my mind, Sonya indicates my suitcase,
already lying on the luggage rack alongside my handbag, with
an unfamiliar box on top. 'We've brought your belongings up
here and as Jeremy requested we've also provided you with a
hospital-grade breast pump and milk bags. There's a fridge-

freezer in that cupboard so you can store your milk, and someone will come once a day to collect it so your son can continue drinking breast milk and you can maintain your supply.'

I open my mouth and close it again. Jeremy had mentioned plans to help with breastfeeding, but this is a military operation.

She reaches forward and puts a reassuring hand on my knee. 'We want your time here to be stress-free, and we've worked closely with your husband over the last few weeks to ensure everything is thought of.' She keeps talking, outlining the daily schedule, wake-up time, where to get coffee, how to do laundry, but I've stopped listening.

Over the last few weeks.

He's been planning this for a long time.

She removes her hand from my knee and stands up. 'It's a lot to take in, I know. I'm around all day, every day, so if you have any questions, let me know, OK?'

I try to nod, but can't make my head move.

'Let's get you some lunch.' She opens the door, holding out an arm to wave me out into the corridor.

I glance at my suitcase and handbag. 'Can I check my phone?' This is the longest I've ever been away from Samuel, and I want to make sure that Jeremy got back OK.

But Sonya shakes her head, not moving from the doorway. 'I'm afraid you can't. We've removed your personal devices and stored them securely for the first part of your time here. Our programme is about recovery and relaxation, and your mind can't rest if you're always contactable, always checking your devices. That's why we open the multimedia room for a short window every day; that way you're not cut off from your family and friends, but you're contactable on your terms, not theirs.'

I frown. 'But it's not on my terms, is it? It's on yours.'

She smiles again, but this time it doesn't meet her eyes. 'Our research shows this approach is very effective, Miriam.' She opens the door wider.

Still sitting on the bed, I scan the room, taking in the thick blackout curtains at each side of the window, the picture hanging over the bed, the mirror above the desk. There it is, in the top corner by the window.

Another camera.

13

I follow Sonya through the endless corridors, feeling like I'm dragging a great weight behind me. Every step is a huge effort. I want to sink down onto the floor and howl; kick and scream and bang my head like Liv used to when she was tiny.

Liv.

Samuel.

Their names echo through my mind, over and over. I thought I'd be able to call them, to see their faces on my phone whenever I needed them.

I walk quietly, hold my breath. Hold it in.

My goodbye with them was perfunctory, not enough. Nothing would be enough. Not enough cuddles, not enough kisses, never enough *I love you*s. And my mum, bundling us out of the door, repeating, 'Don't fuss, don't fuss.'

My arms ache for my babies.

We get into a lift, go up two floors. Everything is black and white, like my eyes are broken.

I'm a shell of a person without them, my arms empty, my breasts full to bursting. They're a part of me, taken away.

I clamp my mouth closed, grit my teeth. If I loosen my jaw, I'll scream and scream and never stop.

The doors slide open to reveal a huge, bustling room that finally ends the eerie quiet that has hung in the air since I arrived. Here are other people: chatting, eating, looking out of the window. A couple of faces glance up from their lunch trays and nod in greeting.

'Here we are,' Sonya says. 'It's buffet style, so grab a tray and help yourself. You might not feel too hungry, but try to eat if you can. Our chef used to work at Le Poulet Heureux in Harrogate. You know, the one with the Michelin star?'

I give a half-smile in acknowledgement. I've never felt less hungry in my life.

Sonya waves goodbye and leaves me at the lunch counter, where I add a mozzarella and roasted vegetable ciabatta to my tray, along with a parfait cup.

I turn to face the room, trying to decide where to sit. I hadn't realised I was nervous about meeting the other patients. All I'd thought about was myself, my kids, my life.

The tables are long, with benches, like in a school dining room. At a table by the window, someone catches my eye and gives a small wave. A woman about my age. A ponytail and a nose ring.

The iron band around my ribcage loosens slightly and I cross the room towards her.

'Can I join you?'

She grins. 'I hoped you would. You look fairly normal.' She lowers her voice and glances around with a twinkle in her eye. 'Everyone else is a nutter.'

I laugh, and again I'm reminded of school. The cliques, the cool kids, the weirdos. I wonder which type she is. 'I'm Miriam.'

'Katy. And I'm just joking about everyone being a nutter.' She takes a massive forkful of jacket potato. 'First day?' she asks through her food.

I nod. 'You?'

She swallows. 'I've been here about a week so far. But it's not my first rodeo.'

'You've been here before?'

'On and off for a few years, yeah. I'm like a vintage car, you know. I've come in for a tune-up.'

I pick up my ciabatta and take a small bite. I want to ask why she's here. But I don't know if it's impolite, like asking someone in prison what crime they committed.

As if she can read my thoughts, she says, 'Agoraphobia. And a bit of OCD.'

I nod, trying to keep my expression neutral. As if I meet people in mental hospitals every day and am used to them blurting out their diagnosis. As if it's normal for me to be here, too.

When I don't say anything, Katy keeps chatting, unfazed by my reticence. 'Everyone's pretty OK. You haven't stepped into *One Flew Over the Cuckoo's Nest* or anything. There are a few addicts, some anorexics. They stick together. The nervous breakdowns and depressives keep to themselves, generally. And then there's a few people who don't talk about why they're here: they're probably court-ordered or referred. I'm guessing kleptos and psychotics, that kind of thing.'

'So you're here out of choice, but some people are sent here even if they don't want to come?'

She nods, shovels more food into her mouth. 'Generally the self-admitted people do better. They're ready to get well, you know. The others... they're riding out their time waiting to go home. If they can.'

I wonder which category I fit in. 'If they can?'

She shrugs. 'So there was this girl who came in last time I was here. She'd been self-harming, I think, and her family sent her here, trying to fix her or whatever.' Katy rolls her eyes. 'She didn't join in with anything, spent her days in her room.

Anyway, it turned out it's great here if you admit yourself, but if someone else has signed you up, you're completely under their control, especially if they strike up a good relationship with the staff.'

My stomach clenches as I remember how pally Jeremy was with Dr Stokes. How they'd been talking for weeks before today. Planning this.

'So what happened to her?'

Katy puts down her fork. 'I don't know. Her time here ended, but I know she didn't go home. I think she was sectioned, sent somewhere more long-term.'

I feel sick. My sandwich sits on my tray half-eaten, the oily vegetables glistening. 'My husband admitted me here. He thinks I'm imagining things, postnatal psychosis.'

'What do *you* think?'

I can't answer. I shrug.

'I've no idea what's going on in your head. You seem pretty sane to me, but then so do I and I haven't left my house in ten years.' She takes a big gulp of water. 'Want some advice? I think you need to be very careful. You've seen the cameras?' She moves her finger in a circle, pointing at each corner of the room in turn.

I hold in a sob of relief. They're real. I'm not imagining them.

She angles her head towards the edge of the room, where a couple of nurses lean against the wall, chatting. 'You're being watched all the time. Even when you're alone, which would probably be illegal if not for the lawsuit-proof consent form everyone signs on their way in. If you want to get out of here and get home to your baby, *perform*. Do everything they say, participate in the organised fun, make them think you're spilling secrets in your therapy sessions, and smile, smile, smile.'

I hang my head over my tray and take a deep breath. Under the table I clench my fists, my fingernails digging into my palms.

I look out of the window, squinting at the sky and trying not to let tears spill from the corners of my eyes.

'You miss your baby.'

I swallow, willing myself not to cry. It takes a moment before I can speak. 'Babies,' I croak.

She places a hand on my arm.

'I've got two. Liv and Samuel. Liv's five and Samuel's not even two months old.'

She blinks back tears of her own. 'Oh, Miriam.' There's so much emotion in her voice, I know she understands. She knows how empty my arms feel, how desolate I am. What I would give to hold my baby in my arms, hear his little grunts as he suckles at my breast, the warmth of his skin against mine. Most of all, I know she understands what I'm losing by being here. I'm missing so much that I can't get back. Liv's slipping away from me, and Samuel transforms every day, growing and developing.

His first smile will be for someone else.

14

The smell of essential oils hovers in the corridor, coating my clothes in lavender and lemon balm. My skin feels greasy with it, and I yearn for a bath. We're in a new part of the building I haven't yet seen: treatment and therapy rooms on the third floor.

I read the signs on each door: *Massage Room*, *Meditation Suite*, *Sensory Deprivation Tank*, and an exercise studio, its door standing open to reveal wooden floors and a whole wall of mirrors.

'Shall we?' Dr Okeke, the Hermitage's head psychiatrist, waves me into his therapy room, which is similar to Dr Stokes's room on the ground floor: comfortable leather sofas and a wall of bookshelves.

I bring a hand to my nose, try not to sneeze. The essential oils have permeated even here. 'You get used to the smell,' he says, as if he can read my mind. 'We're next to one of the more... holistic therapy rooms.'

I enjoy the slightly derisive expression on his face, which he quickly stifles as he sits in the armchair opposite me. 'So as you know, I'm Dr Okeke. But you can call me Frank.' His hair is completely white, including a large beard that makes his eyes and teeth shine brightly. I like him immediately. 'And you're Miriam. It's lovely to meet you.' He smiles, and a little piece of my brittle shell breaks away. He's about the same age my dad would be now.

'Thank you.'

He holds up a sheaf of papers. 'So I've read your intake report, written by everyone who spoke with your husband before you were admitted. It outlines his concerns about your health and why he thinks you would benefit from a short stay here.'

I wrap my arms around my stomach. Part of me desperately wants to know what's in that report, and part of me wants to burn it to nothing.

'This is our first meeting of many; I'll see you every afternoon and we'll chat. Nothing nefarious or invasive, just a normal counselling session while we establish how you're feeling and where you want to be at the end of your stay.' He glances at the paperwork on the arm of his chair and then leans forward, looking me right in the eye. 'Miriam, I know this is hard. You must be missing your kids.'

My breath catches in my throat.

'And you've been having a tough time of it since Samuel was born.'

For the first time, I don't argue. Whether that 'tough time' has been caused by my own brain or by my husband's actions and lies, it's still true. 'Do you decide whether I'm well enough to go home at the end of this?'

'I submit a report to Dr Stokes, who'll review your case. You're not a prisoner, though. We can't keep you here indefinitely.'

'But you can get me sectioned?'

He shifts in his seat, a small frown crinkling his brow. 'Is that what you're afraid of?'

'Wouldn't you be?'

'I can see from your intake report that you feel you're mentally well; that others are imposing a diagnosis on you. Could you tell me more about that?'

I do want to tell him. I want to tell him everything. I open my mouth, about to blurt it all out, and then I remember. I glance up at the ceiling, and there it is, its little red light blinking at regular intervals, the lens pointing right at me. 'There are cameras everywhere.'

He follows my gaze, and then his eyes flick to me. He nods. 'It's for the safety of the staff and guests. Do you find that uncomfortable?'

'I feel like I'm being watched all the time.'

'If it helps at all, the camera feeds aren't constantly monitored. No one's watching you like a *Big Brother* contestant. They're recording so we can refer to the footage if there's an incident.'

I inhale, my shoulders loosening. 'It does help. Thank you.'

He taps a pen on the sheaf of papers. 'Look, it's my job to help you find some balance, to ensure you get the help you need, whether that's an ongoing therapy plan once you get home, some short-term medication to help you regulate your thoughts, or something else.' He clears his throat and taps his temple with the pen. 'I can't read your mind or know what's going on in there, good or bad. I can only ask questions. But I know what you want, Miriam. You want to be a good mum, and you want to be with your kids. So that's what I want too.'

I feel like I might cry. 'Thank you,' I whisper. 'How do I get home?'

'Forget about the cameras. Be a model patient. Attend your appointments, take your prescribed meds, participate in group sessions, get lots of fresh air.'

I nod. I can do almost all of that. Almost.

I will be a model patient. But I won't forget about the cameras.

15

I am a model patient.

The first five days pass in a blur of performance as I act exactly as I imagine a sane person would. Even though I *am* already sane. I no longer smile at myself in the mirror, in case I look delusional. If I catch myself singing under my breath, I stop immediately. Wouldn't want them to think I was talking to myself. And I certainly don't rehearse my next conversation with Jeremy. *How could you? Why would you? You lied to me.*

I wake every morning around seven and shower in my en suite, before the twelve of us on my ward trickle out to the living area to drink coffee together before heading to breakfast at eight. Most days after breakfast I walk around the pond, making sure I'm visible from the windows. *Look how healthy I am*, I try to show with my brisk walk and my deep breaths. *How wholesome. How normal.*

Then it's group therapy, a different subject every day. Mindfulness, anger, assertiveness. My fellow inmates are a mixed bag, ranging from Katy – who seems perfectly fine until faced with the prospect of going outside – to a woman whose name I don't know because she won't speak. But her facial expression is permanent anguish, as if her brain tortures her from the inside. Sometimes she hums, sometimes she rocks. But she never speaks. I wish I could hug her, or help in some way.

I learn to participate in these sessions, revealing little truths and admissions like Hansel and Gretel dropping breadcrumbs through the forest. I talk about my father's death in my early teens, my relationship with my mother, my long-lost teenage angst. None of these things upset me now; I've processed them and moved on. But in these sessions, they're my currency, offered in exchange for trust and my eventual release.

After group therapy, it's our choice of holistic therapies. I bounce between them, a different one each day. Meditation is dull, but I spend the time wandering through the halfway world between wake and sleep. I try to think about Liv and Samuel, about what I'm fighting to return to, but their faces distort and all I see on the back of my eyelids are the blinking lights of the cameras that surround me. Free writing, art therapy, acupuncture, music therapy, gym classes: I try them all. I am a model patient.

I make sure I'm in full view of the cameras at lunchtime, so they see me eating a robust amount of food and chatting with my new friend Katy. Laughing, even, sometimes.

And between meals, activities and therapy sessions, I return to my room and hook up both breasts to the breast pump, filling two bags with milk, which I store in the small freezer as instructed. Every day someone comes into my room while I'm out and takes them, somehow gets them to my son, who drinks from a bottle now instead of my breasts.

I feel a prickle of envy for whoever collects the milk. Do they deliver it personally to Samuel? Are they a direct conduit between me and my son? I wish I could somehow send a message via them, pass to them the power to hold him while he falls asleep, remind him of the smell of his mother's skin.

In the afternoons, I have therapy with Dr Okeke. I like him.

It doesn't seem like he's trying to catch me out or trap me. He asks me to talk about the differences between how I felt when Liv was a baby and now, with Samuel. He asks how I define 'healthy' and 'unwell'. He asks me how it feels to be rejected by Liv, how it feels when she says 'I hate you' or 'you don't love me'. I answer these questions honestly. I cry. I smile. I have nothing to hide.

After therapy, the multimedia room opens for three hours and the patients on our ward wait in the living area, filing into the room one after another. While we wait, we watch game shows on TV, trying to shout out the answers before the contestants. The oldest patient, Tilly, who's in her sixties, gets the most answers correct. She doesn't use the multimedia room, just joins us for the game shows. I don't ask why she has no one to call, or about her family and friends on the outside. I hope she has some.

Jeremy picks up within a few seconds every time. He's always sitting on the sofa, a muslin cloth over his shoulder, Samuel sleeping on his lap. I fake a smile, tell him it's good to see him. He always looks pleased to see me, and asks questions that betray his eagerness to hear I'm feeling better, that I'm 'me' again. He tells me what I've missed, the small changes in our baby I should be there to see. Samuel's first smile.

And every day, Liv refuses to come and say hello.

Some days she's playing in the same room and I hear 'Don't want to talk to Mummy' in the background. Some days she's in her bedroom and won't come out. It hurts every time, my chest searing with pain. But I never lose hope that the next day, the camera will flick on and she'll be there, smiling at the prospect of seeing me.

'Please tell her I miss her and love her,' I beg Jeremy.

'She loves you too,' he tells me, even though her actions indicate the opposite.

She's been spending a lot of time with Grandma, he tells

me. And Jac. They take it in turns to come over and help lighten the load. I swallow the sting: they can see that Jeremy needs help, but they wouldn't help me. Jac entertains Liv, my mum cooks. My mum, who served me ready meals five nights a week until I learned to cook for myself to escape it.

Some days he packs both children into the car and they go and see his foster parents. Where Jeremy gets another break and Liv gets stuffed with sweets and presented with boxes of toys from Jeremy's youth. Sharp edges, choking hazards and rust from decades in the loft. She has the best time, he tells me.

I lean away from the camera so he can't see me wipe away tears.

In the corner of the multimedia room, by the ceiling, a red light blinks for the duration of my calls. I wonder if the computer records our conversations.

At the end of each day, I retreat to my room, pump milk again for Samuel, then lie in bed staring at the camera in the dark. Tears trickle from my eyes and into my ears.

I ache.

My face aches from fake smiling.

My shoulders ache with tension.

My muscles ache from yoga, or Pilates, or circuits, a deep-tissue massage, or whatever physical activity I've participated in that day.

My arms ache to hold my children.

My breasts ache to feed Samuel.

My heart aches for my babies.

I am a model patient.

I will get home.

16

My sixth day is visiting day. I wake up before the alarm and lie in bed, staring at the ceiling, grateful that I packed make-up and earrings. I must look nice today. For Jeremy. But mostly for Liv. I want her to see me looking pretty. A pretty mummy.

I barely choke down my toast and scrambled egg at breakfast.

Katy looks at me, concerned. 'It's your family, love. Why are you nervous?'

I can't respond. I don't know the answer. What happened that my child no longer loves me? What did I do wrong? I know the key lies with that baby monitor and the voice that talks to her in the dark. But saying that out loud got me here in the first place; I can't say it again until I'm free.

So I shrug, sip my coffee, and chew my eggs and toast until it's paste in my mouth.

When it's time, I take the lift down to the ground floor and wait in a large room that spans the width of the building. Instead of the tables and chairs in my mental image of a prison visiting room, it's a comfortable space filled with sofas, beanbags and a little toy corner for kids. Liv will love that.

There's a coffee and tea station, with fresh croissants and Danish pastries laid out in shiny rows.

Katy didn't come. She says she's been isolated for so long because of her agoraphobia that her friends are all internet friends. She gets her visitors every day in the multimedia room. A few other patients mill around, watching out of the window for their own families to arrive, sipping coffee and chatting. They all seem so calm, like they've got nothing to prove. They can accept they're here, they're getting better, they can leave when they want. They don't need to pretend to be fine. Or even to actually *be* fine and have no one believe them.

I pace from window to window, watching the cars pull up and park in the courtyard. People take a moment to gather themselves before they open their doors. No one wants to be here. It's a rare sunny day, and I wish I could be outside with the November wind on my face and the blue sky above my head. But more than anything else, I look forward to feeling my children in my arms, seeing their smiles, smelling their hair.

Every day of struggle, of pretending, of performing for the cameras will have been worth it for this moment.

The visitors are varied: an elderly couple arrive to see their son, a recovering addict in his late twenties. A man and his teenage daughter greet a woman about my age; she doesn't speak much, so I assume she's here with depression. Some people come with young kids, but none as young as mine.

Finally, after everyone else seems to have welcomed their visitors, gathered coffees and pastries and settled on one of the many sofas dotted around the room, I see our car roll through the archway and into the courtyard, its back end as new and shiny as if that crash at the soft play centre never happened. I confessed that to Jeremy once I realised I had no chance of fixing the car without him finding out. I wonder if that was the day he first contacted the Hermitage. The day after we brought

Samuel home. So early. But possible. I have no idea what to think any more.

I back away from the window so he doesn't see me waiting like a prisoner with her face pressed to the bars of her cage.

I quickly sit on an empty sofa, pat down my hair, pinch my cheeks like someone in a costume drama. I try to look nonchalant and calm, when I'm anything but.

Minutes pass and the door stays closed. What is Jeremy doing? Why aren't they here yet? It doesn't take long to park a car. Visiting time is trickling away while my children are on the other side of a wall. I swallow my rising panic and remind myself that it takes a long time to gather a baby and the changing bag, and put Liv's shoes on, as she'll have inevitably removed them during the forty-minute journey. Yes, that'll be it.

But when the door finally opens, it's only Jeremy who steps through, the car seat in his hand. I get up from my carefully posed seat on the sofa and rush across to check over his shoulder for Liv. The corridor behind him is empty.

He goes to kiss me on the cheek, but I barely notice.

'Where's Liv?' I ask, unable to lean in or open my arms to him.

He shakes his head. 'I'm sorry, Mim. She couldn't come.'

My eyes sting. 'Couldn't come?' The phrasing is bizarre, as if Liv had an important work meeting she couldn't reschedule. 'How was a five-year-old not able to come?' I try to keep the hysteria out of my voice, but other visitors look up at my high-pitched tone.

I ignore their stares, grabbing the car seat and rushing to the nearest sofa so I can remove Samuel. I unclip the buckles with shaking fingers.

'Samuel, my baby,' I whisper. He looks bigger, his cheeks even rounder and the hair on his head thicker and darker. He's grown, his toes almost reaching the end of the legs of his onesie.

He'll be in the next size up within a week. It's only been six days and he's a different baby.

I coo at him, grin, tickle his tummy. No smile. Nothing. He's smiled for Jeremy while I've been here, but he won't smile for his mummy.

I press my cheek against his, feeling his cool skin. His cheeks are always colder than the rest of his body, and I love the way they feel against my hot face. He smells slightly of sour milk. Jeremy needs to clean out his neck folds more often.

I unbutton my shirt and offer him my breast. The relief when he latches on and begins to suckle. It's like stepping into a hot shower after a twenty-mile hike. I close my eyes and my muscles release a tiny amount of stored tension. I can finally breathe.

But where is my Liv?

Jeremy strides to the table and pours two coffees from the urn. He takes his time adding milk and selecting pastries, a frown furrowing his forehead.

By the time he returns, Samuel has released my nipple and is staring at the ceiling, his slate-grey eyes wide open. They're getting lighter, drawing closer to their permanent colour. Another little change I've missed.

'He didn't want to feed for long,' I say, trying not to cry. I wanted to see that he's missed me, that he knows his mother offers the best option.

Jeremy shrugs. 'I gave him a bottle before we came in.'

'What?' I run a hand through my freshly washed hair, but my fingers get caught in a tangle. 'Why? You knew I'd want to feed him myself. I haven't seen him in days.'

He reaches for a croissant and breaks it in two, flakes of pastry falling onto the plate and the coffee table. 'I didn't know what medications you'd be on and if it'd be safe for you to feed.'

'I've been pumping milk this entire time, Jeremy. Are you

not getting the frozen bags they've been sending you? What has he been drinking?' My voice gets louder again.

Jeremy winces, flicking a glance around the room. 'They're in our freezer at home. I haven't thrown them away.'

I stare at him, open-mouthed. 'I spend hours every day attached to a breast pump like a cow in a dairy farm. For what?'

'I wanted to double-check before I fed them to him. He's been doing fine on formula.'

'He's an exclusively breastfed baby, Jeremy. There was no need to—'

'I know now, don't I?'

'We talk every day on a video call. You could have asked this any time. I don't understand—'

'I'll feed him your breast milk from now on.' He groans and rubs his hands over his face. His palms scrape on his stubble. He didn't even shave for me. 'Just drop it, OK? I'm dealing with a lot while you're gone.'

My mouth falls open. I could scream. I didn't ask to be here. I didn't ask him to send me away and take sole charge of our children. I could be at home right now, witnessing these changes in my newborn baby as they happen. Rebuilding my relationship with Liv instead of begging her to say hello to me through a laptop camera once a day. He's taking so much from me and acting as if he's the martyr.

I am a model patient. I am a model patient. I repeat it to myself while I hold Samuel tighter. Time for more role play. Model patient. Perfect wife.

I reach towards Jeremy and place a hand on his knee. He flinches at my touch.

'Thank you for arranging this. It's doing me a lot of good.'

He hides his surprise with a tired smile. 'I'm glad to hear it.'

'It sounds like things at home are a lot. Two kids; double work.'

He nods.

'I've got a lot out of this first week. I could come home today.'

'What? Miriam, I—'

'A week's plenty of time. I feel rested, relaxed, happy. Like my old self. I do, Jeremy.'

He looks down.

I realise I'm still gripping his leg. I let go and stroke Samuel's hair, pull him closer.

Jeremy shakes his head, and his cheeks flush in that familiar way they do when he's stressed or angry. 'You're booked in here for two weeks. It's the minimum.'

I try to keep my tone neutral. 'And after that?'

'You come home. They explained it to me when I booked you in: the second week cements the work of the first. You won't get everything out of your stay if you leave now.' He downs his coffee. 'Gotta drink it while it's hot.' He nods at me holding Samuel.

'I'm sorry it's been a tough week for you.'

'We're doing OK, Mim. I'm loving being with the kids all the time. I'll be a better dad after this, you know. I did understand how hard it was for you while I was at work. But doing it solo for days really brings it home.'

I suppress a triumphant laugh. I've been begging him for years to take some time off and immerse himself in our day-to-day family life. But every year we use his annual leave on foreign holidays and Liv's sickness bugs. And now I have what I wanted: an involved, aware husband who knows exactly what it takes to look after two kids with no break while your partner's away. All it took was for him to commit me to a mental institution, apparently.

'Here, let me take him so you can have your coffee.' He reaches for Samuel and I hand him over, my arms empty without him.

I take a sip of coffee and a bite of apple Danish. And then I ask the question that's been running through my mind on an endless loop since Jeremy walked through the door. 'Why isn't Liv here?'

He wipes Samuel's lips with a muslin and finds a dummy in the changing bag.

I don't move. I'm not going to let this one lie. I've been waiting for a week, rejected over and over again on those video calls. If I'm lucky, I get to see the back of Liv's head as she walks past the computer. I needed to see her today.

He sighs. 'I'm sorry, Mim. It must be a phase she's going through. You know how kids have a favourite parent for a while. She'll soon get over it.'

'I'm guessing you're the favourite.'

'I think she's got this idea in her head that Samuel has replaced her somehow. That there's not enough space for her.'

'That I don't love her any more.'

He won't meet my eye. 'New baby brother, feels a bit pushed out, you know.'

'Not with you. Only me.'

He fusses over Samuel, straightening his onesie. 'It'll get better so quickly and she'll be back to normal.'

'Not while I'm locked away here it won't.'

He looks over his shoulder. 'Want another coffee or anything?'

Model patient. Get home. 'Where is Liv today? Who's looking after her?'

He smiles. 'Jac came over. She's been amazing, actually. Pops in on her way home from work most nights to check we're coping. She even brought some fresh milk and eggs from one of the farms near her parents' old place.'

'That's nice of her.' I can't help but feel a sting of betrayal. My best friend. All my friends, involved in my committal here. Zain, Nicole, Jac. My own mum. All sitting there in my living room, looks of concern on their faces. Yet no one thought to talk to me about it, to warn me or ask if I was all right. They went straight to intervention.

'Oh, she said to say hi. I think she's missing you.'

'Tell her thanks for her help. It won't be long now and I'll be home. Right?' I try to keep the fear from my voice.

He nods. 'One more week.'

'Tell Liv I love her.' My voice cracks. 'I miss her so much.'

I manage to keep the tears at bay until I get to my room after visiting hours.

The apple Danish sits in my stomach undigested, slopping around with the coffee. I rush to the en suite and vomit until I'm hollow and empty.

Then I sit with my back to the ceiling camera, tears running down my face, silent sobs racking my shoulders. To the camera I look like I'm sitting on my bed thinking. Even in the depths of darkness, I perform for the cameras.

After a while, emotion wrung out of me like I'm a used washcloth, I hook myself up to the breast pump with shaking hands and pump the milk Samuel wouldn't take.

A model patient.

17

Dr Okeke sits across from me, legs crossed, in the same position he's sat in every afternoon for the past seven days as we pick apart my life, my mind, my childhood and my deepest, darkest secrets. Most of them, anyway.

My mug of tea steams on the coffee table between us. Fresh milk, not those tiny long-life plastic pots. The benefits of private healthcare.

I swallow the hard lump in my throat. It's time. 'I forgot about it. I blocked it out, somehow, and didn't remember until a couple of weeks ago. I can't believe it happened. It's like I stood on the edge of a building and nearly jumped.'

He looks at me, holding eye contact. He's calm. There's no pressure. I can talk if I want to, or we can sit in comfortable silence. 'Tell me about that day, Miriam. The day it changed for you.'

Tears flow down my cheeks and my chest heaves with sobs as I tell Dr Okeke about Liv's cries in the park; her never-ending colic and reflux. My nightly insomnia and hallucinations in the dark.

I'd read the articles: 'Good mums walk away when they

need a break'. The articles that talked about shaken babies, and how crying babies were preferable to dead ones.

I tell him about turning away from her pram, telling myself she'd be better off without me. Someone would find her in a minute, I knew. A dog walker, a parent taking their kids to the swings, office workers on their lunch break. She wouldn't be alone for long. There was no danger.

The pram brake was on, a blanket tucked around her, a hat on her little head and mittens on her hands. Despite everything I'd given her, everything I'd tried, her face was red and her mouth wide with her screams. Nothing worked. I was useless.

I imagined her life without me, released from the burden of me as a mother. I imagined Jeremy's next wife; someone better suited for him. Someone calm, whose five senses could be trusted. A better mother for my baby, who would love her and care for her in a way I couldn't. Liv's new stepmother. He'd pick well, I was sure.

And I walked away from that bench.

I abandoned my newborn daughter. I put her down and walked away. But I couldn't walk away from myself, from my thoughts.

Dr Okeke's eyes shine as the words pour out of me. Are therapists allowed to cry for their patients? I don't know, but I do know this is why I like him. He's a genuinely nice guy and not a robot. He doesn't ask 'How does that make you feel?' or let monstrous silences fill the room. He listens and he feels along with me, and I know he understands who I was in that moment and why I hated myself so much.

When I finish, he folds his hands on his lap, over his untouched notebook. 'Oh, Miriam,' he says. His tone is like a warm hug. 'I'm so sorry that happened to you. And what a burden to carry for so long.'

I shake my head. 'I didn't remember.'

'Part of you did. You carried it with you every day for years.'

I reach for a tissue and wipe my face.

'There's one thing I want you to remember, every single time you think about that day, OK?'

I nod.

'You went back.'

My face crumples into tears again. 'I did.'

I'd got about ten feet away when her cries stopped. Sometimes silence is scarier than anything else. I froze, listening.

And then I rushed back to the pram to find her fast asleep, her mouth open in a tiny 'O'. Not caring if I woke her, I scooped her up in my arms and kissed her pillowy cheeks, rubbing my nose in her hair, feeling the warmth of her skin against my face.

Dr Okeke shifts in his seat. 'You didn't abandon Liv. You were suffering with a very serious mental illness and no treatment. You didn't do anything wrong. You were unwell.'

I open my mouth but I can't speak. I shove my hands under my thighs, the soft leather of the sofa beneath my palms.

'Our sessions this week have been very positive, and today's in particular feels like a true breakthrough. You confided something to me that you've never told anyone before. I appreciate it and I know it wasn't easy.'

I exhale through pursed lips. I feel like I've parachuted out of a plane and my feet just landed on grass.

He reaches for my file. 'I'm going to report to Dr Stokes that you're on track to go home at the end of next week, as planned. There's no reason to recommend further inpatient stay, whether here or elsewhere.'

My heart soars. I'm going home to my babies. 'Thank you.'

'I'm also going to tell Sonya that you're allowed mobile phone access. She'll return your mobile to you, but we insist you keep it in your bedroom and restrict yourself to maximum one hour a day. We know the damage of social media use if not regulated. This is to facilitate your contact with friends and family; no "doomscrolling".' He laughs at my raised eyebrows. 'I've got grandchildren; they tell me I'm very up to date.'

He writes a few lines in his notebook and slams it shut. 'And you can now have visitors outside of your immediate family. If you'd like some friends to pop in, just let them know to come between three and seven p.m.'

I raise my eyebrows. Do I want to see any of them? My betrayers?

'OK. Well done today. More tomorrow.'

I resist the urge to shake his hand. I'm so grateful that he'll still meet my eye even after everything I've admitted to him. I square my shoulders as I open his office door, ready to walk down the corridor, head held high for the cameras.

I am a model patient.

One week to go.

18

My phone has blown up while I've been here. It's only been six days, but when I switch it on, it buzzes and pings for what feels like minutes. I feel a trill of anxiety at all the notifications, and remember what Dr Okeke said about social media. Keep it to a minimum.

I swipe away what's not urgent and am left with an email from work and texts from Jeremy, Zain, Nicole, Jac and my mum.

From Jeremy:

> Central heating on the blink. Have called plumber.

> Boiler fixed. £300!!!?

> Liv says she wants the white cereal bars. Can't find any. What is she talking about?

> What size nappies is Samuel?

> Never mind re nappies

> Hello? Did they take your phone?

His texts stop the same day he dropped me here, when he realised I couldn't reply. I guess he said everything he needed to say on our nightly video calls after that.

My friends' messages are friendly and ingratiating in equal measure. I know they're feeling guilty about their presence at my lowest point.

From Jac:

> Hey mate. Hope you're doing OK in the clink. Went on a couple of dates: got tons of juicy gossip to tell you when we catch up. I'm keeping an eye on your fam: all good. Jeremy coping, Liv perfect, Samuel angel. Hope you're in the jacuzzi every day wearing a mudpack while someone massages you. J xx

From Nicole:

> Thinking of you. I'll pop over this week and see how Jeremy's doing. Coffee and soft play as soon as you're back! x

From Zain:

> Sounds like we have work news to catch up on! Let me know if they let you have visitors in the retreat – I'll come say hi.

I read their check-ins with a half-smile on my face. I try to turn it around: if a friend of mine had had some kind of breakdown after giving birth, I would be sympathetic and understanding. No judgement. So why do I expect different from my friends? They're texting me like normal; they're all still here.

Relief.

I reply to them all with a few lines to reassure them I'm

doing OK, that I'm on the mend. Then I follow up with a second message:

> They just said I can have visitors! 3–7 any day. xx

As instructed, I put my phone away. I hook myself up to the pump and gaze out of the window while the machine tugs at my breasts. It's not always an unpleasant feeling, but it's mentally uncomfortable. Still, it's worth it if it's feeding my baby, even when I'm far away. Even if Jeremy was giving him formula. He knows now. Samuel will have my breast milk now. Jeremy promised, and I believe him. I have to.

The vibration of my phone is almost inaudible beneath the hum of the pump, but I see the screen light up from the corner of my eye.

Incoming call from Zain.

'Hello?'

'Hey, Mim! Just a quick one, I saw your message about visiting hours. I've got some time this afternoon, if it's not too short notice?'

I frown and glance at the clock on my screen. It's already 3 p.m. 'I'd love to see you. I've got no other plans.'

'Great.' I can't quite identify the tone in his voice. There's a strange enthusiasm, maybe. Or relief? 'See you in about an hour, depending on traffic.'

I busy myself with make-up and pinning my hair back. It's Zain. He won't even notice. But I'm doing this for me, really. It feels important that I look well for my first non-family visitor, similar to how it feels important to look good for a school reunion or meeting a friend you haven't seen for a decade. I make sure my eyeliner is even and my mascara doesn't smudge. A little blusher and I'm done.

'Wowee,' chirps Katy as I pass her on my way to the visiting room. 'Got a hot date?' She's curled up on a sofa, book on her lap, while she waits to use the multimedia room. She's sitting with her back to the TV, which is playing mid-afternoon quiz shows to a rapt audience of two depressed patients and one former addict.

'Just a visitor.' I smile and don't stop, and Katy doesn't ask any more questions. I'm sure she'll be full of them at dinner.

Zain's already there when I get down to the ground floor, a muffin, a water and a coffee in front of him at one of the sofas. He stands up as I walk into the room.

There are two other people with him, their backs to the door. They turn when Zain stands, and a smile breaks over my face. It's Jac and Nicole. I gulp at the lump in my throat.

There aren't many people here today. Two elderly ladies sit in one corner talking to a girl in her early twenties. They're leaning forward, heads almost touching as they chat. They don't turn when I come in.

In the toy corner, a toddler plays with plastic dinosaurs, roaring and smashing them together. I smile at him as I walk by.

'Nice place you've got here.' Jac smirks, her arms outstretched. 'I'd heard it was posh, but wow.'

I hug her, then Zain kisses me on the cheek before sitting down and taking a bite of muffin. He leaves crumbs on the table. 'You getting a cake or anything?'

I shake my head, letting Nicole pull me into her arms. 'What a lovely surprise! You got here quickly,' I say when she releases me.

'Well, lots to catch up on.' Zain raises his eyebrows and looks at me expectantly.

'Is there?' I gesture around the room. The boy lies on his back on the floor, holding a stegosaurus in one hand and a T rex in the other. He manoeuvres the T rex's plastic jaw so the stegosaurus's head fits in its mouth. 'Not much happening here, unless you want to hear about the lunch menu or my ability to hold various yoga poses.'

He shakes his head. 'All right, Ms Mysterious. If you want to play it like that.'

I frown, confused.

'How are you doing? Is it OK in here?' Nicole asks, reaching out and laying a warm hand on my knee.

I tell them about my days, about how I'm feeling. About the cameras but how I've got used to them now. About how Liv won't speak to me on the video calls and didn't come with Jeremy for the family visit. And how they're going to let me come home at the end of the two weeks.

'You thought they'd keep you here?' Jac asks, incredulous.

'Well, they could, apparently. The people who don't admit themselves have less control. The ones who check themselves in can leave when they're ready.'

In the toy corner, the boy abandons the dinosaurs and runs sobbing to his family. His cries echo off the high ceiling as he shouts about the T rex biting him on the face. He climbs into his mother's lap, curled into her shoulder with his thumb in his mouth.

Zain takes another bite of muffin. 'Jeremy wants you better, but he also wants you home.' He leans back, arms along the top of the sofa.

Jac nods in agreement. 'He won't solo-parent two little kids for longer than he has to. I've seen it this week. The man's drowning without you; don't let him tell you otherwise.'

I nod. I know they're right. I shake off the little worm of paranoia that curls up in my brain sometimes. It's hard work looking after a five-year-old and a newborn, and Jeremy is not a natural stay-at-home father. No. Given the choice, he would have me home in a heartbeat to share the load. He didn't choose this, I admit to myself for the first time. There's no way he would. I take a deep breath and let it out slowly, trying to visualise the tension leaving my body like they tell us in the yoga sessions.

Nicole gives me an encouraging smile. 'We're here for your whole family. I'll pop in tomorrow and check Jeremy's doing OK. Maybe bring some dinner.'

I lean my head on her shoulder. 'Thank you all,' I whisper.

'OK, I can't wait any more.' Zain claps his hands. 'Tell me what's going on.'

'What do you mean?' I ask, confused. 'I just told you everything.'

'At work, dummy. We've heard your news.' He glances at Nicole, whose face stays impassive. Whatever it is, she doesn't find it as exciting as he does.

Jac shifts in her seat and glances around the room, sipping a glass of water as she tunes out of the work chat. She still hasn't said much to Nicole, but it means a lot that they've put their differences aside for me. They're here together, even if they don't have much in common any more.

I frown. 'Work news? I'm on mat leave. I don't have any work news.' Then I remember the email I haven't read yet. The one with a red exclamation mark next to the subject line. 'Has something happened?'

The skin around Zain's shirt collar blossoms an angry red. He glances at Nicole again. 'Your mat leave cover... I heard her talking to someone in the staff room. They've offered her the permanent contract.'

My stomach twists. I haven't thought about work in weeks, but I was looking forward to returning. I care about those kids, and I love using art to open their worlds. That job is an important part of me.

'I shouldn't have been listening, but I was the only other one in the staff room and the IT guy's invisible to the teaching staff.' He laughs. 'I'd be a great spy.'

I don't laugh with him. I bring both hands to my forehead, dig my fingernails into my hairline. 'What?'

Zain looks even more confused. 'How do you not know?'

I shake my head. 'I haven't spoken to anyone from work since I went on leave. Just you two.'

'They've given your job away?' Jac leans forward, tuning back into the conversation. 'Isn't that illegal?'

Zain puts his head in his hands. 'This is effed up.'

'What's going on?' I ask. The little boy runs to the toy corner to pick up his dinosaurs. He gives me a wave as he walks towards the exit with his family, holding his mother's hand. I don't wave back.

'They were saying you'd offered your resignation. The head said she was disappointed to see you go, but your email was clear that you didn't want to return, nor did you want an exit interview. You wanted to focus on your kids and spend time with your family.'

'Oh my God.'

'That's one of the reasons we came to see you, Mim,' Nicole says.

Jac flashes her a look. 'And to check you were OK in general.'

Zain nods. 'We wanted to say congratulations or whatever it is you say when someone makes a big life decision.'

I swallow the bile rising in my throat. 'But that's the thing, Zain. I didn't make this decision. I don't want to leave. I didn't resign.'

'WTF?' He spells the letters out like a teenager. 'That's crazy.'

'Someone else sent that email?' asks Jac, disbelief on her face.

'I'm so sorry, Mim,' Nicole adds, draping an arm around me and pulling me into her chest. She smells of laundry detergent. 'We'll work it out. There must be a way to fix it.'

My friends stay for another fifteen minutes after that, but I've no idea what we talk about, or if we talk at all. I'm itching to get to my room and check my phone, look through the sent folder in my emails. Zain drains his coffee and eats the last crumbs of muffin, and everyone stands up to leave. I mumble a vague 'thanks for visiting' as I rush to the lift.

I sit on my bed and unlock my phone with shaking hands, and there it is, in my sent items:

From: Miriam Thorne
To: Crawlington School, Head Teacher
cc: Crawlington School, Administration
Subject: Resignation

Dear Ms Ryder,

Please accept this email as notice of my resignation from the position of head of art and art therapy at Crawlington School. I have enjoyed my time in the role, but my maternity leave has allowed me time to spend with my family, and while my children are small I feel that is where my focus is best placed. This decision is final and I don't wish to discuss it further or attend an exit interview.

As my notice period is one month, I believe my last day will be 15 December. Please let me know how much accrued holiday and pay I am owed.
Thank you for the support you've given me during my time at Crawlington. It has been a pleasure to work with you.

From today I won't be checking this email address regularly.

Please send future correspondence to the postal address
you have on file, addressed c/o Jeremy Thorne.

Best wishes,

Miriam

I can't stop reading that final sentence, over and over. *Please send future correspondence to the postal address you have on file, addressed c/o Jeremy Thorne.*

I swallow, my face burning with confusion and shame. Is it possible I sent this and forgot? Maybe I blocked it out, like everything from the first months of Liv's life?

I shake away the thought. No.

I love my job. I fought hard for it: art college, teacher training, further education in art therapy. I care about the kids, love watching them get absorbed in their art, learning to express themselves in new ways. It can help them so much. Putting a pencil or a lump of clay in their hands gives them a voice. I care about Elliot, who stammers until he talks about the robot he made from old recycling. And Paige, who draws pictures of traumatic things she can't find the words for. And myself, for finding true calm when I'm sketching, eyes flicking from subject to paper, subject to paper. It may not be as high-flying as Jeremy's job, but it's mine and I love it. *Loved* it.

No, I didn't send that email. Not even in the darkest depths of amnesia.

Someone hacked into my emails and resigned me from my job. And told the school not to contact me again.

I slide off the bed and onto the floor, hugging my knees to my chest. I'm shaking all over.

I check the date. This email was sent seven days ago. The day I arrived here at the Hermitage Wellbeing Centre. After my phone was taken. After Jeremy drove away and left me here. He knew they'd taken my phone. He knew I couldn't check my emails.

I remember the email from the school that I haven't opened yet, the one with the red exclamation mark. I click into my inbox.

It was sent the same day, arriving a couple of hours before someone tendered my resignation. The subject line reads: *Return date: can't wait to welcome you back!*

So whoever sent my resignation saw the message about my return to work and immediately emailed them to say I was resigning. Someone didn't want me to go back.

Someone is screwing with my life.

I don't know how long I sit there, reading that resignation email over and over. I'm trying to see any clue to who did this and why: patterns or odd turns of phrase. I remember what Zain said in the soft play, weeks ago: a hacker might not be watching a child. They might be using the baby monitor as a back door into other devices connected to the router, like phones and laptops.

This could still be a total stranger ruining my life. Just because they can.

But they know Jeremy's name. They requested my mail be forwarded *care of* Jeremy. I mean, maybe they know Jeremy's name from hacking our devices or watching us every day through the monitor.

Or maybe it's Jeremy, and he wants me to stay at home so he can keep an eye on me all the time. Is it possible that a normal level of concern and worry about his wife has morphed into full-on scary control and... well, imprisonment?

Jeremy has never been a controlling husband. He was always fine with me going out with my friends, never quizzed me when I got home or complained if I was late. He's never gone through my phone when I wasn't in the room, or been jealous about former partners or male friends.

If Jeremy sent that resignation, it's a very different Jeremy to the one I married. But then... I swallow a sob. The Jeremy I married wouldn't have sent me to a mental hospital either. And yet I'm here, and he put me here. He planned it for weeks and then pretended it was a spontaneous decision for my own good. And my future is still in his hands: he could keep me imprisoned here indefinitely if I don't play the game.

I rush to the en suite and kneel over the toilet bowl, holding my hair back as spit pools in my mouth. My stomach heaves, but I don't vomit. After a couple of minutes, I stand up and splash cold water on my face at the sink.

In the mirror, my face stares back at me. My eyes are sunken and hollow. I look haunted. I *am* haunted.

From the bedroom, I hear my phone buzzing over and over. Message after message arrives through every app I have installed: WhatsApp, Facebook Messenger, text... everything. When I check, each app shows five or ten new messages.

I click into WhatsApp: they're all from unsaved or withheld numbers, and the previews show numerous insults and slurs: they call me a whore, a home-wrecker, a slut. They tell me they know where I live. They tell me I deserve to be raped.

It's the same in Messenger and Signal.

> Fuck you. Bitch.

> I know where you are. You can't hide in the loony bin for ever.

I don't even open my text inbox. I know it'll be the same.

And then, as quickly as they appeared, they disappear. Timed messages, allowing me to see them for sixty seconds before they self-destruct. Like a slap, over in a moment and leaving behind only a sting.

I throw my phone on the bed, as far away as I can.

What the hell is going on?

19

I need to escape. I wish I could turn off my brain. I wish I could just run away, listen to the pounding of my feet on the ground and feel the wind against my skin. But the early evening has brought rain, and in any case, I know that no matter how far I run, I can't outrun my thoughts.

I can't even show anyone the messages, as they've disappeared from my phone. Telling someone will make me look more crazy than I already do.

But I'm in the best place in the world for people who need help with their thoughts. The Hermitage is like a Disneyland for mental health.

It's time to try the sensory deprivation tank.

I put on my swimming costume and wrap myself in the Hermitage-branded white dressing gown that hangs on the back of my door. I step out into the corridor, feeling more like a hospital patient with every step, roaming the halls in my nightgown. I pass no one on my way to the lift, and the hallways on the floor below are also empty. Everyone must be at dinner. I ignore the rumblings of my stomach and press on. I can eat later. I need to fix my brain first. I need to cleanse myself after those poisonous messages.

My footsteps echo as I walk from the lift and knock on the door. For a moment I fear I'm too late, that I'll have to wait until tomorrow. But after a few seconds, I hear movement within and the door opens. It's a nurse with red hair in a bun on the top of her head. She slips a mobile phone into her pocket and fixes a smile on her face.

'Hello. Come in. Are you here to use the flotation tank?'

I nod and sidle through, glancing around the stark room. There's a leather armchair, the shape of the nurse's buttocks still imprinted on the cushion. And in the opposite corner, what looks like a giant pod, the size of a small car. New Age music hovers in the air, along with the scent of essential oils that permeates this entire corridor.

The nurse introduces herself as Val. 'Have you used the tank before?'

I shake my head.

She launches into her memorised introduction speech. 'So, you're going to experience flotation therapy, or "REST": restricted environmental stimulation therapy. It's been proven to assist with depression, anxiety and insomnia. It helps the brain enter a more relaxed state, like the mindfulness of meditation but with even fewer distractions.'

I nod, and shift from foot to foot. I just want to get in the tank. I don't need more stuff in my brain. I need *less*.

She doesn't notice and keeps talking. 'The water is saturated with Epsom salts to aid floating, and is heated to body temperature so after a few moments you might even forget you're in water. If you can relax into it, you'll feel like a new person by the end.'

I nod. 'How long is the session?'

She opens up the pod to reveal a small pool of water, lit by blue lights. It looks inviting, like a jacuzzi. 'I'll put you in for twenty minutes to start and then I'll check on you. If you're doing OK, we can extend that for another twenty minutes. But some people find one short session is enough.'

She points to three buttons in the underside of the lid. 'Underwater lights are on the left and lid lights on the right. The large middle one is your panic button. It's ridged so you can find it in the darkness. Press that if you need to get out. It'll set off an alarm and I'll open the lid immediately.'

I swallow. 'So I can't open it myself?'

'There's an emergency release catch here,' she indicates a little lever on the side of the lid, 'but it resets the whole system, so it's best if you wait for me. If you can.'

If you can. I'm starting to question my decision to try this.

She helps me off with my robe and hangs it on a hook on the wall. 'Psychologically, we believe this therapy puts us back in the womb: dark, quiet, floating in liquid. It's where we first developed, so returning to that state can promote emotional growth.'

I turn away so she doesn't see me roll my eyes. This was a bad idea. I should have stayed in my room and tried to work out who's sending me abuse. Screenshotted some of the insults before they disappeared. Called Jeremy to find out what the hell he's doing screwing with my job. I ball my hands into fists against the sides of my bare thighs. But I'm here now. Might as well try it.

I step into the tank, which is about six feet wide. She signals for me to lie down, and I comply, the water in my ears dulling the sound of her voice. 'Twenty minutes, OK?' she shouts.

I nod.

'I'll close the lid. Then after one minute I'll turn out the lights. If you need them back on, your know where the button panel is.'

The lid closes, and the blue underwater lights dim, replaced by a starscape of tiny LEDs. Then those go out too, and I'm plunged into total darkness and silence.

My senses are on fire, yet dulled all at once. I feel nothing, but everything. The water feels nonexistent. I hear only the sound of my breathing. At first I can smell the vague scent of chlorine, but after a few seconds it disappears as my nose gets used to it. The view from behind my closed eyelids is the same as when my eyes are open. Darkness. Darkness.

I try to remember what I've learned in the meditation sessions I've attended this week. Focus on your breath. Empty your mind. Acknowledge your thoughts and let them go.

But I have no job. My husband has taken it from me.

My elder child hates me and my younger has already forgotten me.

I am a prisoner in a gilded cage, at the mercy of doctors and the person who put me here.

And strangers on the internet wish me dead for reasons I don't yet know.

My breathing speeds up, short gasps that don't fill my lungs with air. Empty your mind, I mentally shout at myself. Stop it. Stop thinking about what a terrible mess your life has become. Let it go. *Relax, damn you.*

I realise with a shock that I have no idea how much time has passed. It could be five minutes, it could be fifteen. What if Val leaves me in here longer than she said? What if she forgets I'm here and goes home for the day? What if she has a stroke and can't let me out, and no one finds me for hours?

I try to breathe slowly and deeply. In for four, hold for four, out for four. Box breathing, they called it in the meditation session.

This isn't working. I reach up to the button panel to turn on the lights, but my hands find nothing but the smooth underside of the lid. The light switches are gone.

I shudder and grope at the lid. Nothing. It remains cool and even against my palms. I leave my hands there for a moment, resting on the surface inches above my face. It's nice to feel *something*.

I lift my head from the water, clearing one of my ears. It's so silent that the air feels heavy, like it's filling my ear canals.

I flail and flap, trying to find the buttons again. Finally I locate them and press. The tank illuminates, the dim blue lights under the surface of the water making my legs and arms look other-worldly, long, stringy and gaunt. My fingertips are puckered.

I'm getting nothing from this experience.

Then the lights go out. I'm in total blackness again. The darkness around me feels alive, like it's a being in the tank alongside me. Watching me. Crouched in the corner.

They know I'm here. The ones who hate me. They've found me and they've trapped me.

I'm done. That's enough.

I hit the panic button, expecting an alarm to sound and Val to open the lid. But nothing happens. No alarm sounds. The lid stays closed.

'Hello?' I call, but the silence sucks my voice from my mouth. The pod is soundproof, I realise. The tinkly New Age music playing in the room is inaudible. And so am I.

I wait for the pod lid to open. *Immediately*, she said. As soon as I pushed the panic button. But she's not coming.

My brain can't process space and time. The seconds turn to hours, the minutes to days.

I hit the button again and again. Nothing happens.

I'm stuck. Abandoned in the dark. I will die here.

My breath turns to sobs, my chest shuddering with terror. She said she'd check on me after twenty minutes, and I've been in here much longer. Double that, even. *Where is she?* I need to get out.

She told me about the emergency release catch. I don't care

if it resets the whole system. I need to get out of here. And when I do, she'd better be lying on the floor having had some kind of medical emergency that prevented her from freeing me from this dark, silent prison.

I slide my hands around the sides of the lid. I'm scrabbling, my breath coming in ragged pants, when the lid jerks and slides up with a hydraulic whirr. Cold air whooshes around my shoulders like a chilled shawl. I look up, and there's the nurse, lifting the lid with one hand, phone in the other.

'That's your twenty minutes...' She stops when she sees me huddled in one corner like an animal caught in a trap. 'Are you all right?'

I stand up, water running in rivulets down my thighs. I can't stop shaking. My legs buckle under me and I sink back down. 'No, I'm not OK,' I hiss, between panicked breaths. 'I was trapped.'

She frowns in confusion. 'I was right here. I could have opened it. Why didn't you press the—'

'I pressed the damn panic button. Nothing happened.'

'I'm so sorry. This hasn't happened before.'

She continues to apologise as she wraps a towel around my shoulders and calls Dr Okeke, who gives me a pill to stop the shaking and the hyperventilating. 'Just don't store your breast milk for ten hours or so,' he says, patting me on the shoulder. 'Straight down the sink, OK?'

20

The next morning there's an 'Out of Order' sign on the door to the sensory deprivation tank room when I walk past on my way downstairs. Jeremy's bringing the kids, including Liv this time. I made him promise on our last call.

I still feel floaty and strangely calm, like I'm watching the world at a remove. But that's the effect of the pill, not the flotation tank. It was so strong I went straight to bed as soon as I returned to my room, and slept through until seven this morning. I was too dazed and drugged to call Jeremy or read any more vile messages. Just uninterrupted, deep sleep for the first time since Samuel was born. Bliss.

Who needs holistic therapies when you can take drugs? I wish I could get more of those magic little pills.

I hold out some hope that Liv will sense my calm, drug-induced though it is, and be calm too. No tantrums. No shouting. Just affection for her mummy, who loves her so much.

I fix a smile to my face and open the door to the visiting room. They're already there: Jeremy sitting on a sofa with Liv on his knee, the baby's car seat on the floor at his feet. I rush across the room, trying not to run.

'Hello, family!' I open my arms to them, but they stay sitting on the sofa, looking at me. Liv has her thumb in her mouth, her eyes glassy as she gazes at me with no emotion on her face.

'Come on, say hi to Mummy,' Jeremy mumbles in her ear.

She shakes her head and buries her face in his chest. I drop my arms and wrap them around myself.

He gives me an apologetic look. 'She fell asleep in the car, just woke up. She'll come round in a minute.'

I busy myself unbuckling sleeping Sam from the car seat, surreptitiously wiping my eyes with my back turned. My milk is already coming in, and I'm unbuttoning my shirt when Jeremy reaches out and puts a hand on my arm. 'Stop.'

I frown.

'The medication,' he says.

My mouth drops open in surprise. I'll have to make do with cuddles and Samuel's smell, his skin against mine. 'They said it was fine after ten hours,' I say weakly. I try not to cry.

'I'd rather be cautious.'

Liv slides from Jeremy's knee and wanders away, touching every chair and humming to herself. She's making her way towards the toy corner but trying to look nonchalant about it, like she doesn't know it's there. I feel a rush of love for her, my funny little daughter. And immediately afterwards, a rush of loss. Loss of her love.

'How did you know? About the pill?' I ask as soon as she's out of earshot.

'They update me on your care. There's an app.'

My skin prickles. 'That's... invasive.'

He shakes his head. 'It just tells me what treatments and medications they prescribe.'

'Does it tell you what I talk about in my therapy sessions?'

He laughs.

'It's not funny, Jeremy. This is my life, and I'm not in control.' My voice breaks. 'You are, apparently.'

The smile slips from his face. 'Sorry.' He gets his phone from his pocket and taps the screen a few times. 'Here.' He hands it to me, open to the VirtualHermitage app. *Miriam Thorne, therapies and medications w/c 20 November 2023*, it says at the top of the screen, and then there's a list:

- Person-centred counselling (Dr Okeke)
- Yoga (Santi)
- REST (Val)
- Diazepam 10 mg (guest advised no breastfeeding for ten hours, Dr O)

I hand the phone back. 'Right. I see.'

'Do you want a pastry or something?' he asks, indicating the refreshment table.

'In a minute. If we get them now, Liv will want one, and I need to talk to you before she comes over.' Against my chest, Samuel flails his arms and gurgles, little staccato babbles. New sounds he couldn't make a week and a half ago when I came in here. He's changing and I'm missing it. My heart aches with what I'm losing.

Jeremy nods. 'Sure. Talk away.'

I take a deep breath, grateful for the calming after-effects of last night's pill. One thing at a time. I tell him about the resignation email I didn't send, but I don't tell him about the abusive messages yet.

He looks stricken. 'Why would you resign? I thought you enjoyed your job.'

I try not to groan. 'I didn't resign, Jeremy. I didn't send that email.'

He shakes his head. 'I'm so sorry, Miriam. This is such a hard time.'

'What do you mean?'

'You must have sent it when you were deep in the darkest part of things. To blank it out like that.'

'I didn't send it, Jeremy,' I hiss. 'Someone else did.'

He flinches. 'I know you don't remember. But that's the most logical—'

I swear under my breath. 'They took my phone away when you dropped me off. I didn't even have access to it when that email was sent.'

He looks at me, thinking. He seems genuinely perplexed. I want to believe him. I really do.

'Just tell me, please.'

'Tell you what?'

'That it was you. That when you got home from dropping me here, you sat at your desk and you thought, "Miriam is unwell and needs to be at home. I can protect her and make her better if I simplify her life and take one responsibility away."' I try to make it sound like he was doing me a favour, in the hope he'll admit what he did.

But he shakes his head, a dumbfounded expression on his face. 'If you don't want to return to work, that's OK. My job makes enough—'

'Jeremy, you're not listening. I don't have a choice now. I did want to go back, but you've taken that choice away.'

He stands up. 'I didn't send that email, Miriam. Perhaps you're more unwell than you can admit.' He crosses to the refreshment table and grabs a plate.

From the toy corner, Liv spots him and runs over, wrapping her arms around his waist and eyeing the pastries.

I sit cradling Samuel, who stares at the ceiling and won't meet my eye. I feel a stab of envy as I watch my daughter wrapped around Jeremy, her scuffed shoe standing on his toe, her fingers hooked over the back of his belt as she carefully selects the stickiest, sweetest pastry.

She follows Jeremy back to our sofa, her mouth full already, icing across both cheeks and a trail of crumbs behind her.

I smile and pat the sofa next to me and Sam. 'Coming to sit down?'

She looks at me for a moment, shakes her head once and then sits next to Jeremy, her body angled away from me and towards the toy corner. She'll run off as soon as she's finished that pastry, I know it. 'I've missed you, Liv.'

She doesn't acknowledge me.

I look down at Sam, stroke his cheek.

Jeremy bites into his croissant and nudges Liv. 'Your mum spoke to you.'

Liv doesn't respond.

He forces a smile. 'She's been doing great, Mim. She was excited to come. Weren't you, Liv?'

'No,' she mumbles through pastry.

'She even picked out her outfit. The visiting Mummy outfit. Didn't you?'

Everything she's wearing is patterned with flowers, a riot of different colours on each garment. Leggings, T-shirt and hoodie are a clashing, bright mess. My heart swells with love for her. 'You look amazing, Liv.' And I mean it.

She shakes her head. 'Not this mummy.'

I lean forward. 'What do you mean?'

She stands up, the remains of her pastry dropping to the floor. 'I thought we were visiting my other mummy.' She stands on the crumbs, grinding them into the carpet.

She's got new shoes, I notice. Glittery silver Velcro trainers. Her feet must have grown. Jeremy must have taken her to get measured. Another thing I missed.

He reaches out to stop her, but she wrenches herself away from him. 'I don't want this one.'

It's a kick in the gut. 'What other mummy, Liv? I'm your mummy.' I feel so pathetic, sitting here hunched over on the couch, rejected by my daughter. The parenting advice would tell me to let her have her feelings, not to show the pain she has caused me. Not to turn it around so she has to worry about my emotions. But where's the line? Am I supposed to listen over and over to how much she hates me and how she wishes someone else were her mother? I can't live like this. I won't survive it. I want to crawl off into a hole and die.

Instead, I straighten up and plaster a fake smile on my face. I pass Samuel to Jeremy and follow Liv to the toy corner, crouching next to her as she plays with the wooden beads on the metal loops, a staple of every waiting room ever. She ignores me, which I see as progress. At least she isn't telling me to go away.

I reach out and run a red bead along a track. 'What's your favourite colour, Liv?' I ask. It used to be yellow, but everything changes so fast.

She ignores me. I push a yellow bead.

'No.' She bats my hand away.

I cup my hands in my lap, kneel on the floor. Muster again. 'I've missed you, Liv. Are you having fun with Daddy and Samuel while I'm on holiday?'

'Yes.' She slides stacks of beads violently from one side of the toy to another; the whole table shakes.

'Can I have a hug?' I put a hand on her skinny shoulder, try to pull her towards me.

She freezes at my touch. 'No hugs.' Before I can react, she raises a fist and smashes it into my nose with a crunch.

A starburst of pain. I double over, cupping my hands around my nose. Blood drips into my palms. I try to open my eyes, but my vision is fuzzy, like TV static.

'Liv!' roars Jeremy from across the room. I hear his footsteps as he strides towards us, the rustle of his shirt as he kneels next to me. 'Liv, we don't hit. We use our words. Say sorry to Mummy.'

She folds her arms. 'But I'm not sorry.' Her voice is cold and toneless.

'You should feel very sorry. You hurt Mummy.'

'I'm the boss of my body.'

'What?'

'I'm the boss of my body and she tried to touch me.'

'Liv, that's not—'

'I'M THE BOSS OF MY BODY AND SHE TRIED TO TOUCH ME!' Liv screams.

The conversations around the room stop. Without looking up, I can feel eyes on my back. My face is slick with tears and blood. I try to wipe some of it away, try to clear my vision. I sit on the floor, my back to a toy box. My head throbs. My heart is broken.

More footsteps. Someone crouches next to me. I open my eyes. It's Sonya, blurry. She speaks quietly and quickly. 'Mr and Mrs Thorne. It seems like today's visiting session hasn't gone very well. Not to worry, these things happen.'

Jeremy forces a chuckle. I see from the corner of my eye that Liv is holding his hand and clinging to his leg, hiding her face in the folds of his jeans. She won't let me touch her, but she'll hide behind Jeremy.

'I want to go home.' I try not to sob. 'I need to be with my babies. Liv needs me; she needs her mummy.'

Sonya hands me a tissue. 'This second week is crucial, Miriam. Let's not stop your progress when things are going so well.' She turns to Jeremy. 'I think it's best we cut today's visiting session short. We'll take care of Miriam.'

He nods.

'No.' I wipe my face with the tissue and stand up, stuffing it into my pocket. 'There's still time left. There's still things to talk about. I need more time with my children.' I haven't had a chance to tell Jeremy about the abusive messages, and I still don't know why he sent my resignation. I haven't cuddled Liv.

I haven't kissed her cheek. Or stroked her hair. Smelled her skin.

But Sonya is already leading me away. My lungs constrict with panic. Any after-effect of last night's pill has gone now. I try to shake her off. 'No, visiting hours aren't over.' My voice echoes through the large room. I know everyone's staring, but I don't care. 'You can't do this. I haven't seen my children in so long. Jeremy, Liv needs...'

Blood trickles out of my nose and hits my top lip. I taste the tang of iron on my tongue.

Sonya holds out another tissue. I take it and swipe at the blood, smearing it across my face. I feel eyes on me from every angle. And in each corner of the room, a little LED light flashes as the cameras watch and record.

'We'll speak to you tomorrow, love,' Jeremy says. 'On the video chat. And I'll take extra care of Liv.'

'Let me at least say goodbye to my children.' I pull away from Sonya and take a step towards Liv, still half hidden behind Jeremy's legs.

She shrinks back. 'No no no! Get away from me. I hate you. I HATE YOU!'

I recoil, pushed away by the screams and shouts. The air leaves my lungs like she's hit me again.

'I love you, Liv.'

She doesn't respond.

I turn away, walk towards the sofa where we sat earlier. Samuel's in his car seat, burbling and batting at a colourful toy that Jeremy has hung from the handle. I unclip him and pick him up, hold him to my chest with the love and care I needed to give to two children, not one. But he writhes against me and begins to howl. I kiss his cheek as he pushes his hands against my chest and arches his back.

'Everything OK?'

At Jeremy's voice, Samuel wails louder and reaches for him,

pushing his body away from mine with as much force as his tiny muscles will muster.

Snap. Something inside me breaks in two.

I turn to Jeremy. 'He wants you.' My voice is devoid of emotion. I am a robot. I hand the baby to Jeremy and turn to Sonya.

Sonya gives me a big smile, as if none of this has happened. As if she hasn't just watched my whole world implode.

In my calmest voice I say, 'I'm ready to leave now.'

21

The messages pour in. *Bitch. Waste of skin. Fucker.*

I block every number, but they keep popping up like whack-a-mole. I try to take screenshots, but some tech in the disappearing messages blocks me from doing it. I silence my phone, but I still hear the buzzing. It echoes through my brain. There are so many messages that they obscure any others that might come through, from people who actually care about me.

I don't sleep that night. I switch off my phone, but I know it's there, the messages still arriving.

I lie awake in the dark, staring at the glinting red LED light in the corner of the room. I imagine someone in a control room somewhere watching the screens. Watching the patients – *guests* – as they sleep. Or don't, in my case.

Around 3 a.m., delirious with tiredness, I wave at the camera. I wonder if anyone sees.

In my half-awake, half-asleep dreamlike state, my brain runs through what I might have lost. I have a list in my phone of books I wanted to read with Liv when she was old enough. Books I loved as a child that I was excited to share with her, to see the wonder in her eyes as her mummy showed her a world of stories: *The Secret Garden*, the Famous Five, Narnia, *Journey to the River Sea*, *What Katy Did*. The list represented a new phase of our relationship: the transition from toddlerhood to childhood. But Liv hates me now. She won't want to lie in bed with me and dive into new worlds.

My own mother was difficult to grow up with, expecting me to parent myself while she recovered from losing Dad. She didn't have enough headspace to look after anyone but herself, and I suffered for that. Coming home from school to an empty fridge because Mum wasn't hungry so hadn't thought to shop. Taking myself to the school nurse when my period started because she hadn't realised it was time to tell me about that yet.

I always vowed to be there for Liv in a way my own mum couldn't be for me. I'd be her confidante, her guide through the pitfalls of adolescence. A strong role model with clear boundaries. Always mother and daughter, never best friends. A clear line. Defined roles. I planned it all.

Have I lost it all, somehow, before she's even old enough to know me?

I remember Sonya's wide smile at the end of yesterday's disastrous visit, as she ushered me away from the wreckage of my family. Can't anyone see that Liv needs help as much as I do? What good is this place if my time away from them destroys the family I left behind?

I think about this in a daze like I'm watching myself at a distance. I shower, washing my hair and combing the conditioner through. I glance in the mirror, note the dark shadows of bruises gathering in the inner corners of my eyes from Liv's blow yesterday. A mark on the outside mirroring the pain on the inside. To an extent, I'm grateful for the physical proof.

I dress in head-to-toe black, the softest clothes I can find in my suitcase. I can't stand the idea of denim, zips and seams against my skin.

I go to breakfast even though I'm not hungry. I don't think

I'll ever be hungry again. But the cameras are watching. I must keep going. Yesterday was a disaster, but I can't fade away, can't lock myself in my room, can't scream and cry and howl with loss.

I sit with Katy, but I tell her I'm not in the mood to chat. She understands.

I sip a coffee. Move toast around my plate. Try to stay alive. Breathe in. Breathe out.

I perform for the cameras. A model patient.

I whisper this to myself over and over as I sleepwalk to Dr Okeke's office, black coffee sloshing around in my empty stomach. The incense smell of the corridor hits the back of my throat, and suddenly I'm back in the tank. Trapped. I suppress a gag.

I'm looking forward to seeing him. I like his smile, his pressure-free manner. Maybe I'll tell him how I'm feeling. I trust him not to use it against me somehow. It feels like he's on my side. But when I knock on the door to his office, it's not his friendly 'Enter!' that greets me.

'Come in,' says an unfamiliar voice.

I push the door open. Someone else sits in Dr Okeke's chair, hands folded over his crisp white shirt, grey suit jacket open. 'Dr Stokes,' I say, my heart sinking.

He half stands and indicates the sofa opposite. 'Call me Niall, please.'

'Where's Dr Okeke?' I ask, sitting down.

'Dr Okeke kindly stepped aside today to let me speak with you. There are a few things we need to go over.'

I frown. 'I thought Dr Okeke was my therapist for the duration of my time here?'

He nods, rubbing a hand over his designer stubble. The scratching sound jars my brain. My sleepless night has made me sensitive to everything. Sounds, lights, smells. The smallest thing could make me vomit, or cry, or curl up into a ball and die.

'It's unusual that we change your routine, certainly. But a few things came up, so I asked to see you today.' He opens the folder in his hand, with my name on the front, and clears his throat. 'Sonya tells me you had a tough visit yesterday.'

I nod. I'm not ready to talk about that. Not with him, anyway.

'And your daughter is expressing an aversion to you at the moment.'

I close my eyes and dig my fingernails into the leather of the sofa under my thighs. 'It's perhaps just a phase.' My voice cracks. I cough.

He shakes his head and looks down at my file. 'Sonya said it seems more than that.' He lets a silence hang in the air.

So do I. I stare at the carpet, which is a lot thinner and more worn than the one they show to visitors. Like the walls, it's the same shade of grey as Dr Stokes's suit. I wonder if he does that on purpose.

'Miriam?'

'Mm?' I refocus and look up at him. He's staring at me expectantly. 'Sorry, say that again?'

'We've received a phone call from someone who knows you. In the outside world, so to speak.' He twirls his pen in a slow circle.

I frown. Who would call the Hermitage? Only a handful of people know I am here. But who knows what's been going on outside of these walls? Something has happened that means I'm receiving death threats. And someone resigned from my job on my behalf. I have no control over anything. A thin film of sweat breaks out across my forehead and upper lip as I realise I have no idea what he's going to say next. I stare at him and hold his gaze. He has very pale blue eyes, I notice. Almost grey. Almost translucent.

'Is there any reason why someone would suggest that you use physical punishment to discipline your daughter?'

I inhale so sharply I choke on some saliva. I start to cough.

Dr Stokes slides a glass of water across the coffee table. I sip it. My heartbeat doesn't slow even when the coughing stops.

'What?' I croak when I can finally breathe. I want to get up and grab him by his stupid expensive grey suit and shake him until he tells me everything. But sadly, physical violence might not look too good in the face of what he's just asked me. 'No. I have never disciplined Liv like that. I wouldn't. It's not right. And it's not effective.'

He pauses for a moment. 'And what methods of discipline do you deem... *effective*?'

I shake my head. 'Why ask me this? What was this phone call?'

He looks down at my notes, his expression neutral. 'Tamara received a call yesterday afternoon—'

'Tamara?'

'Our receptionist and administrative assistant.'

I nod and gesture for him to continue.

'From someone who didn't leave a name. They wanted to report that you physically abuse your daughter... Liv, is it?'

'Liv. Yes,' I whisper, feeling again like a spectator in my life and not a direct participant.

'Now, we don't normally receive calls like this. We're not a mandated reporter, nor do we have connections with the police. So I'm not sure why this individual felt it necessary to make such an allegation to the Hermitage. Ordinarily we would disregard this kind of thing, as our priority is our clients and their wellbeing. But after speaking with Sonya about your family visit yesterday, I felt it was important to check in with you about the situation at home and how it might be impacting your recovery.'

'I don't hit my child. Oh my God. I have never...' I gasp for breath. I can't get enough air into my lungs. 'I would never. Never never never.'

He leans forward, puts a hand on the coffee table. I have a

feeling that if the table wasn't there he'd be trying to put a hand on my shoulder or knee. I'm grateful for the barrier. If someone touched me right now, I'd shatter into a thousand pieces. 'It sounds like you're having some connection issues with your daughter at the moment. Am I right?'

'She hates me,' I mumble. 'Since the baby was born. I don't know why. She says she wants a new mummy. That I don't love her.'

'What would make her believe this?'

I shrug. 'I don't know.' But I do know. I do. It's the voice on the baby monitor, pouring poison into her ears. Telling her stories about replacing her, giving her away, not loving her, about new and better mummies than me.

'This must be hard for you.'

I scoff. An understatement. 'I love her so much.' A tear creeps from the corner of my eye. 'I don't think I've done anything to trigger this. And the phone call...' I shake my head and drop it down between my shoulders. 'I have no idea.'

He gazes at me, unmoving. I miss Dr Okeke, who wouldn't leave an ominous silence hanging like this. Who would help. Who would care.

'I think someone is trying to sabotage my life.'

22

The hum of washing machines is comforting somehow, like white noise for a baby. It's also – crucially – an excellent background noise to mask our conversation if the Hermitage's CCTV cameras can record sound. Everything here is so high-end, I suspect they can.

'Why do we have to do our own laundry?' Midway through stuffing my coloured clothes into a washing machine, I pause and sit back on my heels. 'You'd think, somewhere this posh, they'd have a service to do it for you.'

Katy laughs as she folds her clothes into neat piles at the workbench in the middle of the room. Behind her, banks of tumble dryers shiver. 'It's rehabilitation, isn't it?'

I give her a quizzical look as I stand up and twirl the dial on my machine. I love the smell in the air: cotton and detergent. It's comforting.

'Gets you used to the real world. If everything was done for us, we'd find it hard to go back. Some places even have kitchens, and you do your own cooking.'

'I forgot you're an institution veteran.'

'I prefer to think of myself as a connoisseur.' She throws a sock at me.

I duck and it hits the wall and falls to the floor. The room is humid. I look around, hoping there might be a stack of blankets still warm from the dryer. I'd curl up in it and make a nest. Safe.

Katy notices me zoning out. 'What's going on with you? You look exhausted.'

I pretend not to know what she means and give a shrug.

'You seemed to be doing great. I thought you were a hundred per cent on your way out within two weeks. And then something changed...'

I turn away, pretend to be looking for something in my bag of whites that's just come out of the washer. 'What, you think I won't be going home at the end of the two weeks now?' I try to sound nonchalant, but I can't keep the tremor from my voice.

I turn my head so I can see her from the corner of my eye. She's a blurred figure but I can tell she's stopped folding. She's leaning over the workbench, her head propped on one hand, thinking. 'I don't know. I've seen a lot of people go through these places and I could have sworn you were one of the easy fixes. In, out, and I'd never see you again. Whereas some people return again and again like it's their holiday home.'

'And now?'

'Something more complicated is going on, isn't it? I can't work you out.' She's frowning. 'It's like your madness isn't coming from in your head.' She taps her temple. 'The phone call isn't coming from inside the house.'

I stop pretending to look through my laundry bag.

'You OK?'

I turn around and sit on the tiled floor, leaning against one of the washing machines. It's cold against my back. 'You really get it, don't you?'

'I mean, you don't fit the mould of the normal crazies.'

I glance at the door. It's closed, its little reinforced window showing an empty corridor on the other side. We're alone. In the corner, the camera blinks. I stand up and grab the bag of whites, dumping them out on the table between me and Katy. 'Keep folding,' I say, grabbing two socks and pairing them up.

Katy picks up one of her own T-shirts and gives me a funny look. 'Why are you folding those? They're still wet.'

'Just look busy.' I push her laundry basket towards her. 'I don't want them to think we're talking about anything interesting. Look at your washing, not at me.'

She laughs, bending over with the force of her amusement. 'God, Miriam. I wish you'd been locked up with me here earlier. You're hilarious.'

I don't join in with her laughter. 'I'm serious. We're being watched all the time and I don't want anyone else to hear what I'm about to tell you.'

Her smile disappears, replaced with a serious expression. She nods.

As I fold my wet clothes, I tell her about the baby monitor, how it taught Liv to hate me, that no one believed me. And then I talk about the job resignation and the abusive disappearing messages on all my accounts.

By the end, we've both folded and refolded our clothes at least three times, and Katy's face is pale. 'This is insane,' she mumbles, and then catches herself. 'Sorry. You know what I mean. I don't think *you're* insane.' She pauses for a second, flapping out a shirt and then doubling it over. 'I mean, I did when you first started telling me about it. It sounded like classic psychosis. But then there are things you can't possibly invent in your head. The messages, for one thing. You're not doing that to yourself. You didn't even have your phone for a week.'

Every muscle in my body relaxes. Someone believes me.

'Someone's really trying to mess with your life.'

I nod. The relief is immense.

'But why? What do they want?'

I stop folding. 'I can't work it out. I've gone over this again and again since the start, when it was just the monitor. What's in it for them?'

'Wait, so you think the person who was watching you through the monitor is the same person who resigned from your job and they're also sending the messages?'

I pause. It's all been happening simultaneously, so I assumed they were connected. Is it possible they're separate, that the monitor hacker has nothing to do with my fake resignation and the abusive messages? I rake through the pile of white laundry, barely seeing it as I fold and refold, flap and straighten. Then, bizarrely, I come across a little white o–3-month baby vest, stuck inside the arm of one of my shirts. I've no idea how it got into my case and came all the way here with me to the Hermitage. It's a sign. I hold it to my chest, wishing my baby was here. Wishing both my babies were here. 'Yes,' I say, decisive. 'It's the same person. Someone's trying to ruin my life. And I can't let them.'

Katy slaps a hand on the pile of clothes in front of her. 'So what are you going to do?'

I shake my head, defeated. 'I need to get out of this place. I need to go home. All I want is to fix things with Liv. To get my babies back.'

She nods. 'Right then. And your final psych assessment is tomorrow?'

'Yep. With Dr Okeke, I hope.'

'OK, Miriam. It's time to perform the role of your life, and you've got the best coach for the job. I know these places inside out. Do everything I tell you, and you'll be the sanest, most reasonable patient they've ever seen at the Hermitage Wellbeing Centre. We'll get you home to your babies.'

23

I walk to Dr Okeke's office the next day with a stone of dread in my stomach. For him, this is just another day at work. For me, he holds my future, and the future of my relationship with my children, in his hands. I need to get home; I need to rebuild my relationship with Liv. I need to remind Samuel he has a mother. And if I have to sit on my single bed and hook myself up to that huge milking machine for another day, I'll scream and scream and never stop. I need to get out of this place.

I need to not be watched on cameras every moment of the day.

I knock on his door, swallowing hard at the odour of essential oils and incense hovering in the halfway. It's pungent today, as if they've been pumping it even more than usual to really mess with my tenuous grip on my last meal.

'Enter!'

My heart lifts at the familiar tone and I shove the door open. 'I'm so glad it's you...' I stop.

Yes, Dr Okeke is there, his smile broad and his white beard glorious. But so is Dr Stokes, a thin smile on his lips and a coffee in his hand. The two men both sit behind the desk, a few feet apart, Dr Okeke in his normal place and Dr Stokes perched awkwardly at the corner. In any other circumstances it would be quite funny: Dr Stokes has brought a desk chair from another office and placed it next to Dr Okeke's, as if he couldn't bear to sit in the patients' spot, nor concede authority to the other man.

'Good morning,' I say, sitting on my usual sofa but pushing myself as far to the side as possible. As small as possible. As far away from Stokes as possible.

In my mind, I've created a strange narrative, I know it. Dr Okeke is on my side. He believes me, wants to help me get better and get home. Dr Stokes, on the other hand, spoke to my husband right at the start. He imprisoned me here in the first place, separating me from my babies. And presumably persuaded Jeremy that an inpatient stay was the best thing for his mad wife. As director of the centre, his profits increase if I have to stay longer.

I understand that in normal circumstances this kind of twisted thinking would be something to talk to my psychiatrist about so they could unpick all the knots in my tangled mind. *Ha.* This isn't normal circumstances. This is a fight to get home, no matter what the cost to my sanity in the long run.

Following Katy's instructions, I plaster a smile on my face and try to give off sane vibes. The two psychiatrists glance at each other. Dr Okeke nods at Dr Stokes, and the younger man clears his throat.

I decide to get ahead of him. 'How can I help, Dr Stokes?'

'Miriam. As you know, your original period of inpatient care officially comes to an end tomorrow, and this is your final appointment with our psychiatric team. When both myself and Dr Okeke have spoken to a client in a therapeutic capacity during their stay, we share the final discharge appointment to ensure we cover all bases, so to speak.' He shifts in his chair and takes a sip of coffee.

His last, unspoken line hangs in the air: *But the final deci-sion belongs to me.*

I glance over his shoulder at the wall of books behind the two men. All giant volumes, some leather-bound and some looking like university textbooks. *Diagnostic and Statistical Manual of Mental Disorders, Maudsley Prescribing Guidelines, Fish's Clinical Psychopathology.* I wonder if they've found a diagnosis for me in one of them.

'First, I want to thank you for your time here and your coop-eration during your stay. We've seen a distinct improvement in your symptoms since your arrival—'

'Which symptoms are you referring to, Doctor?' I can't help but interrupt, and quickly paste on a warm smile again. *Be polite*, says Katy in my head. The sheaf of papers in his hands is about me and the inner workings of my mind, and no one has talked to me about symptoms of any kind. Before this, everyone has pretended that my stay at the Hermitage was nothing more than a nice little holiday away from my family. Even the refusal to call us patients smacks of denial. And every time I have talked about my fears of being sectioned or kept here indefi-nitely, the staff members have looked at me like I'm making stuff up. I pick at his words like a scab. 'So this *is* a hospital. And I *am* a patient?'

Stokes frowns. 'This is a wellbeing centre. And you are a guest.'

'A guest with "symptoms".' I make air quotes.

He rustles his papers, his expression icy, then reaches to the fountain pen in the breast pocket of his suit jacket hanging on the back of his chair.

Dr Okeke catches my eye and gives a tiny shake of the head. I think back to our very first meeting. I am a model patient. That's how I get home.

I reach forward and pluck a tissue from the box on the table. 'Sorry. I'm just confused by the terminology. I'm not used to it.'

Stokes nods and his expression clears. He puts the pen back in his jacket. I must have used the right combination of words to reset whatever I'd done. 'Your sleep patterns seem healthy.'

I open my mouth to speak. No one has asked me about sleep at any point. So they've been watching me on the camera in my room. So much for what Dr Okeke said in our first meeting. They aren't just recording in case there's an incident. They're watching. I knew it.

Dr Okeke catches my eye again. I close my mouth.

'We haven't seen any continuation of the delusions you exhibited at your admission, and your mood has seemed steady, with consistent participation in appointments, therapies and activities across the two weeks of your stay.'

Dr Okeke smiles at me, but it doesn't reach his eyes.

'However...'

My stomach twists.

Stokes clears his throat and flips to another part of the paperwork. 'We've seen some evidence that your home situation is not entirely stable, with your daughter... Liv, is it?'

Why can't he remember her name? I nod, unable to speak.

'With your relationship with Liv being strained and at times fractured. She refuses to attend your daily family calls and showed a physical aversion to you when she visited. This – compounded with the anonymous call we received – does give me pause in your discharge process.'

I stand up from the sofa, but catch myself and sit back down. 'I don't hit my daughter.' I manage to keep my tone steady. 'I love her.'

He nods. 'Dr Okeke and I have spoken about this at length. I recommend you extend your stay here and we run a series of family counselling sessions. Sonya is a trained family counsellor and would sit with you and Liv while you work through your issues.'

I can't move. I stare at the camera in the corner of the room, its red light blinking as the lens watches me, the black shiny crow eye. A sweat breaks out across my body, slick and sticky. They can't make me stay. They can't make Liv come here too. I want to go home. I need to get home to my babies.

'I do believe you would benefit from some additional treatment, and I have recommended a further week's stay here at the centre.'

Another week.

I want to vomit, or faint, or cry, or scream. I want to stand up and pull the bookshelf from the wall, those textbooks raining down on the heads of these two doctors who hold my future in their hands with such careless thoughtlessness.

I feel like I will die here.

24

I walk into the living room on shaky legs, like I've run a marathon. I'm exhausted.

Katy sits on one of the sofas, her hands clasped together. When she sees me enter, she sits up, her whole body on alert. 'Well?' she calls across the room.

Another patient looks up from their game of solitaire, and then quickly back down at their cards. I haven't managed to make any friends except Katy. But that's OK. She's enough.

I nod and plop on the sofa next to her, expelling a huge lungful of air, and then in a rush I tell her about the last few moments of my conversation in the psychiatrist's office; about how Dr Okeke sat forward and interrupted Dr Stokes, his arms resting on his desk.

'Miriam, Dr Stokes and I don't agree on this. But because I am your treating psychiatrist, I am the one who makes the official recommendation. I think your wellbeing and your relationship with your daughter will improve if you return home to your family. I have recommended that you're discharged tomorrow.' And the immediate feeling of relief. I could breathe again.

Katy claps her hands and bounces on the sofa cushion, jostling me where I slump. 'You're going home tomorrow!'

I should feel elated, but I'm numb.

'Here,' she whispers, sliding a box of Thorntons Continentals over to me with a furtive look around. 'We're not allowed booze in here, so this is the next best thing I could find. To celebrate.' She removes the lid and we both select a chocolate: me a Viennese truffle, her an Alpini praline. We touch them together and say 'cheers' like they're glasses of wine, and as the sugar hits my system, I start to feel better. Optimistic, even.

A nurse walks past and we turn our faces away to hide our chewing, stifling giggles like kids who've stolen from the tuck shop. I don't even think chocolates are banned, but rebellion feels important.

The multimedia room door bangs open as another patient leaves. 'Katy, you're up,' she says as she walks past.

Katy nods her thanks. 'I forgot I've got a session booked. Want to come in with me?'

'Am I allowed?'

She shrugs. 'What will they do, expel you?' She grabs the box of chocolates and walks backwards towards the multimedia room door, waving them at me like she's trying to lure an animal. I laugh and stand up from the sofa to follow.

She shows me a selfie of her boyfriend, who lives in Seattle and who she has never met in real life. He's cute in a geeky way, the kind of guy I could have dated in my early twenties, before my tastes shifted as I realised I needed to settle down soon if I wanted enough time to have fun together before kids.

She tells me a little about him: he's called Tom, and they met on a support forum for agoraphobics. They've been talking for years, and after some vigorous inpatient programmes, Tom now has a job in an office and has taken his first flight across the US. He's ready to meet, but Katy's not there yet. 'It's why I keep checking myself into places like this. Otherwise, I'd be happily at home in my little bubble, only seeing the Tesco delivery guy and the postie.'

He's not online, so she closes the chat app. 'He's seven hours behind, so he's about to go to work, I think.' A look of sadness passes across her face before she catches it and forces a smile.

I wish I could help. This last two weeks away from my kids has been torture. I can't imagine being halfway across the world from someone you love and not able to travel to see them. 'Do you know what caused your agoraphobia, Katy? Was there a trigger, or did it happen gradually?'

She closes her eyes. 'Both, actually.' She opens them again and looks at me. 'It did creep up on me gradually. But there was a trigger too.'

'What was it?' I pause. 'If you don't mind me asking. You don't have to tell me. I know it must be—'

She holds out a hand to cut me off. 'Him. The trigger wasn't an "it". It was a "him".' Her eyes are wide in the darkness of the multimedia room, her eyes reflecting the computer screen in two perfect blue squares.

'It was a bad relationship. A bad man. He made me fear the outside, and by the time I realised that the scary thing was already *inside* my house – I had invited him in – it was too late. My mind was damaged. He broke me.'

I shake my head. 'I'm so sorry.'

She grabs the box from my lap and shoves a chocolate in her mouth whole. She doesn't even look to see what kind it is. She speaks with her mouth full, trying to sound cheerful. 'It's fine. It happens. And we don't know – maybe I would have ended up like this anyway. Even if I'd found a guy who was all flowers and surprise dates rather than threats and outbursts.' She swivels the desk chair to face me and swallows the chocolate. 'So tell me about these messages you've been getting. Can I see some of them? While we're here.'

I glance up at the camera in the corner and fold my arms.

'What's the point? I don't want to give it too much attention. It's already infiltrated my brain enough.'

Her face is lit white-blue by the screen. The room behind her is in darkness except for the little red LED blinking in the corner. 'I spend a lot of time on computers, Mim. I'll take a look and see if I can work out what's going on.'

I wheel my chair across to the PC and log into my email. Even though the most horrific threats have come through on the apps, where they can disappear, over the last few days some have made it into my email inbox. Attacks from all sides. There they are: line after line of abusive emails. The subject lines are awful:

Crawl back into the hole you came from
Whore
Die, bitch!
Screwwwwww youuuuuuuuuuu

She blinks a couple of times and then lets out a low chuckle. 'Wow.'

'Yeah.'

She goes to click on one, but I reach a hand out to stop her. 'What if it's got a virus in it or something?'

She shrugs. 'It's not my computer. Plus, I'm not going to click any links or attachments or anything. I'm not a noob.'

I laugh at the geekspeak and let go of her arm.

She twirls her fingers like she's perusing a tasting menu, and then clicks on *Crawl back into the hole you came from*. 'Looks like the most eloquent, to be honest.'

I glance away. I don't want to read it.

She's quiet for a moment, her eyes scanning the text. I watch her face, trying to work out what she's thinking. Her eyebrows rise high on her forehead as she reads.

'What?' I can't wait any more.

She frowns, then minimises the browser and turns to me. 'This isn't a normal viral hate campaign.'

My stomach twists. 'What do you mean?'

She puts a hand on my arm. 'They know stuff about you and your life. Stuff they shouldn't know.'

My skin prickles with goosebumps. I move my arm away from her hand. 'What sort of stuff?'

'Give me a second.' She turns back to the computer and clicks around, typing things into a search engine over and over. 'I'm seeing if I can find the origins of this. You know, like where your details were posted that triggered the onslaught. With as many emails and messages as you've got, it must be quite a popular site, and someone must have posted your contact info somewhere.'

'Can we do anything if we find it? Like try to get it taken down or something.'

Katy keeps her eyes on the screen, her face a mask of concentration. 'Let's see what I can find first.'

I sit back, but I can't relax. This isn't in my head and now it's a real threat. This means danger. *What do they know?* Do they know where I live? My children's names? Do we need to call the police? Suddenly the internet feels like the Wild West: an unregulated landscape where anyone can ruin anyone else's life on a whim. Of course, the dark web is even worse, from what I found when I researched baby monitor hackers. That feels like a lifetime ago now.

She sucks air through her teeth in a hiss. She's found something.

I sit forward, trying to see the screen.

She shifts and shields it with her shoulder. 'OK, so first. Many of these messages are sent from burner accounts and bots. They're created by a computer and they send a pre-prepared message and then self-destruct. So you can't trace them.'

'Not all of them, though?'

'So some of them are real people. Which tells me this is a campaign orchestrated by someone who's really trying to ruin you. They're the one making the bots. But in doing so, they have inadvertently recruited other people – stupid people – to the cause.'

'I don't understand.'

'It means that somewhere on the internet there's some information about you that's public. And it shouldn't be.' She turns back to the screen. 'Give me another few minutes.'

I sit as still as I can, waiting. I watch the LED blinking on the camera. It flashes every four seconds. I watch it like I watch the light in my room in the middle of the night when I can't sleep. Sometimes the pattern alters and the light stays solid for ten seconds. That must be when the feed broadcasts live to Security. When that happens, I look away from the camera, watch what Katy is doing over her shoulder.

She's using a search engine, but it's not Google. It's not one I've seen before. It looks like something that belongs to an earlier version of the internet. It's blocky and dark and pixelated.

I realise she hasn't moved for a minute or two. She's staring at the screen, reading something. 'What have you found?'

She places a hand on the side of the monitor and swivels the display so I can't see it. 'I don't know.'

I tilt forward, trying to look. She puts a hand out to stop me. 'Seriously, Miriam. I don't know what this is. Give me a minute.'

She clicks around, her eyes scanning the screen. After what feels like hours, she stops reading and looks at me.

'It's a Reddit post.' Her face quivers. I can't tell if it's the reflection of the screen, but it looks like she's trying to hold back a lot of emotion. 'It somehow went viral and made it to the front page, where the most upvoted posts appear to everyone who opens the site.'

'Whoa.' My stomach twists. I've stumbled into Reddit a couple of times, witnessed the toxic groupthink, unfounded anger and cruel bullying that comes with anonymity and lack of fact-checking. 'Why did it go viral?'

'Well, the writer claims she's having an affair with a married man.'

I inhale. 'And the married man is... Jeremy?'

'She doesn't give a name. But she mentions kids. A little girl and then, recently, a baby boy.'

I gag. 'What about them?' I croak.

Katy flinches. 'Listen, Reddit loves a pile-on; the chance to tell people they're right and everyone else is wrong. And the reason why you've been getting these threats and messages... in the comments below the post, someone has claimed to know you. They posted your name and address. The mods got there and removed it, but, like anything on the internet, it's not *gone* gone: some websites archive deleted comments.'

I shake my head. 'Please, Katy.' I can barely breathe. 'Tell me what it says.'

She bites her lip, her eyes scanning the text. 'There's a lot of justifying her actions: they're soulmates kept apart by circumstance, he's unhappy in his marriage, his wife doesn't give him what he needs, he travels a lot for work so the mistress joins him on his work trips...' She rolls her eyes.

'What about my children?'

She can't meet my eyes. 'I'll read you the worst bit.' She clears her throat and whispers: '"I've been waiting so long to get them away from their abusive mum, and it feels like we're finally getting there. All he needs is proof that she hurts them. Enough to block any custody bid she makes. And then this amazing man and his brilliant kids will be all mine. He's finally going to leave her."'

25

The next day, I travel home by taxi, alone. I'm not even sure whose idea it was, but when I called Jeremy to talk about my discharge plans, we both agreed a taxi would be easiest. That way he wouldn't have to wrangle two kids on the journey both ways, and they'd be rested when I got home, ready to spend time with me. Or so I hope.

Jeremy sounded normal. He said he was looking forward to having me home. Back to our usual routine. He didn't sound like a man planning to leave me and take the kids. A man having an affair.

Katy waves at me from the window as we pull away. Sonya and Dr Okeke stand on the step outside the main entrance. Dr Stokes doesn't appear.

The taxi driver tries to chat with me, to ask about the Hermitage and why I was there. His questions probe me like needles. 'I had an aunt go there once. Back in the nineties. Pulled her hair out in handfuls. Nervous exhaustion, they said. Six kids'll do that to you.'

I stare out of the window, watching the raindrops wind their way across the glass as we charge past the Pentland Hills back into the city. I ignore his questions. I don't care if he thinks I'm rude.

After a few minutes, he realises I'm not going to talk, and we lapse into welcome silence. I glance around, looking for cameras out of habit. Nothing. No one can see me except the driver in his rear-view mirror. I sink down in my seat and heave a sigh of relief. For the first time in months, no one is watching me.

When the taxi pulls up on our street, engine idling, I don't want to get out of the car.

I heave myself out of the seat with difficulty and tap my debit card on his machine. *Beep.* I feel a distant hum of surprise that the card still works, as if Jeremy might have frozen my accounts or something. Who knows? I don't know him any more.

My key still works, sliding into the lock and turning smoothly to open the front door. The house smells so familiar that I almost burst out crying as soon as I step inside. A mixture of our laundry detergent, my favourite Penhaligon's candle, and a woody undertone from the parquet floor.

I stand still and listen. I can hear the TV chattering from the living room, and the occasional burble of Liv's voice, matched moments later by the deep rumble of Jeremy's in reply.

For a moment, I consider turning around, straight out of the door and away. Jeremy would be fine. They all would be. My hand rests on the door, holding it open. I have only taken two steps into the house.

I could go to Mum's, stay there until I worked out what to do next. She'd baulk at first – anyone would, at a mother leaving her children behind. But she'd understand eventually. She's never been the most maternal type. And then Jeremy would be free to continue his relationship with this Reddit woman.

This Reddit woman who told the internet I abuse my children. My hand tightens into a fist. I can't let anyone believe that of me.

Just then, a series of shrill beeps emanates from the kitchen. I flinch, consider backing out and closing the front door, but I'm too late.

'That's the oven timer,' I hear Jeremy say to Liv.

There's the sound of movement as she runs to the living room door. 'Ooh, cake, cake, cake!' she shrieks.

And then Jeremy steps out into the hallway, Liv skipping at his heels in excitement. He stops as soon as he sees me, a grin transforming his face. 'Mim! I didn't hear you come in. Mummy's home, Liv!' he calls, and strides towards me, arms outstretched for a hug.

'But the oven timer...' I stumble.

He shakes his head and pulls me into his embrace, enveloping me. 'I'm so glad you're home. We missed you.'

Over his shoulder, I frown in confusion. He's so convincing. If Katy hadn't found that Reddit post, I would have had no idea he is cheating on me. That he is planning to leave. He seems every inch the faithful, kind husband.

He pulls away, still smiling. 'I do have to go and rescue that cake.' He turns to Liv, who dances from foot to foot in excitement behind him. 'Say hi to Mummy while I go and get the cake.'

She stops hopping around and I crouch to her level, my knees on the hard wooden floor. For a moment I think she'll reject me again, but to my absolute joy, she steps into my arms and I feel her spindly arms wrap around my waist. She rests her head on my shoulder and I could weep with happiness.

I bury my nose in her hair. 'I love you so much, my baby,' I whisper. 'I missed you every minute.'

Her hair smells of oranges. It's a new smell, unfamiliar and tart.

She pulls back. 'We're making lemon drizzle cake.

Mummy's favourite.' She flashes me a smile and skips towards the kitchen.

I follow slowly, my brain chewing over what she just said.

Lemon drizzle is not my favourite. I'm not the mummy she's talking about.

The kitchen is warm and smells heavenly from the cake. Jeremy admires it as it cools on the rack. 'I baked it from a pre-made kit thing, but I thought it would be nice to have a little welcome-home cake for you.'

Liv skips around, frustrated by the patience needed before it can be iced and eaten.

There are flowers in a vase on the worktop, too. A huge bunch of lilies, already dropping their orange pollen. Jeremy sees me looking. 'From Jac, for you.'

I smile. 'She's very thoughtful.'

'I think she missed you.'

I'm glad someone did. I don't say it out loud, but I want to.

I nurse Samuel and watch as Jeremy helps Liv make the icing, ready to apply when the cake has cooled. He's good with her, patient and permissive as she smears icing up her arms and across the worktops, a happy smile on her face.

'Seems like this couple of weeks together has done you guys a lot of good,' I say, smiling.

He glances up at me, catches my eye and then looks away, back to watching Liv. Before this, his temper was short, his tolerance for chaos low. He'd come home from work to find toys strewn across the living room and didn't understand why I wouldn't force Liv to tidy up after herself fifteen times a day.

'It's been nice, in a way. Looking after them by myself. I feel more of a dad than before, if you see what I mean. Like I could do it on my own if I had to.'

But you won't have to, will you? I think. Even if I wasn't

here. There's someone waiting in the wings. Waiting for me to go.

I look down at Samuel, his face pressed into my breast. He feels bigger in my arms, more solid, even though it's only been a few days since I last held him. Like Liv, he smells different. 'Did you change their shampoo?'

Jeremy nods. 'We ran out. I couldn't remember what brand you used, so I picked whatever was cheapest.'

I swallow.

'What's up?'

I shake my head. 'Nothing.' I can't even begin to explain. 'Thanks for handling everything while I was gone.'

'Daddy looked after us,' Liv says, licking her sticky fingers one by one. 'He let me sleep in the big bed.' Her eyes glint with mischief.

Jeremy nudges her. 'Hey, you! Giving away my secrets.' He chuckles. 'She had nightmares a couple of times, so I let her sleep in with me and Samuel. For a treat.'

'Wow. Liv, what a grown-up girl, sleeping in the big bed. Was it comfy?'

She grins and nods enthusiastically.

'You've started something there, Jem,' I joke. Samuel finishes feeding and I button up my shirt. 'I'll take him up and check his nappy.'

Jeremy and Liv aren't listening, debating whether the cake is cool enough to add the icing or whether they need to wait longer.

I climb the stairs, glancing around for evidence that someone else has been here while I was gone. But there's nothing; everything looks the same as it did before. And if he let Liv sleep in our bed, it's unlikely he invited his girlfriend in there with him.

In Liv's room, I step over dolls, discarded clothes and a tea set to place Samuel on the changing table. He coos and smiles up at me, and I lean down to blow a raspberry on his little tummy, the umbilical cord healed now. A perfect little button.

He squirms at the tickles, but he doesn't smile for me.

I change his nappy and fasten him into his onesie. Just as I snap together the final popper, the hair on the back of my neck stands on end. My whole body prickles. I'm being watched.

I straighten up and turn, Samuel cradled against my chest, my hand on his head.

The doorway is empty; I have a clear view into the corridor. I can still hear the murmur of Jeremy and Liv chatting below.

I glance around the room. The baby monitor is gone. In its place is a teddy bear, its shiny black eyes twinkling in the fairy lights.

I sigh in relief. It was my imagination.

I head to the door and flick the light switch, plunging the room into darkness. Jeremy hasn't opened the curtains yet today. I cross the room, narrowly missing the obstacles in my way. As I reach up with one hand to open the curtains, I see something flash from the corner of my eye. A red LED, hidden in the fur of the teddy bear's face.

I turn, almost tripping on an Elsa wig tangled around my foot.

I want to grab the bear, peer into its twinkling black eyes. But I can't let them know I know. I can't look straight at it. I can't pick it up or move it. He'll see. He'll know.

It's another camera. And this time, I won't be able to turn it off.

I jiggle Samuel, singing softly. *You are my sunshine, my only sunshine...* I'm not concentrating, my eyes darting everywhere. Looking. My words blur together until I'm humming.

I prop him up on my shoulder, pat him on the back as if I'm burping him. I stroll around the room, scanning every wall, every corner. Nothing else in here that I can see.

Still singing, I step out into the hallway, every movement casual and studied. I'm a normal mum, singing to my baby.

There. In the bookshelf on the landing, half hidden between *A Room with a View* and *Howard's End*. A tiny lens, aimed towards the top of the stairs.

I glance at it out of the corner of my eye, not moving my head towards it directly. I won't show them I know.

I want to scream and run from the house. But I keep singing and humming, a half-smile plastered on my face. *You make me happy, hm hm hm hm.* I open our bedroom door, glance around the room. The quilt is thrown back where Jeremy got out of bed this morning. The curtains are half open, a shaft of sunlight slicing in.

I perch on the bed, bouncing slightly for Samuel, who's resting his head on my shoulder, his eyelids floating. My head faces the door, but my eyes scan the room, looking for lenses and blinking LEDs. I know I'm being watched; I just need to work out where from. It's like being back at the Hermitage.

'Miriam?' Jeremy calls from downstairs.

I stand up and walk to the door. 'Just coming,' I call back. I turn and face the room, and there it is: on top of Jeremy's wardrobe, pointing down at our bed. It must be able to view the whole room from there.

I feel sick.

On my shoulder, Samuel grumbles. He's getting bored. I sing and bounce a little more, but he's too grizzly. We need a change of scene.

'Miriam, can you come down here, please?'

I take a deep breath. *Think, Miriam.* I press my cheek against Samuel's. *Think.*

I review what I know: Jeremy is cheating on me. He's been having a relationship with someone else, and that woman wants my kids. He sent me away to a private mental hospital, and when I came back, the Wi-Fi baby monitor was gone. He wants me to think it's over, that he's not watching any more. Yet even without looking further, I know the whole house is riddled with hidden cameras. The kitchen, living room and his office will be the same: a blinking red light in every room.

It's all clear now. They're trying to gather evidence that will give them full custody of Liv and Samuel. Any misstep, any transgression on my part and it'll be used against me.

Despite everything, all I want in the whole world is my kids with me, every day. I can't lose them. I won't. I thought the performing was over, the watching. It's not. But I've learned a lot in the last couple of weeks. I'm stronger now.

A new plan starts to form, curling around my consciousness like smoke from an extinguished candle. I descend the stairs, gathering my courage to re-enter the kitchen and face my husband with a smile.

I can't let him win. I will love my husband. I will be the perfect mum to my kids.

I was a model patient. I can be the perfect wife and mother.

26

At the sound of the front door, I leap to my feet, ready to present Jeremy with a glass of wine and his favourite home-cooked meal: lasagne. The golden surface bubbles in the light of the oven, a baton of garlic bread nestled on the rack next to it. On the stove top, plumes of steam escape from the hole in the pan lid where broccoli boils. I've decanted the Argentinian Malbec, lit candles at the table.

I'm the perfect wife. The best mother. And it's all on show for the cameras, every single day. The children are in bed, with a new monitor set up to alert me if they cry out. This one is a non-Wi-Fi-enabled video monitor that no one outside our home can access. Jeremy bought it while I was away, and the old one disappeared. A strange acknowledgement that what I was saying was true: that someone had hacked it. But then he rigged the whole house up with cameras instead. He doesn't need to watch the baby any more. He needs to watch me.

Even the teddy cam watches beadily from next to the microwave. Jeremy must have moved it downstairs to have extra eyes on me.

But I'm used to surveillance; two weeks in the Hermitage got me accustomed to being monitored twenty-four hours a day, and now these cameras are my friends: I'll use them to my advantage. Look at me cooking dinner for my husband, watch me playing tag with Liv along the upstairs corridor.

'Helloooooooooo?' The voice in the hallway is not Jeremy.

Jac blusters into the kitchen in a whirl of shopping bags, wild hair and the smell of winter on her coat. 'Smells amazing in here! Sorry for dropping in unannounced.' She takes in the two glasses of wine, the candles, the lasagne cooling on the side. 'Did I interrupt something?'

I slide a glass of red towards her with a shake of my head. 'It was supposed to be a special meal for Jeremy, but he's had to work late.'

Tomorrow is Jeremy's first work trip since I returned from the Hermitage. It's been an unspoken condition, hovering in the air: *I will only go if you prove you can look after the kids.* And I have proved myself over and over again. He didn't need to cancel his trip, or even threaten to invite my mother to stay. He's been watching me every day as I perform for the cameras, and I have played my role to perfection.

So his bag is packed for tomorrow's flight to Lyon. He's really going to go. I wonder if *she* is going with him.

A look I can't interpret crosses Jac's face. 'Working late again?'

I suppress a grimace, my face pointed away from the camera hidden in the recipe books. Tabitha likes to call impromptu meetings that run for hours. Perhaps she's doing it on purpose. She knows it's his last night at home before a week-long trip; perhaps she knows I'm sitting alone at the table, wondering if she is the one watching through the cameras, planning to wreck this family, take my kids away.

I shrug. 'It's the trade-off, isn't it? More money and security, less time at home.' I can't tell her any of it. The abusive messages, the Reddit post detailing Jeremy's affair, the cameras, his plan to take the kids... If Jac is ever called upon to make a statement about my sanity or my ability to look after Liv and Samuel, I need her to tell her version of the truth. I need her to think I'm a happy, functioning wife and mother who has no idea she's being watched every moment of the day.

She doesn't look convinced, and slides a finger around the rim of her glass. She won't make eye contact.

'It's fine. It's not his fault.' I feel a sharp stab of pain in my chest. I wish it were true. I pour some peanuts into a little bowl and put them in front of her. Time to change the subject. 'How are you, anyway? This is a rare opportunity to have an uninterrupted conversation, so you'd better give me the headlines.'

We talk about her love life, which elicits a smirk and a few stories of false-start dates. I always try to pay attention and be a good friend, but her trysts meld together into one faceless early-forties divorcee with a fear of commitment. Her hair shines in the light as we chat, her cheeks still flushed from the cold. She's striking, has no problem getting dates, but doesn't seem inter-ested in settling down.

I ask about her new job, which she describes as 'too boring to talk about', but she happily brandishes a business card at me.

'Senior vice president?' I raise my eyebrows. 'Impressive.'

'Incomprehensible.'

'What else is new? Any more gossip?' I need to distract myself or I'll blurt everything out in front of the cameras.

She shrugs, and pulls her arms tighter around herself. It's a small movement that someone else might not notice, but I know her too well. 'Not much to report.'

'Jac.' It's clear there's something on her mind.

Her eyes sparkle in the kitchen spotlights. 'It's...' Her voice croaks with the effort not to cry. 'Today would have been Mum's birthday.'

I want to stand up, to step forward and put my arm around her, but I know that if I do, she'll burst into tears. I wait, quiet.

'I'll be all right. It just takes time. And the bureaucracy doesn't help. Insurance company and probate. So much faff.' She shakes her head. 'I just want closure, you know?'

I nod. I wish we could talk about this more, like we would have before I had kids. I know she's needed to talk for months, since the day she got the call that shattered her world. The same day Jeremy and I had our twenty-week scan and found out we were expecting a boy.

As soon as we walked in the door brandishing the grainy pictures of black-and-white blobs that only parents and ultrasound technicians can parse, I knew something was wrong. Instead of the joy-filled laughter and chaos that we usually find when we return home to Jac's babysitting, the house felt empty.

We found them on the sofa, Liv transfixed by the television, Jac staring blankly at her phone screen, trying to process what she'd just been told. What she'd just lost. She hasn't been the same since, like a part of her hardened that day.

She sits up straighter on her stool and rolls her shoulders, as if shaking off her grief. 'Anyway, change of subject, please.'

I smile. She's still so... Jac. I point to the lasagne. 'Want some?'

She shakes her head. 'I ate in town. Got some amazing cheesy garlic potatoes from the Christmas market.'

'Ooh, the Christmas market. Was it fun?' I feel a rush of envy. It's so festive, with its mulled wine spices filling the air and the twinkle of lights on each little hut.

She smiles. 'Rammed, though.'

'Remember when Mum took us when we were teenagers? Glühwein for her, hot chocolate for us.'

Jac grimaces. 'Nicole always stole your marshmallows. No one can ever have nice things around Nicole. She wants them for herself.'

I shrug and ignore her barb. 'But there's no way I can go now, with a baby and a five-year-old. Too crowded. Too noisy.'

She murmurs her agreement. Her face pulls that weird expression again, the one I can't quite place. Like she's keeping a secret.

'Jac. What's going on?' I turn to look at her, but she won't meet my eye.

She stares down at her hands, gripped together on her lap. She picks at a piece of skin alongside her fingernail, pulling at it until a drop of blood blossoms like a little ruby.

I place a hand on her wrist to stop her. 'Jac.'

She stops moving, releases a slow, quivering breath. She shakes her head, silent.

'You can talk to me about anything, you know. Whatever it is. Whatever you've done. I'll help you bury the body and wipe up the evidence.' I laugh, and she gives me a weak smile in return.

'I know you would. But for once, this isn't about me.' She laugh-sniffs, and wipes her nose on her cuff.

I wait. After everything that's happened over the last few weeks, I can cope with pretty much anything.

She puffs out a big breath of air, steeling herself for whatever she's about to say. 'I just want you to know how important you are. How much your friendship means to me.' She swallows.

I let out a half-laugh through my nose. No wonder she looked strained: Jac's not comfortable with sentimentality. 'Yours too, Jac. I couldn't have got through the last few weeks without you.'

She holds a hand out to stop me. 'You've been through so much. A new baby, Liv's behaviour, and then the retreat...'

Tears prick my eyes. 'It has been...' I trail off, my head spinning. I'm so mixed up. I wish I could tell her about Jeremy's affair, but I can't, not with the cameras listening to our every word. What would happily married Miriam say now? Deflect. Don't confide. Yes. 'Thank you so much for being here for me, Jac. Really.'

My skin itches all over with the sense of being watched. I hate this so much. I want to curl up into a ball, pull my hood over my head and howl. Since I returned from the Hermitage, there's been no space for me to feel sorry for myself. It's been go-go-go: the baby maintenance, repairing things with Liv, smiling for the cameras. But it hasn't worked. It was all a waste.

I want to rip out the cameras from their hiding places and stamp on them. I need to not be seen. I wish I could walk out of the door and get away from this house of horrors. But I can't leave. I need to stay and take care of the kids. Anything I do that's out of the ordinary will be twisted and used against me to show I'm an unfit mother.

I shiver, suddenly chilled.

The new baby monitor lights up, as if reminding me that the whole house is rigged. Samuel's stirring. I peer into the little screen for a few moments, waiting to see if he will go back to sleep. After a few moments, his mewls turn to cries. 'Sorry, Jac. I've got to go and see to him before he wakes Liv.'

She pulls on her coat and gathers her shopping. 'I'll get going.' She puts a hand on my shoulder. 'If you need to get away for a few days, my parents' farm is always free. There's enough space for all of you. And it's safe.'

My heart swells. I know how much that offer means, with everything it represents and how raw things still are.

'You're doing brilliantly,' she says, looking like she's fighting tears.

'I'll be OK. Really,' I say, kissing her cheek. 'I've loved our catch-up.'

I see her to the door, feeling guilty that I don't have the energy to probe her, to find out what's going on. She clearly came over to talk to me about something, but I guess she's not ready yet. I can't make her spill her guts in a heart-to-heart when I know how much I'm keeping from her.

27

Jeremy doesn't return home until after ten. I'm in bed, lights off, my breathing steady and even. He might have seen Jac's visit on the camera feeds, but I don't know if he watches everything. I'm glad I managed to keep quiet about his affair, no matter how much I wanted to confide in her.

He stumbles around the room, getting undressed, tooth-brush in his mouth. I pretend not to hear. I can smell his deodorant and his normal scent; no woman's perfume, no alcohol, no romantic dinner. My husband covers his tracks well.

I lie awake listening to him until he gets into bed beside me and pulls me close, his chest against my back. His arms enfold me and I close my eyes against the tears. I try to keep my breathing even, feeling the pressure on my lungs as my body wants to sob and howl. How can he do this to me? How can he spend a night with another woman and then get into bed next to me? Who is this man?

'Love you,' he mumbles into my shoulder.

'Love you too,' I whisper back, affecting the underwater tone of someone asleep. The cry imprisoned in my throat makes me sound authentic.

.   .   .

The next morning, he's totally normal. Packing his bag with one hand, a piece of toast in the other. He glances around the bedroom. 'Got my passport, toothbrush, socks...'

'Clean shirts?'

'Yep, and pants.'

'Then you're fine. As long as you've got your passport and your wallet...'

'... I can buy anything else I need if I've forgotten it. I know.' He glances up with a smile, zips up his suitcase and carries it downstairs. I follow, Samuel propped up on my shoulder, snoozy after his morning feed.

Through the open living room door, I can see Liv sitting on the sofa, gazing open-mouthed at the blaze of colour on the screen, a bowl cradled in the well of her crossed legs. A thimbleful of cereal milk swills from side to side as she moves.

In the kitchen, Jeremy brushes crumbs from his hands over the sink and takes a gulp of coffee. He pulls a face. 'Gone cold.'

Without speaking, I take his mug and put it in the microwave for twenty seconds. He gives me a grateful smile.

I hand him the warm mug and close the microwave door. Casual and quick, I say, 'The new baby monitor seems to work fine.'

He freezes, mug halfway to his lips. He takes a moment to gather himself. I watch him try to look calm, loosening his shoulders, taking a careful sip of the hot drink. 'You were right about that old one. I didn't like that it might have been hacked.'

I flick on the kettle for my own coffee, my back to him. 'But this one's not Wi-Fi. I thought you wanted to check up on us while you're away. Make sure we're OK.'

From the corner of my eye, I see him put down his mug. Does he glance towards the camera hidden behind the cookbooks, or is that my imagination? I can't tell. He clears his throat. 'You seem a lot... better. Since you came back from the Hermitage. Do you feel better?'

I nod, not wanting to interrupt what he's about to say. Will he admit to the cameras all over the house? Or will he pretend they're not there? They're hidden so well, I wouldn't have noticed them if I hadn't got used to the ever-present lenses in the Hermitage, their little LEDs blinking at me day and night from a corner of every room.

'I'm so glad,' he says, a self-satisfied smile on his face. He thinks he's fixed me. 'Look, I know it's not easy looking after two kids on your own. I'll call every night at six, so I can speak to Liv before she goes to bed. And please answer your phone when I call, so I don't worry. OK?'

I raise my eyebrows, considering the updated terms of our deal. I suppose he has to pretend he can't watch me any time he wants. 'Yes,' I concede. At least I'm not being observed by countless eyes through a compromised baby monitor now. Just by Jeremy. Small mercies.

'I've spoken to your mum.' He pauses, as if bracing for impact.

I try not to react. 'Why?'

'She knows I'm going away. And she's around if you need help. So call her if things get difficult, all right?'

I nod. I know the subtext here: if I don't answer my phone, he's going to send her over. His personal spy. 'I'll call Jac, too. Or Nicole, or Zain. If I need help.'

He smiles. 'That's great. It takes a village, right? As long as you're not afraid to ask for help, it doesn't matter who it is. Just keep me in the loop.' He pecks me on the cheek, and touches Samuel on his sleepy head. Then he pops into the living room and breaks Liv's hypnotic stare at the TV to give her a hug. 'See you soon, family.'

He grabs his suitcase and heads out on his work trip, pulling the front door closed behind him with a bang.

Samuel starts to wail. I'm on my own.

28

'Can we play our game, Mummy?' Liv's already pulling closed the old baby gate at the top of the stairs. We installed it when she started crawling, and never took it down. It's been propped open for the last couple of years, but recently she's discovered it again. 'Our game' involves closing the baby gate and racing each other along the upstairs corridor: the winner is the first one to touch the gate with both hands. If I don't feel like joining her, or I'm feeding Samuel, then it's a solo time trial using the stop-watch on my phone.

It's a strange game, but one that brings me joy. I've got my daughter back. No more *I hate you* and *I want a different mummy*. I just have to put Samuel in his cot for five minutes a few times a day and sprint along the corridor pretending a five-year-old can run faster than me.

It's a bonus that the camera sees it all. Look at what a good mother I am, Jeremy. Hear how much she giggles when we play. Look how safe I am, closing the baby gate so she doesn't fall down the stairs. It takes some restraint not to stick my middle finger up at the camera in the bookshelf as I run past.

I agree to one game in exchange for her getting herself

dressed for school straight after. She squeals with delight and sets off along the corridor before I've even said 'Ready, steady, go!'

She wins. Of course.

While Liv hums to herself in her bedroom, I wrap myself in the baby sling, pulling it tight around my ribs. I hold Samuel close and he rests his head on my chest, cooing happily. He gazes up at me, all gums and drool.

I beam at him, my face pulled into an exaggerated grin. Still nothing. No smile for Mummy. *It'll come*, I tell myself.

'Ready, Mummy!' She stands in her bedroom doorway, coat already on. I help her zip it up and tie her shoelaces, and then we're ready to go.

I catch a glance of myself in the mirror as we open the front door. Holding Liv's hand, her cheeks still flushed from our game, baby strapped to my chest. Supermum. I wish it had been like this from the start.

The morning air is so crisp I can almost taste it. The woody scent in the air mingles with frost and takes me back to my school days: scrabbling around the hockey pitch or sneaking cigarettes behind the cricket pavilion, hands balled into fists against the cold.

For a moment I feel almost normal again, like I've been standing in a dark corridor for the past ten weeks and someone just cracked open a door, sending a streak of daylight into my soul. Are the one hundred days of darkness over early?

I glance down at Liv, who's skipping along the pavement beside me. She's singing to herself, a wild made-up melody I wish I could record and keep for ever.

Just as we round the corner, a woman faces us on the narrow pavement, feet planted, unmoving. I stop, unable to manoeuvre Liv into the busy street, expecting the woman to step aside to let us past. But she doesn't.

She stands there staring at us. Staring at Liv. A smile creeps over her lined face, which looks crinkled, like an old sailor who has spent too much time outdoors without sunscreen. She must be in her mid sixties, but something – smoking, sunshine, drugs? – has aged her.

'What a beautiful little girl,' she says, bending down to Liv. 'Little angel,' she whispers.

Liv flinches, moves closer to my legs.

'She's a bit shy with new people,' I say, careful not to apologise for her. I pat her shoulder, reassuring. I want her to be shy of new people. It's a good trait, which will protect her from creepy old ladies in the street.

'I could eat you up, take you home for dinner.' The woman laughs, and winks up at me.

Liv shrinks further into my legs. 'No.'

I move one step forward, to signal that I need to get past. The woman still doesn't move, blocking the pavement. A mew from the baby sling draws her attention away from Liv. 'And another little beauty in here.' Her gaze falls on Samuel's blue jumper. 'A boy. One of each, lucky, lucky.' She reaches towards him as if to touch him.

'Leave him alone!' Liv shouts, her hand gripping my arm. 'He's ours.'

The lady chuckles and looks at me, lowering her hand. 'A feisty one you've got there. She'll be a good older sister, looking out for her little brother like that.' She glances at Liv, and her hand twitches, as if she's about to reach out towards her. I pull Liv behind me, stepping between the two of them.

'You're special, aren't you, Olivia?' the woman says, and my whole body clenches. How does she know Liv's name? Does she hunch over a laptop watching children on hacked monitors? Did she read that hateful post, believing I'm an abuser? Or is this all in my head? I could be standing on the street talking to myself. Maybe Liv's not afraid of this person; maybe she's afraid of her delusional mother.

Liv hides her face in my side. Enough's enough. Even though this encounter has lasted only twenty seconds, it feels like we've been standing here for hours, this woman blocking our path and creeping over my children.

I step forward, forcing her to move aside and off the kerb. 'Excuse me, we're late...' I stop myself before I say 'for school'. I don't want her knowing where we've gone. Where I'm leaving this child she thinks is so 'special'. My skin crawls. I've had the bump-gropers and the baby-kissers, but this lady is another level of creep.

I pull Liv away, walking faster than her little legs can move. 'Ow, Mummy, you're hurting me.'

I continue until we reach a lane that leads to the network of cycle routes that traverse the city. I look behind us: the woman is still standing there, watching us leave. I step into the tree-lined path and out of sight. In the sling, Samuel is still happy, peering out at the world when I glance at him.

Liv is howling now, her face red and tear-stained. I crouch to her and pull her into my arms.

She's saying something. 'Donnlettertaykme.' She shivers like a little bird fallen from her nest.

I kiss her cheek and hold her away from me, my hands on her arms. 'What did you say, baby?'

She takes a breath. 'Don't let her take me.'

'Let her take you?'

'Because you have Sam now.'

My heart beats against my ribs. This again. I try not to show my reaction. It's just like before. *They said you won't want me any more now you have Sam.* Has the voice got back inside, somehow, pouring poison into Liv's ears again?

'Don't give me away to the scary lady.'

I swallow my panic and focus on my daughter. 'I love you so much, Liv.' I hug her again. 'I need both of you. You're mine for ever, no matter what. Like you said, Sam's ours. And you're ours. We belong to each other, sweetheart.'

She pulls back and gives me a soggy kiss on the cheek. That's when I see it: her coat is undone, the zip almost to the bottom to show her purple T-shirt: *OLIVIA* printed across the front in that 1970s disco bubble font. The customised pyjamas, a birthday present from Jeremy's foster mum, Liv's name written there for perfectly friendly strangers to read on the street.

How did I not notice she was still wearing her pyjama top? Thank goodness she managed to get into her jeans, at least. What an idiot I am. A paranoid, neglectful idiot. Baby brain indeed. I tug at my hair, a little punishment Liv can't see. The perfect mum is gone.

I grab her hand. 'Come on, let's get you to school.'

The house feels strange when I get home from Liv's drop-off. I can't put my finger on what's different, but there's something in the air.

'Hello?' I call, feeling stupid. Jeremy's not here. He's on a plane or a train, speeding towards a work meeting. I wonder if his lover is travelling with him, lounging around naked in his hotel room while he's out, like a woman in a film. Or is she a colleague, booking a separate hotel room for appearances' sake and leaving one unused as they shack up together every night under the noses of their colleagues?

I shudder and close the front door behind me, checking to make sure it's locked. It feels like someone's been here.

Everything is the same as when I left: breakfast dishes still sitting on the kitchen counter, clothes strewn about the floor in Liv's room. I'm sweating after my walk, despite the cold, and I yank off my coat and then pull Samuel from the sling. He's sweaty too, his little neck folds sticky and damp. Are we getting sick? That'd be the worst timing, just as Jeremy's gone away.

I lay Samuel on the floor while I remove the layers of elasticated fabric wrapped around my ribs, stripping down to my T-shirt. I'm still boiling hot. I put my hand on a radiator, and immediately tug it away, my skin stinging.

That's why it felt so strange when I got home: the heating's on full blast and the house feels like a sauna.

The thermostat reads 35. 'Holy heck,' I mumble. I turn the dial to 18 and push to select that temperature, but it flicks straight back to 35 again. I try again. Same result.

I pick up Samuel and climb the stairs to the boiler cupboard. Inside, the boiler squeals with the strain. I scan the buttons, but everything looks normal. There's no setting out of place. I press a few things on the bottom panel, but the humming and groaning continues. *What's going on?*

I'm sweating again, and Samuel is getting frustrated, his skin sticking to mine where I'm holding him. How much is this costing us? How will we sleep?

I put him down on the ground and take off his jumper, and his grumbling stops. I don't pick him up again – let him have some space to cool off. I turn my attention back to the boiler, hitting more buttons. At my third poke, the entire bottom panel falls off, buttons, dials and everything.

I swear under my breath as I pick it up, try to replace it. But the cables aren't connected any more. Oh God, I'm going to have to call someone. Who do I call? A plumber? An electrician? A heating engineer? I've no idea. I'll talk to Jeremy tonight. For now, I can't think in this heat. I press the power button, and the boiler purrs into silence.

Relieved, I sink to the floor and lie next to Samuel, both of us staring at the ceiling, sweating.

I turn my head and look under the boiler at the part where

the panel once was, trying to work out if this is an electrical issue. Samuel coos beside me.

There are no exposed wires there, which is weird considering a whole chunk of the boiler just fell off. Instead, the cables that must once have connected to the panel are hooked up to something else: a sleek black box with a digital display.

I wouldn't have seen it before the panel fell off, as it was hidden. Even now, I can only see it from low down on the floor. The display winks and blinks, a little Wi-Fi symbol glowing green in the corner. There's a logo on the box, one I can't quite read.

I get up on my knees and grab my phone from my pocket, shining the torch into the dark space under the boiler. I can see the logo now: SmartHomeTech.

No wonder the downstairs thermostat doesn't work. It's some kind of smart device, controlled remotely. Probably on an app.

Is Jeremy cranking up our heating while he's away? Why?

I swallow, a sick feeling in the pit of my stomach. I wipe the sweat from my forehead with the back of my hand and stare down at Samuel with my hands on my hips. *What shall we do, baby?*

Jeremy's always been interested in technology, intrigued by the idea of automating various parts of our lives for convenience. But he'd always talk to me about it. At length. For weeks. We'd have to research every provider and get a temporary subscription to *Which?* magazine so we could pick the exact right one.

But now he's installed a new smart home heating gadget and didn't tell me. What is he planning?

29

I can't sleep when I crawl into bed that night. I thought Jeremy's first work trip would be a milestone: an acknowledgement from him that I'm doing better. That I'm a good mum.

But instead, he's watching all the time, and I'm apparently so untrustworthy in his eyes that he has to control the heating system from his trip too. I hate knowing I'm being watched. My skin itches and crawls with it, like I'm covered in ants. I want to scratch and scratch but nothing will get this feeling off me.

This has been my world for weeks: constant monitoring, never being truly alone. Since the day I walked into the Hermitage.

No. Before that.

My breath catches in my throat. I remember the baby monitor swivelling on its stand, weeks ago, the day we brought Samuel home from the hospital. Watching, always watching. *Mummy doesn't love you.* The memory of the hissing voice echoes around my brain in the darkness.

In the end, around 1 a.m., I stack pillows under the quilt in the shape of a human form, then, keeping my head under the covers, slide across the bed and onto the floor along Jeremy's side, furthest from the door. Here, I'm squashed in the two-foot gap between his wardrobe and the bed – and out of sight of the camera.

I can still hear Samuel in his crib on the other side, so I know he's safe. I'm here if he needs me. And if Jeremy looks at the camera feed, he'll think I'm in bed, sleeping soundly.

I pull down a spare pillow and drag a dressing gown over myself, and for the first time since returning from the Hermitage and finding the cameras, I relax enough to fall into a deep sleep.

Less than an hour later, screams wrench me from sleep. Both kids are howling, Samuel in my room and Liv from hers. I leap up in panic, desperate to check on my babies.

'Mummy! Mummy!' Liv shrieks.

I scoop up Samuel, patting his back and shushing him gently. He settles as soon as he feels my hands on him, and rests his head on my shoulder. But in my half-asleep state, it takes me a few moments to realise what's strange: the bedroom light is on, and the bedside lamps, too.

The en suite door stands ajar, light showing through the gap.

I rush to Liv. The landing light is on, and in her room every bulb is ablaze. She's sitting up in the middle of her bed, hair everywhere, hugging her beanie toy cat. 'Mummy, what's happening?'

Every single light in the house is blazing.

I check the time on Liv's alarm clock. It's 2.15 a.m.

I turn off her lights and settle her back into bed, stroking her hair and singing a lullaby under my breath. I tell her that some-times electricity goes funny and it's nothing to worry about.

It's not long before her eyelids start to float closed, her long lashes resting on her cheeks like perfect crescent moons. I tiptoe from the room and carry Samuel around the house, turning off every light until we're in darkness again. I stand at the kitchen sink for a few minutes, gulping a glass of water and staring out of the window into the garden. An old, grizzled fox emerges from behind the shed, its tail huge and bushy. It sniffs the over-grown lawn for a moment and then disappears into the hedge.

I'm wide awake now, but I need to get more sleep if I'm going to function tomorrow. I trudge up the stairs and into our bedroom, where I catch sight of the rumpled covers on the bed, the human-shaped pillows I arranged earlier. And my little nest in the opposite corner of the room, the dressing gown poking out around the side of the bed.

And now I realise what happened. Why the lights were on.

Jeremy couldn't see me on the cameras. So he lit up the whole house to find me.

I don't sleep any more that night.

I abandon the nest I made, the one safe space in the house. As soon as I leapt up to check the kids, my cover was blown. I get back into our bed, in view of the camera, and lie awake in the dark staring at the LED on top of Jeremy's wardrobe. It blinks at me and I blink back.

The next morning, I'm a zombie. Everything feels difficult.

The milk is off, little chunks slopping into Liv's bowl as I pour. I have to chuck away her cereal, despite her protests. She refuses to eat the toast and honey I make her instead. It goes in the bin.

Samuel bites my nipple while he's feeding. I'm so tired I don't even scream. I just cry, my tears plopping onto his head as he continues to suckle, the milk around his mouth tinged pink with my blood.

After I've taken Liv to school, a banana shoved in her back-pack for break time, I return to the house with Samuel. It's hot again, the thermostat creeping up since I switched the boiler back on for showers this morning. I turn it off again and contemplate calling a heating engineer, pretending I don't know my own husband is messing with the system remotely.

I put Samuel down for a nap in his bassinet in the living room and head to the kitchen to make myself a cup of tea, forgetting the milk is off until again little clumps slosh into my mug.

I can't cope with today. I pour the milk down the drain and make a note to buy more when I pick Liv up from school. My stomach rumbles and I remember Nicole's advice before Samuel was born: when you can't sleep enough, eat more to compensate. Calories can temporarily replace sleep to keep you going.

I slide two pieces of bread into the toaster and grab a block of butter from the fridge. As I carry it across the room, my fingers sink into its foil-covered sides, and a drip splats onto the tiled floor. The butter is soft.

'What the...?' I turn to the fridge and open the door again. No light comes on.

I stick my hand in, right to the back. It's not cold. The fridge is broken. Everything is ruined. No wonder the milk was off.

The butter drops to the floor with a splat as I remember: my breast milk, in the freezer. Pints and pints of it, each labelled with the date and lined up in chronological order. Hours of my time. Sitting alone in my room at the Hermitage, telling myself I was doing this for Samuel, for his health, for our relationship, for his comfort and happiness. Literal weeks of feeding my baby by proxy, telling myself I needed to.

The pain of the pump nipping at my breasts, leaving blisters on my nipples. The hum of the motor making my ears itch.

Wasted. I'll have to pour it all down the sink.

I can't even compute how a broken fridge-freezer could take

so much from me. So much waste. So much loss. It's ridiculous. I shove the thought to the back of my mind. Process it later.

As I'm reviewing the wasted contents of the fridge, wondering what I can salvage, a shrill squealing fills the house. The smoke alarm.

I whirl, my first instinct to protect Samuel's sleep from the noise, but my second instinct overrides that. Protect the baby from the fire.

There's no smoke in the living room, but his nap has been ruined. He's wide awake. I pick him up and walk back to the kitchen through the haze in the hallway. The toast. I've burned my toast and it's triggered the smoke alarm.

One-handed, I pop the toast – charred black charcoal now – and grab a broom to reach up and hit the button to turn off the smoke alarm. How did I not notice the toaster dial was turned right up to max?

Then the doorbell rings.

I swear under my breath and open the front door.

It's a police officer. A very young one; mid twenties, maybe. Another stands at the bottom of the path, outside the gate. He glances at his watch.

My stomach churns. Is Jeremy OK? Liv? My mum? My mind flits through a series of horrific scenarios.

'Mrs Thorne?' the officer says. Her tone doesn't sound serious. Not like she's about to tell me someone died. She sounds... bored.

'Yes. Is everything OK?' I try to keep the tremor from my voice. Samuel coos in my ear.

When she smiles at him, she looks even younger, university student age. 'I'm Special Constable Sarah Neville. We were nearby and got an alert that your smoke alarm was going off.' She points at her phone.

'An alert? I burnt some toast.' I step back. 'Do the police get alerted when you burn food now?' I try to laugh but it catches in my throat.

Her smile slips. 'Not quite. I'm a voluntary officer, training to be a police officer. We were in the area.' She nods to her colleague at the gate, who doesn't even look up from his phone. 'Some users of home security systems can set their systems to alert emergency services when their alarms go off. We got a ping from your house.'

I open my mouth and close it again. I don't understand what she just said. 'Sorry... home security systems?'

She nods, a look on her face that she probably wears when she talks to her grandma about modern tech. 'Do you have a smart home, Mrs Thorne?'

I swallow. 'I don't...' I stop myself. My throat constricts with humiliation. I think about the last twenty-four hours: the sauna-like heating, the lights coming on in the middle of the night, the cameras everywhere, the fridge that turned itself off. I gulp air into my lungs. That must be it. 'Yes, I think so.'

She smiles sweetly, her youthful skin barely crinkling at the corners of her eyes. 'It sounds like you've got guard mode activated. That means your system listens out for things like smoke alarms, carbon monoxide alarms and breaking glass. On the more high-tech systems you can request that local services are notified in the case of an emergency. In this case, you got me.' She holds out both hands, palms up. *Ta-dah.*

I shake my head, my hand wrapped around the brass door-knob. My cheeks burn. I want to close the door and retreat, but my own home is against me. It's no sanctuary. It's a trap.

I shift the door slightly. 'Doesn't seem like a good use of police time.'

She makes a quiet hum in the back of her throat, a subtle agreement. 'It's worth checking what settings you've got activated. If you set off your smoke alarm regularly or, for example, steam from your shower sometimes activates it, then it's not a helpful setting for you to have switched on.'

I nod, trying to pretend I know what's going on here. In my own home.

'I'll make a note it was a false alarm.'

'Thank you.'

She lifts her phone, but then pauses. 'Everything *is* all right?' She looks me dead in the eye. I feel observed, like the moment in your first midwife booking-in appointment when they send your husband out of the room to ask you if he's abusive. They always pause for a moment, leaving a silence for you to fill if you need to.

But with a start, I realise it's not my husband she's assessing. Her eyes scan Samuel, roaming over his face, checking for signs of unhappiness or pain. I hold him closer, give him a peck on his little head. Her eyes settle on his mouth, his lips still ringed with my blood from where he bit my breast.

'Yes, absolutely.' I wave a hand over my shoulder, into the house. 'New system. Teething issues. We'll get our heads around it.'

I silently give thanks that she doesn't automatically assume I have no idea any of this is even possible. That she doesn't say something awful like 'Ask your husband.' Even though that's exactly what I have to do.

She gives a closed-lip smile.

I start to shut the door. 'Sorry for bothering you.'

But I won't ask Jeremy yet. First I need to work out what I'm dealing with here.

I know what I need to do.

30

It's a relief to see a friendly face.

Zain and I sit on the patio, cups of tea in front of us, while Kai and Liv poke in the soil under one of the bushes by the gate, hunting for treasure with last year's seaside bucket and spade.

Samuel is fast asleep in his pram, swaddled in blankets, his little red nose poking out beneath his hat.

Zain pulls his coat around himself and blows air out in a puff of steam. 'Al fresco tea in winter. Interesting choice, Mim.'

I pick up my mug and wrap my hands around it. 'I thought it would be nice. Thanks for bringing fresh milk.' I glance up. 'The sun will be on this patch of garden in a few minutes and it'll be worth it.'

He flashes me a disbelieving look and reaches for his own tea. 'So, how are things? Managed to get your job back?'

It feels like a physical blow. In the madness of home and the mental effort of keeping the kids happy while my own life falls apart, I haven't been thinking about the other half of my world, which has been wrenched away from me. A key part of who I am.

'No. I suspect that ship has sailed.' I look around me, a

habit I can't break even when I'm outdoors. But there are no cameras out here. They wouldn't survive the wet Edinburgh winter.

Zain shakes his head. 'If you want to come back, Mim, I'm sure they—'

I hold out a hand to stop him. 'I found the resignation email, Zain.'

His frown deepens as I tell him about the email and its final line. *Please send future correspondence to the postal address you have on file, addressed c/o Jeremy Thorne.*

'What the eff?' he says when I've finished.

I smile weakly at his pseudo-swear.

He shuffles forward on his garden chair, leaning over the table towards me. 'What's going on? Do you think Jeremy resigned on your behalf? Pretending to be you?' He shakes his head, baffled. 'Is that... that can't be legal. What's he playing at?' He rubs a hand over his jaw, his day-old stubble rasping against his palm.

A cold stone sits in my stomach. I sip tea, trying to dispel it, but the feeling's been there for days. 'I need your help, Zain.'

He sets his mug on the table and rubs his hands together for warmth. 'Anything.'

I want to wrap my arms around him to thank him for believing me, for not asking the question I asked myself when I saw the email in my sent items: *Are you sure you didn't send it yourself?*

I glance at the kids, who have moved away from their treasure hunt under the hedge and switched to a fighting game, where Kai wields the spade as a sword and Liv holds the bucket as a shield. 'Getting violent over there,' I mutter with a nod towards them.

Zain turns in his seat. 'We'll be here to wipe up the tears and blood,' he says with a chuckle. He tugs his zip up to his chin. His fingernails are blue, despite the warm tea. 'Remind me why we're freezing our balls off out here? Well, my balls, anyway. You don't have any.'

'Oh God, Zain. You're going to think I'm insane.'

He flashes a smile. 'More than I already do?'

I don't return the smile.

He sits back in his seat. 'Sorry. No more jokes. I can tell this is serious.'

I clear my throat. 'While I was at the Hermitage, Jeremy did some stuff to the house.' I glance over my shoulder. The windows glow orange with the reflection of the setting winter sun. The Scottish stone looks warm in the afternoon light, but it glitters with frost in the shade.

Zain frowns. 'Did some stuff?'

'The Wi-Fi baby monitor is gone—'

'About time, Mim. Those things are dodgy as f... fudge.'

I shake my head. 'But now the whole house is rigged. That's why we're sitting outside.'

'Rigged?'

I nod, and drain my tea. In the corner of the lawn, Liv and Kai crouch over the grass, looking for worms now. I tell Zain about the camera in the teddy bear, the cameras in every room, the heating system, the fridge, the lights, the visit from the police when the smoke alarm went off.

He doesn't move as I speak, his gaze never leaving mine. When I finish, he's pale. 'So we're sitting outside because you think Jeremy can listen to your conversations.'

His phrasing makes me bristle. 'I don't just *think*. Zain, did you not hear what I said? The whole house is wired, he's trying to set me up—'

'Whoa, whoa, whoa.' Zain holds out his hands to stop me. 'I meant we don't know if these cameras can record sound. They might just be visual.'

'But it heard the smoke alarms...'

He shrugs. 'It sounds like he's upgraded every electronic

device that could be smart. It's possible your smoke alarms are smart alarms. And your fridge, your lights, your boiler... everything.'

I nod slowly. 'That's what I think, too. I'd like your help. Can we test this? But if Jeremy's watching...'

'We need to do it without him knowing.'

'Exactly.'

Zain pauses, thinking.

After a minute or two, I can't stand it any more. 'So, what do you think?'

He wraps his arms around himself with a smirk. 'I think we're going to need to stay outside for a bit longer to make a plan. And I'm going to have to borrow a hat and scarf.'

'Ready?' I ask. I'm crouched in the cupboard under the stairs. I don't think there's a camera in this corridor, so with any luck Jeremy won't have seen me duck inside.

'Yep!' says Zain's voice, tinny and small through my phone speaker. He's still in the garden with the kids. He can't come into the house, not yet. Not until the power is off.

I push on the chunky black switch, flicking it into the off position. There's a whirr, like a spaceship powering down, and then the house is silent.

I take a moment to revel in the knowledge that for the next two or three minutes, no one can watch me. The cameras are blinded. Then I say into the phone: 'Go!'

I hear the door open and Zain's footsteps as he walks into the kitchen. I leave the cupboard and walk past him with a salute on my way into the garden to watch the kids. 'Good luck,' I whisper, even though the cameras can't pick up my voice while the power's out.

He's already rummaging among the cookbooks as I close the door. I keep my phone connected to his, listening to him mumble to himself as he wanders through the house, looking for cameras, assessing what's bugged, what's smart and what's creepy.

In the garden, Kai and Liv are using a bubble sword as a weapon. 'I knight you!' they shout, giggling as bubble mixture sprays in all directions with each hit. I pretend not to notice.

'Miriam?' My mobile crackles to life on the patio table in front of me.

I switch off speakerphone and put the phone to my ear so the kids can't hear. 'How's it going?'

'I'm in your bedroom.'

'Mm?'

'What's going on with the pillows and stuff down the side of the bed?'

I swallow. 'Ah.' He's found my nest. My cheeks grow hot. 'Erm... I wanted to sleep somewhere no one could see. You know, out of camera range.'

There's the briefest of pauses. 'Gotcha.' He doesn't sound convinced.

I put the phone back on the table. As I stare at the wintry blue sky through the bare branches of the copper beech, I dare to think the thing I've been flinching from for weeks. What if he finds nothing? What if it's all in my head?

I feel a glimmer of relief. If it's all in my head, I'm just unwell. I'm having a mental health issue; nothing to be ashamed of. I'll get treated for it, and then eventually – hopefully – I'll be back to my old self. Happily married to a faithful husband I love, with two children we both adore.

But it's not in my head. Katy saw the messages; she found the Reddit post. The words circulate through my brain on a permanent loop:

All he needs is proof that she hurts them. Enough to block any custody bid she makes. And then this amazing man and his brilliant kids will be all mine. He's finally going to leave her.

I didn't imagine that. There's a witness.

But then the little devil on my shoulder prods at me again. What if Katy doesn't exist either?

Next to me, Samuel is still asleep in his pram, wrapped up against the winter chill. And Liv rolls around on the lawn, the knees of her jeans soaked through with mud.

Am I safe to be their mother? Are they safe with me? Or would they be better off with someone else after all?

I would fight for them until I have nothing left, but is that best for them? Or is it better to let them go and continue alone? To let them go for their own good and battle through life without them, *for* them?

I brush away a tear.

'Mim?' Zain's voice through the phone drags me into the present.

I sniff, trying to inject some kind of normality into my voice. 'Doing OK?'

'That's me done. I'll come out and you can turn the power back on.' I stand up, flick a glance at Liv and Kai. They're still whacking each other with the bubble wand, and neither has yet taken it too far. Thankfully.

As we agreed, Zain and I cross over at the door. Back in the cupboard, I flick the switch on the fuse box and listen as the house whirrs to life. The smart spaceship powers up. I check the time on my phone.

Zain was in the house for three minutes. Enough to shrug it off as a brief power cut if Jeremy notices the gap in the feeds. Much more effective than my first idea, to switch off the Wi-Fi. As Zain pointed out, if the cameras still had a power feed, they could continue recording and upload footage once the electricity was back on. The only way was to cut the power to the whole house: Wi-Fi, cameras, everything.

Zain's sitting at the patio table again when I come outside,

Kai on his knee sucking his thumb. He smiles as I walk towards them. 'There was a bubble sword incident.'

Liv rushes over to me and wraps her arms around my waist. I stroke her hair and my heart bursts with love. My sweet, affectionate girl has come back to me. No more shouting, hating, asking for a different mummy. Even if the house is riddled with cameras, no one is pouring poison into her ear through the baby monitor any more. And I'm so, so grateful for it.

I sit down and pull her onto my knee. 'What happened?'

Zain shrugs. 'Not sure. Someone whacked someone a little too hard, I think.'

I smile. 'No harm done?'

He shakes his head. 'The tears stopped immediately. They're tired. Lots of fresh air today.'

'So...?' I lean forward and nod towards the house, hopeful that the kids' presence at the table won't stop him from telling me what he found inside.

His expression is blank. I can't read him at all.

'Miriam,' he says, an apology in his voice.

My heartbeat escalates, and sweat breaks out all over my body, despite the cold. I know what he's going to say.

'I didn't find anything.' He clears his throat. 'No cameras. Nothing.'

31

So it's all in my head.

I stand up, surprising Liv. She stumbles off my lap, grabbing onto the table for support.

I pat her shoulder in apology, but I don't take my eyes off Zain. 'You didn't find anything?' I croak.

I feel sick. I look around for somewhere to vomit. The flower bed. I bend double, hands on my knees. Breathe, Miriam. Breathe. My head is fuzzy. Maybe I'll faint. Better to faint than vomit.

But the house is full of cameras. I've seen them. The fridge turned off. The heating went to max. All the lights came on in the middle of the night. I shake my head. There's a whining in my ears, like a siren. It gets louder and louder, drowning everything else out. I can't hear the birds, the traffic on the main road two streets over. It's a high-pitched shriek. If I've imagined this, I'm in so deep it'll take me years to come back.

'Miriam?' Zain sounds like he's underwater.

'Mummy?' Liv starts to cry.

I straighten up and then drop to my knees beside her, pulling her into my arms. 'I'm so, so sorry, Livvy,' I mumble into her hair, trying to catch my breath. 'I'm not feeling well, love.' And I mean it. She wraps her arms around my neck and sinks into me. This feels like a goodbye.

Because even though I said to myself that maybe it would be OK if it *was* in my head, because it would mean I could be treated, if I'm so mentally unwell that I'm hallucinating cameras and imagining a haunted smart house, then it's likely Jeremy and his lover can get me sectioned and have the kids to themselves. Full custody. Like she said in her Reddit post.

'Miriam?'

I shake my head. I want him to go away. I need to be with my kids now. 'Please, Zain. Thanks for your help. But I can't...'

I feel his hand on my shoulder and close my eyes, burrowing further into Liv, who's whimpering now, confused by what's going on. 'I'm so sorry, baby.'

His hand grips my shoulder harder. 'Miriam, I was joking.'

The siren in my head starts to fade as I process what he just said.

He gives me a little shake. 'It was a joke. A terrible one. I'm so sorry, I shouldn't have said that. There are cameras, and loads of other things. Someone's watching you all the time.'

Another cup of sweet tea in front of me, and a huge number of effusive apologies from Zain later, and the two of us are still sitting in the garden. The kids have given up and gone to Liv's bedroom to play in the warmth, and Zain keeps flicking hopeful glances towards the door as he blows on his reddened hands. He knows, now, that we can't talk about this inside.

'You've got a completely smart house,' he says, his breath puffing with every word. 'Every electrical item that can be upgraded to be controlled remotely has been. And the ones that would need complete replacement to be smart – like your fridge

– have been plugged in through smart plugs. So they can be switched on and off remotely.'

I nod, thankful that we don't have to replace the fridge.

'Your boiler has an add-on: the wiring underneath has been removed so your normal panel – the one with the dials – isn't connected. Instead there's a little digital box that allows you to make it essentially a smart boiler. But the panel is still in place even though it's disconnected, so everything looks normal.'

I take long, slow breaths to calm myself, and process what I'm hearing. 'And the smoke alarm thing?'

'So guard mode, the thing the police volunteer mentioned to you, is activated through a listening device. Like Alexa, or Siri, or whatever. I couldn't see anything like that, so it's probably hidden. And yes, it can listen out for alarms and contact the emergency services, et cetera. And that can also be set to be super sensitive.'

'What does that mean?'

'It sends notifications at tailored noises, like footsteps or a cough. Or a baby crying.' He glances at me and away again. 'I'm not saying that's what's happening here, but it's possible.'

I shudder and gulp my tea.

Zain takes his laptop from his backpack. 'Can I...?' he mumbles to himself. 'Yes, I can.' He types a few things and then looks up at me, triumphant. 'I've got an open-source piece of software on here that lets me scan your router. It provides a list of everything sitting on that same Wi-Fi connection.'

He turns the screen. The list I see makes very little sense to me, with each item containing letters, numbers and some partial words. A few things look vaguely familiar. I point at *Zain-X531LAPTOP*. 'So that's you?'

'Yep, that's my laptop. It's connected to your Wi-Fi right now, so it's on the list.'

I run my finger down the screen. 'And there's mine. And Jeremy's.' I move further down. 'And these?'

He shrugs. 'These look like normal devices that are either connected now or have been at some point in the past. Work laptops and mobile phones, for example. Nothing suspicious here.'

My stomach contracts again. 'No cameras? No listening device? And what about the fridge? And the lights?'

He holds out a hand to stop me. 'Hold your horses, matey. I'm getting to it.'

'OK...?'

'Whoever set up this system is quite tech-savvy.'

'Well, Jeremy works in tech.'

Zain pulls the computer towards him and nods. 'Makes sense.' He clicks a few times, types something and then swivels the laptop towards me. 'Here.'

There's a massive list on the screen, so long it has a scroll bar to the side. 'What am I looking at?'

'Your hidden network.'

My mouth drops open. 'What?'

He shakes his head. 'I won't go into what I did to find this, because it won't make any sense to an art therapist.' He smiles to show he's teasing. 'I have a tool that can spot them and tell you their SSID, encryption and password.'

I nod, but he's already lost me.

He smiles again. 'It's like a second Wi-Fi router in your house, but it's not findable through normal channels.' He points at the list. 'And see? Here are the cameras, the smart plug for your fridge, the lights...'

'Wow. So he'd have to know a lot about this kind of tech to be able to set this up.'

Zain nods. 'I'd say so. I can detect this, but I couldn't set it up. What's Jeremy's job again?'

'Systems integration consultant.'

'For what kind of company? I'm surprised he'd have this kind of specialist know—'

There's a shrill scream from the house, from upstairs. Liv's room.

We both freeze.

Another scream.

I stand and make to run, then stop: I can't leave Samuel. I gather him up from his pram and rush towards the house.

'Miriam!' Zain shouts, his face anguished.

I pause at the back door.

'I'm not here, remember? The cameras.'

I shake my head. 'You can be here now we've stopped poking around. It's a normal playdate.'

We both run up the stairs. Zain gets to Liv's room first. 'Is everything OK?'

I follow, panting, Samuel wriggling in my arms. The kids are sitting on Liv's bedroom floor. Liv is cradling her pink bunny toy and crying. Kai's crying too.

I scan the room. No one is injured. There's stuff every-where. They've emptied Liv's drawers, strewn her clothes across the floor. The teddy-cam lies on its side, its beady little camera eyes pointing under the bed.

The two of them talk at once.

'Mummy, Kai stole my purple pyjama top. The one with my name—'

'I didn't steal anything! Why would I want your stupid girly top?'

Zain and I look at each other and share a smile.

'OK, Kai. It's time for us to go home. I think everyone's tired.' He meets my eye. 'We'll talk more later,' he mumbles, nodding at the teddy-cam. 'When we're not being watched,' he adds with a shudder.

32

I feel lighter tonight, like I've been for a massage and had the tensions worked out of my knotted muscles. I hum to myself as I cook dinner for me and Liv: roasted vegetables, rice and fried salmon fillets. A weekday staple in our house.

Liv's playing with her plastic horses at the table, making them clip-clop around and using an old shoebox as a stable.

Samuel's tucked up in his bassinet in the corner of the kitchen, batting at some colourful toys I've hung from the canopy and chattering away to himself happily.

I've turned on the radio, and the murmur of voices and the occasional tune adds to the companionable atmosphere in the room. As I turn the vegetables with a spatula, I wonder to myself why I feel better after learning how riddled with spy technology our house is.

It's the vindication, I realise as I slide the roasting tray back into the oven. It's knowing I'm not making it up, it's not in my head. I'm not facing years of therapy and medication.

Instead, I have to face the reality that my husband would go to such extreme lengths to manipulate my life and get custody of the kids when he leaves. Or when he manages to drive me to leave. A cleverer person would know how to play this. I've always thought this about myself: my lack of guile sometimes disadvantages me when I'm pitted against someone more manipulative and calculating. I'm not that type of person. I can't think several steps ahead.

I flip the salmon, which is golden and crispy on one side, then I look over at Liv. She has tied a tissue around the head of one of her horses and is now acting as the officiant in a horse wedding ceremony. She sings a wedding march as she clip-clops the horses down the aisle.

Maybe I need help. To talk to someone who can help me play Jeremy at his own game. The thought of admitting this to another person, right from the beginning, makes me feel a little sick. I could talk to Zain; he already knows most of it anyway, after today. And he believes me.

I shake my head. Zain's as guileless as me. He doesn't think like a lawyer, doesn't know how to play games. He's a good person. He said himself he wouldn't know how to rig this up.

No, not Zain. I need someone spiky. Someone calculating. Someone who's always gone for what they want without a second thought. Someone who's never been walked over in their entire life. I tap out a text:

> You free to come over tonight? Got some wine! Wrap up warm. We'll light the fire pit in the garden.

Jac bustles into the house, filling the hallway with her perfume and whispered swearing. 'Kids already in bed?' Her whisper emerges even louder than her ordinary voice.

I nod, and pat my pocket where the new non-Wi-Fi monitor hums, watching both kids sleep in Liv's room. I'll fetch Samuel when it's time for his next feed, and hopefully he won't disturb

Liv too much in the meantime. I can't handle another argument about a lost pyjama top. 'There's something nice about both my babies sleeping in the same room,' I say to Jac.

She smiles. 'I getcha. I'm glad you texted, actually. I needed a chat.'

I wonder if she's decided to talk about whatever was bothering her last time.

She starts to remove her scarf to hang it on the hook, and then pauses, flashing me a wary look. 'What's this about a fire pit? You're going to freeze me to death?'

'I've done us some mulled wine. Does that make it OK?'

She high-fives me. 'If you can't go to Edinburgh's Christmas market, you bring the Christmas market to us. I like it.'

I lead her through to the kitchen and ladle the wine into two insulated mugs that Jeremy and I used to take on our commute every morning, when we both worked across town and left the house together. Before maternity leave and Jeremy's new high-flying job. A lifetime ago.

Now these mugs are going to keep mulled wine warm while we huddle against the cold in the dark garden, hiding from the surveillance system Jeremy's set up to ensnare me. I shudder.

'Oh!' I clap my hands. 'I have some mince pies, too. I warmed them up in the oven.' I put four of them on a plate and hustle Jac into the garden.

We call it a fire pit, but really it's a cheap metal bowl we got from B&M a million years ago. I've stacked it with crumpled paper and wood, and pulled two garden chairs up as close as I can, doing my best to make this feel like an occasion, like it makes sense to sit in the garden in the dark in December.

Jac lowers herself into a chair, taking a moment to check its stability before she commits. She laughs to herself and wraps both hands around her mug. 'We've done some crazy things in our time, but this is another level, Mim.'

I light a match and touch it to the paper underneath the

sticks. The flame creeps through and finally catches the fire-lighters underneath. 'We'll warm up soon,' I say, taking my own seat. I pull the monitor from my pocket and check the feed. Yep, there's enough signal even in the garden. I can see both my babies in black and white, sleeping soundly. I smile. I've got my best friend here and my kids asleep upstairs. This is all I need.

But there's a pang of sadness in my chest, too. For what I've lost. Or, more accurately, for what I once thought I had but never really did: a good, kind husband who loves me as I love him.

My heart is broken. And I know that eventually it will hurt so badly that I won't be able to breathe. But for now, all I can think about is how I keep the kids. I'll deal with the hurt later.

'Everything OK, Smidge?' asks Jac, blowing on her mulled wine. 'This is fun and everything, but it's not our usual Friday night.' She chuckles.

I grab a mince pie from the plate and remove the foil cup. I take a big breath, and Jac and I speak at the same time:

'Jeremy's having an affair.'

'But I did want to talk to you about something.'

My declaration wins, and Jac's mouth drops open. 'No.' She leans back in her chair, a look of resigned horror on her face.

'And I need your help.'

I tell her everything. The Reddit post that Katy found. The cameras. The smart house.

The only part I don't manage to articulate is the spoiled breast milk in the freezer. The awful, hollow tragedy of pouring it all down the sink. The waste. The loss. I can't say it out loud. I'd cry, and Jac would never understand.

She sits in silence, sipping at her mulled wine and staring at me in shock. 'But... but it's Jeremy. Good old happy-go-lucky

Jeremy.' She lifts one corner of her mouth. 'He's just so... steadfast.'

I nod and lean forward to prod the fire. She's right. One of the things that has prevented me processing the extent of his betrayal is that I never once believed this could happen. From the moment we met, I trusted him. He's never given me a reason to doubt his love, his fidelity. Even when Liv was born and everything went wrong, he was still my Jeremy. He still loved me and helped me and wanted to be married to me. I could tell. And even this time, he's been trying to help in his own clumsy way.

I flinch. I'm getting too close to the abyss, the thoughts that will cause me to fall over the edge and into grief. I need to focus on the kids. They're my priority now.

'So I need to play him at his own game. I need your help. I've been the perfect wife, ideal mother, trying not to give him anything on the cameras that he could use against me. For custody, you know. But he's already...'

She gasps, the colour draining from her cheeks, then sits back, her whole body defeated. 'He could use your hospital stay against you,' she mumbles, almost to herself.

'Yeah. Which he arranged.'

Her shoulders slump further. 'Wow. He's been planning this for so long.' She looks at me with sadness in her eyes.

I nod slowly. 'I think so. Possibly even when I was pregnant.'

She pulls her coat around her tighter. 'Maybe this was his mistress's idea. That would explain why it feels so uncharacteristic of him. This whole thing has "woman" written all over it.'

'You think?'

She grins. 'I mean, it's clever. It's evil-genius-level planning. Mastermind. Watching everything you do, trying to make you feel like you're going mad. Or even trying to drive you mad?' She blows air from her lips, a big cloud forming in the cold air. 'I don't think this was all Jeremy. He's very intelligent, but this? Nah.'

'He's gone along with it, though.'

She sips her mulled wine. 'What a bastard.'

I half smile, wishing there were even appropriate words to encompass what Jeremy is. 'Anyway, what did *you* want to talk about?'

She shakes her head. 'No way. I can't follow that. You've got enough going on. I can deal with it myself.'

I'm about to protest and insist I want to know when the baby monitor buzzes and whirrs. I take it from my pocket and check the feed.

Liv's bed is empty.

'What the...?'

'Everything OK?'

I stand up. 'It's Liv, she's—'

The door flings open. 'Mummy! Someone woke me up. Mummy? What are you doing?'

I walk across the garden towards the back door. 'Don't come out here, baby. It's cold.'

'I still can't find my favourite pyjamas. The purple ones with my name on,' she says, silhouetted in the doorway with the kitchen light behind her illuminating her curls like a halo. She rubs her eyes and yawns.

I sigh. The pyjama top has probably been missing for days. 'I know, baby. We'll keep looking. It'll turn up.'

'Why are you outside?'

'Auntie Jac and I were—'

'Auntie Jac's here?' Her face transforms into a smile and she bursts out of the kitchen door and into the garden. 'I knew I heard someone.'

'Liv, it's too cold.' I grab a blanket from the armchair and follow her back to the fire. When I get there, she's already on Jac's knee, bundled up in her coat.

'She can stay for five minutes, right?' says Jac, kissing her curls. 'It's not a school night.'

'Please please please please please, Mummy,' Liv whines, snuggling closer to Jac. 'I haven't seen Auntie Jac for a million zillion years. And I asked nicely.'

I tuck the blanket round her legs. 'Five minutes. And then up to bed, OK?'

She grins. 'OK!' She stares into the flames for a few seconds before she starts to wriggle again. 'Mummeeee?' she says, in the voice she uses when she wants something.

'Mm?'

'Can I have a hot chocolate? It's so nearly Christmas and that can be my present.'

I laugh. 'Little chancer.' It's tempting, and I want to give her what she wants, especially as we're sitting outside, so the cameras won't see her drinking a sugary milky drink after night-time teeth brushing. But I also don't know what the cameras *did* see: a five-year-old wandering outside at 10 p.m. isn't a good look. Oh, but she finally loves me again. Despite all the parenting advice, I want to give her everything she wants, every moment of the day. I want her to keep loving me like she does in this moment. I blink away a tear. 'I know.' I clap my hands in mock-excitement. 'How about Jac takes you upstairs and tucks you in?'

Liv squirms in delight. 'Yes! And a story.'

Jac tickles her sides. 'You're pushing your luck tonight, young lady!'

Liv giggles and wriggles until she slides off Jac's lap.

Jac stands and holds out a hand to her. 'Come on. I'm going to tuck you in so tightly you'll turn into a little burrito. Say night night to Mummy.'

Liv shakes her head.

My heart sinks, my mind flashing back a month or two. *I*

don't love you. I wish I had a different mummy. Please don't let that be happening again.

But she holds out her other hand. 'Mummy come too.'

Relief floods my body. And gladness. But I shake my head. 'I have to stay with the fire. It's not sensible to leave it unattended, you see.'

Jac nods at the flames and turns towards the house. 'Let's put it out and move inside. I've got frostbite.' A look of concern crosses her face. 'Unless you have anything else to talk about out here? I'll stay here longer if we need to.'

'Nah.' I slosh water over the embers. 'I'll gather the glasses and see you guys upstairs.'

When I get upstairs, Jac is sitting on the floor outside the bathroom door. She rolls her eyes with a smile as I walk towards her.

'Bathroom emergency, apparently. She's been a few minutes.'

I slide down the wall to sit next to her and stifle a giggle. 'Cheeky. I bet it's a ruse so she can stay up later.'

Finally the toilet flushes and Liv emerges, her hands still wet from the tap. 'Ready for bed?' I ask.

A smile plays on her lips as she shakes her head and runs towards the stairs.

I suppress a groan. 'Come on, Liv. It's late.'

She pulls the stair gate closed, creating a barrier across the top step. 'One game?' she asks.

Jac looks confused. 'A game?'

'Liv's invented a new game. But Liv, it's late...'

'Is it a quick game?' Jac asks.

Liv jumps up and down. 'Yes! It's so quick. The quickest game ever. Eleven seconds, but I'm going to get it down to ten today. You'll see. I run really, really fast and then—'

'OK, Liv. One game, and you can show Auntie Jac how fast you are.' I open my phone at the stopwatch app and Liv rushes to the far end of the corridor, by the bookshelf.

'Auntie Jac, I'm going to run to the gate, put both hands on it and run back to high-five Mummy in less than eleven seconds!'

'And then it's bedtime,' I say, mock-stern. I walk to her and kiss her on the forehead. She's rocking back and forth, her arms in a running stance and a very serious expression on her face.

'Ready?' I keep my voice quiet, conscious of Samuel sleeping in the next room. But he's still a newborn and can sleep through anything. 'Steady! Go!'

I hit 'start' on the stopwatch and Liv bolts along the corridor. But when she gets to the stair gate, instead of touching it with both hands like normal, she throws her whole weight against it, like a wrestler in a ring.

There's a hideous cracking sound, and the gate detaches from the wall.

Liv plunges down the stairs, screaming.

33

Liv's sobs fill the house as we wait for the ambulance, her head cradled in my lap at the bottom of the stairs. Soon Samuel's cries join hers, filtering through the closed bedroom door. But I don't move. I can't move. Liv needs me.

She's got a graze on her forehead, and some marks on her shoulder where it hit the wall on the way down. But it doesn't look like she has a head injury, and she can move. In fact, it's hard to keep her still while we wait.

'Lie still, please, baby. We need to keep you still until the paramedics arrive, in case you've hurt yourself.' I stroke her forehead.

She writhes, tears running from her eyes and into her hair. 'My arm hurts, it hurts, Mummy.' Her left arm is curled into her chest, her right arm crossed over it, holding it. The wrist hangs at an unnatural angle, her fingers turning a strange blue-white colour.

I flinch. I can't look at it. Her pain is my pain. My whole body aches for her. 'You'll be OK, baby. I'm here. And we'll get you help.'

'Make it stop, Mummy.'

Jac appears at the top of the stairs, holding Samuel. Her face is pale, her eyes dark and sunken with worry.

I give her a half-smile. 'She'll be OK,' I mouth. I don't know why I say that. I'm not a doctor. I don't know anything. But she's talking, she's conscious. She can move her extremities, so she hasn't broken her neck. That's all I know.

Jac's cheeks flush in relief. 'I'll stay here with Samuel. I'll call Jeremy. Don't worry about anything, OK?'

I nod in gratitude.

It all passes in a blur: the ambulance ride and the wait in the Sick Kids A&E department, Liv in my arms, my cheek against hers. They let me hold her and no one tries to take her away. For that I am grateful.

Everyone we see asks the same questions: Has she vomited? Any blood or fluid from her nose or ears? Did she lose consciousness?

And over and over again: how did it happen?

Once they've established she doesn't have a head injury, they leave us to wait.

Liv clings to me, her eyelids floating as she battles sleep. Midnight. This is the latest she's ever stayed up.

'You're so brave,' I whisper, while people rush past us in the waiting rooms and corridors. 'I'm so proud of you.'

'I love you, Mummy,' she mumbles with her thumb in her mouth. 'It hurts.'

I wish I could take the pain away. I wish I could feel it for her.

My phone battery sinks lower and lower. Jeremy texts to say Jac called him and he's on his way to the airport to try and get a flight. I can't parse his tone. Does he blame me? *Should* he blame me? He doesn't call, and I'm grateful for that; I want to be one hundred per cent present with Liv, and I couldn't bear to hear accusation in his tone.

Jac texts:

> Your breast milk stash went sour, right? Have to take Samuel to the 24-hour shop to pick up some formula. Not kidnapping him, promise xx

Of course. No breast milk stash. I feel a pang of guilt and gratitude for my friend.

I turn off my phone to conserve the battery, and rest my head against the wall behind my seat. I scan the waiting room posters: flu vaccinations, don't shake your baby, signs of sepsis, symptoms of type 1 diabetes in kids... a collection of horrors for me to contemplate while I wait to find out if Liv's OK.

I'm grateful it's quiet, not many other parents and kids waiting. There's one mother and her son, who looks about twelve years old. He's reading a book, and it's not clear what's wrong with him and why they're here. I'm thankful for that. So thankful that I don't have to look at a parade of sick and injured kids. Happy they're home and safe in bed.

After what feels like hours, we're called through and Liv is examined, X-rayed and given a bed. A broken wrist, that's all.

'Six weeks in a cast and she'll make a full recovery,' says a friendly nurse with a grin. 'The same can't be said for Mum,' she adds quietly.

I force a laugh that threatens to become a sob. It's too true.

'Ordinarily we'd send you home and get you to come back tomorrow to the fracture clinic. But it's so late and we have a bed, so we'll keep her here overnight. She should try to get some sleep.' She turns to Liv and puts on a sing-song voice. 'It must be past your bedtime!'

Liv gives a mischievous grin; even after everything, she's delighted to be up so late.

'Can I stay? Or do I need to go home?' The thought of

leaving my baby here alone is unbearable. I can't. I won't. I'll sleep on the grubby lino under her bed if I have to.

The nurse gestures at the chair next to Liv's bed, an upright pleather-covered armchair with wooden arms. 'Not very comfy, I'm afraid. But all our bedside cots are taken.'

I force a smile and thank her, grateful I can stay. I glance at my phone, but the screen is blank. I try to switch it on but the power button does nothing; the battery is dead.

'Call if she needs anything,' says the nurse, and swishes the curtain closed.

I glance at Liv, who's almost asleep, her thumb in her mouth and her other arm in a sling resting outside the blanket. There's a coin-sized carpet burn on her cheek. I rest a hand on her forehead as she drifts away.

My own eyes are about to float closed when the curtain is drawn back again. It's a familiar-looking woman, who must have been in the throng of faces when our ambulance first arrived at the hospital. She's in her early forties, wearing a tweed suit, with her auburn hair up in a bun. She looks like a headmistress.

'Can I have a word, please, Mrs Thorne?'

I sit up and rub my eyes. I glance at Liv, who's fast asleep.

The woman signals for me to follow her out of the cubicle. 'We're down here in one of the offices.'

Dread pools in my bones. 'What's going on?'

She leads me out into the hallway. 'We'd like to talk to you about Liv's accident. Just a few routine questions, nothing to worry about.'

I follow her click-clacking heels to an unmarked door. She pushes it open and waves me through, as if she's trying to hurry me along. It's the middle of the night and I guess she wants to get home.

The poky office smells of stale coffee. There's a plastic aspidistra in one corner, dust gathering on the leaves.

The source of the smell sits on the table in front of her: a disposable cup from a dispenser, spots of dried coffee dotting the white plastic. If I worked in this hospital, I'd bring my own coffee and mugs. I wouldn't drink that terrible stuff every day.

She stands in front of her chair and holds out a hand to shake. Her grip is weak and clammy, but her hands feel surprisingly rough and callused, like the hands of a carpenter or a gardener.

'I'm Ms Hodge.' She reaches up and smooths one side of her hair with the palm of her hand. The auburn is threaded with streaks of grey. 'From social services.' She reaches into her pocket and brings out a lanyard and flashes it at me, too fast for me to read anything on the ID.

I'm so exhausted my body feels like it's buzzing. 'I'm Miriam Thorne.' I sit down opposite her. 'Liv's mum.' I try to get her onside. 'Sorry it's so late. Were you here already or did you get called in?'

She waves the question away. 'This is fairly routine. Nothing to worry about.' Her voice is clipped. Her words are reassuring, but her tone is not. She's too serious. I wish she would smile. 'The hospital call us in when they see a child with recurrent visits, or injuries that may not tally exactly with the story of how they happened. I'm here to double-check your explanation about how Liv broke her wrist.'

My hands are shaking, I realise. My whole body is shaking. 'But I've told the nurses what happened. A friend of mine was there; she can tell you the same.' I need to breathe. I don't know whether I'm cold, tired or terrified. I lay my palms on my legs, trying to still my shivers. 'What doesn't add up? It's a straight-forward break, they said.'

She checks her notes. 'A straightforward break could be a

normal childhood accident or something more sinister. Liv's account and the injury do line up.'

I release a breath. 'So why...' I trail off when I realise what she said. 'Liv's account? It was a game. Liv told the nurses that, surely?'

The social worker takes a sip of her coffee and grimaces. Then she looks at her notes again. 'Has Liv had any other injuries lately? Anything that might lead us to consider neglect or,' she pauses, clearing her throat, 'give us cause for concern?'

My mouth turns dry. I look around the room, but there's no water dispenser. I force a swallow and close my eyes. Liv's feet, the broken glass. Her hand, the scissors.

'We have to check things out to make sure she wasn't coached to tell a story. That she wasn't pushed down the stairs, for example.'

I wish I had some water. I wish Jeremy was here. But the Jeremy I once knew is gone. My supportive, kind husband is nothing but a memory. The one I have now is trying to make me look like an unfit mother, trying to get sole custody of my children. My chest convulses with the effort of suppressing a sob. 'Can children be coached the other way too?'

My hands twitch with the urge to cover my mouth. As soon as the words come out, I wish I could take them back.

The social worker frowns, two parallel creases forming between her eyebrows. Her face is craggy, the skin freckled by years of sunshine. She looks at me but doesn't meet my eyes, her gaze resting somewhere around my right cheek. 'Coached... the other way?' she repeats, sounding dumbfounded.

'I didn't do anything to Liv. But could someone coach her to say I did? Like, perhaps someone asks a leading question and it plants something.'

She shakes her head. 'I'm sorry, Mrs Thorne. I'm not following.'

I shift in my seat, trying to redirect her away from my question. I can't let them win. I can't make myself look paranoid like this, even if my paranoia is valid.

'Let me tell you exactly what happened, from start to finish.' I lay my hands on the table, palms flat on the cold surface. I hope somehow my body language and openness will help my case. And I tell her again what I've been telling people since the paramedics arrived at our house: the game Liv and I play, the race along the landing, the stair gate.

The social worker purses her lips and sighs, her coffee breath hitting me in the face. She checks her watch. 'Look, Mrs Thorne. It's been a long night for you. And it's late. One childhood accident doesn't make you an abuser.'

I lose control and start to cry, covering my mouth and nose with my hand to stop the noise.

She slides a box of tissues across the table towards me. 'We'll consult Olivia's GP and check in with you in a few days to make sure she's recovering well. It's possible we'll have another chat with her when she's not so tired. In the meantime, no more games on the stairs.'

I blow my nose, nodding into the tissue. 'Thank you.'

The next morning, while Liv eats toast and jam and chats through the curtain to the little boy in the next bed, I wander to the overpriced M&S café and get myself a sandwich and a coffee. I feel like I've been flying long-haul, my eyes gritty and my skin slick with dried sweat. But my daughter will be OK. Just a normal childhood accident.

And my son is in good hands, looked after by Jac. She'd call if there was anything wrong. I stop in the corridor, causing the lady behind me to almost crash into my back.

'Sorry,' I mumble.

She shakes her head and strides onwards, her heels clip-clopping on the hospital lino.

I pass the nurses' desk on my way back to Liv's bed and someone lends me a phone charger, a My Little Pony sticker on the plug. I connect up my phone and it comes to life: missed calls and texts from Jeremy, Jac and my mum. I frown. How did my mum find out about this?

Liv is absorbed with the little TV mounted on a stand attached to the ceiling. She's pressing buttons on the remote and scrolling through the menu trying to get cartoons. A futile goal, as she'd need my credit card details. I don't tell her that. If there's a way to get cartoons without paying, Liv will find it.

I call the house phone. It rings and rings. Maybe Jac doesn't want to pick up the phone in our house, thinking that's overstepping. But this is the woman who just lets herself in without knocking. Where is she? And where's Samuel?

I flick to my speed dials and am about to call her mobile when the curtain scrapes back with a metallic screech.

34

'Miriam?'

I close my eyes for a moment, steeling myself. 'Hi, Mum.'

She backs into the cubicle, pulling the pram along with her. At the sight of Samuel, my whole body relaxes. I've missed my baby. I stand up and start to pick him up, ready to feed him.

Liv sits up straight in her bed. 'Grandma! You came to visit!' She holds out her sling. 'Look at my arm! It hurts. They're going to give me a cast.'

'A cast; you lucky girl.' Mum takes the chair I just stood up from and turns her attention to me. 'Where have you been? I've been worried sick. What's happening? Is Liv OK?'

'She's going to be fine, Mum. Just a broken wrist. Didn't Jac tell you? She's excited to get a cast, as you can hear.' I perch on the end of the bed. Samuel latches on with a grunt and stares up at me while he feeds. Even though I'm annoyed that Mum is here, I'm so pleased she brought Samuel.

Please smile for me. Please. But his expression stays blank. I feel a flash of desperation, of loss. And then rage at how much Jeremy has taken from me.

I take a breath. *Soon,* I tell myself. *It'll happen soon.*

I take a moment to glance between Liv and Samuel, delighted to have both my babies close. Me and them against the world.

'Grandma, I want you to sign it. No! Draw a bunny on it. A bunny wearing sunglasses.' Liv jiggles with excitement and nearly knocks over her orange squash.

'Careful.' I reach out a hand to settle her.

Mum smiles and ruffles Liv's hair. 'You've been very brave, little trooper.'

'We're waiting to go to the fracture clinic, and then I think we'll be discharged. Is Jac still at home? I'd like to have a word.'

'She had to leave, had to go to work. Jeremy called this morning, about five. He couldn't get hold of you.' She frowns at me.

'My phone was dead.'

'He's stuck in Paris: been waiting for a flight all night, and it was another couple of hours until the next one.'

I purse my lips. 'Poor Jeremy. He didn't have to come back. It was a big work meeting, I think.'

Mum murmurs in agreement. 'He sounded stressed. Give him a call, reassure him that Liv's OK. He works hard.' Something about her tone stings. As if she's implying I don't work hard, or that Jeremy's days are worth more than mine. As if our daughter's injury is an inconvenience to my high-flying husband. I wonder if she really thinks that. I wonder if Jeremy does.

I shake off my strange, sleep-deprived thoughts and tap out a text to Jac:

> Thank you so much for last night. I hope you're not too tired for work today xx

She replies straight away:

> Any time. I hope Liv's OK? Give her a kiss from her fairy godmother xx

Once Samuel has finished feeding, I hand him to Mum and leave the cubicle. I walk down the corridor and into an empty waiting area. Then I grit my teeth and call Jeremy. He answers after a couple of rings. I brace for impact.

'Thank God. Miriam, I've been calling you all night.'

He sounds... he sounds scared. There isn't the anger or the recriminatory tone I was expecting. He sounds like a worried dad stuck in an airport, not able to get home to his daughter.

'My phone died. I'm so sorry you had to come home, Jeremy. She's OK. Just a few bruises and a broken wrist. She's most excited about the cast.'

His laugh is full of relief. 'When I couldn't get hold of you, I thought... Well, you know how it goes. The imagination fills in the gaps. Jac was great, answered her phone every time I called, even in the middle of the night. It's been a nightmare trying to get back. No direct flights, and I finally got a route through Paris, but there's a strike today. Air traffic control. The whole terminal is rammed full of people sleeping on the floor.'

I sit down in a cracked pleather seat. It groans and hisses with expelled air. 'Jeez. What a mess. And you missed your meeting today?'

I can hear the exhaustion in his voice. 'I dialled in for the first part earlier this morning. They're on a break right now. Tabitha's been very understanding. She knows I'd want to be back for Liv. She encouraged me to come home when we heard what had happened.'

My stomach twists. There's so much to unpack there. I texted Jeremy as soon as I knew Liv wasn't in danger. It must have been after 11 p.m. That *when we heard* tells me he was with Tabitha. And the time difference with Lyon makes it after midnight. He was with his boss after midnight.

So of *course* she's understanding. And of *course* she encouraged him to come back. She needed him to come back and make me look like an abuser so she can take my kids. She's the one. I know it.

'Miriam? Are you there? I think my signal's gone.' I can hear the frustration in his voice, his temper short with exhaustion.

'I can hear you. I'm glad your boss is so nice.' Inside my shoes, I scrunch up my toes until they ache.

'I just want to get back to you. I can't believe I'm stuck here in this stupid airport when I could be at home with you and our kids.' He sounds upset. He's a good actor, my husband. Although I'm sure there's a grain of truth in it: he does love our kids, even though he no longer loves me. I blink away a tear. I'm so angry with him, yet so sad at the same time. Sad at how much I've lost, and how much I might still lose.

'Maybe I'll try and get the Eurostar.'

'Back to Scotland?'

He sighs in exasperation, as if I'm the one trapping him in France through my own stupidity. 'I don't know, Miriam. I can't find any information here.'

I grit my teeth and push my husband towards his lover. 'Is it worth going back to the meeting? Liv's OK, and if the strike action is twenty-four hours, then maybe...'

He's quiet on the other end of the phone, thinking.

'I can cope here. I mean it.'

He takes a sharp breath, but when he speaks, I can tell he's made a decision. His voice is already more clipped, back in work mode. 'All right, Mim. I'll see what I can do. It'll take me a couple of hours to get back, if there's a train, but I can dial in again, and then I'll be back for Tabitha's second presentation after lunch to field any questions...'

He's not talking to me, I realise. He's running it through in his mind, planning what to say to his boss. His girlfriend.

I swallow. 'We'll see you when we see you. But we're OK, Jeremy. Go to the meeting if you need to. We'll be fine and it's important you are too.' And I mean it. I still care, even after all this.

'Can I say hi to Liv before I go?' he asks, and I walk back to the cubicle and hand over the phone.

Mum stays with us for the rest of the morning, entertaining Liv with a game of snap using playing cards that have materialised from somewhere. Probably her handbag.

As much as I'm annoyed that she's here to meddle, I'm glad to have an extra pair of hands to keep Liv entertained while we wait. After what feels like hours, a nurse comes and fetches Liv, who practically skips out of the cubicle to get her cast. Mum and I exchange an amused glance.

'Thanks for being here,' I mumble. 'I know it was an early start for you.'

'Miriam, love. Anything for you.' She reaches out and puts a hand on my arm. I want to pull away. She's not a motherly type, and this caring touch is uncomfortable. Why is she being so nice? 'Why didn't you call me? I would have been here. And poor Jeremy, not knowing what was going on...'

I lean forward, ostensibly to check my phone but really to dislodge her hand from my arm. 'Do you need to head off? We've disrupted your plans.'

She grabs a cotton handkerchief from her handbag and dabs it under her nose. 'I've got a clear day, so I'm all yours.'

I shake my head. My mother never has a clear day. 'But what about your clubs and classes? I know you had to cancel something.'

'Nothing that won't keep.' She tucks the hanky into her sleeve like my grandma – her mother – used to do. And suddenly I see it: my mother is an old lady now. Yes, the dyed hair and the bright clothes and the huge social calendar are the acts of a younger woman, but the way she stuffed a cotton hanky up her sleeve was one hundred per cent old lady. I just couldn't see it until now.

Her martyr act doesn't last long. 'It was a life-drawing class with Denise. We were going to focus on light and shade today. With charcoals. You should see the abs on our model, Mim. It's not a six-pack, it's an eight-pack. Lots of shadows.' She winks at me and then gives a little sniff. 'When you work out the cost, it's eighteen pounds a lesson. Can you believe it?'

'That's expensive.' I suppress a smile. This is more like my mother, making sure I know what she's sacrificing to be here.

'Luckily Denise and I get the senior discount. But it's only ten per cent.'

'What time's the class? You might still be able to make it.' I glance at my watch. Yes, it's only 10 a.m. Time operates in strange ways when you've been up all night and ward rounds started before six o'clock.

She shakes her head, her perm bouncing. 'No, no. I promised Jeremy—' She cuts herself off.

I lean forward, the drawing class forgotten. 'You promised Jeremy what?'

She roots around in her handbag and comes out with a packet of mints. She offers me one and I take it gratefully, but keep looking at her, not letting her change the subject.

'You promised Jeremy what?' I say again, even though I know the answer.

'Well, he thought you might need help with Liv. You know, getting her home when she's discharged.' I watch as she frowns, thinking, and then her expression clears. 'I brought the car. You came in the ambulance, didn't you?' She glances pointedly at the pram and Samuel. 'Just let me help, Miriam.'

She's got a point. Getting home with two kids, one with an immobilised arm and the other in a pram, doesn't sound like an easy prospect. Whether a promise to Jeremy or not, I could use the lift.

Mum stands up and glances out of the curtains. Satisfied that no one's coming, she sits back down. 'Is everything OK with you and Jeremy? I'm sensing some tension.'

She's peering into a little round mirror, applying bright pink lip liner to the edges of her lips in tiny strokes, her mouth hanging open. She glances at me and notices I'm watching.

'Do you want some of this, Mim? You're looking awfully pale.'

I shake my head. No way can I tell her anything.

No, the person I want to tell is the one person I can't: Jeremy. My best friend. The one I chose to spend the rest of my life with. I lost him, somehow, along the way, and I can never get him back.

35

We're discharged around lunchtime, just as I run out of nappies in Samuel's changing bag. Mum drives us home at thirty miles per hour, and I leave her with Samuel in the kitchen and take Liv upstairs to attempt a nap.

On the way upstairs, I notice Jac has cleared away the broken stair gate. She's so helpful. I peek at the wall on the way past, at the drill holes where the gate once hung.

And in that moment, I get a strong flashback to the moment Liv fell. It's true what they say about time moving in slow motion when devastating events take place. I saw everything.

The pure, raw fear in Liv's eyes as her shoulders hit the barrier and didn't bounce back. The way her hands reached out, grasping at empty air. The shape of her mouth as she tried to call for me: her lips forming the 'M' of Mummy before a scream of terror overtook her.

But I also saw something else. Something almost as horrifying as the sight of my daughter falling down the stairs.

Loose screws at the hinges of the stair gate. And a red screwdriver tucked in beside the skirting board at the top of the stairs.

Someone planned this. Someone wanted Liv to get hurt.

'I fell here, didn't I, Mummy?' Liv stops walking and puts her hand against the holes. She'll dine out on this story for a long time, I can tell. 'We were playing a game and I fell down the stairs.'

It's not Jeremy. There's no way he would endanger his daughter like this. He wasn't watching through the cameras. He didn't loosen the gate. It was his mistress. She knew about the game we played, alone at home when no one else could see. She was watching.

She planned to hurt Liv.

'That's right. And you were so brave,' I say, swallowing my panic.

'I was *very* brave. I barely cried, did I? And the nurses gave me an award for being the bravest.' She holds out her arm, showing me the purple cast sleeve she chose.

'Well, you certainly deserve it.' The words emerge from my mouth without my awareness, like someone else is talking for me. Meanwhile, my eyes scan the skirting board, searching for that screwdriver. Was it really there last night? Or did I make it up?

She knocks her knuckles against the cast's hard surface, once, twice. Then she stops and stares me in the eye with a puzzled frown. 'Did you push me?' she asks.

My blood runs colder. 'What?'

'Mummy pushed me down the stairs?' she says again, the question morphing into a statement before my eyes. Was this Jeremy? Did Jeremy say this to her on the phone?

'No, Mummy didn't push you. You fell. It was an accident.' This is how kids operate, I tell myself. If I make a big fuss here, it'll cement the incident in her brain. Create a false memory. All she needs to hear right now is what really happened, and how brave she was, and it'll override whatever storytelling her brain is trying to do. I take a breath and reach down for her free hand.

'Come on, let's get you into bed for a little rest. And while you're falling asleep, I'll tell you a true story about what happened last night.'

'About Liv being brave?'

'Exactly.'

The screwdriver is gone, taken after Jac took Samuel to Mum's. Evidence removed while the house was empty. She's been in our home.

Ten minutes later, I finally have a chance to lie down, leaving Mum downstairs with Samuel while I try to rest in bed. But my brain won't stop whirring, replaying the incident over and over again: the expression on Liv's face as she fell – betrayal and shock. The grasping of her hands. Her crumpled body at the bottom of the stairs. The odd angle of her wrist.

I text Jac:

> It wasn't an accident. Someone loosened the screws on the stair gate.

Every time I nearly fall asleep, my brain jolts me awake with a new horror. What if Liv injured her head and we don't know yet? Some kind of delayed-onset injury. What about internal bleeding? Why didn't they X-ray her whole body, just in case?

Eventually I give up on sleep and flick through my phone, enjoying the knowledge that Liv is safe in bed and Samuel's safe with Mum.

As I scroll through stories on Instagram, my phone buzzes with an incoming email. Zain. I click on it, my breath catching in my throat as I see the subject line: *Over and out.*

I pull myself up to a sitting position and open it.

Hi Mim,

Sorry it's taken me a while to get back to you after I came over. I've been thinking about my visit and everything going on with you. You've been under so much stress lately and all the smart tech can't be helping your paranoia.

I keep thinking back to the pile of pillows and blankets I saw next to your bed. And your panic attack when I said there were no cameras (a bad joke, and I'm still very sorry). It's been niggling at me for days, because I don't think those things are the behaviour of someone who's doing well mentally.

I hope you don't mind, but I talked to Nicole and she agrees with me. I'm not going to try and hack this system to find out who's doing it (I don't think my tech skills are good enough anyway, tbh). I think what you should do is let it go, disconnect as much as you can and get some help – a therapist or something. Whatever is going on in your life, hacking this won't fix it. But a mental health professional and a lawyer might.

All my love,

Zain xx

I splutter. A mental health professional and a lawyer. What a joke.

I thought Zain was my friend. I thought he believed me.

I flop back and let my phone fall from my hand onto the quilt. I'm so tired. Tired from my all-nighter at the hospital, yes, but also tired of fighting against an invisible force that seems to always be one step ahead of me.

A mental health professional would take one look at my history and commit me. They wouldn't believe me for one second. I'd be back in the Hermitage before you could say 'Jeremy's new girlfriend'.

And a lawyer. Well, for one thing I'm an art therapist on maternity leave. No. I catch myself. I'm a former art therapist and now unemployed. I can't afford to hire a lawyer.

They knew this. Jeremy and his girlfriend. When they sent me to the Hermitage and took my job away. They were disarming me before combat. I've been on the back foot right from the start, with no way to defend myself.

What would a strategic thinker do now? For the first time in my life, I wish I was a chess player. I wish I could look at a game board and see several moves ahead. But my brain has never worked like that. Not like Jeremy's.

Should I be playing him at his own game? Setting traps to make him look like the unfit parent? He's never here; surely that counts during a custody battle?

I pick up my phone to google something, but what? *How to frame your husband?* And if he's as good with technology as it seems, maybe he'll find my search history and use it against me. I put my phone down. There. Good. Thinking ahead, predicting his next steps. I'm learning.

From downstairs, I hear the trill of the doorbell.

I pause, listening to my mother's shuffling steps and the click of the front door as it opens. Probably an Amazon parcel.

But then I hear the hum of voices, my mother's getting louder and more insistent.

I sit up in bed.

'You can't do that,' I hear her say. She sounds terrified.

I push back the covers and run into the hallway, pausing at the top of the stairs, where I can see the front door.

It's the woman from last night, Ms Hodge. She's wearing the same clothes, her auburn hair still up in its neat bun.

She's stepping into the house, but my mother bars her way. 'You can't come in. Don't you need a warrant or something?'

Mum looks wild-eyed and panicked in a way I haven't seen before. 'Show me your ID. You could be anyone.'

Behind her, Ms Hodge looks calm and resigned. Like she does this every day.

'Mum, what are you doing? This is the lady from social services.' I rush down the stairs, trying to stop whatever is happening. We need to make a good impression. 'Just let her in, you can't—'

'She's here to take the children, Miriam. She says she's taking them into protective custody. Jeremy called her.'

My legs fold under me, and my hand grips the banister, just stopping me from plummeting down the stairs. 'What?' I whisper.

'But she hasn't done anything.' Mum's tone is shrill. 'It was an accident, for God's sake. This isn't normal. This isn't how it's done. There are real monsters out there, hurting their children. Go and find *them*, don't fuss around with my Miriam. She doesn't hurt them. They're happy, fed and warm and loved. She's a good mum, damn you.' Tears trickle down her cheeks, wearing grooves in her foundation. She swipes them away with the back of her hand.

Over Mum's shoulder, the social worker gives a tight-lipped smile. 'It's a precaution while we investigate the incident. They'll be placed with a foster family overnight, and in ordinary circumstances they'll be back with you within a day or two.'

I wish I could cry, like Mum. But I'm frozen in shock. 'Ordinary circumstances,' I mumble. 'These aren't ordinary circum—'

'If you can pack a bag for both of your children, please, Mrs Thorne. Include any comfort items you think will help the transition. Favourite teddies, familiar blankets. Milk and nappies for the baby. You want them to be comfortable, don't you?'

I sit on the stairs, the treads digging into my spine. 'Both of them,' I repeat in a monotone. I can't function. My brain is frozen. 'You can't. Please.'

I want my children. I need them in my arms.

'What about Christmas? It's three days away.'

She shakes her head, non-committal. Samuel's first Christmas.

I've just got them back. I've just learned how to be their mother, two at once.

I love them. Both of them.

And now they're being taken away.

36

'Mummy, why are you crying?'

Liv sits up in bed, her face wrinkled from her pillow. She was fast asleep when I came in, but the social worker said I had to wake her, that they had to leave soon.

I have fifteen minutes to pack for them.

I sniff hard and force a smile. 'Just a runny nose, Liv. Not crying.'

'What are you doing?' She climbs out of bed and comes to stand beside me, peering into the suitcase, where so far I've stacked underwear, pyjamas and her bunny. 'Is it time for a holiday? Did you find my purple top?'

Inside I'm falling apart; outside I'm holding it together for my babies. My feelings aren't important. They need to feel safe and they need their stuff, wherever they're going. 'That's right, it's time for a holiday. You and Samuel are going on a holiday. But not for long; you'll be home with Mummy really soon.'

She reaches into the suitcase and pulls out her bunny. 'And Daddy, too?'

I can't answer, so I nod and gently remove the bunny from her arms, sliding it back into the case.

'I don't want to go.' Her lower lip trembles.

I drop to my knees next to her and reach over to her bedside table, pulling open the drawer. 'Do you remember when Samuel was born and I gave you a present?'

She shakes her head, but a smile plays on her lips. 'I like presents.'

'I know you do.' I pull the little box from her drawer and open it, showing her.

She leans over, her hair brushing the silver heart bracelet. I stroke her hair and tuck it behind one ear. Then I take the bracelet from the box with shaking fingers. 'You see how this heart fits into my bracelet?' I show her again how her charm fits into the one around my wrist, interlocking. I've worn it every day since I gave it to her, as I said I would.

'One for Mummy and one for me?' she asks, doing a little jig of happiness.

I smile and blink back a tear. 'That's right.'

She holds out her chubby wrist – the one without the cast – and I fasten the catch. She waves her arm around, admiring the way the silver glints in the light.

'Wear it every day, and I'll wear mine. Wrap your hand around it when you want a hug from Mummy, OK?'

She clutches her wrist and then steps forward to give me a proper hug, melting into my arms as if she knows what's happening.

I can't watch as they're led away down the path to the social worker's car. Away from me.

This has to be a mistake.

37

I hear Jeremy arrive home later that day, but I don't move from our bed, the curtains drawn against the low winter sun. Mum left long ago, after I screamed at her that I needed to be alone. That she'd fulfilled her promise to Jeremy and not left me on my own with the kids. That she should get lost. Then I burst into incoherent tears. Mum's whole face shut down, and she backed out of the room, hands raised like a shield.

'Hello?' Jeremy calls from the entryway. 'Anyone home?' His voice echoes through the empty house.

I can't pretend any more. I can't act the perfect wife, and the option to be the perfect mother has been wrenched from me. All I feel inside is hate.

I bury my face in my pillow and scream myself hoarse.

'Miriam, what's going on?' Jeremy's voice comes from the doorway.

I don't look up. I don't move. What's the point? As if viewing us from a distance, a part of my brain wonders if I could murder him. If I'm capable of it. I imagine picking up a knife from the block in the kitchen and driving it into his chest, between his ribs. I experience a surge of adrenaline just thinking about it. Wounding this man who has hurt me so much, who has taken away the most important things in my life. Who has schemed against me and set traps for me. Yes, I think as I lie unmoving on our bed. I could stab him to death very easily.

The bed sinks at one side as he sits down and lays a hand on my back.

I recoil, backing away until I'm as far away from him as I can get while still on the bed. I sit up and wrap the quilt around my shoulders like a layer of protection.

'Are you ill?' he asks, sounding concerned. Again I'm struck by how good an actor he is. How guileless I would find him if I didn't know better.

I glance at him, ready to look away if the urge to hurt him takes over. He looks tired. His brow is clear, his eyes open and untroubled. He looks like a husband and father who just flew across Europe to get home to his family. He doesn't look like a scheming sociopath who's plotting with his mistress to over-throw his wife; even through my fury I can see that much. He looks... worried. My resolve wavers. *What if I'm wrong?*

He loosens his tie. 'Where are the kids? Out with your mum?'

I scoff. That's too far. Too much. There's acting and then there's taking the piss. 'Are you kidding me?' I ask, sarcasm drip-ping from every syllable.

He frowns, his tie halfway over his head. 'What?'

'I've had enough of your games, Jeremy.'

He pulls the tie free and picks at the knot, loosening it with his fingers, his gaze not moving from me. He breaks eye contact first. 'I'm sorry I called your mum. I know you don't like her being involved. I just...' He takes a shaky breath. *Give this man an Oscar.* 'When I couldn't get hold of you and your phone was off, I panicked. I need you to know what that was like for me,

Miriam. Getting Jac's message that there'd been an accident and then getting your voicemail over and over for hours while you were at the hospital. That wasn't nice. I need you to think about me.'

'You need me to think about you?' I repeat, my voice robotic. I say it again. And again. '*You* need me to think about you?' And again, until I'm shouting it.

Jeremy stands up, leans over the bed and puts his hands on my shoulders, weighing me down. 'What's going on, Miriam? Where are the kids?'

I flinch at the weight of him. His sheer physical presence. He's a strong man who could hurt me if he wanted to. I remember Katy's words, talking about the relationship that triggered her issues: *the scary thing was already inside my house – I had invited him in.*

I try to shake him off, but his hands won't budge. I stare at him, unblinking. 'You think you deserve to know?'

His face pales. For the first time, he looks afraid. 'What have you done with them?' he whispers.

I laugh in his face. 'What, do you think I did something insane? Do you think I've become a self-fulfilling prophecy? That your plan to take them from me has gone awry somehow?'

He releases my shoulders and I almost fall backwards off the bed. He opens and closes his mouth, like a fish.

'Yes, I know about your plan. You and your girlfriend, trying to take everything. Was the social worker part of it, or have you hit a little bump in the road on your journey to happy families?'

His hands shake as he pulls his phone from his pocket. 'What plan, Miriam? I don't know what you're talking about. What girlfriend? Just tell me where the children are, please.' He unlocks his phone and opens up the keypad, presses nine three times. His finger hovers over the call button, but he doesn't press it. It's a bluff. It's always a bluff with Jeremy.

For a moment, my resolve wavers again. *What if it's not*

true? What if there are no cameras, no girlfriend, no plan to take the kids? If this is my imagination, to Jeremy I must look like a madwoman. A woman who left the kids in the car on a hot day, or drowned them in the bath.

But then I see his finger still hovering over the call button. He hasn't pressed it. If he believed I'd harmed the kids, if he really doesn't know where they are, he would have pressed that button already. Because he does love our kids, even if he doesn't love me any more. And he wants them to be safe.

'I know everything, Jeremy,' I say in as calm a voice as I can muster, watching his face.

He shakes his head, looking at me warily like I'm a crazed animal.

'Was it your idea, or your girlfriend's?'

He shakes his head. 'What are you talking about?'

I groan in frustration. 'Stop! Stop pretending you don't know. You sent me away to that fancy hospital because you needed me out of the way. So you could—'

'I booked you into the Hermitage so you could recover from Samuel's birth. Because I was worried you might get post-natal psychosis again. Because my new health insurance covered it and I wanted to do everything I could to help you be OK. So I could go back to work and earn money to support our family.'

'To *dismantle* our family.'

'I love our family.'

I shake my head. 'You love our kids. That's different.'

He puts his head in his hands. 'I do love you, Miriam. But I don't know who you are right now. What is happening? Where are Liv and Samuel?'

'They're safe, Jeremy. Exactly where you expected them to be when you called social services.'

He stares at me. 'I haven't called social services. The only people I've spoken to in the last twenty-four hours outside work are you, Jac and your mum. Your mum was supposed to be here, giving you a hand with the kids. What's going on?'

He looks so haggard, so lost, that I believe him. I believe he didn't call social services. I don't trust anything else he says, but on this he's telling the truth. Can I trust him again one day? Could we return to where we were before all this?

I rub my hands over my face, feeling the scrape of my palms against my skin. 'Something was flagged at the hospital, with Liv's accident. They said it looked suspicious, or she said something... I don't know. They interviewed me about what happened. And then, after Mum and I came home, they turned up on the doorstep and said you'd called them, that they were taking the kids into protective custody.' I swallow a sob. 'That I had hurt Liv. But it wasn't me, it—'

'But Jac was here when she fell. She could confirm it was an accident.'

I nod. He believes me. He knows I wouldn't hurt them.

He straightens up from his hunched position on the bed, squaring his shoulders. He reaches for my hand and I don't pull away. 'This doesn't sound right, Miriam. That isn't how it works.'

My body turns to stone. If anyone would know social workers, it's Jeremy. Bounced around foster homes as a teenager after his mum's breakdown. Caring for his little brother. He's been one of those kids, interviewed about incidents. Just like Liv was.

'There's a massive load of procedures involved – police, court orders, referrals, investigations. They don't just take kids away from their parents.' He pauses, thinking. 'You said she turned up at the hospital in the middle of the night? To ask you questions about Liv?'

I nod.

'Was anyone else there? Any nurses, any other social workers?'

'No.' My voice is a whisper.

'Did she show you ID?'

'Yeah, she had a badge thing.'

'Did you look at it? Did you read it properly?'

'I don't...' I screw up my face, trying to remember.

'Miriam.' He lets go of my hand and grips both of my shoulders. 'Think.'

I swallow back tears. 'I didn't look at her ID properly. It looked like the local council colours, but it could have said anything.'

'And what did she ask you? Did she have Liv's medical records? Her X-rays?'

I'm frozen in place, trying to remember. 'She had notes, but no X-rays. She didn't...' I shake my head, at a loss. I can't remember anything she said. She let me talk, make my assumptions. *Oh my God.* I walked right into the trap. 'She asked questions. I told her about Liv's fall. She didn't seem to know much, but I assumed she hadn't had time to read the file because she'd been called to the hospital so late.'

'Social workers don't take kids away because of an accident like that. Not unless there are injuries that can't be explained by the incident. I don't even think they come to hospitals any more. Especially not in the middle of the night.' He puts a hand over his mouth and looks like he's trying not to be sick.

He pulls me into his arms and holds me tight. I sink into him, my brain on overdrive. 'It's OK. It's not your fault. You're a victim of a crime.' It sounds like he's trying to convince himself rather than me. Or maybe he's rehearsed this speech.

After all this, I wonder if he's still acting, if he's still pretending he loves me. But even the world's best actor couldn't keep this up. And why send a fake social worker and then tell me it's a fake? Will he blame me for this, too? I'm so bad at thinking two moves ahead, and I can't work this out.

Then he does the thing that surprises me the most: he looks

at his phone again and presses the call button. Almost immediately I hear a voice on the other end of the line:

'Nine nine nine, what's your emergency?'

He clears his throat. 'Police, please. My children have been kidnapped.'

38

I sit frozen on the sofa while Jeremy talks to the police officers, who arrived with blue lights and sirens just minutes after his call. I can't move, can't speak.

The two officers take our statements. They talk into their radios a lot, relaying information to colleagues across the area and at the station. They ask for a recent photograph of the children, and a physical description. Distinguishing features. If they take any medication or have any medical conditions.

Jeremy tells them the basics, then clears his throat and looks to me for help.

'Liv's cast is purple, on her left wrist. On her other wrist she's wearing a bracelet. The opposite of this.' I hold out my own wrist to show the charm, and then wrap my hand around it, hoping that somehow Liv will feel it.

Jeremy describes Samuel next.

I rock back and forth, hugging myself. I can't stop shaking.

'A freckle,' I croak. 'He has a small freckle on his lower back.' I close my eyes and pray to whatever power might exist that no one will ever find that freckle except me. 'And he's wearing a light blue onesie with a pattern on it. Animals. Lions, giraffes and stuff.' My speech slurs as if I'm drunk.

My babies. Someone has taken my babies.

One of the police officers speaks but I can't understand what she says. It's like we're underwater, liquid stopping up my ears.

'Miriam.' Jeremy shakes me by the shoulder, his eyes pleading with me. 'You need to describe the woman who took them. What did she look like? Did you see her car?'

I mumble about red hair and a tweed suit. 'She said she was a social worker. Does this happen? People impersonating social workers to steal children?' It sounds so far-fetched to me, the stuff of cheap Netflix thrillers.

The younger officer shrugs, but the older one raises her eyebrows in recognition.

'It has happened?'

She nods. 'There were some reports in the nineties. People attempting to abduct children from their parents.'

A shudder racks my body.

'Police forces looked into it – including Lothian and Borders – but they couldn't find any real cases or victims. Operation Childcare, I think it was called. In the end, they said it was all made up. Media panic.'

Jeremy leans forward. 'But now it has happened. Our children have been kidnapped.'

'I'll pass on your descriptions. All available officers will attend the area to look for the children.'

I shake my head. 'Why don't you show them the camera footage, Jeremy?'

A frown crosses his brow.

Sitting next to each other on the sofa across the room, the police officers exchange a glance. The older officer makes a note in her little notebook. On her shoulder, her radio beeps and crackles and she mutters into it then looks up at us.

The other one leans forward. 'You have security cameras?'

'We have cameras everywhere. It's a smart house,' I say.

But Jeremy talks over me. 'No, we don't have any cameras.' He leans into me, his shoulder pressing against mine. 'What are you talking about?'

I shift away from him, clasping my hands together to stop them shaking, and glance up into the corner of the room. Where a red LED once blinked at me, there's now an empty space. The camera is gone. *What...?*

I stand up and walk into the hallway. That one is gone, too.

I run up the stairs. The books sit at an odd angle, tilted into each other where they used to shelter the little lens that watched as Liv tumbled down the stairs. Empty.

'Miriam?' Jeremy stands at the bottom of the stairs, his hand on the banister as he looks up.

I lean over the banister. 'They're gone.'

He looks into the living room. 'Sorry about this. My wife's... Well, this is a very stressful situation.'

'No,' I say out loud. 'Don't apologise for me.' The tiny, burgeoning kernel of affection and trust disappears in a *poof*. I feel a rumble of fury deep in my stomach and swear under my breath. I'm not going to let him do this. He's been screwing with my life for so long, and I can't let him make me look insane to these police officers. I run down the stairs, my feet pounding on the treads. 'Don't you dare, Jeremy.'

I stride past him and into the living room, my mind sharp with fury. I stand in front of the fireplace and address the officers. 'Until yesterday, there were cameras in almost every room in this house. Every single movement I made was recorded.' I point at the corner of the room. 'Even the smoke alarms were smart. And the fridge. The boiler. Everything was wired and monitored and watching. There was a camera up there. You can see the hole where the wire was hidden. But they've all been removed.'

I turn to Jeremy, who's standing in the doorway, his mouth agape. He looks at me as if I've really lost it. 'Miriam, that's not... We don't have any cameras.'

My voice grows shrill. 'We don't *now*, no. You've taken them all away.'

The police officers stand up, the older one tucking her notebook into her pocket. They talk to Jeremy and ignore me. 'We need to search the house anyway, to look for anything that might help us find your children. Perhaps your wife can show us where she thinks the cameras were.' She smiles at me, her expression bland. Her tone is placatory. She's humouring me.

Jeremy shrugs and waves them out of the living room and towards the kitchen. He's removed the evidence. The cameras are gone. I bet the fridge's smart plug has been replaced, the boiler back to normal. Was that what he was doing when I thought he was stuck in an airport in Paris? He knew the house was empty – he would have seen on the cameras that Jac had left with Samuel and I was at the hospital. Did he come to the house instead of straight to the hospital to check on the welfare of his injured daughter? Did his lover come too, to make sure no one knew she'd tampered with the stairgate? Does he know she injured Liv on purpose?

He leads them through every room, and I hover in the doorway, scanning for evidence of the surveillance. But there's nothing. It's all gone. They open Liv's drawers, push her underwear aside. They peer into her toy box and look under her bed. They take her hairbrush, sliding it into an evidence bag to preserve her DNA.

In our room, they lift the blankets up from the side of the bed, glancing at Jeremy with a puzzled look on their faces. My nest. My attempt to protect myself from him, which has made me look even more unhinged. He's attacked me from every angle. Removed everything I ever cared about.

Eventually they head to the front door and shake hands

with Jeremy. A family liaison officer is on their way, apparently. And scenes-of-crime investigators, to look for that woman's fingerprints.

'We've got enough to start preliminary searches. We'll contact your family and friends and Olivia's school, and put out an alert on social media.' The officer glances at me, one eyebrow up to show her concern. 'I'd call your GP, see if you can get something to help with the stress.'

Jeremy opens the front door, and that's when I remember: another police officer standing on the doorstep, peering into the house. The smell of burned toast.

I gasp in recognition.

They all turn to look at me, with expressions of indulgence: give the madwoman a moment of your time so you don't set her off again. I can see it on their faces.

I shake my head. 'There *were* cameras. The house was full of surveillance devices. And there's proof. You can check your records.' I tell them about the day the smoke alarm went off, the special constable who came to the door and explained to me about the guard mode system and the setting that alerted the emergency services.

Jeremy stares at me as I talk, shaking his head. 'Miriam, we've never had that kind of technology. It's not something I would...' His voice fades and he rubs his head with his hand. 'We'll call the GP, officer. Thank you for your time.'

I step forward and touch the officer's sleeve, make her meet my eye. 'Please check it on your system if you can. I'm telling the truth.'

She holds my gaze and then looks away, making a note in her book. 'I'll have a look, Mrs Thorne. But I'm sure you'll agree our priority is to find your children.'

Then Jeremy closes the door and we are alone.

39

As soon as he closes the door behind the police officers, Jeremy whirls around to face me. His eyes are dark with anger.

I step away, until my back touches the wall.

He leans in, his face a snarl. 'Where are they, Miriam? What have you done with them?'

I flinch and try to move away, but there's nowhere to go. I'm pinned. He isn't touching me, but his body is a barrier. I reach up and place a hand on his chest, trying to push him away. As I feel the warmth of his skin through his shirt, I remember how long it's been since I've touched him. How long it's been since *he* touched *me*. And something inside me breaks.

'No, Jeremy. You don't get to do this again. Enough.'

He blinks and snaps out of it, stepping back to give me space. 'What?'

I move forward, trying to get to the kitchen, the living room, anywhere.

But he holds a hand out to stop me. 'I don't get to do what again?'

I look up at him, aware of his physical strength, his quivering muscles, the slick of sweat on his upper lip. I frown, shake my head once. I have nothing left to lose. I ball my hands into fists.

'Since Samuel was born, you've dismissed me over and over again: you told me the baby monitor wasn't hacked but then you got rid of it anyway. You knew I would struggle with a new baby, but instead of helping me, you—'

'I did help you! I got—'

'You sent me away to a mental hospital.'

'A retreat.'

I shake my head, not bothering to address the semantics. 'And you'd been planning that for weeks. Where was the planning when I was pregnant? When we first brought Samuel home? We could have talked it through together. You could have asked me what I needed instead of insisting on stupid deals that let you spy on me. You left me to flounder alone. You don't listen, you don't believe me, you blame me for what goes wrong and then you make decisions without me. So *of course* when that woman turned up here and told me you'd called social services, I believed it. I let them take the kids because it fits with everything else you've done to me.'

He's quiet for a moment, his shoulders rising and falling with his breath. He closes his eyes, then opens them slowly and looks at me. His voice vibrates with suppressed emotion. 'So you're saying it's my fault the kids are gone.'

I groan in frustration and turn away.

He reaches for my arm and pulls me back. 'There's no time for this, Miriam. If our kids are somewhere and we can save them, I need to—'

'If we can save them? If they're *somewhere*?' I pause, wheels turning in my brain. Then I realise what he's implying, what he believes I'm capable of. 'Jeremy, I wouldn't hurt our children. How could you—'

He rears back in frustration. 'I don't know you, Miriam,' he roars. 'I don't know who you are, what's going on in your head, what you might be capable of.'

'You know exactly who I am, you're just choosing not to see me. I love our kids.'

'I believe that. But you're mentally ill.'

'No I'm not!' I sink to the floor in despair.

He looks down at me. 'That's what you said last time, too. You had no idea how ill you were until you were given treatment. Until you were better. You said it yourself at the time. That even with medication and therapy, it was months until you could look back and see you weren't OK.' He brushes a tear away with a fist. 'You told me you didn't want Liv any more, don't you remember? You convinced yourself she'd be better off without you.'

I wrap my arms around my knees and hug them to my chest, rocking back and forth on the wooden floor. 'That was a different time, Jeremy. I was different then. I admit I was ill when Liv was a baby. I did think those things. But I don't now. I love our kids and would do anything for them. You'd know that if you just talked to me, even once.'

He hunches over, his hands on his thighs, wheezing, as if just thinking about this causes the breath to leave his body. 'I don't know, Miriam. I don't know how to believe you.' He sits down on the floor opposite me, his back to the wall. Even when he turns his head away, his eyes don't leave mine. Watching for my reaction. 'Some people... some ill people can convince themselves that no matter how much they love their kids, for some reason their kids need to leave this world. To go to a better place. And that somehow they're doing that *for* their kids.'

My stomach contracts. 'Doing what?'

He leans forward, as if he's going to be sick. For a moment I imagine what we'd look like on one of those cameras: two adults balled up on the floor, facing each other across the hallway. Two exhausted fighters in a ring, too tired to get up for the next bout.

'They think they're doing *what* for their kids, Jeremy?' I ask again.

He doesn't say anything, just shakes his head.

I bang my head against the wall behind me, just to feel something. My husband thinks I could murder our children. 'Jeremy, I—'

He holds out a hand to stop me. 'I never wanted to believe you would do that, Miriam. I know you love them. But you were so secretive that first time. You pretended you were fine. I didn't know you were having mental health issues until it was too late, until you were broken. I felt so useless that I hadn't noticed, that I couldn't help. So this time I didn't want to give you the chance to keep secrets, to pretend to be fine. This time I wanted to treat you as if you'd already said it.'

I frown, not understanding. 'Said what?'

He clears his throat. 'That they would be better off somewhere else. Without you.'

I close my mouth, tuck my chin into my knees. If I could disappear into nothingness, I would. Because I did say that, then, when Liv was a baby. I think back to that day, the day I walked away from the pram in the park. The day no one knows about except me and Dr Okeke. I look up at Jeremy. 'You think me capable of that? Of hurting them?'

He shakes his head. 'Not you, not the Miriam I know. The Miriam I love. The healthy, happy Miriam. But honestly, I doubt you can remember that time. How it was, those first weeks of Liv's life. You weren't... you.'

'But I'm me now.'

He nods. 'I thought this time was better,' he says, his voice hardening once more.

'Thought?' Past tense.

He gestures around the empty hallway. 'Where are our kids, Miriam?'

I stand up, the moment shattered, any progress undone.

He's not my husband any more. He hasn't cared for me, hasn't loved me the way I deserve. And even when presented with the evidence, he refuses to see it.

I turn towards the kitchen. 'You tell me, Jeremy,' I yell over my shoulder as I walk away. 'You did this.'

40

For the next couple of hours, our front door barely closes for more than a minute. As promised, Ann, the family liaison officer, arrives and traps us in the kitchen with endless cups of tea while the scenes-of-crime team scour the house for forensic evidence of the kidnapper everyone believes I've invented or imagined.

Ann is kind and no-nonsense, in a maternal sort of way. I wish I knew her in another world, another life, so I could laugh at her tame jokes and ask her about her life outside work.

Jeremy and I don't look at each other, don't speak except to answer the FLO's questions. Something between us has fractured.

Ann tells us what's happening outside our four walls. 'The attending police officers have gone back to the station for a case conference, where the senior investigating officer presents to the inspectors, sergeants and CID. They'll give out jobs for the next steps in trying to find Liv and Samuel.'

Her voice is soothing and calm, even though nothing could be a balm to my spiky soul right now.

Jeremy nods, his eyes unfocused, his face pale.

'Meanwhile, all available officers are scouring your little corner of the city. Even traffic officers, dog handlers and special constables. Everyone's looking for your kiddies.'

I remember that young woman who turned up on our doorstep to respond to the alert about the smoke alarm. I wonder if she's out there searching.

'And the Passport Office, Interpol, the National Border Targeting Centre... they'll all be alerted.'

My stomach twists. I hadn't even processed the idea that someone could take them out of the country, even when the police asked about their passports.

'We'll find them,' she murmurs, slopping milk into three mugs. 'If they're out there, we'll find them.'

She settles in our kitchen armchair and drinks her tea, tapping her feet on the tiled floor. I wish I was her. I wish I was anyone but me.

Jeremy wanders off. I hear him opening and closing doors upstairs. Assessing the damage done by the search and the scenes-of-crime team.

I stay on my stool, thighs turning numb while I call everyone I know, begging those who answer to look everywhere and help in any way they can think of. I don't touch my tea.

The doorbell rings again, but from my seat in the kitchen I hear no movement. Jeremy isn't going to answer it. We're both paralysed with pain, fear and frustration. And distrust of each other.

But it might be some news. Our children might be on the doorstep somehow.

Ann starts to stand up, but I shake my head. 'I'll get it.'

When I open the door, Zain rushes at me, arms wide. 'Oh my God, Miriam. Oh my God.'

I let him hold me, but I don't wrap my arms around him. I can't. I asked for his help and he wouldn't give it.

'I'm so sorry,' he mutters into my hair. 'I should have been there for you. But I talked to Nicole and—'

I step away from him. 'And what? A therapist and a lawyer, I think that was what you decided I needed?' I can't keep the bitterness out of my voice. 'Will *they* find my kids?'

His cheeks flush and he breaks eye contact. 'I got it so, so wrong. Please, let me help now. What's going on? What's happened?' He's breathless with panic. I know he's imagining how he'd feel if it were his own child who was missing. That's what I would be doing too, were our roles reversed. And weirdly, it would feel more real to me if it was someone else's kids. This kind of thing is so horrific, so abnormal; it doesn't happen to me or the people I know. It happens to people on the news, in stories and films. Not to me, Miriam Thorne. Never like this. Never my children.

'I keep thinking it must be a mistake,' I mumble, almost to myself. 'That they're just upstairs, Liv playing with her horses and Samuel batting something colourful hanging above him. Or she was a real social worker after all, and the police checks and follow-ups just... missed her. And they're safe.' I'm desperate to find a kernel of hope to cling to, no matter how minuscule.

Still standing in the hallway, I tell Zain about Liv's accident, the social worker, the home visit to take away the kids, and then Jeremy's revelation that it doesn't work like that. The social worker was an impostor. Tears of self-blame and remorse roll down my cheeks as I sink to the stairs. I tell him I didn't check the ID properly, that a sleepless night and panic combined to make me careless.

Zain sits down on the floor, his back to the wall. Almost exactly where Jeremy sat just a couple of hours before.

None of this would have happened if my husband had been here for me, I want to say. But I don't.

'What can I do, Mim?' he asks, shaking his head. 'Anything.'
'I need you to talk to Jeremy.'

Jeremy sits on the sofa in the living room, his leg pulsing and his face haggard with exhaustion and worry. He's still wearing the shirt he wore for his work meeting, what feels like days ago. It's crumpled now, and the material under the arms is grey rather than white.

I feel nothing when I look at him.

Zain clears his throat and leans forward in the armchair, resting his forearms on his thighs. 'When you were away, Miriam asked me to come over and insisted we sit in the garden. She felt someone might overhear our conversations if we talked in the house. She thought you were controlling everything remotely: the heating, the alarms, the cameras. Trying to make her look crazy.' His cheeks flush. 'We cut the power to the house and then I scoped the whole place while the cameras weren't recording.'

I hear Ann in the kitchen, talking on the phone. Her voice is low. She's reporting back to the station, telling them the information we've given her since she arrived. And anything else she's observed, no doubt. I wonder what she thinks of us. If she believes us.

Jeremy shakes his head sceptically. He doesn't look up from staring at the rug. 'You should have called me, mate. I needed to know she was heading down this road again.' His voice is flat, disinterested. He's given up on me. He's not hearing anything that will lead him to the kids, so he's just waiting. Waiting for news. For information.

Zain leans even further forward, interlocking his fingers like he's saying a prayer. 'That's the thing, though, *mate*. She was telling the truth. I saw the cameras.' He pauses, giving Jeremy a moment to process.

Slowly, Jeremy focuses his gaze. His eyes flick up to Zain, and then to me. His mouth opens, then closes again. 'You saw what? We don't have any cameras. No security system. No smart boiler, or whatever Miriam told you about. It's all in her head.'

'No, Jeremy.' Zain's tone is icy. 'It was very real.'

I can't help it. I start to cry. *It was very real.* Great big hacking sobs that wrench the air from my lungs.

Zain reaches over and places a hand on my quivering back. 'You weren't imagining it,' he says.

I wish I could record him so I could play his words over and over and prove it to everyone.

Jeremy shakes his head, an almost imperceptible quiver. 'How...' He stops, frowning, and looks around the room, his eyes scanning the cornicing, the bookshelf. I can tell he's beginning to believe Zain like he never believed me. 'I never set up any cameras. I threw away the Wi-Fi baby monitor. Miriam was right, it was a creepy thing.'

I dig my nails into my palms. *Miriam was right.* Why couldn't he have said that sooner?

Zain looks at him. 'You weren't watching her? Playing cruel tricks on her while you were away?'

He shakes his head, his expression open and baffled.

Zain raps his fingertips on his kneecaps. 'Well, someone was. Someone was spying on Miriam and your kids. They came into your home. They were watching your family.'

I take a shaky breath. 'There were at least seven cameras in the house, Jeremy. And now they're gone.'

Jeremy folds his arms, hunching his shoulders, still not ready to change his view of the world, of me. 'Why, though? What did they want? How did they get in?'

I wipe the tears from my face with my T-shirt. 'Fine, Jeremy. Maybe you didn't set up the cameras. Maybe this wasn't *your* plan. But you know who masterminded it. You wanted to discredit me, to take the children away. Haven't you done that? Isn't it enough now? I don't even know why you're pretending to be worried. She's got the kids, clearly. And whatever footage she needed. So go to her. Just tell me where they are.'

He shakes his head violently. 'Who are you talking about? I don't know anything.'

I groan in frustration. 'Stop this. I saw her Reddit post.'

'Whose post? Seriously, Miriam—'

'Enough, Jeremy. It's your turn to listen.' Something in my voice silences him at last, and I tell him about the Reddit post and the abusive messages that bombarded me for weeks.

He stands up. 'Let me see it.'

I call Katy on WhatsApp and watch the happy smile slide from her face as I tell her what's happened since we parted ways. Behind her is a bookshelf, spines arranged into a rainbow of colour. She must be back home now, her stay in the Hermitage over.

She listens, her mouth set in a hard line, her eyes anguished. 'I'm so sorry, Miriam. Whatever I can do...'

I introduce her to Zain so they can collaborate in their technological detective work, and then I ask her to find the Reddit post again. She nods once and gives a little wave as she hangs up.

Jeremy walks to the window, gazing out onto the street. Drops of rain dot the window pane.

Within moments, my phone chirps with a link, which I forward to Zain's email. A text message follows it:

> I'll keep poking around online, see if I can find anything else. Text me if I can help. xx

Zain leans down to pull his laptop from his bag and opens it. Then he clears his throat and hands the laptop to Jeremy, who pores over the screen, his body tense and still. After a minute, he shudders and reads aloud the words that have haunted me since I first heard them in that poky little computer room at the Hermitage:

"'I've been waiting so long to get them away from their abusive mum, and it feels like we're finally getting there. All he needs is proof that she hurts them. Enough to block any custody bid she makes. And then this amazing man and his brilliant kids will be all mine. He's finally going to leave her.'"

There's silence once he finishes.

'This post isn't about me,' Jeremy says finally, not looking away from the screen. 'It couldn't be; there's no way. And "their abusive mum"? You wouldn't touch them.' He looks at me for the first time in hours. Tears collect in the corners of his eyes, threatening to spill. He closes the laptop and hands it back to Zain.

I give him a weak smile, and shrug. 'My name was in the comments, Jeremy. Before the mods removed it. All my contact details. She set them on me, hundreds of them sending threats and death wishes.'

'Who is *she*?' he asks.

I try not to sigh. I'm so tired of his pretending. 'Your girl-friend. The one you've been planning a life with. Once you leave me.'

He whirls around and rushes at me. I flinch, but he sinks to his knees in front of me and grabs my hands. A tear breaks free, glinting as it slides from the corner of his eye and down his cheek. He wipes it away with his forearm, not letting go of my hands.

He believes me, at last.

Zain slips from the room.

'Miriam...' Jeremy sniffs. 'You're right that I haven't been listening. I've been so caught up in this new job, in the stress of making sure our family's all right now there are four of us. Four seems so much harder to manage than three somehow.'

I give a wry chuckle of agreement.

'I should have dealt with things better after Samuel was born. You're right: we should have planned better. Talked to each other. I was panicking about you, terrified that the same thing would happen again. I thought if I just sent you to the Hermitage you'd be OK, because professionals could help you. Because, God knows, I felt totally helpless last time. Having a new baby in the house made me remember those feelings again. I just... I couldn't do it on my own, a new baby and a new job. So I thought, quick blast of therapy and we'd prevent the post-partum psychosis this time.'

'But I'm not ill, Jeremy. We talked about this when I got pregnant: what the warning signs are, how you could check in with me. We were prepared. We didn't need the Hermitage. All you had to do was talk to me, for God's sake.'

He closes his eyes. 'I know. I know that now.'

'You haven't listened to me.' I try to remove my hands, but he grips harder. 'Even now, even today... Why did it take Zain to prove to you that I'm telling the truth?'

'I'm sorry.' He rests his head in my lap and his shoulders shake. He takes a big breath and gathers himself. 'I'm so sorry. But I haven't been unfaithful. I don't have a girlfriend. I don't want you to leave, or for someone else to get custody of our kids. I want more time with you, more time as a family.' He wipes away another tear.

I believe he's telling the truth. But I don't know yet whether that's enough, whether I can trust him again after all this. And whether he can trust me too.

'I hate going on these work trips. I hate what I'll miss of our kids growing up while I'm on planes and in meetings. I come home and Samuel's learned something new, or his babbles sound more like words.' He closes his eyes to trap the tears.

I feel a sharp stab in my chest when I think about all the things I missed in the two weeks I was at the Hermitage.

Samuel's eyes changing, his body becoming more solid. His smile. I've experienced that feeling of missing out, and it's torture.

He draws a long breath and lets it out slowly. 'I want to be at home more, not less. I wouldn't jeopardise that by sneaking around with someone else.' He rubs his hands along my forearms, and my skin prickles at the warmth of his touch.

'Then why does someone say they're in a relationship with you?'

He shakes his head and gets up, sitting next to me on the sofa, his thigh against mine. 'I have no idea. None at all.'

'Is there someone at work, someone who might have a crush on you? Your boss, maybe?'

'Tabitha?' He sounds incredulous. He leans back, both hands on his forehead. His shirt rides up to show a sliver of bare stomach with a scattering of dark hair. 'Where? How?'

'It doesn't matter.' I stand up and flick through my phone, checking for messages, refreshing my inbox. Nothing. I call Jac again, but it rings out and eventually hits voicemail. She rarely answers when she's at work, but she'll call back when she's free. 'None of it matters. How could it, when our children are missing?'

He pulls his own phone from his pocket and clicks a few things before passing it to me. It's open to LinkedIn, a profile page for Tabitha Darwin. Her picture shows a smiling middle-aged woman with postbox-red hair. 'That's Tabitha.'

She's about twenty years older than Jeremy. She looks very friendly but not the husband-stealing type.

'Do you recognise her?' he asks. 'Was she the social worker?'

'No.' I pass the phone back to him.

He groans. 'Something in me hoped it was. Right age bracket. Red hair. That she was some kind of nutter who'd imagined a relationship with me and thought...' He trails off with a shake of his head. 'At least that way we'd be able to find them.'

In my hand, my phone vibrates and I snap to attention. It's a text from Katy:

Found something.

41

'Knock knock.' The living room door swings open and Ann steps in with an apologetic smile. 'Sorry to interrupt, but I just wanted to check in and see how you're both doing.'

She sees us hunched over my phone on the sofa and gives a nod of approval at our closeness. I wonder how we compare to other couples she's seen going through this hell. I wonder again if she believes us.

'I'm going off duty, but I'll be on call all night.' She hands Jeremy a business card with her mobile number, tells us to call with anything at all, any time.

Jeremy stands up and sees her out while I stare at my screen, waiting for Katy to send over what she's got. I feel raw and exhausted, like the top layer of my skin has been peeled away, leaving me exposed and in pain.

My phone buzzes again.

Zain'll show you what we found.

When Jeremy returns, Zain follows him into the living room, his open laptop balanced on his hand. 'Katy and I just dug around in some of the back-end stuff I accessed last time I was here. See if we could find who accessed your cameras. She's good with tech stuff, your friend.' He sits down on the opposite sofa, his laptop on his knee.

Jeremy joins me again, his weight on the sofa pulling me closer towards him. 'Did you find something?'

Zain gives us a grim smile. 'Maybe. I don't want to promise anything, but...' He types and then swings the screen around to show a list of numbers. 'So we tried to get into your hidden network, but it's wiped. Nothing there any more. As if it never existed.'

'What the...' Jeremy scratches his head. 'There was a hidden network?'

Zain nods. 'It was running all the smart devices so they weren't detectable through your router's network.'

Jeremy's eyes widen. 'That's sophisticated stuff. Not many people could set that up.'

'Exactly what I said. Even someone – no offence – in a techy line of work like yours, it wouldn't be something they'd necessarily know how to do.'

'And it's completely gone?'

'Not a trace.' Zain taps his finger on the top of his laptop screen, still facing us.

I hug myself, trying to keep warm. Since Liv and Samuel were taken, I haven't been able to stop shivering, little tremors running up and down my limbs. I can't rest. I can't relax. I can't think.

'But we managed to get into your old baby monitor account.' He beams. 'You need to enable two-factor authentication, by the way.'

I close my eyes. He mentioned that ages ago. I still don't understand what it means, but he's right and I should have paid attention. I thought changing the password would be enough.

Zain taps the screen where the list of numbers runs down

the page. It looks just like the list of devices he found on our hidden network. It's all gibberish to me.

Jeremy leans forward. 'Fascinating.'

'What is it?' I ask.

Zain raises his eyebrows. 'Where did you get that Wi-Fi monitor?'

I shrug. 'Jeremy picked it up from somewhere. He set it up while I was in the hospital with Samuel.'

Jeremy's face pales. 'I didn't buy that monitor.'

42

My skin crawls, and even though the cameras are gone, I can't shake the feeling of being watched. And no matter how convincing he is, I still can't trust Jeremy.

'So...' I pause and take a breath, trying to steady myself. 'Someone set up this baby monitor so they could watch us. And then when Jeremy threw away the monitor, they came in and set up cameras and smart devices. Then they came back and removed them all.'

The three of us stare at each other. Zain and Jeremy look haunted, their eyes wide.

'I don't know where that monitor came from, but...' Zain shakes his head. 'It has bad news written all over it. It's not secure at all.' He points at the column of numbers on the screen.

'These are IP addresses that accessed the monitor?' Jeremy says.

Zain nods. 'Katy found a back end to your settings, like a developer mode. It's hard to find, but when you get in, there are things like this. I've been looking through these IP addresses.' A look clouds his face that I can't quite read. He looks uncomfortable.

'What?' I ask.

'They're from all over the world. Croatia, Azerbaijan, Romania, Egypt...'

I swallow. 'People were watching us from all over the world? Watching Liv? And Samuel?' I feel sick. Nappy changes, breastfeeds, my little girl getting changed. When I thought it was one person, one disgusting person, it was bad enough. When I thought it was Jeremy's girlfriend, plotting to discredit me and get custody of my kids... that was horrifying. But worldwide logins from hundreds of users? I remember what I found that day I dug around on the internet for information about baby monitor hacking. Traffickers selling details of vulnerable children for these sickos to watch.

And now someone has taken my children.

Jeremy wraps his arm around my shoulders. I feel a comfort in the warmth of his body alongside mine, but I can't lean into it. I stiffen at his touch. I still don't know who he is, my husband.

'Does that mean we were... posted somewhere? Our feed was on the dark web?' I stand up, looking around for Ann's business card. 'We need to get this to the police.'

'Wait a second, Mim.' Zain's voice is gentle. 'I think we've got something interesting here and I want to explain it before we react.'

I sit down, further away from Jeremy than I was before. I don't want him to touch me. Not yet.

Zain scrolls through the list of IP addresses. 'My first thought was the same as yours: multiple users. That somehow your username and password were posted on a creepy paedo site somewhere and all these people were logging in. But Katy looked into some of these IPs, and they're all VPNs. Almost every single one.'

IPs. VPNs. So many acronyms. I raise my hands in defeat. 'Please explain.'

'Virtual private networks,' says Jeremy.

Zain nods. 'Basically, anyone can mask their computer's ID and location by using a VPN. It's like a barrier between your computer and the places you're accessing, and it makes it look like you're somewhere else, using someone else's computer.'

'OK... so what does this tell us about this baby monitor?'

'Even though it looks like you have had hundreds of visits from people all over the world, there are a few key things to note here. The timestamps of the visits are spread out. There are never two logins at the same time, for instance. Or even within a few minutes of each other.'

I nod, still unsure what Zain's working towards.

'And next... this one's a bit more complicated. There are databases specialising in VPN detection, and they list IP addresses and their corresponding VPN provider. You can find them if you know where to look.'

'And you found these IPs?' Jeremy leans forward. I'm glad he's here. I'm lost, but this means something to him.

Zain grins. 'They're all the same provider.'

'So the same person, using a different IP address each time?' Jeremy rubs his face and huffs out a breath.

'Yes. Even though you have logins from multiple IP addresses across the world, it's likely they're all the same person. And finally... Katy's *pièce de résistance*.' He turns the computer towards himself, clicks a few buttons and turns it back, where several rows of the list are now highlighted. 'This is the only IP address that appears more than once. Each time, the user logged off very quickly. Within seconds. Because—'

Jeremy practically jumps off the sofa. 'They forgot to switch on their VPN.'

Zain claps his hands. 'Yes!'

Jeremy is vibrating with energy now, back in his seat next to me. I feel him shift towards me, his thigh against mine. 'And you've tracked that IP, right? Where is it? Who is it?'

Zain's face clouds and he flicks me an apologetic glance. 'Jeremy, it's your office.'

43

My thigh prickles where it touches Jeremy's. I feel him tense.

'Someone in my office has been doing this?'

I get up and cross the room to stand by the window where Jeremy stood not long ago. The rain is heavier now, thick drops falling from a leaden sky. Our garden looks forlorn: the rusty old slide and an abandoned ball peeking out through overgrown grass. No children here to play with them. I clutch my chest. It feels like my heart will burst with pain.

'It's possible it was someone trying to make it look like Jeremy,' Zain suggests, his voice quiet. 'If the company has guest Wi-Fi, for example...'

'Or Jeremy should have been better at covering his tracks, even if his acting skills are convincing.' My voice is cold. I'm done with playing his games.

'Miriam, stop, please. I understand, but we've been through this—' The doorbell rings, cutting him off. He stands up. 'I'll get it,' he mutters, more to himself than anyone else.

I check my phone again. Nothing. No news. Jac hasn't called back. She'll want to know what's going on. The police will have interviewed my mum by now, gathered her description of the fake social worker. I wonder if they're out looking for my babies. I wonder if this has happened before. Are there other kids with mine? Is there someone to hold Samuel? Will they know to feed him a bottle every three hours? Will they change his nappy so he doesn't get a rash? Does he have somewhere safe to sleep?

And Liv. I reach down to my wrist and wrap my fingers around the bracelet like a hug. I hope she gets some comfort from hers. I hope she knows how loved she is. I hope she's OK, no matter where she is and who she's with. I hope she remembers me, if I never see her again.

Zain sits quietly, occasionally clicking his mousepad. I think he knows not to intrude on my catastrophising thoughts. I'm glad he's here. I don't want to be alone with Jeremy.

I hear voices from the hallway, and the living room door swings open. Behind Jeremy, Nicole is shaking the rain from her hair and slipping her coat from her shoulders. She looks around for somewhere to put it, and Jeremy takes it and hangs it out in the hall.

'I can't believe what's happened, Mim.' Her eyes are wide with shock. 'You must be going out of your mind.'

I take her through to the kitchen and boil the kettle for tea while I catch her up on what's going on. She shakes her head, gasps and places a sympathetic hand on my arm in all the right places in the story. She apologises over and over for persuading Zain not to help. 'I just wanted what's best for you,' she says, more than once.

I shrug it off. It's not important now. I don't ask where Lottie is, just like I didn't ask Zain where he's left Kai. I'm just grateful there aren't other kids here to entertain, to remind me of what I'm missing.

Tea made and Nicole caught up, we carry two mugs each through to the living room, where Zain and Jeremy are hunched over the laptop, Jeremy leaning over the arm of the sofa, both so focused on the screen they don't seem conscious of the person next to them.

'What's going on? Have you found something else?'

Zain looks up, his pupils large, his eyes wide. 'We've made some progress.'

Jeremy straightens with a mumbled apology to Zain for invading his space. 'So we looked into this IP address, the one Zain said was for my office. It's not, not quite.'

'What do you mean?' I hand him his tea and sit down on the sofa next to Nicole.

Jeremy crosses to the mantelpiece and places his mug next to the photograph of Jac and Liv with their tiger face paint. He looks at me as if Zain and Nicole aren't here. 'The IP address that accessed the baby monitor was my company, but not the part of it I work for. It was the parent company, Pendant Data Systems. So not me. And not Tabitha either.' He raises his eyebrows at me as if he knew that was exactly where my brain would go next.

'Pendant Data Systems,' I repeat.

Next to me, Nicole gasps.

We all turn to her.

'Where's Jac? I thought she'd be here,' she says in a quiet voice.

I glance at my phone again. No notifications. 'I don't know. I've been calling her, but she's not picking up. I guess she's in meetings or something.'

Nicole coughs. 'When I was here a few weeks ago, when Jeremy...' She smooths her hair with a flat hand. It's still damp from the rain. 'When you weren't very well...'

'The intervention,' I say, with a glance at Jeremy. 'When you all sent me off to a "retreat".'

Jeremy has the grace to look embarrassed.

Nicole picks at a hangnail. 'Yes, then. Well, while we were waiting for Jeremy to get home, we were chatting. And Jac told me where she works now. I'm sure she said Pendant Data Systems.'

The room is silent, everyone processing what she's just said. I nod, remembering Jac mentioning her new posh job. Senior vice president. Too boring to talk about, she'd said.

Nicole shifts in her seat, her cheeks colouring. 'And Jac was here the night Liv fell?'

I nod, picturing the loose screws on the stair gate's hinges, and the screwdriver on the floor by the skirting board. Spit pools in my mouth and I swallow, trying not to be sick.

Jeremy grabs the family liaison officer's business card. 'And she stayed here with Samuel while you went to the hospital with Liv.' He unlocks his phone and keys in Ann's number.

My voice is a whisper. 'The night the cameras disappeared.'

I remember her text from that night, telling me she'd gone out to buy formula because she knew the breast milk in the freezer had spoiled. But now that I think about it, I didn't tell her about the breast milk: I couldn't say it out loud. I said nothing about the fridge. *How did she know?*

I unlock my phone and click on her contact details one more time. I raise the handset to my ear. Straight to voicemail. Her phone is off.

44

'We've got to go.' I stand up and rush to the door, shoving my phone in my jeans pocket. At last, there's something we can do to find Liv and Samuel.

Even now, I'm trying to rationalise what must have happened. *How* this could have happened. Jac is such a good godmother to Liv. She loves her as if she was her own, she's always said that. She's bought huge birthday presents and has always been available to babysit. She offered to stay with her for as long as we needed when I was in the hospital having Sam.

If Jeremy and I weren't around – if we were in some kind of terrible accident – she'd take Liv and raise her as her daughter. She's never wanted kids herself, but Liv is the exception. She's said that many times. Hasn't she? Or did I assume that, based on the life she leads? All the dating, the jokes about keeping her freedom...

If it was her – and I still don't know if it was – logging into the baby monitor from work to watch us through the camera, then maybe she was doing it out of care and love. Maybe she wanted to check we were OK. To keep an eye on her god-daughter.

And now maybe she's just looking after the kids. Babysitting. Maybe it was a miscommunication.

In the hall, I pull on my wellies – no time for laces – and grab my coat from the cupboard. 'Jeremy, come on. We need to go to Jac's. We need to find the kids.'

I stride through to the kitchen and pull open the 'stuff' drawer, the one full of Sharpies, cotton reels, spare buttons, shoe polish and other crap we never know where to put. I push a roll of unused fly paper out of the way and there it is: Jac's spare key.

'What are you doing?' Jeremy comes into the kitchen. He's not wearing his shoes, nor his raincoat.

'Why aren't you ready to go?'

'What are you doing?' he asks again.

I show him the key, gripped between my finger and thumb. 'Jac's flat. She needed someone to look after her key after her parents died. She said we were her closest family once they'd gone.'

She gave it to me at her parents' wake. I was over halfway through my pregnancy with Sam and finding it strange to mark the death of two people while a new life was beginning inside me.

I shove the key in my pocket and fumble with the zip on my jacket. 'Can you get your shoes on, please?'

He doesn't move.

I get the zip lined up and pull it, looking up at him. 'Come on. If there's somewhere our kids might be, we need to go there.'

'The police said someone needed to stay here. I've called Ann, told her what we know. And we don't *know* they're with Jac.'

'We don't know anything. But I can't stay here doing nothing.'

'I'll stay,' says Nicole, glancing at Jeremy. She's standing in the doorway, leaning against the frame. 'Lottie's with my ex for the afternoon, I don't have to be anywhere. You go, see what you can find out.'

I give her a grateful smile, and Jeremy nods, persuaded.

'But call the police if there's any reason to feel something's off. Whoever's done this is unpredictable. Even if she's your oldest friend, Mim.'

'I'll come too,' says Zain, already pulling on his coat in the hallway behind Nicole. 'In case you need an extra pair of hands.'

I realise he's saying we're better in a larger group. In case we need physical strength, or the advantage of numbers. Against Jac.

Jac, who I've known since school. Whose hand I held while she sobbed at her parents' funeral. Whose bed I slept in for countless sleepovers. Who borrowed my clothes and always fancied the same boys as me. Whose make-up I've done thousands of times, her breath on my face as I outlined her eyes with liquid eyeliner.

But if she's done this, she's not the person I know. She's not the friend I've valued. She's a stranger. A stranger who put Liv in danger to make me look like a bad mum. Who rigged my house with technology to make me feel like I was going insane.

Who wants me gone, I realise, so she can build a family with my husband.

Jeremy and I climb into our car, and Zain follows in his own: two vehicles might be useful if we need to split.

Jeremy drives. I huddle in the passenger seat as we cross the grey winter city, watching the rain trail along the window pane.

His forearms look strong and muscular, his hands gripping the steering wheel. I don't know how he can switch off his brain enough to concentrate on driving. I couldn't. All I can think of is my babies, and where they could be. I pray to whoever might be there. *Please keep them safe. Please keep them safe. I'm coming for them. I'll be there soon.*

My skin prickles with gooseflesh as I rethink what I know of Jac, of what she wants in life and who she is. I remember her at eleven years old, wanting two kids and to one day take over her parents' farm and run it with her husband. Fresh eggs and milk for breakfast every day.

Then in her twenties, always picking the wrong boy. The cheater, the one who didn't want to settle down yet, the one who pretended he liked her until they slept together and then ghosted her. The one who stuck with her until another girl broke up with her boyfriend. The one who got her pregnant and disappeared when she miscarried.

I shiver, pulling my raincoat around me. She did want a relationship. She did want kids. It just didn't work out for her, so she put on a brave face. All the dates, the one-night stands, the short sharp affairs and catastrophic break-ups... she was always looking for what I had.

I didn't pay enough attention. I didn't ask the right questions, didn't see past her bravado. I didn't realise she was watching me all the time, planning how to get what she wanted: the handsome, steady guy who was happy to settle down; the two kids, a girl and a boy.

And then this amazing man and his brilliant kids will be all mine.

I had what Jac wanted, so she decided to take it for herself.

I glance across at Jeremy, his gaze on the road ahead. Outside, the grey stone of the city centre's streets flashes by the windows, blurred by the rain. The street lights flicker on.

'Jeremy?'

'Mm-hm?' He blinks once. He looks tired. I wish I could hug him.

'Did Jac ever...' I pause, trying to work out how to phrase this. 'Did Jac ever try anything with you? Anything at all?'

There's no sound in the car except for the rumble of the tyres over cobblestones. Jeremy doesn't answer.

'Jem?'

His cheeks redden. I have my answer.

'Can we talk about this when I'm not driving? When our kids aren't missing?' He sounds angry, but his facial expression is just... sad.

I shrug. I've already lost everything. What does it matter *when* I find out how much more I could lose? It doesn't matter that Jeremy is still next to me. Jac has pushed us so far apart.

Above us, Edinburgh Castle looms, its rocky cliff face streaked black with rain. Behind us, the soaring peak of Arthur's Seat reaches up to the sky, flanked by the swoop of the Salisbury Crags. And nestled in the middle, the tall tenement buildings full of flats, one of which might hold my children.

45

Jac always wanted to live in the city centre. Close to the nightlife, the public transport and decent coffee, she'd say.

Where once she'd wanted nothing but the life her parents had, as our teenage years continued she soon wanted the opposite. Growing up in the middle of nowhere on a farm would do that to you, she'd explain. When there were two buses a day into the city, the city seemed like a prize to be won.

Now, in her late thirties, she still lives in the same tenement flat she bought fifteen years ago, with its wooden floors and high ceilings. A beautiful two-bedroom refuge, with period features, heritage paintwork, and French doors opening out into a private garden.

But when Jeremy rings the doorbell, no one answers.

Behind us, Zain pulls up and lowers his passenger window. One hand on the steering wheel, he leans over and calls: 'I'll find somewhere to park and be right with you.'

I shake my head. 'No one's answering.'

Jeremy holds out a hand. 'Give me the key.'

He pushes the door open and steps into the darkness. 'What the...' he whispers, covering his mouth with his hand.

I follow close behind, and the smell hits me like a wall. The scent of death.

I lift my scarf over my mouth and nose like a mask, trying not to retch.

I flick a switch, and the open-plan kitchen/living room floods with light. There's the source of the smell: the overflowing bin, chicken bones protruding from the propped-up lid. Crumbs litter every surface, and the sink is stacked high with dishes.

I shudder, reviewing the devastation. 'This is...' I pause, stepping over a cereal box, its contents splayed across the tiles. 'Jac usually keeps this place so nice. Something's very wrong.'

The other rooms are no better: her bedroom smells musty, the bed unmade and clothes strewn across the floor. A pile of mouldering towels prevents the bathroom door from opening all the way.

A shuffling noise causes us to startle. We back away from the front door, ducking into the bedroom.

'It's me,' Zain calls.

I release a breath, my hands shaking. 'They're not here,' I call back, stepping into the living room.

'Holy heck.' Zain picks up a mug and shows me the layer of mould growing in the bottom. 'There's a problem here.'

'I've never seen it like this,' I say, surprised that even now my instinct is to defend her. 'She's usually so neat.' I remember various parties from the past decade and further back: raucous games of flip-cup slopping beer across the tiles; Eurovision viewing parties where we heard none of the songs because we all talked across the TV; dinner parties that ended with us piling into the garden to share cigarettes. The flat was always immaculate within an hour of the end of the party, no matter how late it finished.

I shudder at the memories. A lifetime of friendship, reframed in an instant.

'Thankfully I can't see anything that implies our kids were here,' Jeremy says, opening and closing cupboards.

I look around the flat again, turning on lights. The second bedroom is in total darkness, the light switch unresponsive. I stride in and pull open the curtains, the dusky afternoon light throwing shadows across the mess. There's a single bed along one wall, its wrinkled duvet partially covered by a pile of clothes. And a desk with a computer: two monitors with little lights blinking in the half-light like a spaceship waiting to take off.

The keyboard and mouse are the only thing in the room not covered in a thin layer of dust. She's been here recently.

I wiggle the mouse and the set-up comes to life: a password box and the time appear on the screen.

'Zain?' I call.

He appears in the doorway.

'Do you think you can get into this PC?' I ask.

He purses his lips and lets out a low chuckle. 'This isn't a film, so I don't think Jac's childhood cat's name with a "one" after it will cut it, I'm afraid.'

I half smile in recognition. It always annoys me when someone in a book or a film can immediately guess a password.

'Unless...' He reaches out and hits the enter key. 'Some people leave their password blank.'

We watch hopefully, but the 'incorrect password' notification pops up within moments.

He shakes his head. 'Sorry, mate. We'll get locked out if we keep trying. I'll check paperwork, see if there are any passwords written anywhere.' His footsteps recede as he leaves the room. I hear him and Jeremy talking in the kitchen, the opening and closing of drawers as they search.

I puff out my cheeks and look around the room. Below the desk, more lights blink. It's a laser printer; the display reads

PAPER JAM. There are some pages in the tray, printed side face-down. I get down on my hands and knees and snatch them out, rushing over to the window so I can look at them in the light.

As I study them, my breath catches in my throat. I can't move.

'Miriam? Are you OK?'

I start, fumbling the pages.

Behind me, Jeremy stands in the doorway, the light from the corridor casting his face in shadow. I take a step back. 'Don't, Jeremy.'

'What?' He moves into the room. 'What is it?' He holds out a hand for the papers.

I shake my head and hold them to my chest. I don't want him to see. He can't know I know. I need Zain here too. 'Can we go into the living room?'

He frowns, confused, and steps aside to let me pass.

Zain sits at the dining table, a big bunch of keys in his hands. He holds them up to the light, examining them.

'You've found something?' I ask, moving a dirty bowl onto the kitchen counter and sitting at the cleared space. I set the papers in front of me.

Jeremy pulls out a chair with a squeal and sits down.

I shift a couple of inches away from him.

'What's going on, Miriam?' he asks. 'What did you find?'

'Zain, you go first.' I don't look at Jeremy. I can't meet his eyes. I can't believe I almost believed him. For a few minutes – maybe even an hour – I believed that he was as confused and lost as me. That he didn't know where our kids were. That he'd loved me all along and his actions of the past few months came from genuine concern for my welfare. But the papers in front of me, papers from Jac's printer, say otherwise.

Zain holds out the keys. 'I found these in a drawer. I'm

wondering if Jac has access to another house somewhere.' He lies them flat on the table in front of him, fanning them out. 'They look like a normal bunch of keys, except there's a few differences...'

They do look normal. I have no idea what he's getting at.

He points. 'These five are mortice keys, and all different, which says to me they open a number of different doors, possibly all on one old property. And then there's what looks like a car key but isn't.'

I try hard to listen, but the papers in front of me seem to glow. I'm going to have to tell them what I've found, and soon.

Jeremy reaches forward and picks up the keys, studying the one Zain pointed out.

'Could it be a padlock key or something?' I ask, peering over his shoulder.

He shakes his head. 'Too big.'

Zain squints, his eyes crinkling at the corners. 'I'm wondering if it could be for a piece of equipment. A lawn-mower or something.'

And with that, I realise that I know these keys. I lay a palm flat on the table, over the papers. 'It's not a lawnmower. It's a tractor.'

Zain and Jeremy stare at me.

'Jac's parents' farm. It's old and rambling, lots of external doors, outbuildings and farm equipment. Her mum and dad died when I was pregnant with Samuel. A horrible accident, something to do with the boiler. She was devastated. She hasn't sold the place yet; she needs to do some stuff to it before she can put it on the market.'

Jeremy stands up, pushing his chair away from him with another scrape on the tiles. 'We have to go. Now.'

He pulls on his raincoat and strides to the door, yanking it open and gesturing out into the rain.

I start to gather the papers, following him. But then I stop. I lay them back on the table and sit down again.

'Miriam, what are you doing? If we know where they are—'

'They're not at the farm.' I turn over the papers and hold them out to him. 'Admit it, Jeremy. Just tell the truth. Jac's at the airport with our children. And you're meeting them there.'

46

Jeremy releases the door and steps back inside. It swings on its hinges in the breeze, and a gust of wind blows rain into the hallway, splatting on the wooden floor.

He kicks the door closed with his foot, not taking his gaze from me. 'The airport?' He steps under the kitchen lights, which cast long shadows down his face. His eyes are dark holes.

I shiver, and again I'm so grateful for Zain, who's still sitting at the table. He gives me a nod of encouragement and I lay out the pages, three in all.

The first, a plane ticket for Jac. Edinburgh to Palma, leaving in four hours.

The second, the same route but for Liv.

The third, for Jeremy. And in small letters underneath his name: *Infant in lap.*

'Was this the plan all along?' I ask. 'Jac gets a fake social worker to remove the kids and then you meet them at the airport to fly off on a sunny little holiday together? Or did it go wrong somewhere? Was I supposed to be arrested on suspicion of hurting the children? Or was I supposed to go insane with all the cameras so you could send me back to the Hermitage?' I put my head in my hands, my elbows on the sticky table.

'No, Miriam. I don't know anything about—'

I hold up the papers. 'Was this really going to work? How long has it been going on, Jeremy?'

Zain looks like he wants to sink into the ground. He wraps his arms around himself, the collar on his jacket up high past his jawline.

Jeremy leans over the table, a hand on either side of mine. Once again I'm aware of how large he is. How strong. He could hurt me if he wanted to. And Zain. Neither of us is big enough to stand up to him.

But then he surprises me: he picks up the printouts and looks at them, his forehead crinkled as his eyes flick back and forth across the words on the page.

'I have nothing to do with this, Miriam. Samuel doesn't even have a passport. How could she take him out of the country? You heard our FLO: they've alerted Interpol. And why would she think I would go with her? I've never...' He trails off, obviously remembering what I asked in the car. The question he refused to answer. He slumps down into a chair, his frown deepening.

'Go on, Jeremy. Tell me you've never done anything inappropriate with Jac. You've never kissed her, or had an affair. Or planned a holiday to Palma.'

He shakes his head, his face pale and sickly. 'I've never done anything with her. I promise. But I don't know what was going on in her head, from her side. I've always felt uncomfortable around her, like I have to be on my guard. At New Year's parties and stuff, her kisses on my cheek have always felt too close to my mouth. She's winked at me. Hugged me too tight. Always things I thought you'd laugh at me for if I mentioned them. Things she could deny or say I was imagining.'

He takes a big breath, a gasp half of shock, half of realisation. 'When you were in the mother and baby unit, and this time when you were at the Hermitage, she'd drop round almost every day. Way more than she does when you're around. Little excuses, like she'd bought too much pasta in her online shop and she wondered if it'd help with meal prep, or wanting to help with Liv's bedtime so I could have a rest. And she'd stay too late, or offer to sleep on the sofa. But then Nicole would often drop round too, so I thought it was just them being supportive friends. Maybe Jac did...' He blushes. 'I don't know. There was always a slight overfamiliarity with her. But I told myself that maybe she felt a closeness with me because I was your husband. Never that she wanted more. If it crossed my mind, I'd tell myself it was bollocks. I never thought she wanted to play happy families in the Balearic Islands. *God.*' He rubs his face with both hands.

I nod, once. I don't even ask myself what I believe any more. I just want the kids back. Nothing else matters. 'So what now?' I point at the keys and the airline tickets. Our choice to make. 'Is she going to try to take our kids out of the country? Or do we assume not and head to the farm?'

Jeremy picks up the papers. 'The flight is in four hours. We could watch the check-in desk and make sure they don't try to get on the flight.'

Zain clears his throat and sits up. 'Like you said, Samuel doesn't have a passport. And she didn't take the tickets with her. I think this is a red herring or a plan that didn't work.'

'She could have the tickets on her phone,' I say.

He grabs the papers and stands. 'I'll go to the airport, and I'll phone your family liaison to tell her what we've found. You guys go to the farm. Keep your phones on and we can call each other if anything changes.'

I wrench open the front door and plunge out into the dark

evening, pulling on my coat and shoving the farm keys into the pocket. I climb into our car next to this stranger, my husband. Alone together, again.

47

The car bounces up the pitted lane to the farm. The drive reminds me of visits to Jac's house when we were teenagers: the endless summer days spent moping around the fields with Nicole and Jac bickering, desperate for something to do.

There's no sign of those endless summers now, as the car's wheels hit every pothole and muddy puddle on the lane, the hedges whizzing past in the darkness and the rain. Jeremy drives with no care for the suspension. I know he'd say that getting to our kids is more important.

On the other side of the hedges, the fields moulder, neglected. When Jac's parents died, she sold their animals and left the fields to fester. She couldn't be a farmer, she said. If they'd wanted someone to take over from them, they should have specified it in their wills.

We turn a corner and there's the farmhouse, the facade in darkness. It's an old building, from the early nineteenth century, with small sash windows. It's longer than it is high, huddling against the brutal Scottish weather.

The car rolls across the gravel driveway with a hiss as Jeremy pulls up outside the front door.

'They're not here,' he says, defeated.

I know how he feels. The farm looks abandoned, its windows dark and empty. If they're not here, then where? The airport? I check my phone. 'No signal. Zain can't get hold of us.'

He turns off the engine and zips up his raincoat. 'Well, we're here now. May as well take a look around.'

I get out of the car and head for the living room window, where I cup my hands around my face and peer into the room. I see the outline of two sofas, a book on the coffee table, bookmark still between the pages. I draw in air through my teeth with a hiss.

'What? What did you see?' Jeremy's right behind me.

I shake my head. 'Nothing. It's just... it's like they're still here. Jac's parents. Like they've just gone out.'

I wonder if this is where they found them. Their bodies, after the accident. Sitting next to each other on the sofa, a normal evening.

I turn away from the window with a shudder.

I miss them, Jac's mum and dad. Jac and I would joke that we should swap parents: I'd be happier spending long, quiet afternoons helping on the farm, while she'd sneak into pubs with my mum for underage drinks and a flirt with the barman.

Something in my brain shifts. If I'm right, it's been there this whole time. Since we were teenagers. She's always wanted what I had, even then.

Next to me, Jeremy pushes his face against the glass and squints into the empty room.

'I can't believe they're gone,' I say.

He wraps an arm around my shoulders. 'What was it again? Gas leak?'

I wipe at my cheek even though there are no tears there. Jac and I simply call it 'the accident' and she doesn't like to talk about it, so Jeremy doesn't know the detail. 'Carbon monoxide. A dodgy boiler. At first it looked like someone had tampered with it. Like it was done on purpose. For a while the police considered a murder-suicide, but eventually they dropped it.' I can't say any more. It's too much to imagine. We knew Jac's dad wouldn't do that. He was so steady, so good.

But I see everything in a new light, now that she's taken my children. I remember how much pressure she felt from her parents to have kids. How they held me up as an example, especially once I told them I was expecting my second. 'They'll never accept my choices, Smidge,' she'd say. 'One day I'll give up trying to get their approval.'

Was it really an accident? I wonder. Or was the investigator's initial hunch correct? Not a murder-suicide, but just straight murder. I can't imagine her capable of that, but then...

I take a sharp breath and Jeremy looks at me, concerned.

'This started months ago,' I hiss at him. 'The day her parents died.'

'The day of Samuel's twenty-week scan.'

My throat swells and my skin prickles. *A boy and a girl.* I had what they wanted for her, and she couldn't let them find out. I nod. Pete and Aileen. Their kind smiles fill my head. 'I think she killed her mum and dad.'

His eyes widen, his pupils huge in the darkness. He steps away from the window and peers into the darkness. 'We need to find Liv and Sam. Is the barn over here?'

I nod, and he strides away. 'We should check around the back...' I call, but he's already disappeared into the darkness.

The large barn is only a few metres from the house. One side held equipment, the other animals, I remember. It has large double doors big enough for a tractor to drive in and out. Jeremy uses the keys we found in Jac's flat, getting the right one on the second try.

We peer into the dusty darkness. Hulking metallic shapes loom along the back: the rusting remains of a tractor and various other pieces of equipment. It smells like straw and manure. A warm smell, somehow.

'They were very isolated out here,' I say, glancing around the dark space, empty of animals now.

Jeremy steps inside, grabbing his phone from his back pocket and turning on the torch. He disappears behind a wall of hay bales. 'Miriam. You need to come and look at this.'

I follow, stepping over the scattering of straw that covers the concrete floor.

As I approach the bales, Jeremy pops his head round the corner, startling me. 'They're here.'

My heart pounds, and I rush forward, arms ready to hug my children. Instead, I grind to a halt when I see what he means. It's not them.

But it is Jac's car, with two empty child seats in the back.

48

At the sight of the car seats, I crumple to the ground.

They're brand new, labels still affixed to their fabric covers. One is small and faces backwards, a protective shell to surround my baby and keep him from harm. *My* baby. Liv's is colourful and bright, covered with cartoon sea creatures. It's exactly the type of pattern she would love.

I wail, my body racked with sobs.

I've spent the last few weeks struggling through day by day: Jeremy growing distant as he believed I was descending into mental illness again; the deep betrayal as he sent me away and separated me from my children; the cold, steely dread when I found that Reddit post and realised his betrayal was even more complex than I'd thought. And now this exhausting uphill battle to thwart Jac's plans and keep my kids. A fight I shouldn't have to have.

They're mine. They began their lives inside me as I nourished their growing bodies. And Jac has taken them.

What does she think she's doing? What's going on in her head?

Does she really believe she can just step into my family and make it her own? That she can take anything from me if she wants it enough? I pause. Yes, that's exactly how she's always thought of me and our friendship. She's always done this. No wonder Nicole distanced herself as soon as she could. *Why couldn't I see it?*

And now it's my husband, my children.

I imagine Jac walking into the shop, telling the assistant she has two children. Fitting the new seats into her car, ready to receive my babies as if they're her own.

'I can't...' I try to speak, but it's not possible to articulate everything going through my head. 'What did she...'

Jeremy places a hand on my shoulder. 'Shh, it's OK. It's going to be OK. Our children are here. We're here.' He pulls his phone out of his pocket.

'What are you doing?' I brush the tears from my face.

'I've just got signal.' He holds the phone to his ear. 'I'm calling the police. We need them here.'

'Good.' I pull my coat around me once more and stride towards the doors. The wind whips through the gap, catching my hair and pulling it across my face.

'Wait, Miriam. Where are you going?' Jeremy stares at me, the phone still at his ear.

'I'm going to get our kids.'

He rushes after me, muttering into the phone: 'Just a moment, please.' He pauses. 'Yes, this is an emergency.' He holds the phone away from his body and reaches for my arm with his free hand. 'We need to wait here. The police will be on their way. Let them do their job.'

I look at him, standing with the phone in one hand, the other arm outstretched towards me. Imploring me to stay. The last months of my life have been at the mercy of other people. Imprisoned by Jeremy, surrounded by Jac's web of cameras and plotting, told over and over that I was imagining it all, that I just needed to be kind to myself and everything would be fine.

But everything is not fine, and when it comes to the welfare of my kids, being kind to myself is not even a consideration. I don't matter. They are all that matters. Liv and Samuel. My babies.

I pull away, tearing my arm from his grip. 'Our kids are here. I can't sit here doing nothing. I'm going to get our children and bring them home.'

I don't wait for his response. I walk away into the dark.

49

The rain whips at my face, blown across the hills in huge sheets. I pull my hood over my head and wrap my arms around my body.

I can barely see, but it doesn't matter. I know the way.

The front of the farmhouse is still in darkness, but I head around the back. To where the kitchen is, its windows looking out over the hills. As soon as I turn the corner, I see golden light beaming over the landscape. The lights are on in the kitchen.

I walk quietly, keeping to the grass verge instead of the gravel driveway, and stay close to the building, running my hand along the damp stone as I inch my way towards the window and duck low. The kitchen looks warm and inviting: there's a bunch of flowers on the worktop and the Aga is polished to a shine. Jac stands with her back to me, watching something in a frying pan on the stove. Her hair is up in a clip, just how her mum used to wear hers. And at her back I see the strings of an apron tied in a knot.

She looks up, laughs.

I flinch, but it wasn't directed at me. She won't notice me. I stand to see into the room.

There at the dining table, Liv sits quietly, surrounded by coloured pencils and an old Disney colouring book. My heart wants to burst out of my chest. I could smash this window, launch myself through it and grab my child. I want to press her to my body, bury my nose in my hair.

The tip of her tongue protrudes from her chocolate-smeared lips. Next to her is a half-eaten stack of pancakes, knife and fork propped on the edge.

It pains me that she looks happy and content. Why isn't she crying and screaming for her mummy?

'It's bedtime, Liv.' Jac turns towards the window, and I wrench myself away, stepping into the shadows. And then I see Samuel: strapped to Jac's chest in a cosy sling, his little cheek pressed against her bosom as he sleeps. The perfect little family. *My* perfect little family, which she has stolen.

I suppress a growl of rage. I need to go inside. I need to get my children.

I turn away from the window, in a rush to get around to the front door. As I do so, I collide with someone else.

'Oof,' says a woman's voice.

Someone has been following me. Watching me watch my family.

We both tumble to the ground, the gravel scraping my knees and hands.

I scrabble to get to my feet, but she's just as fast. As I try to run, she catches me by the arms and holds me in place. I look into her eyes and my breath catches in my throat. It's the woman who stole my children.

Close up, she looks older than she did when she came to my house. Fifties, not forties. She's not wearing a suit this time, and her hair isn't up in a neat bun; it's in a long plait straight down her back, loose tendrils framing her face. She's not dressed like a social worker. She's wearing a battered wax jacket, the zip undone.

'You,' I hiss, shuddering with rage. *Ms Hodge.* If she wasn't gripping my arms, I'd claw her face like a wild cat.

She holds me tighter, strong for a woman so slight. 'It came from a good place, Miriam. She was trying to help your family.'

I attempt to pull out of her grip, to wrestle away, but she pushes me against the wall of the farmhouse, my head banging on the stone. For a moment, the world turns blurry with the impact.

The light from the kitchen window catches the side of her face. I stare at her. This close, I can see the coffee stains on her teeth. I recognise her, I realise. And not only from the last couple of days.

'You... you were at the retreat.' Not just a faux social worker, but also a nurse.

The room behind me falls silent on the other side of the glass. The kitchen is empty, the children gone.

I pull against her grip on my arms, but she holds fast. 'Yes, I work at the Hermitage. I'm a friend of Jac's.'

'You trapped me in the sensory deprivation tank.'

'That was a malfunction.'

'Who the hell are you?' I hiss through gritted teeth. The wind whips my damp hair across my face. 'You think you can take my kids?'

'Jac will explain everything.'

I feel a surge of rage and try to raise my hands. I want to hit her, to tug at her hair, to push her down, to trample her body as I run to my children.

I lift my leg and thrust my knee into her crotch. She yelps.

As I strain to free myself, the sound of footsteps on gravel distracts her. Jeremy. She glances over her shoulder, and her grip loosens.

I wrench myself out of her grasp and with both hands I shove her shoulders.

She topples backwards, hitting her head on a stone with a sickening thud.

I don't stop to see if she's all right. I step over her body and run around the house to the front door.

'Miriam?' Jeremy calls as I pass him.

I ignore him. The only thing I need is my kids.

The front door is locked, our keys still in the barn door, but I find a spare key under the faded garden gnome beside the path. It's been there for years.

The house smells the same as it always did, as if Jac's parents have just gone out for dinner and will be back later to fill the place with laughter, the murmur of the radio and the aroma of freshly baked bread.

I remove my wellies in the hallway so my socked feet are silent on the wooden floorboards. It's cold – the kind of cold that builds in an uninhabited house, that deep chill that filters through to your bones – and beneath the familiar smells, the tinge of damp hangs in the air. Jac didn't plan to bring the kids here; I know it instinctively. Something went wrong. This is her plan B. She must be panicking.

I wait in the hallway until I hear sounds from the kitchen. Jac has returned. There's the low rumble of the radio, and the occasional clink of dishes as she clears up from making pancakes.

My feet itch to rush up the stairs and scoop my babies into my arms.

Not yet. Jac first. I need to override my instincts and think several moves ahead, like she has done this whole time. I need to play her at her own game.

I feel the damp air enter my lungs. I wrap my hands around the cold brass of the door handle, but then I hear the clunk of another door opening and closing.

I freeze, listening.

'Jeremy,' Jac says, happiness filling her voice. He must have entered through the back door. 'I'm glad you came. I had to get you out here, away from everything, so we can think straight. We're safe here. I have a lot to tell you.'

She wants to show him how his life could look with her instead of me. I curl my toes against the hard wood floor, trying not to burst in. Something tells me to stay where I am, wait here and gather as much information as I can before I act. A final test for Jeremy to pass.

'Tickets to Palma, Jac? We found them in your printer.'

I hold my breath. For a moment, I wonder if he's been tempted. If there was ever a world in which he might choose her.

Jac's voice gets higher, indignant. 'It was a surprise, from ages ago – I thought we could get away together. You know, before...' Silence. The air prickles. 'But then Mim was struggling and you sent her to the Hermitage, so I cancelled it. Then my new job got crazy busy and I didn't have time to fix the printer – or clean my flat... God, I'm so embarrassed you saw it like that.'

'I'm not here to talk, Jac.' I squeeze my eyes closed at the sound of Jeremy's voice. 'You kidnapped my children.'

'I rescued them, Jeremy. Liv's fall wasn't an accident.'

I dig my fingernails into my palms.

'They didn't need rescuing.' I feel a rush of relief at Jeremy's words. He sounds angry, commanding. 'Move out of the way, please. I need to get the children.'

There's a scrape of chair leg against tile as Jac backs away from him. 'Please listen. Everything I've done, I've done for you; your whole family.' Her voice is high-pitched and pleading. 'Is Miriam here? I want to explain to her, too.'

'The things you've done to Miriam over the past few months... it's despicable. The cameras, the tricks—'

'No tricks!' she interrupts. 'We needed proof. She sent the house haywire, the breast milk got spoiled, your boiler was tampered with. I had to do something. I needed the teddy-cam to document what was going on. All the other cameras were her—'

'Stop,' Jeremy barks. There's a violence behind his voice that chills me to the bone. 'Whatever you thought you were doing, whatever crazy rescue mission you thought you were on, you've made a mistake.'

'But—'

'No. And the new car seats, the holiday tickets... Did you believe I would leave her for you? You're living in a fantasy world if you think you can replace her. I'm married to Miriam. She's the mother of my children.'

She sighs, a resigned acceptance. Her voice is quiet when she continues; the fight has gone out of her. 'I bought a ticket for Miriam, too. There was a paper jam...' There's a pause, and then her voice filters through the door to my hiding place once again: 'You're not getting it. I need to talk to Miriam. She'll listen to me.'

I slam into the kitchen, the door swinging on its hinges. 'Go on then, Jac. This is over. Talk.'

She looks at me, her eyes pleading. 'Miriam, thank goodness. I should have been a better friend. I should have talked to you earlier, helped you realise what was going on. But Samuel was so tiny, and you were so lost. You were dealing with so much already.' She looks almost sad for a moment.

I scoff, disbelieving. I look around the kitchen, taking in the pile of chocolate chip pancakes, the bouncy chair on the floor that's the exact design of the one we have at home. The steriliser, the bottles. She bought this stuff for them. She thought she could step into my life and take it. Make it hers. How long has she been planning to steal my family?

'Miriam, we've been friends our whole lives. We've been

through so much together. I need you to listen to me, quickly, before—'

'Not any more, Jac. You've not been my friend for a very long time. Nicole and Zain, they're my friends.'

'Oh, perfect Nicole—'

I cut her off, no patience for her teenage feud now. 'Nicole's in our house right now, waiting by the phone, in contact with the police for us.' I shake my head. 'And what were *you* doing? Spying. Kidnapping. Messing with my mind.'

She shakes her head as if trying to get rid of a mosquito. She steps closer to Jeremy, and I see that in her left hand she's holding a kitchen knife, her knuckles white where she grips the handle. Jeremy flinches away from her.

The back door handle rattles and the door starts to open, bringing with it a blast of cold air and rain. Ms Hodge stumbles inside, her hair wild and her face muddy.

Jac greets her sidekick with a small smile. 'This is Valerie, an old family friend. She's been helping out around here, and she kept an eye on you for me at the retreat.'

Valerie gives Jac a warning frown and crosses to the radiator, testing the temperature with her hand and yanking it away when she feels the heat. In the corner, the old boiler hums and the pipes creak as water floods through the system.

Valerie glances at Jac and nods.

'I'm glad it's working.' Jac gestures upstairs. 'It was so cold when we arrived tonight, Miriam. I didn't want the kids to freeze to death.' She turns to Valerie and mutters some instructions, something about getting something before the police. I don't parse it completely because suddenly I realise what she said before that.

The heating is on. My body turns to stone. I swallow the panic rising in my throat.

'The faulty old boiler.' My voice comes out in a croak.

Jeremy stares at me, his eyes wild with fear. Then he makes a sudden lunge towards Jac. 'Go, Miriam.' He grabs her wrist.

I turn and run, ignoring the scuffle in the kitchen. Jeremy can look after himself. My kids can't. Jeremy was my first choice, my first love. But Liv and Samuel are the loves of my life. The ones I would go into a burning building to save. I understand now how a mother can find the strength to lift a car if her child is trapped underneath. I am that mother.

I hear a shout and a thump from behind me, but I don't stop. I take the stairs two at a time, feeling the chill of the rest of the house in contrast to the warmth of the kitchen.

It's dark upstairs, the smell of damp permeating my nostrils. The old house creaks as I rush towards Jac's parents' bedroom. My shoulder nudges a painting on the wall, and I hear it crash to the floor.

I pull my jumper over my mouth as I run, to protect me from the fumes. I can only hope there hasn't been enough time for them to build up, to poison my children like they poisoned Jac's parents.

The bedroom door is closed, and my sweating hands slip on the doorknob as I try to turn it. For a moment, I think it's locked, and I whack my shoulder against the wood until it flies open. But I don't even notice the pain. It doesn't matter.

Nothing matters. Nothing will ever matter again.

Because in that double bed where Jac's parents died just a few months ago, my two children lie still, cold and lifeless.

'Liv!' I run to the bed, where the quilt is pulled up over the familiar hump of Olivia's motionless body. On the other side of the bed, Samuel lies still, his arms flung above his head.

My breath heaves in my chest, catching in my throat. I rush to the window and push it open, desperate to clear the air.

I throw back the quilt to find Olivia curled up, one foot on top of the other. I sit on the bed and scoop her floppy body into my arms. Her weight is so familiar.

'Wake up, baby. Please wake up.' My breath comes in short gasps, my lungs straining for oxygen.

She doesn't move.

I gaze at her lifeless face, her eyes closed and expression peaceful. She's perfect. Everything about her. I love the golden honey colour of her hair, the tiny kink in each ear at the top, like a little chip. The milky-biscuit scent of the crook of her neck. The way her hand feels in mine. The curve of her tummy after she's eaten a big meal. The gap between her baby teeth at the front.

She is a piece of my heart, out in the world, and I never

want to live in a world where she doesn't exist. She makes me whole. Her and Samuel.

'My baby. Please wake up.'

I pull her closer, reach forward for Samuel and gather him up too, a baby in each arm, my face pressed into their bodies, drinking them in. Everything aches.

Beneath my ragged breathing, I hear a whimper. I freeze, holding my breath.

Samuel stirs, mewing like a cat. He's alive. 'Oh my God. My baby.' I feel his chest; his skin is warm, his heart beating.

His eyes flutter open.

Maybe I'm not too late. Maybe there's still a chance to save him. Both of them. If I can get out of here, into the fresh air, maybe I can revive Liv too.

I stand up, my legs shaking under their combined weight. But I can do it. I could lift a car if I had to. I heave Liv over my shoulder in a fireman's lift, with Samuel propped against my other shoulder. We'll get out of here. I'll get into the corridor and down the stairs, into the fresh air. I can do anything for my children.

I squeeze through the door, knocking Liv's head against the frame.

Suddenly she moves, her arms flailing, and takes in a big breath like a shout.

I nearly drop her in surprise. I stumble to the floor in the corridor, lying both my babies on the ground. Then I kick behind me, shoving the bedroom door closed and trapping the gas inside.

Liv's eyes open wide. 'Mummy?' She smiles as she realises it's me. Her face has that scrunched, crumpled look it gets when she's woken from a deep sleep. And her sleep is always deep, especially when she first drifts off.

I can't hide my tears, my sobs of relief. She was just asleep. A deep sleep, like always.

Next to her on the carpet, Samuel reaches out with his little starfish hands and grabs a handful of Liv's hair, with a happy coo.

My babies are alive.

A shout from below drags me into the present. Jeremy, still in the kitchen with Jac and that woman. I need to help him.

But Liv hears him too. 'Daddy!' she squeals, and scrambles to her feet.

She's off down the corridor before I have time to stop her. I grab Samuel and run after her, but she's too fast. 'Liv, wait!'

She thunders down the stairs and straight towards the kitchen. 'Daddy! Look at my arm! I broke it. Will you sign my cast?'

I reach her in the doorway and grab her shoulders, pulling her behind me as Jac steps forward, blocking our way into the room. I peer over her shoulder and catch a glimpse of Jeremy. He's doubled over by the back door.

My stomach lurches. *Is he injured?* I've spent the last few weeks believing he's my enemy, trying to outsmart him like he's been outsmarting me. Now I know I was wrong. I've wasted so much time. I need to get in there, help him. But...

'Liv, baby.' Jac smiles, but her face is pale and sweaty. She looks ill. What's been happening down here? I try to see around her into the kitchen, to check on Jeremy, but she bars my way and shuts the door, enclosing the three of us in the hallway and cutting us off from him. She kneels to Liv's level, her hands shaking as she reaches out. Her fingers are stained with blood, and I see the rust-coloured tip of the knife where it's pushed up her sleeve. 'Come here for a cuddle.'

Liv steps forward.

'No.' I reach out to pull her back, but I'm not fast enough and she's already enveloped in her godmother's hug.

My mouth falls open as Jac meets my eye over Liv's shoulder. She pulls Liv closer, exposing more of the knife. She raises one eyebrow: a challenge.

I'm not going to play tug-of-war for my child. I can't let Liv see that. I take a breath, decide to let her have this one moment with Jac. A goodbye. I straighten up, trying to stop my legs shaking.

Still restrained by Jac, Liv frowns and looks back at me, sensing that something's amiss. Her bottom lip trembles.

I smile at her. She's more important than anything. 'It's OK, Liv. You've done nothing wrong.'

She relaxes, leaning into the hug. I fight the urge to rush over and wrench her from Jac's grip. It's too dangerous. That's not the way to win.

'Whatever your sick game is, don't involve Liv,' I hiss. I hold out my arms to my daughter, but Jac gathers her even closer, a protective arm around her narrow shoulders. A protective arm that holds a knife.

Liv's smile begins to falter, and she squirms, trying to ease out of Jac's tight grip.

'Kids can sense when people are good and when they're bad,' Jac says. 'Liv loves me, Miriam. And so does Samuel. You should listen to what they're telling you with that love.' She gestures to my chest, where Samuel has started to root, trying to feed. Soon his murmurs will turn to wails.

Liv pulls away, Jac's arm still around her shoulders. She's discomfited, even though she doesn't fully understand what's happening. Jac steps closer and grabs my arm, her fingernails digging into my skin. She tugs me towards her, her bloodied grip painful as she twists. She nods towards the window. 'We're running out of time.'

At almost the same moment, the light in the hallway shifts, the golden hue replaced with flashing blues, filtering in from outside.

I turn. Through the darkness I see silhouettes striding towards the house. Two... no, more. I hear the muffled slam of a car door and heavy footsteps on the gravel. The low hum of voices. My heart lifts with the hope that help has arrived.

'Liv, the police are here. We need to get Daddy and go home.' I hold out my hand and my fingers brush hers.

But Jac gasps as if I'm the dangerous one, and tugs Liv away from me again. Liv's face falls and she looks between us in confusion.

Jac crouches down to her, her lips next to my daughter's ear. 'Don't go home,' she whispers. 'It's not safe.'

51

I ignore Jac and focus on Liv's perfect face gazing at me with love and confusion. That's when I see it, and I realise my chess pieces have been in the right place from the very start.

I shift Samuel's weight onto my shoulder and wrap my hand around my wrist, feeling the heart charm under my palm. I speak quickly, desperate to lure Liv to my side and get her away from Jac. 'Liv? Do you remember what I told you when I gave you this bracelet, when Samuel was born?'

Liv looks down to her own wrist, where the bracelet still sits. No doubt if Jac had known its significance she'd have removed it in moments. Her face breaks into a smile. 'Hugging Mummy even when she's not here!' she says with a laugh.

'That's right. The bracelet is a way to hug me when I'm far away. But when you're with Mummy, you can hug her in real life too.'

Before Jac can stop her, Liv breaks out of her grasp and runs into my arms. The knife clatters to the floor between us. The blade is covered in blood.

Jac looks up, tears glistening in her eyes. 'Smidge, listen to me. I—'

I flinch at the old nickname, an echo of a long-gone friend-ship. 'No, Jac.' I shake my head in disbelief. 'I don't want to hear it.'

The door behind her swings open with a blast of cold air, and I see the devastation in the kitchen: Jeremy lying next to a pool of blood, another knife beside him on the floor.

I scream and rush forward, knocking Jac out of the way. I crouch over his body, the blood spreading across the terracotta tiles. Next to him, the back door stands open, the winter air bringing a chill to the room.

He opens his eyes, pulls himself up to a sitting position, leaning against the kitchen cabinets, and reaches for Samuel. I pass him over and Jeremy cradles the baby to his chest, kissing his head.

Liv crouches by my side. 'Daddy? Are you hurt?'

He shakes his head and pulls her to him too. 'Just tired, baby,' he whispers.

I don't know if he's telling the truth. 'But what...'

He nods towards Jac, who I see now is leaning against the door frame, one hand pressed to her shoulder. 'It's Jac's blood. She caught her arm on the knife when she tried to grab me.' He glances at the open door. 'The other one gave me a good punch in the stomach and ran as soon as she heard the police. I'm just winded.'

At that moment, two policemen stride through the open back door.

'Jacqueline McKeighan?' They cross the kitchen to Jac, who barely moves from her position, her face still clammy and pale. 'I'm arresting you on suspicion of child abduction. I'll caution you that you're not obliged to say anything, but anything you do say will be noted down and may be used in evidence.'

She stares at me as the officer speaks, her eyes not leaving mine. It's as if she doesn't hear.

As they take her arms, she opens her mouth and hisses at

me: 'It wasn't me, Smidge. Please believe me. I did everything for you. It was Nicole.'

I turn away.

52

A lifetime later, and yet only an hour has passed since they slipped handcuffs around Jac's wrists and radioed for an ambulance.

We answer questions huddled outside in the December cold. There was no carbon monoxide. The police checked straight away: the boiler was replaced weeks ago. Still, I breathe deeper in the fresh air, as if the farmhouse and its tragic secrets were sucking the oxygen from my lungs.

Soon Liv squeals that she needs the toilet, and I take her behind some bushes, unable to face that house again. Then Samuel starts to wail in the sling on Jeremy's chest. The police let us go, promising more questions tomorrow.

'Mummy, it's past my bedtime, isn't it?' asks Liv as I strap her into her car seat. On the other side of the car, Jeremy smiles as he settles Samuel into his.

I nod, and boop her little button nose. 'It's very late,' I agree. I tighten the straps and run a finger underneath. Tight. Safe.

I step back, about to close the door, but Liv grabs my hand. 'Will you sit in the back with me and Samuel? Please?'

I peer at the narrow gap between the two seats. Just enough space for an adult, but not enough to be comfortable.

'Please?'

My chest swells with emotion. 'Of course,' I croak, and climb in awkwardly, Liv collapsing with giggles as I clamber over her with a grunt and a groan.

And there I am, sandwiched between my two babies, one on each side.

Jeremy closes Samuel's door and climbs into the front seat, glancing at me in the rear-view mirror before he starts the engine. He cranks up the heater and the chill fades.

Next to me, Liv wraps her hand around my wrist, enclosing my bracelet. She admires her own version, linking the charms together with clumsy fingers, placing hers inside mine. 'Look, Mummy,' she says with a sleepy grin. 'We're joined together for ever. My heart in yours.'

I blink away tears. Soon Liv's eyelids slide closed. Her fingers slacken but she doesn't let go of my wrist, her charm still slotted into mine. My arm starts to ache, keeping it in the same position. But I won't move it while she holds me. Her other arm lies by her side in its cast. I feel a surge of guilt that my baby got hurt by someone who should have loved and protected her, not competed to win her like a prize at a carnival.

I check my phone and try to call Nicole, but her mobile goes straight to voicemail and our house line is engaged; it must have been left off the hook by accident. I look out of the window as we speed through the dark countryside, the hills looming out of the darkness, my family surrounding me.

On my other side, Samuel's eyes glint in the passing street lights. He's quiet, watching them play on the car ceiling, enraptured by the light show.

In the rear-view mirror, I see Jeremy glancing at me, flicking his gaze between me and the road ahead. 'What was Jac saying about Nicole?'

I'm enveloped by a wave of exhaustion. I shrug. 'Jac's always hated her. She probably thought she could get one last dig at our friendship before she's sent down.'

He sighs and shakes his head, keeping his eyes on the road ahead. 'Poor Nicole. She's been a good friend these last few months; she doesn't deserve that. She was always around for me while you were away, even though she's in the middle of that nasty divorce. And she was like a second mum to the kids, especially Liv.'

He shifts to get a better view of me in the mirror. Headlights from approaching cars light up his face. His eyes are kind, tinged with sadness.

'I'm so sorry, Miriam. I'm so sorry I doubted you. That I wouldn't listen. You're a good mother. And I'm lucky to have you as my wife.' He reaches back and lays a hand on my knee, an affectionate stroke. I don't move away. I want his touch. I love him, even though he put me through hell. He put me through hell because he thought he was helping. The last few months have highlighted the flaws in our marriage, showing our lack of trust. We lost each other somehow. Stopped seeing each other, stopped listening. But this has also shown me we have something worth fighting for. We're better together, Jeremy and I, even after everything.

I suppress a sob, part exhaustion, part relief. We hurtle through the Scottish countryside, heading towards our home, but for a moment I hope we never get there. Everyone I want and need is here in this car alongside me. And I nearly lost it all.

I gaze at Samuel, his tiny hands flexing, perfect little nails on each finger. I hold out a teddy bear, moving its arm so it waves at him. He coos, reaching out and grasping at the bear, his movements jerky like a puppet.

That's when it happens. The thing I've waited for these last few weeks, desperate with loss that it had somehow been taken away from me while I was locked up, separated from my babies.

Samuel looks around, his eyes searching for me. His gaze settles on my face, and his expression transforms into a beaming grin.

My baby is smiling at me.

A tear rolls down my face. I lean over, my mouth inches from his ear. 'I love you,' I whisper. 'I've loved you since the day you were born. And I'll love you every day for ever.'

Samuel holds the bear in his hands, poking at its eyes with his chubby little fingers. Shiny, glittering eyes. Like the eyes of a crow. I gasp, my breath catching in my throat.

'You all right?' Jeremy asks from the front.

'Mm-hm,' I reply, not taking my eyes off the bear. Jac's teddy-cam.

I pull it from Samuel's hands and shove it into the footwell behind the driver's seat. Samuel squawks in protest, but a dummy fixes things straight away.

My relief disappears, replaced by a niggling dread. Jac admitted to the teddy-cam, I realise. Why would she admit to one camera, but not the rest? *It was Nicole.* Her words reverberate through my brain. *Don't go home.*

Unless she admitted to the teddy-cam because that was the truth.

I think back over the last couple of hours: Jac's strange statements, her desperate entreaties to get Jeremy and me to listen, when all we could think about was finding the kids. Of course we weren't going to take any notice of the ramblings of the person who kidnapped our children, who had made my life a nightmare for months. But now, given a moment of peace to gather myself, I try to unpick everything she said, looking at it through a neutral lens instead of one tainted by panic and fear.

'Jeremy?'

'Hm?'

'When we were in the kitchen and Valerie Hodge had just come in, what did Jac say to her? I couldn't hear, but you were closer.'

I watch him in the rear-view mirror, his eyes sparkling in the headlights. His forehead furrows, and he shrugs. 'Something weird. Everything she said was weird, wasn't it?'

'Can you try to remember?'

He taps his fingertips on the steering wheel. 'Something about our house. A dead phone line. Getting there ahead of the police.'

'Why? Jac already took all the cameras. What did she need?' I swallow, shifting in my seat to alleviate the pain where Liv's car seat digs into my side. 'But then Valerie was in one of the patrol cars, wasn't she, when we left?'

'Yep. They arrested her too. Must have caught her trying to run off. Good riddance to both of them.'

I stare down at the teddy-cam where it lies face-down on the car floor, surrounded by biscuit crumbs and half-empty de-icer cans. What if Jac was telling the truth? What if that was the only camera she bought, purchased to catch someone else? Sure, the company she works for produce cameras and their software, but anyone can buy them. Just like anyone can get a VPN, or learn to create hidden networks, if they're determined enough. If they're trying to gather evidence to set someone up. To take their children.

I think back to just a few hours ago, when Nicole arrived to help us. *Jac told me where she works now*, she said, telling us the cameras were Jac's doing without overtly saying it. Without needing to. *And Jac was here the night Liv fell?* she asked, weaving a web of accusation without us even realising.

How did Nicole know that? Unless it was Nicole who was watching.

Nicole, whose marriage started to disintegrate around the same time I got pregnant with Samuel. Nicole, who always wanted two children but never got her second. Nicole, who got a job in the school I worked at and then my job was taken away. And who turned up at my house day after day while I was trapped in that asylum, ingratiating herself with my husband and acting 'second mum' to my children?

Nicole. My stomach churns and my thoughts blur together as I try to process what this could mean.

The car slows as Jeremy turns off the bypass and enters the residential part of town, parked cars along the verges and bins out on the pavements for collection.

Jac's been trying to tell me about this for months, I realise with a start. The night she dropped in when Jeremy was working late. *No one can ever have nice things around Nicole.* And then the expression on her face, like she was holding something back. *You've got enough going on*, she said that night by the fire pit. She wanted to tell me, but she needed proof before she could. She was trying to protect me.

'Here we are,' Jeremy says, his tone jovial as he pulls to a stop at the roadside.

The kids stir from sleep, but they don't open their eyes. Jeremy kills the engine and unclips his seat belt.

I look out of the window, glance up at our house, where every window is illuminated, the stained glass in the front door glowing like a cheerful beacon of comfort. *Don't go home*, I hear Jac say.

'No, Jeremy. Wait.'

While I watch, the front door opens as if the house has been waiting for our return. Nicole stands on the doorstep with a giant smile that doesn't quite reach her eyes. Next to her is her daughter, Lottie, wearing the purple pyjama top I searched for all over the house for weeks: *OLIVIA* is emblazoned across her chest in bubbly 1970s font. Nicole steps towards the car and holds up a hand in a silent wave, and I see the web of straps over her shoulders: an empty baby carrier, waiting to hold Samuel.

'Darling,' she says to my husband, both arms outstretched towards him. 'I'm so glad you're safe.'

I unclip my seat belt and make to move. 'Jeremy.'

He doesn't hear me. He opens his door and steps onto the pavement.

'Jeremy, wait. Stop.' I scramble to reach the door handle beyond Liv, but I'm trapped between the two car seats, unable to get out, unable to stop him walking towards her open arms, ready to lead him into the house. To what fate? What further horrors has she been planning?

Jac's words echo again. *Don't go home.*

My nightmare isn't over yet.

EPILOGUE

NICOLE

The last straw was that day at the soft play. You'll understand when you hear my point of view. Miriam hobbled in looking a total mess, dragging Liv behind her and the new baby all squashed in a sling. She had everything and all she could do was complain: blah blah blah, Jeremy's not here, Liv's being difficult, breastfeeding's exhausting... Cry me a river.

The universe delivers amazing gifts to her doorstep and she takes them for granted. I've watched it happen our whole lives, and frankly I'm sick of it. Perfect husband? Boom. Two gorgeous children? Here you go.

When they called her over the tannoy because her car had smashed into another in the car park, good old Zain was all 'poor Miriam'.

'Is she OK?' he asked, his eyes big and sympathetic. He's always had a thing for Miriam, I reckon.

Anyway, I told him, 'She's three days post-partum, of course she's not OK.' And I meant it. I had no idea how or why she left the house that day, except for attention, although I'd never say that to Zain.

There's a lot of things I don't say, and I was getting a bit sick of holding my tongue, to be honest. So I let my guard down a little bit. Out of concern, you must understand.

'She's never been good at relaxing and taking care of herself,' I said, remembering Miriam's breakdown when Liv was born. No sleep for days, they'd said when she was eventually admitted to the mother and baby unit. 'I'm surprised they chose to have a second, if I'm honest. After last time.'

Faithful old Zain, the golden retriever of our friendship group, decided that he needed to defend Princess Miriam: 'Maybe their family didn't feel complete with just one child.'

Now that was just too much. You know whose family doesn't feel complete? Mine. My useless ex-husband left me for Little Miss Ugg Boots while I'm staring down the barrel of the menopause desperate for a second baby, and nobody gave me a second thought. I didn't get one flash of Zain's sympathetic-big-eyes look or a lasagne on my doorstep. Tough Nicole, she'll be fine, they probably thought; if they thought of me at all. But I express one tiny doubt about Miriam's decision-making skills and I'm the bad guy.

You know what? Miriam has no idea what's best for her, never has. But I know. She didn't understand the value of what she had.

So I told Zain: 'Or maybe she's already heading down the psychosis rabbit hole. Refusing to rest at this stage might be a red flag. Someone should keep an eye on her, make sure she's coping.'

It's lucky I set up that baby monitor before I popped it into Jac's gift basket. That was thoughtful. Like a lasagne. It was even luckier that Jac installed it that very first night while she was babysitting. So helpful. I could really keep an eye on things after that.

So then, because I'm a good friend, I checked on the kids in the soft play. Lottie was scrapping with Kai in the ball pit, not a care in the world. I found Liv high up, swinging from a rope swing alone. *They said you won't want me any more now you have Sam*, she had said when they first arrived. She was terrified her mum didn't love her. What a mess. I had a word with her as she swung on that rope; you know, comforting stuff for a kiddie to hear. I promised I'd be her other mummy if Miriam abandoned her, and that Liv would always feel loved with me. No newborn favouritism from Auntie Nicole. I even promised lemon drizzle cake.

Not long afterwards, she came running out of the soft play structure, her cheeks streaked with tears. 'Where's my mummy? She left me.' Her mouth opened wide in despair. 'She left me.'

I held out my arms to her, and she melted into them, her whole body racked with sobs.

'It's OK, Livvy. It's OK. Mummy's coming back,' I told her. But what if she wasn't? Maybe Miriam had cracked and wandered off? I could look after Liv, and Samuel too. I'd take great care of them both.

Her body felt so tiny and fragile, like my Lottie's but smaller. She was inconsolable. It felt so good to be needed.

'You should take her outside to Miriam,' said Zain, as if I wasn't good enough, couldn't fix it. He's always poking his nose into everything. I just needed more time with Liv and she'd realise I was better than her useless mother. I had more love to give.

But I did as he suggested and stood up, Liv's arms tight around my neck, her weight in my arms. 'Keep your eye on the other kids, will you?' I said.

I watched through the glass doors: Miriam looking frazzled in the car park, talking to a man wearing a Bluetooth headset, the baby strapped to her chest. She didn't want this baby, I knew, as the man flailed his arms in anger at her. She could barely cope with Liv, and she certainly couldn't console her and hold her like I was doing in that moment. There was no space for Liv here.

It was stupid to add a newborn into this mix: now there were two children who wouldn't get what they needed from their mother. What an injustice that children are born to ungrateful parents all over the world when mothers like me would kill for another baby.

I buried my nose in Liv's hair for a moment and then stepped outside into the autumn air. Always unselfish. I'm a good friend. 'See? There she is. Mummy's right there.'

Liv's sobs turned to whimpers and she reached out for Miriam, wriggling out of my arms and into her mother's.

My arms hung empty, not needed any more.

Miriam had no idea she had what some people could only wish for: the perfect family, a handsome, caring husband. But maybe she didn't want those things anymore. She might be happier on her own, with no responsibilities. Perhaps she'd even be pleased if someone stepped in and took her place. A seamless transition for everyone concerned.

Of course, for this to feel truly seamless I'd have to understand how the family operated, really get under the skin of that marriage and those kids. Watching and listening, forging connections with Liv, Samuel and Jeremy. I could even start breaking down Miriam's grip on them early, to make the transition easier for everyone. It's what a true friend would do, given a chance. I would take on Miriam's burdens and set her free. And in the process I'd get what I'd been denied. Lottie's always begging for siblings. Everyone wins.

I stepped towards the mother-and-daughter hug, reaching out for one last stroke of Liv's hair. 'Poor thing. What made you think Mummy would leave you, Liv?' I turned to Miriam. 'What happened out here?'

Miriam explained some stuff about the car, typical inattention of a mother who has taken on too much. I nodded and smiled in the right places, but I only really started listening when Miriam said the words I'd been waiting to hear, sending a spear of joy into my heart:

'Two kids feels like too many right now.'

An invitation.

A LETTER FROM ROSIE WALKER

Dear reader,

I want to say a huge thank you for choosing to read *The Baby Monitor*. If you enjoyed it, and want to keep up to date with all my latest releases, just sign up at the following link. Your email address will never be shared and you can unsubscribe at any time.

www.bookouture.com/rosie-walker

I loved writing about those first days of motherhood when you bring your baby home from the hospital: how magical it feels, but also how terrifying it can be, too. And it was so much fun to write a novel inspired by some of the creepiest news stories I've come across in recent years: hacked baby monitors. I was so fascinated that, like Miriam, I contacted a well-known mum-influencer to ask if she'd come across this type of hacking, and she really did respond like the Instagrammer in the book: she said it was all lies and it didn't really happen. And I wondered: how would it feel if you were the victim of a hacker and no one believed you? And so this book was born!

One of my favourite things about writing books is hearing readers' reactions to my stories. Did you shiver when the baby monitor swivelled on its stand? Were you on Miriam's side? Did you feel Miriam's fear of losing her kids, or her frustration when no one would believe her? Have you seen something scary on *your* baby monitor?

I hope you loved *The Baby Monitor*; if you did, I would be very grateful if you could write a review. I'd love to hear what you think, and it makes such a difference helping new readers to discover one of my books for the first time.

I love hearing from my readers – you can get in touch on social media or through my website.

Thanks,

Rosie Walker

www.rosiejanewalker.com

 facebook.com/rosiewalkerauthor

 x.com/ciderwithrosie

 instagram.com/rosiejanewalker

ACKNOWLEDGEMENTS

First thanks go to my literary agent, Charlotte Robertson. When she read an early draft of *The Baby Monitor*, she knew exactly what I was trying to do, and read countless different drafts as we worked together to get there. Charlotte makes me a better writer, and her (often genius) ideas and suggestions for this book made it what it is today. She's not only a fantastic agent, but also a brilliant editor, mentor, coach and counsellor all in one! I'm delighted that I'm lucky enough to work with her.

None of my books would exist without Suzy Pope, who is always my first reader, invaluable sounding board, hilarious co-conspirator and very important checkpoint to prevent my more off-the-wall ideas from making their ill-conceived way out into the world. I don't know how to – and nor would I want to – write a book without Suzy's editorial eye and ability to make a very strong gin and tonic. Suzy endured almost as many drafts of *The Baby Monitor* as Charlotte did, and gave amazing feedback every time. I'm so grateful for her patience, kindness and brilliant brain.

My family have been a huge support in my writing career, from my parents reading me endless books as a child and my mum continuing to check that I'm stocked in her local Waterstones (so far, so good – thanks, Mum), through to my husband, Kevin, talking through tricky plot knots with me and indulging my need for a wall of scribbled Post-its during the planning phases. On publication day for my second book, my wonderful mother-in-law, Denise, made a cake of my book cover, and not only was the cake delicious, but it was the perfect way to celebrate. I'm lucky to have such great family support. (And a special thanks to Bella the dog, who fell asleep with her face on the keyboard while I was editing this book, and helpfully added a page full of symbols. All errors are hers).

And of course, thank you to Elsie, who was born during the writing of this book. Without her, it wouldn't exist: Elsie's arrival into the world gave me the necessary insight into some of what Miriam goes through during the novel. I now understand her deep fear of losing her kids, her fierce struggle to protect them at all costs, and her ability to keep fighting for them even when she thinks she has nothing left. Having a child is both the most terrifying and most rewarding thing I have ever done, and I wouldn't change anything.

The Baby Monitor is my first book with the wonderful team at Bookouture, and I am delighted to be one of their authors. There's a huge group of talented people behind the book, and I'd like to offer special thanks to Maisie Lawrence, my clever, insightful and enthusiastic editor: I am so pleased to work with her and can't wait to collaborate on more books together in the future. Thank you to Ruth Tross, who spotted the potential in this book right at the start and made sure it made its way into Maisie's capable hands. All my thanks, too, to the rest of the Bookouture dream team, who work so hard to make sure this book and others are as gripping, entertaining and error-free as possible, and reach as many readers/listeners as they can: Helen Jenner, Jessie Botterill, Jenny Geras, Billi-Dee Jones, Hannah Snetsinger, Jane Selley, Liz Hatherell, Alex Crow, Ciara Rosney, Melanie Price, Occy Carr, Jess Readett, Kim Nash, Noelle Holten, Sarah Hardy, Marina Valles, Mark Alder, Lauren Morrissette, Alba Proko, Richard King and Saidah Graham.

It's always a surprise to me how much research goes into a book. *The Baby Monitor* benefited from the expertise of Elle

Dickson, who gave me so much useful information about police procedure, PCSOs and child abduction. Thank you also to Ann Hodson, who donated a Sunday morning to talk me through how real social workers operate, just so I could make up a pretend one instead. This book wouldn't be nearly as robust without your help. Thank you also to Catherine Cho, who wrote so candidly and clearly about her experiences with post-natal psychosis in her memoir *Inferno: A Memoir of Motherhood and Madness*.

Thanks to friends who kindly suggested names for my characters, to avoid me using the initial boring names that pop into my head while I'm hammering away at a first draft. Ann Hodson named Liv and gave her name to our Family Liaison Officer, and Chris Steedman named Jeremy. I stole Jenna Grant's first name for the influencer who dismissed Miriam's fears about hacked baby monitors. Last but not least, Zain Rizvi gave me his own name for Zain, and he chose Kai for Zain's son. I wanted to use Zain's name because every winter for the last twenty-five years, he has slept on the streets for one night to raise money for St Basils, a UK homelessness prevention charity that works with vulnerable young people who are homeless or face the possibility of homelessness. That deserves your name in a book.

One part of being a published author that always brings me delight and gratitude is the overwhelming feeling of community and friendship from fellow authors and book professionals. We may all be separately hunched over our laptops, but there's so much support and companionship both in person and online from the writing community. Thanks to Christie Newport, Russell Jones, Suzan Holder, Colm Boyd, Anna Eberts, Rebecca Alexander, Tana L. H. Boerger, Jacky Collins and Noir at the Bar, my fellow Bookouture authors, and many more, for chats, advice and writerly friendship. Finally, a great big shout-out to the amazing D20 authors: a community of 2020 debut authors who came together to bolster each other through our pandemic-ridden debut year, many of whom have become excellent friends.

Shout-out also to the amazingly talented photographer Joanna Jamrozy, who took my latest round of author photos. She knew the prettiest locations (South Queensferry, an excellent suggestion) and the exact right thing to say to make me smile, even though I don't like having my photo taken. She also knew to take a ridiculous number of photographs so I could be picky.

Massive thanks to the team at Creative Scotland, who saw something special in *The Baby Monitor* early on in the process and provided me with funding for part of the editorial phase of the project. Arts funding is a brilliant thing, which opens doors to allow more creativity into the world.

And finally, a huge thank you to everyone who reads my books. If you enjoyed this book or any of my others, please write a review, tell your friends, borrow them from libraries and/or buy them as presents! If you didn't enjoy them, either keep it very quiet, lie and say you loved them, or send copies to your enemies.

Made in the USA
Monee, IL
13 February 2024

53455774R00194